SHADOW WOMAN

By
Nikki DiCaro

Thrillers:

The Trap
The Outcasts
Paradise Awakening
Larceny U

The Amelia Chronicles:

I'm Nobody's Pancake
What, No Bacon
Pass the Butter
Pass the Syrup
Top Off the Coffee and Leave the Check
Chronicles of an Irreverent Life
Don't Eat the Potato Salad

Shadow Woman

Shadow Woman
By Nikki DiCaro
www.NikkiDiCaro.com

ISBN: 9781696539630

Nikki DiCaro

To those in my family and my heart friends; you supported me during the most challenging period of my life

Chapter 1

DIVORCE. THE WORD RATTLED around in his brain like a steel ball in an old-fashioned pinball machine. The papers had arrived at his office that morning by courier; he was officially divorced. Russell Radcliffe pulled his cherry-red Mercedes Benz convertible into the garage of his modest, low slung rancher and slid the gear shift into park. The faded white clapboard house was a throwback to a bygone era. There was something eerily similar to Russell's situation – the old and the new converging. Stung by the events of the day, he sat quietly, parked in the driveway trying to deal with the cataclysmic changes in his life.

The five thousand square foot McMansion wrapped in white stucco, the kidney-shaped heated pool with elaborate matching cabana complete with wet bar and massage table, the Mercedes and the Range Rover, the country club membership, the well-earned upscale lifestyle—gone. The dream life with his children and the trophy woman he promised to love for better or for worse were now a memory.

When days were rosy and nights sultry, the couple fell for the trappings of opulence. Russell was flourishing in his chosen profession. Life seemed to have dealt him a winning hand, three sevens on the slot machine. To support their lifestyle, the lifestyle he thought would keep his beautiful wife happy, Russell and his wife mortgaged themselves right to the edge; not close enough that a fall from grace was eminent, but close enough that Russell could feel the spray from the waves pounding on the financial rocks below. The last brick in the wall crumbled; the mansion—the dream home his future ex-wife coveted—had a for sale sign with a picture of a 40-

something big-haired, big-nailed, real estate goddess in the front yard. The real estate market had softened, putting a large portion of their nest egg in harm's way. His wife got to remain in the house with their two teenagers, forcing him to relocate. Russell was willing to settle the whole ugly business if he could salvage his car and his secret; the last vestiges of his pride that his ex-wife had shredded. Amanda Radcliffe wanted everything before she would cede his car to him. He wanted that car; he needed that car. He equated the car with his identity even more than the house. She knew it and held it over his head like the sword a Damacles.

Russell replayed those last days of their marriage. In one fell swoop, Mandy revealed she was having an affair and had the divorce papers served to his office the next day. Not only was he not getting any of his wife's pleasures, an interloper had been planting in his garden. He told Mandy that he was willing to forgive her, that she would regret leaving him, that she couldn't stand on her own two feet.

***

"Come to your senses Mandy. Quit this foolishness and think it through."

She laughed. "Do you think I haven't thought this through? Do you think I'm doing this because I want to get your attention?"

"I don't understand why you're doing this to me. I just want you to stop. Adultery is against the law." His voice was strained; he wanted desperately to get through to her. His wife stood arms akimbo, her long sleek legs ran from her blue skirt through nude pantyhose and slid perfectly into navy blue patent leather pumps. She was attractive even after two hard pregnancies. Her auburn hair wafted in sultry waves across her soft shoulders, ending elegantly just short of the middle of her back. Large hazel eyes were framed by high cheekbones, thin nose, and highly sculptured eyebrows. Her complexion hinted at regular trips to the tanning salon.

"When you started wearing my clothes I knew it was over. You were the one who turned our marriage into a farce, not me."

Her tone was accusatory. "And don't think threats will work with me, kiddo. I can ruin you if you put me in that position." Her gaze was cold steel.

Russell looked her over; he would have begged her to stay if his pride wasn't strong. He loved her; she was his female role model; everything he wanted to be in a woman he saw in his wife. But he couldn't condone her desire to find pleasure in another's bed. Looking away he calculated his options; they were bleak. Losing his job wasn't an option. He had worked long and hard to parlay the master's degree in finance into a high-profile position with an investment banking firm. He figured he would be summarily dismissed if his superiors knew he was transgender.

After the divorce, he licked his wounds and decided to buy down-market. The shock of a smaller place on a postage stamp lot made him wish he hadn't been critical when his wife unceremoniously disclosed her extramarital affair. He lost that struggle and was losing others. He would never give up his femininity even though it had meant losing his wife, who realized she wasn't the only woman in his life. This had cut her deeply and she had made him bleed.

As he sat in the car with the engine running, he considered pressing the activator button to bring the garage door down and seal off the garage. Just one click and he would fade slowly into eternal sleep. As he unfastened the seat belt, he became instantly aware of the muffin top above his waist. His expensive figure-enhancing pantyhose were simply no match for this roll of blubber. His wife called them "love handles." He preferred the more feminine "muffin tops." At forty-five, his five-foot eight-inch body was slowly losing the fight against gravity. "Time has a way of feminizing the male body," he mused.

After weighing the consequences, his hands ended the debate raging in his brain by turning the key and killing the engine. Thank God for muscle memory. He had to remind himself he had much to live for: his new life as Allison. His increasingly dominant female side could begin now that the word "wife" was preceded by "former." Fleeting urges to take his life waxed and waned. Those ideations kicked in when the divorce was finalized.

Pressing a button on the visor, the garage door creaked and moaned as it lowered on its tracks. Opening the car door, Russell emerged stretching the kinks out of his back.

Once inside the house he grabbed a Tab from the fridge on the way through the kitchen, popped the top and inserted a thin straw. Tab was getting harder and harder to find, but he loved the taste. Using a straw reminded him that it would prevent him from leaving a telltale lipstick stain on the can when he was wearing his female face. He pranced off to the bedroom. Slipping out of his slacks and button-down shirt, he stood in front of the full-length mirror hanging on the wall across the room from his bed. Reaching down he removed black socks, the last remnant of male clothing.

"There, that's better." String bikini panties under tan pantyhose looked just right. His midsection was becoming a gutter for his sagging pectorals, which to his delight were gradually beginning to look more and more like breasts. *I'm going to need to invest in a form-flattering girdle to help me win the Battle of the Bulge.* He forced his shoulders back; they were slumping from being hunched over the computer keyboard all day. Head up, shoulders back, chest out, his makeover artist had told him.

Salt and pepper hair combed straight back accentuated his widow's peak. He wore it longish on the sides, borderline acceptable in the corporate world of mergers and acquisitions. Mandy had asked him to change his hairstyle. His rising forehead wasn't appealing. He refused to relent, retaining a tenuous control over one thing in his life. His big brown eyes were deep set; sleepless nights left him with dark circles. He put on a bit of concealer to brighten them. His nose seemed longer as his eyes became sunken. Once-firm jaws were starting to form jowls.

Extracting a box from the closet, he pulled off the lid and reverently removed his favorite black patent leather stilettos; five-inch heels. Balancing on one foot and then the other, he slipped them on and posed in the mirror with his legs canted and his hands on his hips, admiring their perfection in the mirror. Russell had a fetish that had taken him to places his wife's lack of attention had completely missed. Mandy was sexy for her lover, but not for her ex-husband.

Walking over to the closet, he picked through his expanding feminine wardrobe. Russell needed the female fix. He needed to be Allison. Getting dressed after work was his nightly ritual. Depending on his mood, he would choose either a sheath dress or skirt and blouse. Checking his watch, he saw he had less than an hour before his two teenagers arrived for dinner. The child custody negotiations were upside down. He wanted alternating weeks. She wanted every other weekend. They settled on four days every other week plus dinner with Dad two nights every off week.

Stepping into the cotton skirt he almost caught his heel on the hem, but deftly flounced it to avoid a potential problem. Positioning the top of the skirt he pulled the zipper, barely getting it to the top without a struggle. *Need to control my appetite.* He had taken to eating as a palliative measure. The home gym was too big to move and he didn't quite have the energy to overcome his inertia. When he told his ex-wife, he had found a home and wanted to send a mover over to pick up the gym, she told him she had sold it.

Walking around the house in the billowy white blouse and navy skirt, he felt refreshed and energized. The gentle hug of his pantyhose-clad legs, the delicious swish-swish they made, and the sound of stilettos on the hardwood floors stimulated his feminine side.

He started to tidy up the living room with his diet soda in one hand. Looking at the picture above the sofa he backed up, caught his heel on the edge of the area rug under the coffee table, and the soda went flying onto the hardwood floor, leaving a puddle that was headed straight for the Persian rug his ex-wife had insisted on purchasing and then refused to take as part of the property settlement.

"Oh, shit!" He frantically ran to the kitchen for a roll of paper towels and caught the puddle just before it reached the rug. Working wood floor polish into the wet areas with a rag he finished the job.

Back to the kitchen; the digital clock on the freestanding,

avocado 70's vintage stove read six forty-five. Fifteen minutes until the children arrived, and no time to prepare dinner. "Shit!" Panic gripped him. "I should have popped that lasagna into the oven. I should be a better parent." Plan B: they would go to the local pub.

He kicked off the shoes, quickly stripped off his outfit, and debated whether to take off his pantyhose. *Better not tempt another disaster.* He picked out a long-sleeved, combed cotton golf shirt in tangerine with horizontal navy pinstripes from the casual section of his closet, where the shirts were arranged by color to form a rainbow. He completed the outfit with a pair of pleated khakis, brown tassel loafers, and matching brown woven belt with a brass buckle.

***

Meghan pulled the Volkswagen Jetta to a stop in the driveway. Mark unbuckled his seat belt before the car came to a complete stop.

"Mark, you're not supposed to unbuckle until the car comes to a complete stop." Her voice was borderline obnoxious.

Mark rolled his eyes. *She's just like mom.*

Meghan blew a breath that caused her bangs to ruffle. "You're just like Dad; you never listen." Meghan blamed her father for the divorce. Her mother told them their father wanted a divorce. She was technically right. Mandy was always technically right.

The kids felt pulled; they loved their father but this dinner gig was eating into their homework time and time with friends. On the drive over, Meghan and Mark had discussed how to break the news to their dad that weeknight dinners were not convenient.

Dinner at the Rusty Rake was a nonevent. The local pub was slow. Tuesdays were an off night and only regulars were there. Russell was preoccupied with the aborted dressing session. The children texted obsessively. Dad, feeling compelled to enforce his "no texting during meals" policy, incited a near-riot before ultimately acquiescing. Dinner was tense, perfunctory conversation was stilted. The kids couldn't wait for it to end.

Pulling into the driveway, Meghan pushed the shifter into park.

"See ya, Dad," she said, anxious to be on their way.

"I want a hug from both of you and not one of those halfhearted hugs. I need some skin cells." He reached over and turned the key, killing the engine. His action deflated the children. "I don't get to see you very often." Russell stopped himself before continuing the guilt trip. They didn't want to hear it. His psychologist told him it wasn't engendering love.

"Dad, we have homework," Meghan said. She was the stronger of the two children. Russell leaned over and placed a kiss on his daughter's cheek. Turning he did the same for his son, who leaned between the two bucket seats to accommodate his father.

Russell watched the white Jetta disappear down the street. Trudging inside he locked the house. *Alone again.* He felt a mix of emotions. Sad to see his kids go; wondering whether they could accept Allison, and relief that he could relax and be himself. In the end, Allison won out; she was winning more of these struggles. Feeling the pull of regret, he apologized to the walls. "I'm sorry, Allison. I didn't mean it. I know you're always here with me."

Retreating to the bedroom he pulled out the nail polish kit and decided to give Allison her due. He wasn't ready for a public manicure and pedicure, leaving him to learn in quiet solitude. Slipping into pink silk pajamas he gathered the hinged plastic container that held the nail files, buffer pads, toe separators, and bottles of polish.

These were the challenging times. Allison was his strength as well as his weakness. He wanted her be primary, but not enough to make her existence public.

Why was he enmeshed in this raging conflict? Why was he condemned to live two genders?

Every time Mandy had pampered herself with nail salon visits or shopping sprees to enhance her wardrobe he had felt jilted, left out. He had even offered to perform a pedicure. She had dismissed his offer as an attempt to keep her from enjoying the treatment at the local salon.

When she went out and the kids were steeped in their activities

11

he had explored Mandy's extensive wardrobe, smiling as he slipped into a pair of her favorite, well-worn shoes. With the assistance of a shoehorn, Russell's feet wedged uncomfortably into the heels. Slipping into a sheath dress he would prance around the bedroom, sit on the edge of the bed, cross legs, and move the elevated foot back and forth in a rhythmic pattern.

Each time he returned the clothes to their home in the closet, the pull of regret strengthened. He wasn't sure how to handle the constant demands the feminine side exercised.

He had tried to explain the whole thing to Mandy. She didn't want to hear it. She laughed derisively. "I married a man. Be a man, Russell, stop trying to be something you are not." He wanted to tell his wife about the feminine side whose name was Allison. He wanted to tell her that Allison made him more sensitive to Mandy and her needs. He desperately wanted to share his emotions with her, his real emotions and the energy he felt femme. His attempt fell flat as Mandy dismissed him with the wave of a hand before turning, leaving him sinking into emotional quicksand.

Chapter 2

RISING AT 5:00 A.M., Russell had begun to rise early to give himself ample time to attend to the things that women must attend to. The morning regimen included a hot shower with body wash, shampoo, and conditioner, facial exfoliation and full-body hair removal. After a rinse cycle, he wrapped himself in a full-length powder-blue terry cloth robe and attended to eyebrows. Keeping them sculpted was a constant battle. Next, he applied skin toner to clear impurities, shrink his pores, control oils, and balance his skin pH. Russell then applied a caffeine-based eye brightener under his eyes to tone down the dark circles under his eyes.

For final touches, he used a brown eyebrow pencil to hide a few grays, a little dab of concealer around his eyes to draw them out, and a couple of swipes of brown mascara. Finally, he applied a coat of clear lipstick. This was his subtle daywear makeup. He wore it every day. Allison wouldn't let him out of the house without it.

Being a woman was hard work but Allison insisted she was in the picture right up front for all to see if one looked closely. There was a level of treachery in the subtle honesty of his presentation. At a casual glance others would see Russell's face in the crowd as a man, but Russell would always see Allison in the mirror.

Slipping on a pair of string bikini panties, Russell gazed into the mirror. He was pudgy, full figured, and the string bikini didn't look right.

Pulling on panties and a camisole, he ignored the tightness around his midsection. Extracting a blue dress shirt and beige slacks, he stepped into the male shell convention demanded. Black dress socks and penny loafers finished the Ivy League look. Walking into the kitchen, he wondered why he insisted on covering up early. He could have flitted around the house unimpeded. *Tomorrow for sure*, he thought.

A light breakfast of a half bagel with smoked salmon and a small glass of orange juice was his daily ration. He was determined to lose weight, and he knew he needed to limit his calorie intake to do it. Allison wanted to look attractive, and eating to relieve stress was not allowed. Shopping for stress relief was another story. Pulling out of the garage, he stopped at the base of the driveway until the garage door closed. *I can't believe I was considering ending my life. What is wrong with me? I enjoy my feminine side. Half the world is female, what's wrong with that? Nothing, nothing at all.* He wanted to lay the blame at Allison's painted toes. Allison reminded him she was his salvation; his deliverer. Perhaps he wasn't a typical red-blooded All-American, dyed-in-the-wool manly man. He had given Mandy all of his attention and support and in return she had turned him into a throw rug and walked all over him.

Even when things had been good they weren't ideal. Mandy had wanted him to "man up." He was sick and tired of hearing that phrase. Why did she have to make it sound like he was less of a person because she would not accept him for who and what he was? She wasn't satisfied with ripping out his heart, she had to stomp on his liver for fun. He thought things would improve when she wasn't around physically. She made a point to be there psychologically.

At first Mandy had made the kids call him every night. They weren't happy about being pressured. She told the kids it was what their father wanted. She knew how to box him in. If he tried to explain it was not his doing, they might think he wasn't interested in them. She knew how to push his buttons, a control freak. Only when Allison was in control could Mandy be held at bay.

His daily drives were filled with reflection. Traffic was moving at a steady pace that required no thought. He gradually emptied his consciousness. Images of his troubled past scrolled across his mind's eye. He had attended an all-boys' school. Most of the teachers were priests. At fourteen he had been sexually molested by one of his high school teachers. Russell never revealed the humiliation he experienced. His parents would not have believed him. The struggle raged like a river's rapids swollen by spring rains. Mandy would not have forgiven him for marrying her with both black spots on his psyche.

The priest only molested him once; the damage had been done. Russell never came close to revealing the problem; he talked himself out of it every time. What good would it do?

The more he fought to keep the feminine side subdued, the more miserable Russell became. Russell had dabbled in cross-dressing since puberty. Along the way, he would binge and purge and binge and purge.

***

The push and pull of gender dysphoria took him back to events leading to his newly minted divorcee status. Viewing himself in the full-length mirror in the master closet, bedecked in black sling backs with four-inch heels, pantyhose and midnight blue sequined dress, he felt fabulous, as though a weight had been lifted from his shoulders. He pointed his hip toward the mirror and struck a pose. "Here I am!" he said, "This is me." The last time the blue dress had been out of the closet his wife had worn it to a wedding reception, and that night he tried to make love with her. Hours of partying had left him in a drunken state and his flaccid member was not up to the task. He loved that dress, but she never wore it again.

Russell had finally surrendered to the siren song of femininity. He had been denying his female side for almost thirty years, trying to deliver the man that Mandy insisted she needed. He had tried all through his roaring twenties and almost twenty years of marriage, but he couldn't resist any longer. His interest in projecting his male ego had dwindled to nothing. When his femininity spoke, the message was clear and unequivocal: Allison wanted equal time. When he saw her staring back from the mirror, he felt a combination of relief and revulsion. Men didn't do this. Men were supposed to be strong, virile, and in control. He was none of those things.

Stripping off his wife's clothes, he carefully replaced

15

everything, hoping he had not tipped his hand. For the balance of the day he fretted that Mandy would suspect; call him on it, start a confrontation. He wanted to explain his need for femininity, which made perfect sense to him. Yet he sensed that she would brush his flimsy logic aside and every counterargument he framed in preparation for the inevitable argument flaked and then crumbled.

Several days passed. A quiet calm settled over their relationship. Russell found himself more attentive to his wife. Sitting and talking at length felt natural. Mandy was pleased by his willingness to forego "manly" things that she regarded as a waste of time. His transition to submissiveness was gradual. It started with dinner and his willingness to help with preparations in the kitchen. She dished about the events of the day; he listened attentively and made thoughtful, supportive comments.

After a month, Mandy began to wonder what had happened to the bad habits. "Russ, dear, you've been helpful lately, and I just wanted to let you know that I have noticed your efforts."

"I'm trying to be more responsive to your needs. You complained about me all these years, and I finally began to see things from your point of view." Mandy wasn't buying it. He was being defensive, as if he were caught doing something untoward. She stared at him, her sixth sense picking up the conflict.

"People don't decide to change on their own. Something's up with you. I think you're hiding something." Russell struggled to retain dignity, restrain the urge to defend.

"I've been thinking about this for months, maybe years. I thought I should take your advice; come halfway." His voice rose, trying to find a redeeming quality to hang on to as he felt his position weaken. At first submitting to her will had been liberating. Although Mandy wasn't the type to blindly understand and accept, he didn't expect her to react with malice. She had a way of dissecting you, carefully peeling off your skin one layer at a time and probing with a needle until the pain was so great you would say anything to get her to stop.

"I'm finding this just a little too good to be true," she said.

"Look Mandy, I'm trying to be a better husband. I thought you'd appreciate it," he lied.

The debate ended in an uneasy truce. Mandy wanted to get to the bottom of his new act, and Russell wanted her off his back.

A few days after this confrontation, Mandy decided that it had been too long since she saw her girlfriends.

"You should go out with them. In fact, you should make this a regular thing. Not every week, but maybe once a month," Russell offered. Mandy smiled. He was trying to accommodate her; maybe it was time for her to acknowledge. Walking over to him she embraced him and placed a soft kiss on his cheek.

"You're really trying, aren't you?" She stepped back and looked into his eyes. Fighting for a façade of sincerity, Russell allowed his gaze to be transfixed.

"I want you to be happy." He took her in his arms and kissed her on the lips. The power and control had shifted; she felt it. Mandy basked in the glow of knowing she had the upper hand. Interlacing the fingers of one hand into Russell's she led him to the bedroom. They made love. Using his mouth and tongue he brought her to several massive orgasms before finishing with her on top. She ground herself into him hard and as she began to climax, she squeezed and pulled his sensitive nipples, which would always make him lose control and climax.

Thursday rolled into evening. As Russell made his way to the stairs, pulling on sweats, the couple passed each other in the foyer of their palatial home. "Have fun, and tell the girls I said hello." She backtracked to give him a peck on the lips before flitting out the door to the car.

"Be back later; I'll try not to be late."

Russell grabbed a quick bite to eat. The refrigerator held delicious leftovers from the last two nights. The kids were ensconced in their rooms working on homework with background music playing loudly. He couldn't understand how kids could focus on important things with distractions swirling around. After kissing them and spending a few minutes with each of them, Russell retreated to the master bedroom. Closing the door, he locked it and checked to make sure the lockset was engaged.

Moving to the dressing area he tore off his clothes, dropping them in his wake as he approached Mandy's extensive wardrobe that consumed three-quarters of their bedroom-sized closet. He had at least two hours to enjoy his femininity. "Let's go all out," he said to himself.

First, he donned a matching black bra and panty set. Then black pantyhose. Next came her four-inch high-heeled sandals, snugly fitting.

Then came the fashion show; he picked out the blue dress and gingerly removed it from the hanger. Placing the hanger back where it had been, stepped into the dress and reached behind to work the zipper up to the middle of his back before reaching over his shoulder to pull the zipper to the top. It was tight, but he loved that dress. It aroused him in ways the clothing manufacturers would appreciate. Standing before the full-length mirror he posed and admired the reflected image. He felt perfectly at ease.

Allison started modeling one outfit after another. When she tired of one look she carefully replaced the dress or outfit back on the hanger, rearrange the hanging straps, and zip the dress up.

Two hours and a dozen dresses later his need was satiated. He returned the last of the garments to its home in the closet, and then perched on the end of the bed in his bra and panties. There was a knock at the bedroom door startling him. Frozen, his heart skipped a beat. He was totally flustered and vulnerable.

"Who is it?" he called in a surprisingly calm voice.

"Who do you think it is dad? And why is the door locked?" It was Meghan.

"Give me a minute," he called back hoping the question of the door being locked would not come up again.

"We're going to bed and just wanted to say good night." Russell let out a long breath.

"Okay sweetie, sleep well."

"You too, Dad," she called back.

Shadow Woman

Stripping off the last of his wife's undergarments, he pulled on sweatpants, tee shirt and moccasins and checked his image in the mirror over the sink. His eyes were bloodshot; the threat of intrusion taxed him. He carefully put away her lingerie and accessories and checked and rechecked under the bed for any stray signs of his modeling session.

He slowly opened the bedroom door and peered out to make sure the coast was clear and tiptoed downstairs and into the garage. He lifted the lid of the trash can and stashed the panties and hose into a bag filled with garbage, arranging a few papers on top for good measure, and headed back upstairs to replace the waste basket.

As he exited the bathroom he reminded himself that being in the bedroom with the door locked wasn't smart. Meghan would say something to Mandy; he knew it. As he stepped into the hallway he felt perspiration forming on his brow. Vowing to control himself, he moved to Meghan's room. He knocked several times before Meghan answered in a bothered voice.

"It's Dad honey, I want to give you a hug and kiss to send you off to dreamland with happy thoughts."

"It's okay dad, I'm already asleep." Meghan was dismissive; she only wanted you on her schedule. *She's so much like her mother it's scary*, he thought.

After spending a few minutes with his son, he retreated to the bedroom. Switching on the television he tuned to one of the weekly drama series. He enjoyed the variety of women guest stars; their wardrobe gave him ideas—ideas he knew he would dismiss before they gained a foothold.

Mandy wandered into the bedroom just before midnight. Her movement caused him to stir. She climbed into bed, kissed him, then rolled over.

The next morning, he prepared for work feeling a sense of calm. On the drive, he realized how important Allison was to him. She relaxed him and released his creativity and energy. He desperately wanted to dress up more often, but struggled with the fact that Mandy would never allow it. He wasn't about to talk with her about it. He had tried to meander onto the topic by asking her how it felt to be dressed sensually. Her response was guarded; as if she had the ability to read his thoughts.

That evening he strolled into the house after a productive day. He could not remember the last time things went smoothly at work. Mandy was in the kitchen preparing dinner.

"Where are the kids?" he asked.

"I sent them to my mother's. I wanted us to be alone tonight." She smiled and offered her painted red lips. He kissed her lightly, feeling need that he knew would overwhelm him. She was radiant wearing a classic white silk blouse with a lacy white bra underneath, short blue linen pencil skirt, shimmery nude pantyhose and navy blue sling backs. Her musk perfume was intoxicating. Her eyes were smoky; long lashes fluttered as light shimmered suggestively off the pearlized white eye shadow painted just below her brows.

She had dinner ready and waiting and walked over to the dining room table to light the candles.

"This is really nice, Mandy. We haven't had time alone for so long. What's for dinner honey? he asked as he noticed the wine glasses on the table. "Red or white?"

"I made your favorite, lasagna with meat sauce." Russell picked out the best Cabernet Sauvignon, uncorked the bottle, sniffed the cork, poured a sample for her, which she sipped and smiled.

"I want this to be a night to remember. We've had few of them." As they ate they discussed the kids. He thought they had finally made peace and he could get back to enjoying his life, rather than wondering and worrying that the sword was about to fall at any moment.

She cleared the plates as he watched. She insisted he sit. "This is my show; you'll have the opportunity to make it up to me later." Her wink and smile made a promise he hoped she would keep.

The dessert course included decadent chocolate brownies still warm from the oven, topped with whipped, sweetened, heavy cream. Before the kids came along they used whipped cream for more erotic purposes. Taking the can of real whipped cream, she created a tower of sculptured white atop his brownie and topped it off with a maraschino cherry. She popped one into her mouth and stood motionless for a second as she tied the stem in a knot with her tongue, which she playfully dropped down the front of his shirt. Russell laughed and began unbuttoning his shirt to retrieve the stem.

"Well, you're easy," she said with a laugh.

After dinner, they cleared and cleaned up. He snuggled close to her and kissed her neck. She giggled like a schoolgirl. When the kitchen was back in order she took his hand and led him to the family room.

"Sit; I have a little surprise for you. I want your undivided attention," she said.

"You've got it honey." She walked out of the room and returned with a tote bag, which she unzipped producing a DVD in a plain jewel case. She stepped in front of the television, bent suggestively at the waist and fiddled with the remote controls for the television and the DVD player. Master remote control in hand, she sat down next to him on the sofa. His mind whirred with possibilities.

She placed a manicured hand on his knee to signal she was in control of the situation. "Now promise you'll watch this whole movie before you try anything." Her sultry eyes melted him.

"I promise." He was on the ragged edge; needing her more than he could remember. He went to put his arm around her but she deftly fended him off, grabbed his wrist and pushed his hand onto his thigh, holding it there.

"No, I really mean it, Russ. I want you to sit and watch this whole movie, okay?" He nodded and said "Okay" in a 'now what's she up to' voice.

"Sit back and relax. That's a good boy." *Relax? Is she kidding?*

"Ready?" she asked ceremoniously and clicked the remote. The movie started with a title: "Exhibit A – Remote Camera 2, Created on April 23, 2012, copied on April 27, 2012," on a blue background. The scene was dark and non-descript and there was a running time and date stamp in the lower right corner. "April 23, 2012 8:35 pm." He made out what he thought was the outline of light around a door.

As the door opened, the scene flooded with light as the camera adjusted to the sudden change in lighting and came into focus. His jaw dropped as he recognized the star of the show. It was him in a bra and panties. He flushed with embarrassment and broke into a cold sweat. He understood in a heartbeat that she knew everything about his cross-dressing.

"Cat got your tongue?" she asked. He had no idea what to say. He had practiced his "I am a worthy husband, but I am a cross-dresser" speech a thousand times.

The pieces of logic that he thought would convince her were swirling around in his head but he could not form words. He sat there frozen and watched. The video had been shot from cameras hidden in various spots in her walk-in closet. There was no sound. He watched himself walk up toward the camera and pensively gaze at her rack of shoes. He slid a shoebox from the rack, opened the box, and sniffed the leather aroma, carefully extracted a pair of navy blue sling backs, and slid the box back on the shelf. He then tiptoed out of the closet dangling the shoes by the straps.

Mandy punched the 'pause' button on the remote. Turning she looked at him; smug and self-assured. "How do you like my little production?" she asked. Russell felt his genitals tighten.

"I can explain." The words fumbled out of his mouth.

She patted his knee. "No need to explain. You get off on wearing my clothes," she said matter-of-factly.

"But you don't understand," he pleaded.

"I understand more than you know." Her smug tone sent chills down his spine.

"When did you… How did you…?" He was trying to understand the implications.

"Look sweetie, if you think those little feminine gestures you make go unnoticed you are naiver than I thought. I began to notice that my clothes had been tampered with and at first I suspected it was Meghan. But then I thought, no she wouldn't be interested in my things at her age. I began to suspect our maid, Arminda. She's been a gem, and she does such a terrific job cleaning everything, but the idea of her wearing my clothes creeped me out. I was ready to fire her ass, but I needed proof. I hired a detective who installed a couple of motion-activated cameras. It was expensive, but I needed peace of mind. I got a call from the detective telling me he had solved the mystery." She paused. "Picture my surprise when he told me it was my husband who was screwing with my clothes."

"You're not mad?" The words slipped out before he could formulate a better response.

"I was mad, I was balling my eyes out as I watched the video at the detective's office. After a couple of days the light bulb came on. My husband plays for the wrong team. I thought, "Why should I be mad? He can't help himself." She paused for effect; loading the next round of verbal ammunition.

"The better question, Russell, is whether I'm upset enough to do something about it." The delivery was stern, causing his spirits to sink. "Clearly, my husband has no balls. The real question is, do I have the balls to do something."

"I know you're upset. I can explain." He tried to take her hand. "My feminine side is…" She pulled away, and cut him off in mid-sentence. Standing she paced in front of the television.

"You're a man, Russell; just be a man and stop trying to pretend that you are a woman. What am I going to do with you?" She crossed one arm under her ample breasts the other bent at the elbow, her index finger tapping her supple lips. Russell started to stand hoping to embrace her.

"Sit down!" Her voice was sharp. His knees buckled and he fell back into the sofa. Trying to calculate the damage, the toll rose dramatically with each passing moment. "How long have you been doing this?"

"Dressing up?" His voice faltered as if the two words would indict and convict.

"No, picking your nose. Yes, dressing up!" Her eyes burned holes in him. "Don't think about trying to lie to me. I am tired of your lies. Our marriage is one big lie."

"But I need you, Mandy."

No, Russell, you need my clothes. Clearly you were in your little world that night. And from the way you slipped into and out of my clothes, I know this wasn't the first time." She stopped pacing, turned and faced him.

"I wanted to experience what you feel; what women feel. You are beautiful; free to express your emotions. You are so..." He struggled for the right punctuation mark. "Very sexy!" She held up a hand to stop any further groveling.

"You want to feel what I feel? Well, I am feeling betrayed, I feel as though I am competing for my husband with another woman." She turned and fiddled with the electronics; extracting the DVD from the player; placing it in a jewel case and carrying it out of the room. He wanted to follow but feared reprisal.

When she returned, she beckoned him to follow. He rose slowly, his knees like jelly. She led him to the bedroom and into the closet. "Show me how much you enjoy dressing in my clothes." She stood with arms folded, determination engraved in her features.

"But I don't want to do this." His voice cracked; humiliation emptied him of strength.

"I don't recall giving you a choice. You just told me that you want to feel like a woman. I want to see how you do this. Maybe I can learn some tricks from you since you've been practicing." Her voice softened. "Here, let me select your outfit." She walked in front of him, her sensuality gone. She was all business. Plucking a skirt and blouse she balanced the hangers on the tip of her manicured finger. He was frozen, indecisive.

"Take them. I'm not going to wait all night." He reached with trembling hands. She let the hangers slip from her finger. He caught them, almost fumbling them to the ground. "That is one of my favorite outfits. Don't you dare ruin it!" She turned and exited the bedroom returning with a garter, bra and silk thigh high stockings.

"I think I'd like to see how adept you are at working with a garter and stockings. I can never seem to get them fastened the first time." Her voice was whimsical. Russell's stomach was doing hula-hoops around his ass. She watched as he stripped off his day clothes. Sitting on the edge of the ottoman, the chill from the leather surface caused him to flinch.

"Now you know how I feel when I sit on that thing," she smiled. He struggled into the garter, next the stockings. His fingers weren't working right; the clasps on the garter were defying his will. When he finally had them fastened he stood.

"Straighten out those lines. You can't go around looking disheveled," she said smugly. Haltingly he adjusted the stockings and the seam running up the back of his legs. "Now the skirt and blouse." He stepped into the skirt and shrugged on the blouse after strapping on the bra. The band of the bra cut into him; she was smaller through the chest and shoulders. Mandy smiled as he struggled to fasten the clasps.

"Let me see you in stocking feet." He tried to stand straight, uncomfortable and embarrassed. "You know men find that look vulnerable." He wondered why she thought that was important for him to know. "Pick out a pair of shoes; nothing lower than four inch heels." Russell could not help himself; desire and sensuality threatened to betray him. Mandy's shoe collection was displayed in painted white cubbies. She insisted on a section of the closet being devoted to her shoes. He labeled it a shrine.

Perusing the vast collection, he was becoming intoxicated by the hint of fragrance from her shoes. Selecting a pair of four-inch sling back pumps with peep toe, he showed them to his wife. He didn't want to appear anxious to step into them, although enthusiasm welled up.

"You have good taste; those are my favorites." Unconsciously he brought the shoes to his face and inhaled.

"I can tell," he said smiling. Her look turned from amused to nonplussed, causing him to blush. She didn't like the fact that he was experiencing enjoyment.

"Put them on," she said as she walked out of the bedroom. Standing, he felt complete, in the open, although he wasn't sure Mandy was going to sanction this long-term. He hoped this exercise would end here. Catching him gazing at his image in the full-length mirror she interrupted his reverie.

"Turn around, sweetie." She spoke in a girl-friendly voice. When he turned the flash of the digital camera surprised him. "Now walk over there. I want to get a full-body shot."

"Don't do this Mandy, please!" His shoulders slumped as he considered the possibility of his pictures circulating around the Internet.

"Don't 'please' me," she giggled at the dual meaning. "Be a good girl and model for me. These pictures are for my amusement." She left the insinuation dangling like the sword of Damocles.

"You promise you won't do anything with them?" he asked, his spirit broken.

"Don't stand like a man. You know how to look feminine," she said. He attempted a lady-like pose.

"That's better." She snapped a few pictures.

"What are you going to do with those pictures?" He was more insistent.

"You needn't worry as long as you do whatever I ask. If you give me incentives to keep your embarrassing secret then you will have nothing to worry about." Her voice was sinister, conspiratorial. He felt perspiration forming in the middle of his back. Turning off the camera she approached him. Walking around him as he stood uncomfortably, she smacked his ass.

She pinched his cheek. Russell felt vulnerable, completely at her mercy. "You look cute; you're my little girlie girl." She pinched his cheek again, noticing the day's stubble rough against her soft skin. What shall I call you; Barbie?"

"Um, it's Ali, Allison." stammered Russell.

"Jesus fucking Christ, that's priceless," she said, her voice dripping with sarcasm. "Now I'm married to Allison."

"Allison is my femme name."

As she walked toward the doorway out of the dressing area she stopped and turned. "You can take those off. Make sure you hang everything where they belong. Wash the garter and nylons by hand and hang them to dry. You know how much I dislike wearing things that have not been washed. Which reminds me, she walked over to her dresser and pulled out a zip lock bag with the panties and pantyhose, she threw them in his lap. I loved your little show honey."

As she stepped across the threshold into the bedroom she turned again. "One more thing, find one of my nighties. You can wear that to bed tonight." She cackled as she turned and left him alone. He felt his loins betraying him. He was becoming aroused. He didn't understand it.

Standing naked in the dressing area he looked at himself in the mirror. When he was in this physical dilemma he would have rushed to his wife and they would screw like rabbits. He didn't think being clad in a silk nightie would prompt arousal in her; at least not the arousal that would result in their union.

Chapter 3

THEY LAY IN BED, each on their side physically separated by a short distance, but separated emotionally by an ocean of conflict. She wasn't interested in him. He hoped it would pass. This wasn't what he had hoped would happen. In his heart of hearts he knew the inevitability of discovery of his hidden desire. He had hoped to ease her into it. *Who am I kidding? How do you ease someone into a bathtub filled with ice water; a pool infested with sharks?* He sank into an emotional funk.

The night passed slowly; when he finally fell asleep the weight of the evening polluted his dreams with dread and discouragement. He awoke feeling drained but sexually aroused. Fecklessness struck him between the eyes. He wanted to snuggle with his wife, but feared a tongue-lashing. He needed to allow things to settle. Slipping out of bed he looked back at his wife's sleeping body. "She's not going to forget this." The voice of dread spoke clearly to him.

In the shower he struggled; nicking himself in several places as he shaved his face. Stepping out he toweled off. He wondered how he could retrieve the video and the pictures. *The calculating bitch. She's my wife! How could she do this to me?* Looking in the mirror as he applied deodorant and aftershave he could not reconcile how his world had been radically impacted.

Exiting the bathroom, he moved to the dressing area.

"Russ?" Her sleep-laced voice startled him. He'd hoped to dress and be on his way before she awoke. He needed emotional distance.

"Yes?" His response was clipped.

"Come here, please." Promise welled up in his heart. Maybe she was going to let this go, explain his failing with a warning baked in. He walked over to the bed naked. Hoping she would invite him to a morning romp was too much to expect.

She turned to sit up. "Good, you're not dressed yet." Her eyes were trained on him drawing him like a tractor beam.

"What can I get for you, Mandy?" His voice was soft almost a whisper. She made him wait for an answer, making him nervous.

"Get me a pair of panties please." He tried to remember whether she wore panties to bed. The kids weren't home; he couldn't figure out what was up unless it was that time of the month.

"Are these okay?" He held out a pair of black string bikini panties.

"They'll do just fine." He held them out to her. "They're not for me silly; they're for you!" Her voice found a playful edge. He was poleaxed; catching himself with an extended arm against one of the pillars that extended from the footboard.

"Go ahead and put them on."

"But Mandy…" He stopped short of pleading. He knew there was no way she was going to relent. She snapped her fingers and made a motion with her hand. Compliant, he slipped into the panties.

"You should be thankful I don't have you wear a camisole and pantyhose, too. You should kiss my feet… Wait, you would enjoy that!" She barked a laugh devoid of humor. He considered objecting, but reconsidered. If he mollified her she might eventually let things return to normal.

The day at work was a blur. He was preoccupied with the events of the prior evening; kicking himself figuratively several times for being caught. As the day wore on and the lack of restful sleep took its toll, Russell concluded that the video and the pictures were his wife's bargaining chips. If he screwed up she would ruin him. That was one hell of an incentive to toe the line. It also meant he would be under her thumb.

That night the kids were home; things were normal. Mandy was cordial to him, almost loving, leaving him to wonder how much was a show for the kids and how much was real.

Several weeks passed without event. Mandy didn't carry on; it appeared she had forgotten since she had not imposed dressing sessions on him. He refrained from spending any more time in the closet than absolutely necessary. He felt his wife's clothing beckoning him. He dared not heed the call. He figured one more time and his life would worsen.

A month after the debacle he decided to approach her. He was love-starved. A dozen red roses and a bottle of champagne accompanied him home. Pulling into the garage, Mandy's bay was empty. She hadn't said anything about being out. He chalked it up to a last-minute errand. She was always running around helping the neighbors.

Placing the champagne in the refrigerator he proceeded to hunt down a vase for the roses. Arranging them, he placed them on the center island of the kitchen. The expansive speckled granite island sat prominently like an aircraft carrier in a pond. Surveying everything his toils had produced, he felt sanguine.

Following the sounds to the second floor he knocked on Matt's bedroom door before entering. They exchanged pleasantries. Matt responded to his dad's hugs. The gangly youth felt no compunction to show affection to his dad.

Parking himself on the edge of the bed, Russell watched as his son resumed the shoot 'em up video game. They had waited outside the gaming store at midnight to purchase it. Tiring of the monotony, Russell moved to his daughter's room. She was on the mobile phone chatting it up while she sent instant messages by computer to three other friends. Meghan looked over to her dad mouthing, "I'm going to be a while."

Russell approached his daughter and planted a kiss on the top of her head. "I love you, Meg," he said, disregarding her conversation. He heard her say, "It's just my dad telling me he loves me," into the phone.

Slowly down the winding staircase, he absorbed the beautiful grand entryway finished in ivory marble, wainscoting and triple layer crown molding. He was fortunate to have so much in such a short period.

Grabbing a snifter from the china cabinet he poured two fingers of cognac. The bouquet was enticing. I don't do this enough, he reminded himself. Carrying the beverage into the living room he avoided the family room; the ill effects of "movie night" still haunted him. As he sat in the overstuffed armchair, feet atop the matching ottoman negativity stabbed at him. He had asked his son where Mandy was. He shrugged.

After thirty minutes of building anguish, he grabbed his mobile phone and called Mandy's number. His thumb massaged the 'send' button quelling the admonition that he was being paranoid. Initiating the call, he raised the phone to his ear. After five rings voice mail picked up. He left a short message ending it with, "I love you, Mandy." Placing the phone on the end table to his right, he took a large sip of brown liquid. The heat in his throat chased the demons, if only for a moment.

Two hours later he began pacing. Three hours later he polished off his third snifter of cognac, dulling his senses.

After checking on the kids and asking Meghan if she knew her mother's plans—she told him "mom said she was going out." The kids turned in just before midnight. He returned to the living room, worried. His mind conjured up dark possibilities.

At 1:00 A.M. Mandy stumbled into the house. Russell roused from a doze, his neck stiff from the awkward sleeping position. Pushing himself out of the chair he approached her. She seemed surprised to find him up.

"Why aren't you in bed?" The words rode a singsong voice as if she was addressing a roommate.

"Where have you been?" Russell tamped down the anger making his question a pleading.

"Out, silly!" she giggled.

"You're drunk!" His voice sharpened.

"Not drunk, just rowdy." Her words acquired long tails. Russell studied her; she looked unkempt. This was the Mandy that never stepped away from the mirror with one hair out of place.

"Where did you go with your girlfriends?" he asked hopefully, his mind filling with questions and dread.

"Girlfriends, that was last week; tonight I went out with my new boyfriend."

The words slammed him like a blow to the solar plexus. Recovering slowly, he thought she was teasing him.

"Let's go to bed I'm exhausted." She started up the stairs after slipping out of her heels, which she dangled from her fingers. On cue Russell cradled them and hustled to catch up to her on the stairs, his free hand taking liberties with her shapely ass. She swatted his hand away. "Hands off the merchandise, mister."

"Sshhh, you'll wake the kids," he whispered loudly.

"Then stop and I won't wake them," she replied.

She bounded into the bedroom and he followed with her shoes and locked the door. She lit a candle on the nightstand and turned off the lights. He went to embrace her and she pushed him away. "Are you wearing my panties?" He wasn't, but replied, "Of course." She grabbed his crotch and squeezed his erection.

"Somebody is glad to see me," she giggled. "Give me a sec to brush my teeth while you get comfortable. And why don't you put my pumps on. I know you want to." She left the trail of words as she headed to the bathroom. Russell stripped off his clothes, which he left in a heap, grabbed a pair of pink panties from her drawer and slipped into her shoes. He wasn't sure what to do as he gingerly perched himself on the edge of the bed and awaited her return.

Mandy emerged from the bathroom. From across the room she asked in a seductive voice, "Wanna play show and tell?" Russell had never seen her in this sex kitten outfit; a departure for her. He was awestruck, simply nodding. "I thought you might. I think you should go first. Why don't you tell me about what's inside your panties?"

Russell thought after years of dull, lifeless sex they were on the verge of engaging the role-playing that he yearned for. Mandy grabbed the antique white wire frame chair with the heart shaped back and red cushion from her vanity table and sat down in front of Russell with her legs crossed.

"On your knees. I don't want to make you do anything that would embarrass you, Allison!" Sarcasm dripped from her delivery

32

causing her submissive husband lost in the moment emotionally straddling between his male and female sides. Making love woman to woman proved Allison's devotion and submission to Mandy. Mandy dominated completely. They had crossed a boundary together and there was no turning back. Allison wasn't thinking about the consequences, she wanted to prove her womanhood to please her lover. Mandy was busy shredding Russell's dignity and asserting herself as the alpha partner.

Mandy's orgasm wracked her body. She announced her climax with moans and groans of pleasure and then quickly pulled away from Allison, who remained exactly where she was as if waiting for command from her mistress. Lying on her back, Mandy fingered herself enjoying the aftershocks while Allison curled up into a fetal position at the foot of the bed and closed her eyes. Mandy contemplated making her husband repeat his performance for good measure. Mandy's defeated husband lay in bed trying to make sense out of what transpired. His manhood was history.

Emerging from the bathroom Mandy was dressed in pajama tops and bottoms, her hair pulled back into a ponytail. "Did you the enjoy sloppy seconds?" The words took precious seconds to register.

"What did you say?" he asked, incredulous.

"You don't know what sloppy seconds are?" she asked playfully.

"You had an affair." He struggled to control his frustration.

"I wouldn't call it an affair." She continued to toy with him.

"Then what would you call having sex with a stranger?"

"He wasn't exactly a stranger." Russell's thoughts collided as he tried to process. "I met him the last time I went out with the girls. You can relate to this; he knows you from your little fashion show." She giggled like a schoolgirl, driving frozen emotional ice picks into his spine. "He thought I needed a 'real man' in my life. I couldn't argue with his logic." More giggles. "He's such a hunk and my girlfriends really like him." She spoke the words as if their acceptance was enough to justify her actions. "He bought us drinks and flirted with us. That's all it was at first."

"You hooked up with him?"

"Yes. After all, you have a girlfriend. I thought it would be fair to balance things." She placed her hands on his chest releasing his limp member. Wrapping arms around him she tried to kiss him. He was repulsed, pushing away and pacing to the far end of the room. Wrapping arms around his chest he stood shivering.

"This is about getting back at me; getting even? All because I wore your clothes? Mandy, I have been faithful to you since before the day we were married." He moved to the night table, retrieved pajamas and threw them on the bed before climbing into them.

"No, Russell, this is about me looking out for myself, I wish I had walked out on you the minute I discovered you were playing for the other team. When I began putting the pieces together it became obvious to me that you live in your little world. I take care of the kids and what do you do? You cheat on me." Her rationalizations were making him crazy. He wanted to reason with her and convince her that his cross-dressing was a wonderful thing; that he could be strong as well as sensitive.

"Mandy, look, I know that my cross-dressing is not easy for you to understand, and maybe you *are* mad at me, but I don't understand why you felt the need to have an affair. His voice rose as he paced his side of the bed. Mandy had moved to her side of the bed watching, calculating.

"Russell, you listen. I know what you want but I am just not that kind of girl. I didn't want to cheat on you, but I will tell you this woman needs a man." She crossed her arms under her supple breasts, showing signs of tears.

"I'm your husband."

"I don't know what you are. You're something between a man and a woman!" She threw her arms up in disgust.

"I'm a man." His voice faltered. He wanted to be a man at that moment, but the woman inside wanted to tell her side of the story. Allison was tired of taking a back seat.

"Men don't wear women's clothes." Her eyes bored into him.

"Maybe you should see a therapist," he offered.

"Me? Really, Russell, you're the one who should see a therapist." She pointed a finger in his direction. He summoned courage before speaking.

"Maybe, we should both see a marriage counselor together. I am willing to forget about this fling you had tonight and I will forgive you. I've been devoted to you all these years, doesn't that mean anything to you?" He crossed his arms in a show of strength. She turned to the side, staring at the lamp before adjusting the shade. Satisfied the lampshade was perfectly set, she turned back to him.

"It's too late, Russell. I'd forgotten what it's like to be with a real man, one who knows how to treat a lady."

"But I'm your husband, Mandy."

"Russell, if you loved me, you wouldn't need to cross-dress. Am I not enough woman for you?"

"That's not it. I like to express my femininity."

"Spare me the psychobabble, Russell. You can call it what you want. Face it, we're done. You don't want to quit dressing up. Do you think I don't know that? It's an addiction, Russell."

"It's not an addiction; it's how I feel."

"All you talk about is your delicate little feminine feelings. Seeing you prance around in my clothes..." She paused to shake off the feeling of regret that threatened to derail her diatribe. "The gestures, the poses; do you think no one notices how you stand. How you gesture with your hands; it's posturing Russell."

"I didn't want to hurt you anymore than I have to but I know that's what I have to do. Sam said it wouldn't be easy. He thought I should give you a little test; see how you would react to finding another man was planting in your garden. A real man would have flown into a rage and vowed to kill him. Russell, women like strong men who will defend their honor. I can't trust you Russell."

It devastated him to hear her words. He tried to recover their crumbling marriage. "That was role playing, Mandy." She cut him short.

"Role playing?" she scoffed. Russell. Look, I get it, you are transgender and you want to be a woman. But I am not a lesbian. It makes me sick to see my husband wearing my clothes. Physically ill, do you hear me, Russell?"

Making what felt like a last stand, he summoned the will to fight for himself.

"What I do in this house stays in this house. You've humiliated me enough. Mandy, I get it. You've made your point. I'll stop cross-dressing if that will make you happy."

"You can do whatever you want, Russell, I am divorcing you."

"What? You screw another man and you're divorcing me?"

"That's right, Russell."

"My God, you are serious, aren't you? But, Mandy, I just…I just don't see why you can't accept me. And what about the kids?"

"It's a done deal, Russell. I am going for full custody. Don't make this harder than it has to be. Remember the evidence I have? Do you think I'm keeping it for fond memories? Those pictures and the video are sitting in a safe deposit box. One look at those and the judge will issue a restraining order against you."

"But you just fucked another man. That's adultery."

"Maybe so," she said with a giggle. Russell's world had collapsed and she was laughing at him.

"Tomorrow is a big day. You have some papers to sign. I suggest that you get some sleep." Mandy, grabbed a glass of water from the nightstand and took a couple of pills from a small pill case in the night stand.

What are those?" he asked.

"Sleeping pills, you want a couple?"

"Um no. Well, yeah sure."

Mandy reached into her nightstand and handed Russell an oxycodone. She had only taken two vitamins.

Russell lay in bed and tried to think of something to say, but in a few moments his mind began swirling and soon he was asleep.

Mandy popped up and shook Russell by the shoulders. He stirred for a moment and opened his eyes. He was trying to raise his head but he felt woozy and weak. He couldn't seem to move his arms. Meanwhile, Mandy grabbed her mobile phone and called Sam.

She put the phone down and hit the speaker button. Walking over to her dresser she slipped into a negligee.

"Did you see the look on his face? It was priceless."

"Yeah, yeah, I got it all on the camera." They both laughed.

"You want to come over for some champagne and a quickie?"

"Of course, sugar. We can move him to the spare bedroom."

Ten minutes later Sam pulled his Corvette into the driveway and let himself in through the garage. Bounding up the stairs to the master bedroom, Mandy was waiting in a lacy teddy with matching panties, thigh high silk hosiery and fluffy mules. They embraced and kissed. Mandy pulled back and gestured over to Russell under the covers.

"Yeah, right." Sam was a massive man; six feet five inches of muscle; 250 pounds of flashing steel and sex appeal. He scooped up Russell like a rag doll.

"Where do you want him, ma'am?"

"The couch seems appropriate. Sam carried him down the stairs and plopped him on the sofa.

"How long do those pills last?"

"Six to eight hours." Mandy had grabbed a pillow, a sheet and blanket and they tucked him in on the couch.

"Sam, you do such nice work," she said as they embraced. He drew her closer grabbing her thighs and lifting until her legs were wrapped around his firm waist just a few feet away from Russell.

"Sam, I know a single man like you has a lot of options and that you don't want to be tied down." She played the vixen to his stud.

"You are different than the others, Mandy. You are a real smart lady and I'd be lying to you if I said that I was just in it for the money. It's more than business this time."

"Are you just saying that?"

"No, Mandy. You are a catch and why Russell couldn't man up and defend your honor is beyond me."

'I'll be set for life after the divorce," she said hopefully.

Sam whispered in her ear. "Let's make a video of us screwing on the coffee table in front of him." Mandy reached down and felt his large package, and smiled.

"Should we? I mean wouldn't that be discoverable?"

"Good point, it's just not worth the trouble."

"How about some champagne?" Sam positioned her so she could grab the bottle and the flutes without letting her go. Mandy fetched the bottle and two crystal flutes she had lined up on the coffee table.

Chapter 4

WHEN THE DUST FINALLY settled, Russell had given up the maximum in return for the video and pictures: most of the marital assets and a significant chunk of his annual earnings as alimony.

The news of his divorce spread around the office. He received condolences from his male colleagues. Two of the women were icy toward him. They thought divorce was a giant eraser for male mistakes. It was a jip, reneging on a promise. Russell refused to entertain their malice.

By the end of the day one of the vice presidents, Barbara Collins, stopped by. She was single and very personable. They had worked on two big deals during the past year. She had come on to him. His lawyer warned him to "keep your nose clean." Russell stopped her advances in their tracks explaining that the ink on the divorce decree wasn't dry. He wasn't in the right frame of mind.

She perched herself on the edge of the desk, one leg dangling suggestively, the slit in her skirt strategically placed to expose a supple thigh. Russell's eyes found her visual offering. She blushed at his attention. Russell processed the color and texture of her pantyhose, the cut of her skirt and the curve of the neckline of her powder blue fitted blouse. When his eyes strayed to her nude pumps she extended her leg to give him a better view.

"I like your outfit, you are really put together; I mean your outfit is really well put together. I mean in a professional way." It was a Freudian slip and he reminded himself that running afoul of human resources policies was second only to having his pictures in a dress circulated around the office.

"I know what you meant, Russ. That's very sweet." She blushed as she replied; shifting to allow her blouse to open enough to reveal tanned cleavage and the rim of her blue lace bra.

"I'd love to chat but I've got a deadline to make." The statement was partially true. He needed her to leave before he lost control. He wanted to feel her softness; to live vicariously through her.

"Would you like to get together for a drink after work, just you and me? We could enjoy a little girl talk. Oh, you know what I mean. You just seem like you could use a little pick me up. How about seven?"

"Seven really doesn't work for me. How about six at O'Malley's?" Russ figured that he could go back to the office if he had to make an excuse to get away.

***

They escaped the usual late night work obligation. They both hated the fact that their boss, Sylvia, could impose her will and suck up their free time whenever she wanted. Sylvia had been called away from the office. That meant a reprieve for all. Settling on a barstool at O'Malley's, Russell ordered something strong, shying away from the fruity drinks that Allison would order. Barb arrived a few minutes earlier. She had already ordered.

"I saved you a seat," she said as she sipped vodka and cranberry through the little stirrer, her ruby red lipstick glistening in the bar lights.

"Thanks." He lifted his drink in a toast to her. "To you." He took a long pull on the bourbon, the heat in his throat radiated into his gullet. Staring at his reflection in the mirror behind the bar his gaze bypassed the rows of liquor bottles that adorned the glass shelves. Turning, he glanced past his colleague observing the patrons to his right and then to his left. Satisfied that he didn't recognize anyone he turned his attention to Barb.

"How do you do it?"

"How do I do what?"

"How do you look just minted after a long day at the office?"

She pondered the question before answering. "I'm not sure I should reveal my little secret. Girls don't kiss and tell." She winked.

He wished he could reveal that he was one of the girls.

Switching subjects Barb wanted to talk shop. "Sylvia is such a bitch."

"Copy that." *But I love her clothes.* He chased the thought before he spoke it.

"She's the one you should ask about looking newly minted. The bitch looks like she just stepped out of Glamour magazine," Barb said.

"I don't need to ask. I know the answer." He sipped his drink knowing he was piquing her curiosity.

"And how do you know this? If you're smart, then you probably think you know my secret." She pinched his arm for good measure causing him to fumble his drink.

"Yo, I almost spilled my drink!" He feigned shock.

"Answer my question and I'll lay off." She barked a laugh.

"She's got the female version of the Portrait of Dorian Gray in her attic. Either that or she's the devil's daughter." A crinkled smile meandered across his lips.

"Very funny. Did you think of that all by yourself?"

Conversation ebbed and flowed for an hour before Barb pulled up stakes.

"I've got to get rolling." She left the balance of the statement unspoken. He wanted to ask but thought it too personal; none of his business. Besides he could make his way home and give Allison quality time.

"Maybe we could do this again. Dinner when you have a free evening?" He was fishing for intelligence on her personal life. He wanted to know if she was seeing anyone.

"Okay, Russ. I'd love to have dinner with you; be a sympathetic shoulder. Not much of that on sale today." She referenced the judgmental people in the office. As she stood, the shoe slipped off her left foot revealing ruby red painted toes. She lingered a moment before finding the shoe with her pointed toes. She watched his eyes, expecting them to fall out of their sockets and bounce around the floor. He was thinking about his feet in similar shoes; he couldn't wait to slip into a pair of pumps when he arrived home.

***

The drive home from the bar with the convertible top down felt liberating. As he walked up the driveway he felt the smoothness of the silk stockings against his legs. The faint swish of the stockings under his slacks comforted him. He had decided to wear a black lace garter to work. After the first night in the garter, when he wrestled with the fasteners he had finally become facile attaching the garter's clasps to the stockings.

He struggled, trying to understand why he was in this twilight area. Catholics call it purgatory. He called it torture. The woman inside showed him a side of life he fought to hide. Single and uninhibited, he wanted Allison to be just as free. He began investigating meet-up groups on the Internet that catered to his passion for wearing women's clothes and learned he was not alone. The promise of connecting with other males with female tendencies filled him with hope, but the process of trying to reach out was awkward and he was wary of hidden agendas.

At home, he rushed to enjoy his version of creature comforts. Most women relax at the end of the day. Allison on the other hand took comfort in turning up the glam. He decided he would let Allison play a bit, running errands femme.

He resolved to wear something feminine to work every day. As a precaution, he kept a gym bag with male undergarments in the trunk of his car. He could never be too prepared. Disaster, in the form of an accident or a traffic violation could strike when he least expected it. He wished he had thought of that before he'd taken those liberties with his wife's closest and made the monumental blunder that landed him in the current situation. Leaving the car in the driveway with the top down he decided to dress and take a drive. He had accessories to keep his wig from being tangled by the turbulence washing over the windshield and swirling around inside the open cabin.

Allison pushed him to be bold. She wanted him to take

calculated risks. She didn't care about the neighbors; she wanted him to enjoy her as often as possible. Tonight was going to be one of those nights. Working through the closet Allison had made him rearrange by purchasing a two-layer closet organizer.

The two-tiered system provided one rack for blouses and tops, and the bottom rack for skirts. Another section of the wall closet was devoted to dresses. Below Allison's clothes a two-shelf system for her shoes was already filled.

Pushing back the male wardrobe he felt his pulse quicken. It happened every time he saw Allison's clothes; the hint of perfume lingering on her clothes tantalized him.

Grabbing a red pleated skirt with a forgiving elastic waistband and a flouncy pale pink top, he placed them on the bed. Grabbing a pair of red patent leather heels, he held them up before placing them on the floor next to the bed.

Stepping into the skirt and slipping into heels he felt the male façade melt away. In the bathroom, he unfolded the makeup case and unrolled the makeup brush kit. Running the electric razor over the stubble he concentrated on the heavier areas. Caressing his now smooth face, he emptied the razor of its handiwork before digging a makeup wedge from the bag. Applying foundation, Allison came to life.

Selecting a bronze concealer, he focused on cheeks, neck and around his eyes. Penciling in his eyebrows he reminded himself to employ the tweezers to shape them better.

Applying eye shadow, Allison came into view. She smiled. Several short strokes with the eyeliner pencil and then mascara; she was almost ready.

A touch of blush on her cheeks and across her jawline and she was ready for lipstick. This was always tricky. Wishing for full lips wasn't going to make a difference. Botox was an option, but finances were tight. There was enough of a challenge to build Allison's wardrobe without breaking the bank.

The transgender makeup artist at an online makeup site had showed how to make lips look full without medical intervention.

43

Following those instructions, the red gloss enhanced what nature provided. Turning to the linen closet in the bathroom, he grabbed the box that held Allison's mane and positioned the wig. In front of the mirror Allison admired herself. Reminding herself to enjoy the look she pushed the criticism that "you could look much better with more practice" to the back of her mind.

Sliding a sleeve of bracelets over her right hand, they jingled as she shook her arm to settle them. Choosing matching clip on earrings, she fastened them and adjusted her shoulder length hair. *I've got to get my ears pierced.*

Selecting four rings she slipped them onto her ring fingers and pinkies. A necklace of interlocking circles finished the look. Digging the Mani Pedi storage bin from under the sink she fished out a bottle of pearlescent pink. Applying one coat to each finger she moved her hands through the air to speed drying, trying not to catch a wet nail on her clothes.

From the opaque storage bin at the top of the closet she grabbed a colorful scarf and the leather cap with the cute brim. Finishing the look with a red clutch, she added the wallet, fold of cash, and car keys before prancing to the car.

Behind the wheel, Allison retrieved her oversize sunglasses from the center console, slipped them on, and checked her look in the visor mirror. Stabbing the key into the ignition she fired up the car. Backing out of the driveway, she felt the twilight of the evening inviting her. The sun splashed its waning light across the horizon in shocks of red-orange hues. Pointing the red coupe toward the horizon, the car jerked as she applied the gas. *I need to learn to drive in heels.* High heels were a new challenge but she refused to drive bare foot, not wanting to break the feeling of completeness.

An hour into the drive Allison decided to stop. She needed fuel and wanted to test herself in a public place. Trepidation engulfed her resolve. Dusk removed the edge from daylight's revealing illumination. "Let's go honey," she said to herself. As one elegantly heeled leg found macadam next to a bank of fuel pumps, a wolf whistle cut the air. Helping herself out of the car, she turned toward the direction of the sound.

"Hey honey, you are hot!" The middle-aged man looked love-starved and desperately in need of wardrobe triage. Allison turned away refusing to acknowledge. Extracting her wallet, she initiated the purchase transaction. The unkempt admirer approached, the grind of gravel between his boots and the warm blacktop replicated nails on a chalkboard for Allison.

"I'll get that for you, honey," he said, grabbing the pump. Allison's temperature rose. She was torn between saying something and exposing her secret or defending her space.

"I'm perfectly capable of doing this for myself." Allison's voice was softer than she anticipated but with enough masculine definition that the interloper froze.

"You're...," he stammered, caught flatfooted.

"That's right; perfectly capable of helping myself. Now get lost before I call a cop." Allison managed the nozzle into the filler port and locked the trigger of the nozzle in the 'on' position.

After completing the fuel transaction, she fired up the car and pulled around to the convenience store. She wanted something to drink. After passing the first test Allison felt emboldened. Stepping up to the front door a male patron exiting the store, held the door for her, and eyed her longingly as she entered. Once inside she pranced around enjoying the sound of her heels and catching stares from other shoppers.

At the front counter, she paid cash for her purchase and thanked the cashier, who gave her a skeptical look. Comfortably seated in the car she sipped from the water bottle, remembering to drink gingerly to preserve her lipstick.

Darkness settled as Allison pulled the convertible up the driveway and into the garage. Sitting for a moment with the engine off and ticking as it cooled, chastising herself for ever considering an end to what was shaping up to be a promising life.

Chapter 5

RUSSELL STOPPED AT BETHANY'S Coffee Shop to pick up coffee and a breakfast sandwich. This wasn't on his diet plan, but after the prior night's adventure he thought a tiny reward for being bold was in order. As he waited for his order there was the woman in grey pinpoint tweed tailored overcoat and black stockings. She had a sumptuous black leather purse and a caramel leather tote bag.

He followed her out of the shop, itching to ask her about the outfit, but uncomfortable approaching a stranger. He watched the beautiful woman pull out of the parking lot. She was driving a red Volvo S40. He felt vindicated sitting in his red sports car. Securing the coffee in the cup holder, he turned his attention to making it to the office in one piece.

"Russell, the boss wants to see you." The voice of Russell's secretary over the intercom cut the silence, startling him.

"Tell her I'll be there in a moment, Katie," he said.

"She sounded tense. I wouldn't keep her waiting." Katie protected her boss as much as she could; her success was directly tied to his. Sparkling charm and disarming smile masked her astute business instincts. Russell fished a piece of dark chocolate out of a crystal bowl on his desk, then stood and stretched.

Exiting his office, he stopped by Kate's workstation and handed her the dark chocolate reward with a smile. She blushed as color rose in her high cheekbones. Her soft complexion answered the straight blond hair that fell to her shoulders. A chill of excitement radiated through her petite and toned body. Blue eyes burned with a mixture of pride and infatuation. Katie was impressionable. She would do anything for him and he knew it, trying hard not to exploit his position.

Shadow Woman

He walked to the end of the long hallway with window offices to his right and cubicles for the support staff filling the interior of the office to his left. The layout was a holdover from the days when every manager had a bevy of secretaries and administrative people to pull the work wagon.

Knocking, he watched Sylvia Hutchison gesticulating as she strolled around the office talking on a wireless headset. She was a mover and a shaker. She'd been accused of sleeping her way to the top. It was easy to understand how jealous peers could make such an assertion. She was a bombshell in a business suit. Her long jet-black hair fell across her shoulders like a waterfall of shimmer and shine that constantly flowed with her movements. Sylvia's oval face carried a clear, dewy-fresh radiance. Her large hazel eyes burned with drive and framed a perfect button-cute nose. She wore bold red lipstick to adorn her full plump lips.

Some of the also-rans at the office speculated that she had Botox treatments, frequent facials, and chemical peels. For a while there was a rumor floating around that she was dating a cosmetic surgeon. Maybe she did and maybe she didn't. Sylvia was not the sort of girl who would reveal her secret to anyone. She used her beauty like a weapon to intimidate women and disarm and captivate men.

Dropping softly into the designer executive chair she placed her elegant French tip manicured fingers flat on the desk on either side of the morning report, and reached up to adjust her reading glasses, which were tethered with a delicate solid gold chain.

"Come in, Russell." Her words snapped him back to the present. As he entered he felt the aura of success. The corner office was cavernous, bordered on two sides with floor to ceiling windows.

Sylvia was rich and successful—at least she gave that appearance. Settling into one of the cushioned contemporary wooden arm side chairs in front of her desk, he focused on her fingers with the perfect French manicure. The nails looked real, natural.

"Russell, are you with us?" Her voice was crisp.

"I'm here and thinking about the project."

"I need you to focus right here, on me." He told himself she had

47

no idea how focused he was on her.

"That was San Jose on the phone." Russell checked his watch. It was just after 5:00 A.M. on the west coast. He was about to respond when she held up a hand to stop him. "There's a problem with the deal." Her words fell hard on him. He had been working for weeks to close the acquisition for their client, an international conglomerate. She fidgeted with the sheaf of papers until she found what she was seeking.

"This is the problem." She pulled several pages from the group and handed them across the desk. As he grabbed the papers he felt something invisible pass between them. Watching her expression it wasn't evident that she noticed anything peculiar. He took the papers and perused them. There was a disconnect in the numbers. This was going to be a big problem.

"How did we miss this?" he asked, hoping he wouldn't be burned at the stake for the oversight.

"Look, you can only work with what you've got and the lawyers apparently just found it buried in one of the boxes of paperwork that had been sitting in their data room for over two weeks."

Russell let out a long sigh of relief. "Exactly! Why are we paying a high-powered firm to counsel us if they can't find their ass with both hands?" Russell knew there was no answer. He sat quietly.

"We can get past this. It's not like we haven't had a challenge before." A smile of reassurance crinkled across his lips. Sylvia stared at him making him wonder what she was holding back.

Her expression softened slightly. Her full lips turned up just enough to break the tension. "I know we can. That's why I called you in. You and I are going to work together to solve this problem. Remember that good managers turn problems into opportunities." That was Sylvia's punch line. He'd heard the refrain several times before, and knew that the only opportunity he'd be given would be the opportunity to work his ass off while Sylvia concentrated on making sure she got all the credit.

"We still have a couple of weeks to pull this together. The problem compresses the timetable, but we should still be okay." He tried to sound confident as he calculated the hours it would take to get the project back on track. He'd have to rearrange visitation, since weekends were now committed.

"We're going to start tonight," she said as she punched up her secretary on the intercom. "Delia, clear my calendar for the next week. And bring in dinner menus. We're going to be working late tonight." Sylvia wasn't the type to allow the personal life of employees to stand in the way of her success. Russell knew better than to object. He valued his career too much for that.

"You're divorced, change of plans shouldn't impact you, huh?" Her question was more a statement.

"No worries. This is an important project and you know I'll do whatever it takes." The words rang hollow from him.

"Grab your files. We'll convene in the conference room in fifteen. Grab Eddie and George. We'll let them do some of the background work."

He stood and turned. "I'm not going to ask Katie to stay until we get to the point when we need admin support." Her silence made him wonder if he had guessed wrong.

After a long pause, she responded. "That's fine. We should be okay for the next couple of nights." Russell retreated to his office. Grabbing the handset, he called his ex-wife. *She's going to love my changing plans. Nothing like being wedged between two hard cases.*

"Mandy, it's me."

"I know, Russ, I have your number in my contacts. What do you want?" She wasn't interested in small talk.

"I need to change visitation. I have a deadline that just surfaced and I'm going to have to work all weekend."

"Why is that my problem? Suppose I made plans."

"Look Mandy, I wouldn't call you if it wasn't an emergency." He was pleading and hated himself for being weak.

"Can't you hire a babysitter?" She had a knack for rubbing sand in an open wound.

"You know I can barely afford to pay you alimony and child support. Hiring a babysitter is not in my budget."

"Maybe you should have thought about that before volunteering to work the weekend." Her words cut him.

"I told you this was not my doing. I was conscripted. I don't have a say unless I want to lose my job." He left the insinuation unspoken. He ran through his options, anticipating another pass of the hedge trimmer over his genitals.

"Let me see what I can do. Sam and I have plans. I need to touch base with him to see if we can shift things around." *Sam, she's got nerve making this dependent on him.* "I'll get back to you." She ended the call, leaving him with the dial tone.

Dropping the handset into the cradle he circled his desk to gather the files. "She's heading to the conference room." Katie's voice carried alarm. She knew the CEO didn't appreciate being kept waiting.

"Can you get Eddie and George to join us? Tell them to grab the Wombat project file."

"Already done." Katie smiled, efficient to a fault. With an armful of accordion files Russell moved quickly to the conference room dropping them onto the long table surrounded by twenty-four leather executive armchairs. Sylvia did nothing conservative. She was already engaged with Eddie and George, the finance version of Simon and Garfunkel. They made numbers sing and their look was eerily close to the soft rock duo.

"Russ, nice of you to join us." She stabbed him with her words. "I was just telling Eddie and George about the problem. They think they can fence the issue and get us an exposure range." Russell wasn't sure whether she was honestly pleased or mocking their admission of the obvious. He didn't say anything as he dug through one of the brown expanding folders. Sylvia watched for a moment before continuing her conversation with the finance version of the dynamic duo.

Extracting a bound report, he placed it on the table, leafing through it until he found the page. Turning the report, he slid it toward the analysts. "I think this would be a good place to start." Eddie pulled the report toward him as George leaned in to kibitz.

"What is that?"

"The valuation with all its provisos. If we start there we can determine the impact of the latest problem." Sylvia snapped her fingers. The report was carried around the table and placed in front of the CEO. Her manicured nails drummed on the polished table. Russell could not figure how she concentrated with that distraction.

Two hours later they all knew the screw-up by the lawyers was worse than anticipated. An all-nighter was on the menu. Russell was the last person out of the conference room. He watched Sylvia's pencil skirt pull tight as she strode confidently in her heels to her office. As he walked by her door she called to her secretary. The lawyers were going to get an earful and more. When she was angry, vitriol poured from her like molten lava.

***

Nine P.M. came and went. George and Eddie were dismissed. Sylvia was on the phone with the west coast while Russell poured through research reports. They had only scratched the surface of the problem after hours of tearing down the spreadsheets and changing the formulas that were wrong. Stretching, he stood. His gaze fell on Sylvia's shapely legs, crossed and propped on her desk, shoes off and lying suggestively at the base of her chair. She was engaged in an animated conversation.

Russell felt his jaws part. He feared that if he looked down he'd see his tongue dangling from his mouth, down his chest and threatening to spill onto the floor. Involuntary sexual reaction coursed through him. *If she looks up she's going to flip.* He turned to hide the moment of weakness. He hadn't had a woman since the split with his wife. Sylvia was hard in many ways, but she was drop dead gorgeous and Russell had more than one fantasy about her.

He wanted to get closer; the soft shimmer of light from the ceiling fixtures coaxed a satin sheen across her sculpted calves. Her toes moved to an internal rhythm as she spoke; the conversation ebbed and flowed. His mind was elsewhere; Allison was feline curious; she wanted to know what color nail polish powerful women wore on their toes. Russell urged himself to relax. His gait could betray the activity in his loins.

Taking a deep breath, he turned, avoiding contact with the crisp edge of the coffee table. Walking slowly, his head down as if concentrating on the tome he held in front of him, he prayed she would not shift positions. He had never seen his boss relaxed and out of character. He wondered what she was like in bed. Allison wondered if she could learn something from the woman who exuded power like an arc of lightning.

Circling widely, he walked by the door and turned. Approaching the desk, he glanced up to calibrate his location. If he could get to the outside of the guest chair to the left of her desk he would have a clear view. Two more steps, he was catching the tail end of the conversation. She was wrapping up. One more step and he would be positioned; she shifted in her chair. Coming up beside the armchair his thigh brushed the padded arm. Looking up and over he savored the view of her shapely body; her legs long and sensual.

Ruby red nail polish was a sultry contrast to her golden flesh. Allison made a mental note to add ruby red to the nail polish collection. He must have been staring. She wiggled her toes playfully. He didn't realize she had ended the call.

"Red Carpet Shimmer is the color."

Her words slapped him. "Are you a leg man, Russ?" He tried to respond; his mouth felt as if it was filled with marbles and oatmeal. "Really Russell, you've got to be more forward."

He wasn't sure what he was supposed to do, supposed to say. *Can I touch your legs? Do they feel as silky and sexy as they look?*

Shaking off the thoughts he fumbled for a response. "Yes, you have such beautiful legs. Can you blame me for admiring you?" The words floated from him as if he had lost control over rational thought. Sylvia smiled. He had seen that smile. Shortly afterwards heads were lopped off, blood spilled, careers imploded. "Sylvia, I'm sorry, I didn't mean to disrespect you." Perspiration blossomed under his arms. He felt the first trickle of sweat run down his back. His face flushed. Sylvia's smile broadened; her eyes like giant clamps held him in place.

"Russell darling, I dress for success. That success manifests itself in how my business operates and just as importantly, how I influence people. I know that men are very visual creatures and can't help themselves. I exploit that weakness every chance I get. It's an edge. All I am looking for is an unfair advantage." He drank her in; as her lips moved he thought he heard music. Despite his awkward advances, she did not dismiss him.

"Once I bring them down, I let them know who's boss, and let them grovel, but I never, ever give them the time of day." She reached down and retrieved her shoes. Holding them on the tip of two fingers she watched his eyes move toward them. She swung them back and forth like two pendulums, as if she were a hypnotist. "Concentrate on the shoes," she said. Her voice seemed distant. He put the report down on the edge of the desk and it spilled to the floor. His gaze did not shift from her shoes. "They are just shoes, very nice shoes, but from the way men act when I put them on, you would swear they have magical powers." She began swinging the shoes into wider arcs and suddenly flung them over her shoulder and they disappeared onto the floor behind her.

She spun her chair around; Russell was not sure what to do next.

"Don't just sit there, Russell. Come help me on with my shoes! You don't expect me to stoop down to pick them up, do you? That's what underlings do, Russell. You are my underling. Aren't you?" Her gaze captured his eyes, holding them hostage. Russell felt his stomach drop. This wasn't what he expected. She was going to make him serve her; humiliation settled over him like a wet blanket. The "how do I do this" look filled his expression. She glanced back at the shoes for a split second, slowly raised her finger and pointed at the shoes. "Fetch!" she commanded. Russell hustled over to the shoes, stooped and gingerly picked them up. "Kneel!" she barked and Russell knelt before her.

"Come now, Russ, you've never helped your wife with her shoes? I'm sorry, I meant ex-wife." Her tongue was sharp; her words were cutting him. He looked down at the labels stitched into the foot bed: Jimmy Choo. The famous Jimmy Choo designer heels that women covet. Navy blue sling backs. Russell longed to try them on, but they belonged to another.

"Do you like my Jimmys?"

"They are fabulous. The craftsmanship is exquisite," he said with reverence.

"You're into shoes aren't you, Russell?

"No, not really."

"Come on now, Russell, that's not what I heard." Russell wasn't sure if she was fishing,

"Mandy and I went shopping the other day. She and I have become good friends Russell, did you know that?"

"No, I didn't." Russell's mind leapt to the conclusion that Mandy had told his boss about his cross-dressing. He was wearing pink panties and kneeling before his boss and wondering if he was in heaven or hell.

"She was worried about you, Russell; worried that I might want to fire you. And then how would you pay her the alimony?" The words pricked him like a thousand needles. It was as if she were injecting him with truth serum. "I told her that your little secret was safe with me." Chills raced down Russell's spine; she owned him now.

Sylvia uncrossed her legs and extended a pointed toe at Russell. Russell gazed between her thighs and caught a glimpse of lacy white panties. Then refocused on the shoes and turned them around to point away from her. He proceeded to arrange them to match the correct foot. Instinctively he cupped his right hand, took her heel and delicately slid the shoe onto her foot. A twinge of regret pierced his heart as her toes disappeared into each elegant and expensive shoe. She placed her shoe on the floor and he carefully fastened the strap. She pointed her other foot at Russell and lifted her left leg until her toes touched his lips. Lightheadedness threatened to topple him. Helplessly he placed kisses on the tips of her toes. As he opened his mouth to devour her toes she pulled away.

"Ah, ah, ahh! Not now sweetie, you've had enough." He

dutifully placed the other shoe onto her foot.
continued to kneel as if in homage to his queen.

"I love the adoration, but we have work to do, sweetie. Let ᵕ
about my priorities, shall we? You are going to do whatever it takes
to fix the report for the account, without whining or trying to win
points with the other partners. You work for me now exclusively.
Yes, exclusively." She stretched the word 'exclusively,' drawing a
pint of emotional blood from her latest subject. "I need you to give
me your best work, Russell. I know all about your little fantasies. If
you prove yourself to me and show me that you can handle the
pressure, maybe, just maybe, I will make it worth your while. Your
loyalty will be rewarded if you prove yourself worthy."

Russell wondered what the reward might be, but was afraid to
ask. "I picked you for this project Russell, because I know that you
have that creative spark to turn that little oversight by legal into an
opportunity. Failure is not an option for you, Russell. Are we clear
on this?

"Yes, we are crystal clear."

She smiled like the cat that ate the canary. "Good, I know you'd
see things my way."

Deep down, Russell knew that he was going to have to tell a big
lie with numbers, and create assets out of thin air if the numbers
weren't right. She was setting him up to be the fall guy if things went
south. She could have any man she wanted, but she craved power.
And turning this around would give her endless power over the
lawyers. She would never let them live it down. Men fell all over
themselves to be close to her, and Russell was going to get an
intimate look. Except for one failed marriage, she never took men
seriously enough to allow them closer than arms-length. This would
be on her terms.

Chapter 6

AFTER RUSSELL SUBMITTED TO Sylvia's need to dominate his male persona, she went back to work as if nothing had happened. Russell was another story. The fragrance from her feet haunted him; the softness of her skin aroused him. He struggled to focus on the financials; he knew he had to perform, but the assertive display had been personal and overwhelming causing his mind to drift.

Around midnight, Sylvia concluded they had gotten a good day's work on the books. Russell was relieved when she dismissed him with the wave of a manicured hand. He felt as though he should express his gratitude and let her know that he would be loyal. But there was no evidence that she had taken their relationship to a new level. She appeared to have forgotten it as quickly as it happened.

He needed to rush home, express his femininity, and let Allison soothe him. Arriving home at 1:00 A.M. he could not expel the male layer fast enough. Standing naked before the closet he felt half-baked, undone, the fringe of emotional stability frayed. Grabbing the first pair of pantyhose and heels he saw, he sat on the bed gathering the right leg of the pantyhose. As he slipped them on, calm quelled anxiousness, a sedative and a stimulant. For an hour, Allison pranced around the house in a red mid-thigh dress with a low scoop neck. Matching red patent leather heels and red belt finished the look.

At 2:05 A.M. the shoes and pantyhose sat in a pile at the foot of the bed. Propped on the edge of the bed with one foot on the night table Allison stripped off the pink nail polish from her toes and after treating the cuticles applied red. Sylvia inspired her. He lay in bed staring at the ceiling as moonlight streamed through the partially open mini-blinds. The digital display on the clock radio read 2:45

A.M.

Finally falling into a fitful sleep, he dreamt Sylvia brought a French maid's outfit to the office for him. She made him dress and parade around the office as his coworkers gawked and commented. Sitting bolt upright his body was drenched in perspiration; he looked at the clock: 5:15 A.M. *It's going to be a long day.* Taking hold of his emotions he forced fear from his consciousness. *How am I going to face her?* He knew he would melt in her presence even faster than before last night's episode.

Climbing out of bed he padded to the kitchen. Coffee would lift the fog. He was going to need caffeine injections to stay focused and not fall asleep.

The long drive to the office brought haunting memories. Sylvia was dangerously beautiful. He missed the exit and had to double back in heavy traffic. Arriving fifteen minutes later than usual, he tried to make his way inconspicuously to his office. "The boss is looking for you. She called twice," Katie reported. Russell's heart skipped a beat.

"Can you get me a cup of coffee and bring it to Sylvia's office please?"

"Good morning," he said in his best "I'm here and ready to work" voice. She extended her right hand with her index finger pointed toward the ceiling. She was on the phone and did not want to be disturbed. He wasn't sure whether to enter or leave. He looked to her for a signal; none was forthcoming. As he turned, Katie approached with the cup of steaming java. Taking it and thanking her, he turned back to Sylvia who was engaged in a heated conversation.

She snapped her fingers and pointed to the casual seating group; his cue to enter her sanctum. Russell felt tightness in his chest as if an invisible corset was being tied around his torso. Sipping from the steaming mug he fought nervousness. He was tired; it was a matter of time before he flamed out. He hoped she would forget the prior night's festivities.

"It seems everything we did last night is worthless. The client is furious." She ended the call and turned her attention to Russell. She needed a verbal punching bag. He was elected. Sitting quietly, he attempted to absorb the heat without reacting. Taking notes, he tried to connect the dots. His brain wasn't processing. The CEO wasn't sparing the rod. By the end of the soliloquy, Russell couldn't wait to retreat to his office.

At least she didn't bring up my servitude. Thank God for small things. Reading his notes, his handwriting was erratic. By 4:00 P.M. he was running on fumes. Coffee failed to have the wake-up effect. Sending his secretary across the street, she purchased concentrated energy drinks for another long night. Pinching the bridge of his nose, he pushed back from the desk. Looking around the average size rectangular office, his gaze fell on the framed pictures of his kids. They were dated. Mark was missing front teeth, leaving a large gap in his smile. Meghan was in pigtails holding a softball bat. He had removed all remnants of Mandy.

The buzz of the intercom recalled him from a comatose state. "Come in and bring your spreadsheets and that report Simon and Garfunkel put together." She punched the 'end' button before he could respond. Collecting the papers as he willed himself to wake up, he scurried to her office. The staff had gone except for a couple of stragglers. As he approached Sylvia's office he hoped she wasn't lounging like the previous night. He wasn't up for it. He needed sleep. He was afraid his feelings might betray him in a moment of physical exhaustion.

"Close the door." As Russell backtracked to do so, Sylvia stood up, kicked off her pumps, and hiked her dress up. Russell was spellbound for an instant. She hitched her thumbs under the waist band of her pantyhose, slid them down to the floor in one smooth motion and stepped out of them. Then she threw them at Russell.

"Russell, darling, I need you to run out and fetch me a pair of pantyhose. These have a run and I usually keep an extra pair in my desk, but they don't match my outfit."

"Do you have a favorite brand?"

"Of course, but we don't have time for you to drive all the way out to Sugartree Mall. You'll have to improvise. Use your judgment, I am sure you'll do just fine."

Russell scooped up the discarded pile of crumpled fabric. "You may keep them, but you are not to wear them." Sylvia called as Russell struggled for composure. His first instinct was to scoop the bundle of fragrance and press it to his nose. "There will be plenty of time to enjoy my haunting fragrances when you are alone. Then you can perform whatever you do to relieve your pent-up need to please me. Now hurry along and get my pantyhose. And buy two pairs. I want to have a spare in case of emergency."

Russell didn't dare ask for money. He knew that she expected him to purchase them; an offering in homage to her. The thought that she could be subtle scared him.

The time out of the office gave him an opportunity to breathe and collect himself. The register clerk shot him a strange look at checkout. Russell refused to lock gazes. *There's nothing I can say that would matter to the kid.*

Back at the office, Russell carried the small package to his boss. Her door was closed. Delia was working away on a document. "Sylvia said you can leave that with me." Sometimes it seemed Delia was practicing for the part of Sylvia's stand-in.

An hour later Sylvia announced she was leaving. Before departing she gave Russell homework. Watching her saunter out he knew that she knew his eyes were glued to her shape.

Chapter 7

FRIDAY NIGHT WAS AN early dismissal from the office. Sylvia ordered Russell to show up at nine Saturday morning with coffee and bagels. Servitude took many forms. Playing the go-for was not the worst, but it came close.

Walking into the office Saturday morning, he was business casual: khaki pants, golf shirt and Dockers without socks. Business casual outfit included lacy pink bikini panties. He'd arrived before Sylvia, and on her explicit instructions he removed the bagels from the bag and placed them on a plate on the coffee table in her office with the veggie cream cheese spread, coffee to her desk and removed the lid to cool. Grabbing his coffee, he headed for his office. Sylvia was sitting at his desk in a pale pink cotton fitted blouse with the top two buttons open, offering a glimpse of her perky breasts. Russell calculated that she was a D-cup; her breasts seemed to be taxing her lacy nude bra to the limit.

"Where's my coffee?" she pouted.

"In your office as instructed." He stopped as she shot him a knowing look. He put his coffee down and minced to her office to retrieve the coffee and bagels. On the journey, he realized he wasn't walking like a man. He was walking like a secretary.

"Close the door," she said as he stepped across the threshold. He did as he was told before delivering her beverage. "Where did you go for bagels?" He was about to tell her when she unceremoniously ripped the bag.

"There's poppy seed, sesame, and an everything bagel with low-fat veggie spread. Take whichever you like." He tried to sound confident, but she had already begun to slice the sesame bagel.

"Thanks." Her tone was soft and easy, but his feminine instincts told him there was an undercurrent, and she was clearly up to something. If he learned anything from working for her, it was to never let your guard down. She was volatile. She used it to keep people off balance.

"So, Russell, how are we doing?" she asked between bites. She took one half of the poppy seed bagel and broke off a small piece. She was adept at protecting the lipstick that covered her full lips. He watched and learned; wondering about those Botox rumors.

"We have a long way to go, but I think we can salvage something for the firm. It's too late for them to change horses; they'll ride us to the finish line," Russell said as she watched; her eyes wide and absorbing. She could look at you in a way that would make you feel like you were the only person in her universe.

Russell stopped to sip coffee. Sylvia pushed the bag across the desk to him. She had taken the mess of papers on his desk and placed them in piles to one side. As he pulled the bag toward him he realized he would have to reconstruct the crude filing system that made his desk look disorganized. Russell pondered what her moving the papers meant. His desk was his personal space; it felt as though she was staking her claim on his territory. She watched as he bit into one half of the whole grain bagel. She sensed something; she had that uncanny ability. When it didn't comfort him it scared him.

Nervously he collected his thoughts. He didn't want to sound scattershot, he was already in a daze from last night's episode. "I was up half the night trying to sort out the mess. It finally came to me at about 3:00 A.M. I wanted to run my idea by you before I did anything."

She watched him, half-interested. "I wasn't talking about the deal, Russell." He stopped mid-bite. His taste buds shut down as his jaw worked the bagel into a pulverized mass. Swallowing felt like a golf ball through a garden hose. "Opportunity is knocking Russell. I'm holding the open door for you, but I am not going to wait all day."

She turned the office chair until she was seated parallel to the desk. He watched her cross her legs. His heart pounded; he felt it in his temples. Rising on rubbery legs he tried to steel himself, torn between wanting to touch her and feeling himself sliding down a slippery slope.

His eyes moved from her face to her legs. She was wearing powder white skinny jeans that ended just above the ankle; frills of embroidery hid the tiny hem. Four-inch heels, sky blue satin to match her eye shadow, adorned her feet. Dropping to his knees, he tried to contain his excitement as she rotated her foot.

"You may go ahead." Her voice was sultry, suggestive. Removing her shoe, he kissed her bare toes. She watched him; her power increasing as he submitted to her.

Ten minutes of fantasy become reality filled him with a toxic mixture of thrill and dread. "That was fun!" she said, in a devilish voice. He was trying to hide the arousal that threatened to cast him further down into her pit of humiliation.

"Was it good for you too?" He looked up, locking gazes with her.

"Yes." His voice cracked.

"You've always been my favorite. Frankly I never understood how your marriage lasted. You clearly like being submissive." She sipped coffee and took another piece of bagel between her lips. "You can get up now." Russell's cock was engorged and felt heavy inside his pants.

"Russell look at you! I see we've made connection. Come closer, sweetie." Color rose in his cheeks completing his embarrassment. As he stood she slipped off the chair and onto her knees. Before he knew what was happening she had his pants unbuckled. Slipping them down she stopped, leaving him with pants at his knees.

"Ha, what's this?" She said with a giggle as she stared at the lace thong. He tried to grab his pants to cover up, but she had a firm grip on them and held them down. "Russell's hard little cock looks cute in those panties. You've got great taste in lingerie." Russell was confused, He expected her to bully him with a degrading comment. Instead she seemed delighted. Russell instantly crossed his hands over his crotch trying to preserve his modesty.

"Relax, Russell. Your underwear is your private business, honey." She cooed before standing to allow him to pull up his pants. "I didn't mean to spoil the fun. I know all about it, remember?" she asked, watching his body language.

"You can't tell anyone. My kids don't know; it would kill me, and damage them," he pleaded. She folded her arms under her breasts and observed him as he fastened his pants, taking small steps backwards to put distance between them.

"Your secret is safe with me." She paused as if to collect her thoughts. "That is as long as you do as I say." Her words were like the iron door of a jail cell slamming shut.

"Please don't do this!" he begged. She placed a manicured index finger against her lower lip.

"Let's see if we can have some fun, shall we?"

"Please, I'm begging you!"

"I like begging; go right ahead. You know begging is best done on bended knees." She shifted, placing one foot in front of the other, tapping her toe. Russell felt constriction in his chest. Dropping to his knees again he felt defeated; his secret exposed to a woman capable of impaling him with it.

"Sylvia, please…"

"Don't you think that addressing me by my first name is not quite appropriate?" She smiled. He thought he saw horns sprouting from her well-coifed head. "It is more appropriate for you to call me Mistress." Her voice was suddenly serious. "Go ahead and try it."

"Mistress." Uncertainty stung him.

"Yes, my subject."

"Please keep this between us."

"What exactly do you mean?" She toyed with him.

"You know, Mistress!" He fought the urge to sound frustrated.

"Yes, I think I do, but I would like you to state it clearly."

Swallowing the lump in his throat he constructed the statement in his mind before verbalizing.

"Please don't tell anyone that you caught me wearing women's panties." He could not believe he said it.

"You haven't made a compelling case yet, Russell. You'll have to answer a few questions before I decide what to do with you."

He felt screws tightening around his testicles as the throbbing in his temples threatened to erupt into a headache.

"Why do you wear panties, Russell?"

"I don't know. It's something I've always felt a desire to do." Her face expressed skepticism. "That's the truth; I don't know why I wear women's clothes." As he replied he realized he revealed more than he wanted to reveal.

"Oh, it's more than panties," she said; a hint of reverence in her voice. "What else do you wear and how often do you dress up?"

"Please, Mistress, don't make me tell you."

"I'm not making you do anything. You want to tell me." Her words fell heavily on him. "You need to tell me, Russell. How can I keep your secret if I don't know what it's all about?"

"But it's all very personal; you're invading my privacy," he said.

"That's not all I'll invade if you don't tell me," she said with a laugh. She was going to badger him until she got what she wanted and everything he told her could and would be used against him. Part of him wanted to confide, he wanted to make a woman-to-woman connection with her, and let go of all the emotions he had been holding back.

"This is unfair."

"Come on Russell, be a sport, I am simply fascinated by male to female transgenders."

"Really?"

"Yes, really, It's all interesting to me."

"Wait, how did you know I'm a transgender"?"

"Oh, let's just say I can tell. I'm right, aren't I?"

"Yeah, um I suppose; it's all shades of gray."

"I mean you're an attractive guy, but your brain thinks you should be a woman, right?"

"Um, yeah."

"See, that's cool. You have escaped the norms set by society and want to establish yourself as a female. Society didn't tell you that you should be female. Lord knows, it's not easy, and yet you swim upstream against the current and struggle to be a woman. What drives you to be a woman, Russell? I want details."

"I don't know where to start."

"What's your femme name?" Russell's heart skipped a beat; he looked away. His femme name was a secret that no one knew except his ex-wife, and Sylvia was asking for it. If he told her, she would have full access to Allison.

"You're blushing, Russell, I know you want to tell me." She put her hand on his shoulder and gently turned his face toward her. "It's okay, you can trust me," Sylvia said looking into his eyes.

"Allison." Sylvia smiled and offered a hug.

"It's okay, sweetie."

By the time she was satisfied, Russell had revealed the depth and breadth of his wardrobe and how he dressed and went out and about.

She asked to see pictures. He knew he was now a hostage.

With her curiosity temporarily satisfied, she shifted to work mode. Russell waited for her to bring up the topic throughout the day, but her focus was singular. By evening they had slogged through the bowels of their faulty proposal. Except for her having him fetch drinks and food, they enjoyed an employee-employer relationship.

At 10:00 P.M. Sylvia stretched. "I think we've done enough for the day. Go home and get some sleep. I'll see you tomorrow."

"Okay, I'll pick up coffee and bagels again?"

"That would be good." As he turned to leave she called to him. "Russ, wear a thong tomorrow under pantyhose and bring a pair of heels. I may want you to wear them around the office." She was working through a stack of papers as she spoke. He knew it would be futile to fight.

"I'll see you at nine tomorrow morning," he said as he left her in her office.

Chapter 8

RUSSELL STRIPPED AND STEPPED into the shower. Hot water baked the chill out of his bones. The day left him wondering how much lower he could sink. He tried to wash away the soil of the day. Thinking about what his boss had done to him, arousal betrayed the dark side of his character. If he could share without screwing up his life maybe there could be a silver lining to the gathering storm clouds.

Plucking a silk nightie from the closet he worked his way into it, the fabric cool against his warm body. Under the covers, he lay staring at the ceiling, the lamp on the nightstand projected a circle of light that mesmerized him.

When he awoke, it was daylight. Panicking he popped up and looked at the alarm clock. He had two hours until another humiliation session. He wasn't sure whether he hated her, or admired her for discovering him. He replayed how she had dropped to her knees before him. She was going to service him orally. He couldn't get that through his head. Powerful woman, world by the balls, and she was going to "do" him.

Must be lonely at the top. That's why she needs to control every aspect of her life. He began to feel sorry for her until he realized how she was using him for her ends. Rising, he decided to shower again. He still felt dirty. As he washed he played her words over in his mind. He didn't like the idea of having to bring pantyhose and heels to the office. *What if someone walks in while I'm wearing them?*

Slipping into pantyhose he selected black, convincing himself that they could pass for sheer men's nylon socks. He cursed when he realized he hadn't put on a thong first. Taking one leg out of the hosiery he stepped into the black lace thong. Stretching the pantyhose over his plump midsection, familiar constriction sent a tingle through him. He fought the dread that threatened to pollute the moment. Fishing through the boxes of shoes he found a comfortable pair of black satin heels.

Walking through the lobby of the office suite, he carried a shopping bag with shoes and food in one hand and two large cups of coffee in a carrier in the other. He hoped she stayed at home. When he didn't see her car in the parking lot, he figured maybe he'd dodged a bullet. He wore old comfortable blue jeans, a buttercup yellow, short sleeved, button down shirt, and black penny loafers. He wanted to feel loafers through pantyhose. He had seen the secretaries wear them and it intrigued him.

In his office, he sat and fired up his computer. Sipping coffee while the machine awoke he pondered his situation. He had sacrificed his marriage for Allison. Now his boss had glimpsed into his private life. She wanted him to dress. Would this be the beginning of a new chapter? Could this be the opportunity to go female full-time without shocking the boss? *I don't think I have the stomach to do it.* He warned himself to go slow. He wasn't out of the woods yet.

Checking the clock on the computer, it was 9:15 A.M. He smiled. *She's not coming.* Opening the bag with the bagels he pulled out the pumpernickel circle and applied butter. He rarely indulged, but this was cause for celebration. As he slathered butter generously, he heard movement.

"Russell?" Her voice grabbed his spine and shattered his mood.

"Fuck!" he whispered.

"Are you here, Russell?" she called again.

"In my office, Sylvia, I mean Mistress." He hoped there wasn't anyone other than Sylvia to hear him.

"I'd appreciate my breakfast." She was unhappy that she had to ask. Grabbing the bag and the second cup of coffee, he moved quickly to her office. She was going to make him pay for his failure to be immediately attentive. He was certain of it. As he stepped in her office he watched her bend over the desk, black leather pants pulled tight to her body. She wore five-inch black patent leather heels. When she straightened up the ribbed white top clung to her curves leaving little to the imagination.

"Put the coffee and bagel on the coffee table. I'll be with you in a minute." She spoke without looking in his direction; she seemed preoccupied with something on her computer screen. He wasn't sure whether to stand or sit; nervous energy coursed through him. She would do this from time to time; ignore until the lack of attention became maddening. She was brilliant and passive-aggressive—when she wasn't active aggressive. Sipping coffee, he almost spilled it on himself.

He could not tolerate her standoffishness. "Are we working on the plan today?" His voice was hollow. She raised a hand to quiet him. He hated when she used hand gestures to dismiss. Grabbing the uneaten bagel and warm coffee he walked toward the door. *I have work I can be doing. I'm not standing around waiting for her.* When he reached the threshold, her words stopped him.

"Where do you think you're going?"

"To my office; I can be more productive there."

"You'll do no such thing." He fought the urge to turn around, keeping his back to her. He heard her move, expecting a physical attack. As she approached he steeled himself. When movement stopped, he turned. She stood in front of him, left foot in front of the right tapping the thin pile carpet, arms crossed under her breasts as if to keep them from sagging.

"Let's get one thing straight. When you are in the presence of your mistress for the first time you will greet me properly." The thought of paying homage to her every day made him queasy. He would become the laughing stock of the office. "You can start now."

Dropping to one knee he took the hand she offered, kissing it gently until she retracted it.

"You may stand." She looked at him, her eyes soft. He wasn't sure why.

"You need not concern yourself about being embarrassed. I would not expect you to greet me that way during the workweek. I will expect you to make it up on days like this." She smiled, he felt no warmth radiating from it. *Shit, she's going to make me work weekends to humiliate me.* Chill settled over him as he awaited her next words.

By 4:00 P.M. they had worked through the entire presentation, tearing it apart and reconstructing it. Sylvia was happy with the work product. Russell was relieved that she had forgotten about his feminine assignment. As they wrapped up she stood and stretched, the definition in her lean body highlighted.

"Where are your heels?" The words caught him off guard. "You did bring them."

"Yes, they're in my office." She hadn't forgotten. He was deflated.

"They're not doing any good in there, are they? Go get them. I want to see your taste." She circled her desk and settled onto the settee, propping her heels on the edge of the coffee table as Russell walked slowly out of the office wondering if he could escape today's fate without repercussions.

Scooping the bag from the floor he carried it back to Sylvia's office. "Sit there and slip into them." As he removed the shoes from the bag, he felt her eyes on him.

"Walk over there," she commanded, pointing toward the far corner of the office near her desk. He stood; Allison was unbridled. She pranced across the room giving Sylvia pause. "My, you do that well." The audience of one clapped for his performance. Allison continued to parade around the office. Russell worried about the repercussions; electricity coursed through Allison. She felt energized, making Russell wonder whether discovery of his secret was such a bad thing.

"You're enjoying this, aren't you?" Sylvia loved the power trip. Allison felt a weird bond to the woman who unleashed her. Stopping and leaning over. Allison rolled up pant legs to makeshift Capri pants. Russell fought for equal time without success.

"This is liberating!" Allison said. Sylvia laughed, unsure what to make of the person who moments ago faced her command with trepidation.

69

"How often do you walk in those heels?"

Before Allison could answer Russell fought to the surface. "Not very often." he lied. No need to tell more than he had already revealed.

"I don't believe it. You're a natural. Is this why your wife left you?"

He chafed as he turned; Russell felt Allison's defenses engaging. "No, my wife decided she wanted to fool around. I wasn't going to allow that and have her sleep in my bed."

"You sacrificed your marriage and your family for an indiscretion?" She was tenacious when she focused.

"I don't call cheating a small indiscretion." Russell fought back. She watched him as he spoke.

"What do you call this?" She waved a hand in his direction. He blushed as the conversation was making him uncomfortable.

"What?" he asked defensively.

"Uh, dressing like a woman; don't you think your wife would see this as cheating?"

"No, because I do it myself."

"So, you're the other woman."

"No, I am me."

"And you want to be a woman."

"No… no I don't." He wasn't convincing.

"Russell, honey, you're not making a very strong case." She shook her head as if disappointed by his denial. He dropped his eyes. "That's better. Now come over here and tell me about your shoes." Russell moved haltingly, suddenly losing confidence and fumbling over his awkward stride.

He sat and removed one shoe holding it up. She commented on the style, grimacing at the brand. "These shoes would never be good for all day wear." She took the shoe and pointed out flaws in design and comfort. He watched as she dissected.

Handing the shoe back to him, she smiled. "Look Russell, I am intrigued by this clandestine life you are leading. I want you to know that your secret is safe with me." Her voice was sincere as she repeated the phrase she offered the last time the subject was broached.

He felt tension release from his shoulders. He started to remove the other heel when her words froze him.

"As long as you do exactly as I say." Her voice was icy. She stared at him.

He tried to muster the strength to return her stare.

"The right question would be, 'What do you want me to do for you, Mistress.'" She laughed as she watched him expectantly.

Needing to break the silence he forced himself to respond. "What do you want from me?" he asked, dreading the response.

"You agree to do what I say, and we're both happy. Refuse to give me what I want and you will be famous, or infamous, before the last words of refusal leave your lips." Her eyes were cold steel. Russell felt Allison's hackles rise; a defensive outburst being loaded into the vocal cannon.

"You're going to hold me hostage because of something you wanted to do to me?" Allison's look hardened as her lips pursed.

"Taking that approach will get you nothing but unemployed. Besides, nobody would ever believe I did anything wrong. You, on the other hand will have difficulty explaining your fetish. Think about that." She punctuated the statement with a wink that was anything but playful.

"What brand of pantyhose do you wear?" she asked casually, making him more paranoid. She was capable of shifting from playful to ball breaker without warning.

"L'eggs; they're affordable." His response was flat.

"Control top or sheer toe?" she asked as if knowing the line of questioning was an ice pick digging into his brain.

He felt a headache ready to erupt. "Control top." He hoped his clipped answers would make her dry up and blow away. She had his leash firmly in her manicured hands.

"Don't they bite into you? Let's face it honey, you've got a muffin in the making." She laughed, grating on his nerves, fueling the headache.

"They're okay," he said, refusing to give her the satisfaction.

"I'll see you Monday." She spoke as if there was quality time between now and then. Rolling his pant legs down he slipped into his male shoes before retrieving his heels. A twinge of regret pulled at his heart. He always felt that way when he had to stow Allison's clothes. He wished he didn't have to surrender to the tyranny of conventional gender roles, but he knew that wearing the heels for all to see would be a bold statement; not one he was prepared to make.

Dropping heavily into his office chair he cursed himself. *Why did I have to wear panties to the office? I never figured she'd make a play for me.* The thought of her kneeling before him, if only for a split second, was enough to make him wish he could have experienced her pleasures. Placing the heels into the shopping bag Russell hustled out of the office before she made another personal attack on his no longer private feminine domain.

Pulling out of the parking lot, he stopped short of the apron that led to the turn onto the public road. Grabbing the bag with the shoes, he pulled off the loafers and slipped on the heels. "Why am I not enjoying this?" he chided. The heels felt natural; more natural than his boy costume shoes. Allison was back and in the safety of her private space. "I'm sorry, girl, that you had to go through that." He spoke to the windshield as embarrassment threatened perspiration on his forehead. Savoring the privacy, he dropped the transmission into gear before pulling away; the initial punch of the accelerator made the car jump.

In the garage, he sat with the engine running; the thoughts of suicide percolated. If he ended it all now, everyone would know he was wearing pantyhose. Turning the key, the engine cut off. Lowering the garage door, he sat: half man, half woman and totally incomplete.

Making a beeline to the bedroom, he tore off the male costume and slipped into Allison. Prancing into the bathroom, he pulled the makeup case from the cabinet under the sink.

Washing his face and running the razor over the day's growth, he felt the familiar burn on this neck. Taking a washcloth, he ran it under cold water, wrung it out, and applied it to his freshly shaved face. The cold soothed. He applied moisturizer and foundation. Watching the slow and steady transformation, he smiled as Allison came into focus. Dotting and blending over his chin and down his neck, the shadow of his beard disappeared. Applying eyebrow pencil over shaped eyebrows he reminded himself there was plucking to be done. He didn't want that to interrupt putting on his face. He needed Allison more than he could remember ever needing her.

Tapping eye shadow onto his eyelids and then brushing the color softly above the eye just below the brow he smiled at the ease at which he was able to create the smoky eye look accentuating his large hazel eyes. He applied a generous line of liquid eyeliner to his upper lash line and counted to twenty to let it dry before moving to the lower lash line, breathing a sigh of relief as Allison pulled off this delicate task without a hitch. After applying mascara, he turned to the closet to extract an auburn wig. Straightening up he pulled the cap down, repositioned the lace line until it was seated properly.

Allison smiled as her image in the mirror stared back, satisfied. Femininity washed over her like the ocean breeze on a hot beach day. There wasn't a day when she didn't reflect on the change in Russell's life that allowed her to emerge and flourish.

At age eleven Russell discovered women—not like most adolescents. He discovered an inner connection that scared him. When he looked at a woman he wasn't attracted to them the way other boys were. They wanted to touch and grab the girls with blossoming breasts and swaying hips. He coveted their bodies because he wanted to feel what they felt. He wanted to ask them about their secrets for attracting the attention of boys. He wanted to know how it felt to put on makeup, slip into sheer and silky undergarments. He understood the power of their beauty and outwardly submissive behavior.

As he watched the older boys he was repulsed by the way they were only after one thing. For them, a girl was simply a sex object. The younger girls were clueless to the power they held. Their need to be "taken" was their primary motivation. When he tried to engage girls in his age bracket he found them flighty and giddy. They didn't understand his interest in them and his unusual interest in dresses and makeup. They didn't understand that he was desperate to be their girlfriend. Uncertainty and misunderstanding on the part of the girls exposed him to their ridicule.

He receded to the safety of his mind; finding solace in magazines that depicted the beauty of mature women; the ones who understood the power in their beauty. In the comfort of his bedroom he gathered magazines his mother enjoyed reading. Pictures of women in form-fitting dresses, shimmering hosiery and heels turned him on. When he superimposed these images on the older girls at school he began to understand that they needed to grow into the power and attraction that only maturity could teach. He admired them. He couldn't bring himself to exploit them like the boys with raging hormones.

Russell struggled through his formative years trying to make sense of his scrambled emotions. When most boys were out romping and rollicking, he favored his mother's company. He heard people call him a mama's boy. He tried to break the stigma without success. His father wasn't much help; working long hours, he didn't have time to be the male force in Russell's life. His three younger siblings were closer in age to each other than to Russell, creating a quasi-generational gap that left him virtually alone in a family of six.

High school wasn't much easier. The all-boy environment isolated him. He had to allow body hair to grow naturally. Appearing in the boys' shower after gym class with a clean-shaven body would summon hellacious reaction. Boys are never more brutal than if one of their kind looks feminine. Christmas break and summer vacation were the only times he could risk shaving, but summer offered its own complications.

As he looked back on those years he realized there were probably others in the same emotional conundrum. The times did not lend themselves to open and honest soul bearing. Revealing his weakness to his tradition-bound parents might have gotten him banished from the family.

Shadow Woman

The house was quiet except for Allison's movement. Settling onto a vinyl covered kitchen chair she nibbled on a 100-calorie snack; good but too small. She patted her tummy, the control top pantyhose promised better days to come.

Deciding to prolong Allison's game of solitaire she slept in wig and makeup after shrugging into a silk nightie to complement her pantyhose. She wouldn't sleep well; Allison wanted attention. She awoke several times, the male portion of her aroused. She wouldn't give Russell the satisfaction of climax. This was her time and nothing was going to interrupt it.

She awoke groggy when the alarm sounded. She had fallen into deep sleep only for the last hour of the night. As she looked at the clock, hair from the wig fell across her eyes. Brushing it aside she sat up, nightie askew; Forcing the covers off she stood at the twilight between the two genders, making the next move tentative. Allison pressed her case; Russell felt remnants of control slipping though his fingers.

Stepping into three-inch red open-toed mules adorned with feathers Allison gained confidence as she walked out of the bedroom. Donning the male shell was going to be more difficult than normal. As she prepared the first cup of coffee of the day, she pondered the surreal experience at the office the prior day. Something shook lose. Presenting hadn't really been embarrassing. Instead it felt like an unveiling, a chance to break out of her shell. Allison felt connected. Russell was petrified. Allison was confident.

Sitting with legs crossed, she sipped coffee between dainty bites of fruit yogurt. Allison insisted the diet be rich in calcium and low in calories. There were several dresses and skirts she wanted to fit into without body shaping undergarments. She knew Russell would never be satisfied with her choices. He wasn't in control, and that was all that mattered.

In front of the bathroom mirror, Allison removed makeup before taking off the wig. Allison slipped back into the shadows. Russell emerged clean-shaven and ready to pass as a male.

He pulled on gray herringbone slacks and a white button down shirt. As he walked over to the bed, he spied the pumps, red panties and beige, thigh-high hosiery. A twinge of disappointment pricked his soul. Unfastening the waistband of his slacks he allowed them to drop to the floor before stepping out of them. Seated on the bed he stepped into panties and methodically rolled the pantyhose up, unfurling them up each leg before straightening the tops. Stepping back into slacks he felt conflict raging. He needed Allison to give him room to work. Her prodding and insistence was going to submarine his employment.

He abandoned the high heels at the foot of the bed and headed to his car. Mondays were not his favorite; a long week ahead. This one was going to be particularly challenging after the events of the weekend. Driving, he tried to rationalize his life. More importantly he tried to handicap how the day would unfold. *She's going to play up the weekend. How do I handle this if she insists on mind games?* He felt suddenly cold although the day was shaping up to be a warm one.

Pulling onto a side street he pushed the transmission into park before engaging the roof. He had left it down hoping to catch fresh air before walking into the pressure cooker of an office. Until the divorce and the unraveling of his personal life, Russell had been happy with the job. Now he wasn't sure. He hoped Allison would help. She provided courage. There was a price to pay; Russell knew it. The law of averages confirmed it.

With the roof up and locked into place, he continued. Stopping halfway to the office he needed a jolt of caffeine. The Coffee Spot, a pad site in a busy strip mall, was buzzing with activity. Their clientele loved the personal attention. Bethany Queralls was the proprietor. She was effusive, ebullient, efficient and all the other "E" words that described the most upbeat of personalities. Russell liked Bethany. Bethany liked everyone, making it a point to learn first names. Customers ate that up like dessert.

"Good morning, Bethany!" Russell called over the line of customers engaged in various conversations. The mood in the shop seemed light; when you walked across the threshold it was as if the problems of the world melted away. That was the way Allison made Russell feel. He wanted that feeling every day, vowing to stop for a refill each morning. Maybe this was the elixir to get him to the next level in his life. He pondered how he could capture some of the magic of The Coffee Spot and spread it generously over his life.

"What can I get you, honey?" She called him honey. He felt sweet as she poured happiness over him. He ordered a double skim latte.

"You look fabulous as always!" He wondered why she never married.

"Same as always?" she asked, shrugging off the compliment. She was engaged in several conversations at once as she took orders and conveyed them to the barista helping her. Russell enjoyed the casual atmosphere as he wondered how Bethany was able to make a good living selling coffee and pastries. The math wasn't working for him. As he waited for his order he mused about her. He thought that maybe he could date her. He dismissed the thought. He didn't think she'd appreciate competitive dressing.

Back in the car he sipped the steaming liquid. *She makes a mean cup of coffee.* There was something about her coffee that he could not replicate. He had asked for her secret. "Honey, that would be bad for business," she told him.

In the office parking lot, he slung the briefcase over his shoulder and retrieved the coffee cup from the hood of the car. Proceeding to the elevator, dread gripped him. Sylvia's unpredictability made him wonder if he would have a job at the end of the day.

Walking through the double glass doors into the suite, the hum of activity was palpable. He heard Sylvia talking with Simon and Garfunkel. The soliloquy was familiar. Russell mouthed several of the words on cue. They were getting a dressing down for failure to be diligent. "Got to keep the subordinates in order. I can't let feelings get in the way; people will just have to adjust to me. If being difficult is the way to maintain order then so be it." Sylvia took pride in telling anyone who would listen this was advocated by management gurus. The people who heard the revelation speculated that the genius who invented such an insensitive management style was martyred for his beliefs.

Russell retreated to his office and closed the door. He was not ready for the day. He fired up his computer, sipped coffee and started to scan his emails and immediately realized that he hadn't responded to emails in three days. People would begin to wonder whether he was still employed. After the weekend, he felt he was living on borrowed time.

Deep in thought as he triaged the most critical emails, he didn't notice his secretary standing in front of his desk. She had a knack for being stealthy. "Damn it, Katie I asked you not to sneak up on me. Knock before coming in. You're scaring me out of years of my life!" He chided her as she blushed with disappointment. *She can't help herself.*

"These are from Sylvia." Russell shuddered. He looked up, hoping Katie was going to give him something benign. "What's wrong? You look like you're scared of something." Katie's expression radiated concern.

"Something with the kids from the weekend."

"Are the kids okay? Is there anything I can do to help?" She dropped into one of the guest chairs sitting on the edge as if she was ready to pounce.

"It's nothing serious, just parent worry stuff. You'll find out when you have your kids." He smiled, trying to change the subject as he leafed through the folder.

"I'm glad. I'm here to help." She smiled as she stood; straightened her skirt and walked out. Russell watched her petite body wriggle and sway. There was a certain energy and vibrancy to her walk. Carefree youth.

He thought about her beauty and innocence and how it was destined to be ruined by the world. Russell rose and opened the door to his office. Sylvia railed against people who insisted on working behind closed doors. She had threatened on more than one occasion to remove all the office doors. He wasn't in the mood for another of her diatribes.

Shadow Woman

Tossing the remains of the tepid coffee, he stretched. His body ached from lack of sleep. He wished he had called in sick. Back at the desk he pulled several papers from the folder and laid them on top. There was new information about the deal. She was brilliant! He wondered if she ever slept. It must have taken her all night to pull the reports together. Part of him wanted to wander down to her office to see if she looked like she had been up all night.

Lunch hour rolled around. Sylvia had not intruded on his work. By noon, he had plowed another four intense hours of research and spreadsheet work into the project. Needing a break, he decided an escape to the outside would re-humanize him. Once out the door, the warmth of the sun reminded him there was life outside of work. He hadn't taken a vacation since before the divorce; choosing to immerse himself in work, shutting out everyone and everything but Allison.

The convertible beckoned. Strolling over to the car, he debated a getaway to points unknown, but he turned around and stepped away from the car, because he knew if he left he'd never return. He was far too submissive to chart his own course. *I am at the beck and call of Sylvia.* After a stroll around the outside of the building, he stepped back into the air-conditioned lobby. Tiny beads of perspiration formed on his upper lip and brow. The elevator ride left him wondering what the afternoon would hold. Preparing for the worst, he pushed the glass door open and stepped inside. The receptionist smiled through a conversation Russell thought was probably personal. He didn't know her well but she seemed to have the telephone headset fused to her head.

Meandering through the support staff cubicles he was curious to see today's fashions. With lots of young women in the office, every day was a fashion extravaganza. He envied them not only for their birthright but also for the fact that they had someone in their life, at least the married ones did. They could come to the office, do their job and go home, leaving the dust from the workday behind.

He settled into his chair and unlocked the computer. There were emails from Sylvia. She had been busy. As usual, each email had a demand and a deadline. She was consistent. She had delegated eight hours of work; another one of her quirks. She had no sense at all that her minions had personal lives. She told him when he pitched a fit that since she didn't have a personal life nobody else should be expected to have one.

By 7:30 P.M. he was spent. Three cups of coffee had propelled him through the afternoon, but he was running out of gas. There was one deliverable that wasn't going to get done. He had to tell her. She'd excoriate him if he left without explaining. Standing, he watched as the computer powered down. He wasn't going to allow her to browbeat him into staying. He needed sleep or he'd be toast on Tuesday morning.

Knocking on the doorframe of her office, he waited while she finished typing a thought into her computer.

"Russell, I haven't seen you all day!" She smiled as she delivered the words in singsong voice.

"Hi Sylvia." He wasn't going to give her the satisfaction of a response.

"Finished everything?"

"All but one item. I'm going to call it an evening. I'll pick it up in the morning." He saw her complexion gray before clearing.

"Come in, and shut the door." He felt the noose tightening around his neck. She wasn't going to let him escape. Closing the door sent an ominous message. She was going to dress him down. He was going to feel violated. He wished he had finished the last task.

Closing the door slowly prolonged the execution. Turning, he looked at her. She didn't look angry.

"You look really tired." She sounded sympathetic.

"I'm beat." He had to work to engage; forcing fear of being fired to the back of his mind.

"Come around here; I want to show you something." He fought the urge to turn and run. His mind played out the possibilities. She wanted him to review her work. But why did he have to close the door? His mind was working as if the gears were coated with oatmeal. As he rounded the desk she swung around in the chair. Her long legs were crossed. Her feet were clad in navy blue sling-backs with a narrow-pointed gold cap toe and four inch heels. Her legs were coated with sheer nude pantyhose; the expensive type that looked like they were airbrushed.

"Wearing anything feminine today?" she said with a playful tone and a smile. The slit of her charcoal gray pinstripe skirt revealed her well-toned thigh. Clearly, she found the time to exercise.

"Just pantyhose and panties." He couldn't stop himself from answering truthfully.

"What color panties?" She was amused.

"Black with lacy frills." Allison answered. She had transformed Russell into Allison in a brief moment. Allison felt the power as Russell's persona wilted under Sylvia's yoke.

"Very nice Russ; or should I say Allison? It is Allison, isn't it?"

"Yes, that's right." Allison said, with a wave of her wrist, trying desperately to sound feminine. Sylvia locked onto Allison's eyes and gave her a mischievous look. Allison was doe-eyed and entranced.

"How do they feel?"

"Oh, I don't know. A little tight, I need to lose a few pounds." He blushed, the statement of a naïve figure-conscious woman slipping from his lips.

"You enjoy telling me about your feminine side, don't you." Her question was more an affirmation. "I've never known a man who dressed as a woman. This is a treat. I'm enjoying learning about the real you." Her words scared Allison. She wasn't sure if Sylvia was cynical or sincere. Allison shifted from one leg to the other like she needed to pee.

"You're mocking me, aren't you?" Allison said as her voice pitched up and female defense mechanisms kicked in.

"Oh, I don't mean to make you uncomfortable, just relax, sweetie. I'm fascinated; curious about why you dress up as a woman." She was adjusting her approach like a big, agile cat stalking its prey. Allison wanted desperately to connect with Sylvia as a woman, but she needed to protect Russell. Allison's mind was swirling; a mixture of excitement, relief, and terror.

"How often do you get fully dressed with makeup?" Sylvia probed.

"I don't wear makeup often." Allison fought for control, not wanting to reveal.

"Come on Allison, it's okay, you can tell me the truth. I'm not going to bite. You dress up and wear makeup and you even go out in public." Her words prompted Russell to step in and defend Allison's honor.

"Why is it important for you to know all of this about my personal life?" He fired back, his delivery edgy.

"Because I want to know if one of my employees can bring disrepute to me or my firm. You understand, I know you do." The veiled threat was not lost on him.

"I would never do anything to hurt you or the firm."

"If that's the case, you won't mind explaining your activities to your employer," she demanded. He wondered how many human resources regulations she was violating and how many laws she was breaking.

"I don't want to be in a position to have to take action to protect my interests and the interests of the firm. You don't want me to take preemptive action, do you?" She was the queen of rhetoric.

"I don't do anything to put the firm at risk," he insisted.

"You're wearing pantyhose and panties. What if you were in an accident and needed to be rushed to the hospital? Do you think there might be a scandal if medical personnel found you wearing women's clothes? I'll bet you didn't think of that, did you?" She was firm. His face drained of color. He hadn't thought of that possibility.

Recovering, he fought for emotional purchase. "I think you're being paranoid." As he spoke her face muscles tightened and her eyes narrowed.

"Don't tell me about my responsibilities. I could fire you on the spot for being insubordinate. You do remember your employment agreement? If not I can pull up a copy of it." Laser beams shot from her eyes; he wilted under her stare.

Regrouping, he tried another angle. "I'm not trying to bring disgrace to the firm." His voice was conciliatory. He watched her, hoping she would soften.

"I want to know what you are wearing and why. I want details on your movements dressed in drag." He cringed at the words "in drag" as if he was trashy.

"I dress when I'm at home. I have wigs and makeup. When I go out, which isn't often, I don't go to places where I go as Russell. I'm discrete."

She considered his statement. "I'm not sure I'm buying your story." She paused before continuing. "I want to see what you look like in drag. I need to know what I'm buying." She drummed into her employees that she bought their services every day. She could decide to stop buying at any time. He knew she was dangling the threat. He could not afford to lose his job.

"You want to see pictures? I don't have any pictures." He thought about the pictures his ex-wife had taken. He had them but he was not in wig and makeup. Fearing she would snatch the pictures, he wanted minimal recognition factor. He looked passable as a woman. If he was totally femme Allison would be conspicuous; Russell would be hidden.

"I find that hard to believe. I want to see pictures."

"I will have to take pictures," he promised hoping she would forget.

"I expect to see pictures by Wednesday. That will give you enough time to comply." She watched his body language. "Do you like my shoes?" She changed the subject as if they were having casual conversation.

"They're stunning. The gold caps really make them pop." Russell felt Allison's envy percolating. He couldn't believe he could respond as if nothing unusual was occurring.

"You can touch them." She flexed the foot at the end of her crossed leg. Struggling to deal with the embarrassment that was about to blossom, he tried to resist.

"I can admire them from here." She wasn't pleased with his

response.

"I want you to touch them. Besides after a day in them my feet could use attention." He felt his knees turn to rubber; he was powerless to resist as she crossed and uncrossed her legs fully aware of the impact of her actions. Dropping awkwardly to one knee then the other, he felt himself giving in to her. She smiled; more power transferred. She placed one shoe on his thigh; pressing the heel into his muscle and causing him to flinch. Cupping the shoe in his right hand he lifted her leg and slipped the shoe off as she wiggled her toes.

Bringing her leg up to his face she pressed the ball of her foot into his lips. The combination of warmth, perspiration and fragrance made him hard. "I see you like that!" she giggled like a schoolgirl. "Enjoy them; show me how much you appreciate being able to worship me." She pressed her toes into his nose. "You are getting a privilege that most men only dream about."

As he massaged one foot then the other he placed soft kisses on the instep of each. Sylvia sat back and enjoyed; purring as he worked over her feet with strong hands.

"That feels good. You do that well. You have a job." Her comment wasn't lost on him. If he performed for her, he'd continue to be employed.

On the drive home, he recalled the events that led to the fragrance on his hands. He admitted that Sylvia was beautiful. He also admitted being that close to her assuaged feelings of need. What she commanded him to do was exactly what he had dreamed of doing to sensually dressed women. She engaged a fantasy as if she knew exactly what he needed. *If it means I keep my job and she keeps my secret then I'll live with it.* The gates of submission opened as he pulled the car into the garage.

Pulling himself out of the car, he was physically and emotionally drained. Trudging into the house, he fell into bed barely removing his clothes before falling asleep. When he awoke the digital display in the clock radio read 3:14 A.M. Getting up, he relieved himself, drank a glass of water, and slipped under the covers.

Shadow Woman

The alarm woke him. He felt like he could sleep hours longer. He needed to get to the office, work his time, and get home; the requirement of delivering photographs weighed on him.

The office was quiet; Sylvia was out at meetings. Her secretary told him she wasn't due in. That didn't mean her overbearing personality wasn't ever-present. At least he wouldn't be giving foot massages.

By 5:30 P.M. he had caught up on several open matters. She had called once with instructions. He took the call and delivered what she needed. By six thirty he had surveyed his closet and picked out a tasteful princess-seamed sheath dress, four-inch pumps with pilgrim buckles, and a matching belt to pull it all together and accentuate his waistline. After a quick shower, he stepped into pantyhose and heels, slipped into the dress and applied makeup. Checking the image in the mirror as he pulled the wig onto his head, Allison stared back looking fresh. She convinced herself that if nobody knew there was Russell, there was no way they were going to come to that conclusion looking at Allison.

Allison was hungry; she had not cooked for days. Checking the cupboard, she found quinoa and canned vegetables. There were a few items in the freezer that were mildly interesting. Reminding herself there was a diet in process she settled for the high protein grain and a side of French cut string beans.

Several days of mail had accumulated on the dining room table. Sliding onto one of the chairs, she crossed her legs. Halfway through the mail the cell phone rang. Sugar Ray's *Answer the Phone* was the ringtone. Meghan had programmed ringtones for her father. She thought he was such a Neanderthal when it came to technology. Rising, Allison moved to the bedroom; the phone's display flashing "Barbara Collins." Allison hesitated. "Why is she calling me?" Allison hoped it wasn't an encore of the earlier discussion at the office. "Shit!" Russell wanted to answer; talking to his beautiful coworker made him feel a little of her sensuality. "What if she wants to come over? What if I win the lottery?" Allison fought the urge to laugh at the stupid joke.

Indecision forced the call to voicemail. When the phone stopped ringing the display changed to indicate missed call. If Russell knew Barb well the next message would be a voice mail notification. When it appeared, Allison picked up the phone and checked voicemail.

Barb wanted to see Russell. She assured him she wasn't trying to pressure him.

Punching the 'delete' button without further thought, Allison's smile was smug. There was no way she was going to permit another female to supplant her. This was her time. Settling down to the meager dinner that would do nothing to assuage hunger, Allison ate daintily to preserve her lipstick.

After cleaning up the kitchen Allison wandered to the bedroom to find her camera. Snapping a few pictures in front of the full-length mirror Allison felt none of the embarrassment Russell had experienced at Sylvia's hand.

Scrolling through the pictures she selected four she thought were acceptable. Uploading them to her personal email account; Russell would access them from the office and dump them to the color printer in his office.

Chapter 9

ACTIVITY IN THE OFFICE was frenetic. It was too early for the usual crazy pace. Sylvia was stirring the pot, portending a long and stressful day. Before he put his briefcase down Katie accosted him. "The boss wants to see you." When she used the term 'boss' that meant Sylvia was in a ripe mood. When she wanted you, you had better be within earshot. Russell was a few minutes late, putting him on her shit list.

"Did she say what she wanted to discuss?" he asked hopefully.

"She said you would know." *What am I a mind reader?* "Do you need me to pull anything together?" *A miracle.*

"I should be okay. I'll let you know if there's anything I need." Katie turned and before leaving looked at him doubtfully. Something had negatively impacted him. She felt the vibes but couldn't put her finger on the problem.

"Good morning." He tried to sound upbeat as he walked into the office. She had gathered three of the key staff along with Simon and Garfunkel. They were pouring over stacks of documents. Sylvia was on the headset wearing a rut in the carpet behind her desk. She didn't seem crisp; the person on the other end of the phone was receiving an unhealthy dose of vitriol. He hoped the tropical storm didn't progress to hurricane status.

"What's on the agenda?" he asked. Charlie, one of the three vice presidents grabbed a sheaf of papers bound with a large binder clip and slapped it into his hands.

"The boss found another major problem with the deal. She's

pissed." *Tell me something I don't already know.* He pulled up an armchair. Several of the pages were tagged with Post-it flags. He flipped to them. As he absorbed what had been outlined his blood ran cold. The entire deal, all of the months of effort, was unraveling, the multi-million-dollar payday headed for the crapper. Sylvia was trying to salvage it by laying off the blame. She had a knack for making people accept whatever she was dishing. This time it seemed less likely that whoever was on the other end of the line was going to bend over and take it.

"Who's she talking to?" Russell had to know.

"Anti-trust counsel in California. Seems they missed something that could fuck this up," Charlie said. Russell winced. Charlie was a decent guy, probably too decent for this environment. Russell wondered if Sylvia came on to Charlie like she came on to him. He wondered if the women knew she was using the office as her private male harem.

Two hours later Russell was back in his office; Sylvia had strafed the group, dropping a carpet of napalm in the form of work on them. "She's right, but she doesn't have to grind her heel into our spleen," he said to Barb, who was part of the triage team, as she rolled her eyes. She despised the woman when she acted the tyrant.

"I get it; she's panicking. If this deal crumbles she's going to have to answer to the gods on Mount Olympus," she replied, referring to the governing board. "They are cut throat. She's a pussycat compared to those sharks."

"I don't feel my heart bleeding for her," Russell said, the embarrassment of the weekend still an open wound.

"You don't have to be such a grump."

"Let's not talk about Sylvia. We've got work to do and I was planning to have dinner with my kids tonight."

"You might want to cancel. I don't think the shackles will be unlocked until we get this problem solved." Barb made a pouty face as Russell steamed. He needed to see his kids, whether they liked it or not.

She moved to the small round table and two chair grouping that was the only surface in the office not littered with papers. The hint of her pantyhose swishing as she moved delivered a tingle to his loins.

Shaking off the thought he joined her. As he sat she reached across and caressed his knee, causing him to jump.

"You can't do that!"

"Keep your voice down. Do you want the office to think we're having fun? You know fun is verboten." She winked and ran her manicured fingers across his thigh. He looked into her eyes and felt himself falling. He loved the attention but at the same time feared his secret might be discovered.

"I called you last night."

"I know. I was wiped out; went to bed early," he replied as he tried to focus. Her perfume was subtle yet distracting. He wasn't sure why she was interested in him. He worried that if he became entangled with her he might learn things that were going to scare him. He knew the axioms, "don't dip your pen in the company's inkwell," and "don't screw the help." Technically she wasn't the help, and they were two consenting adults. What scared him even more was the potential for Sylvia finding out. *Given what she knows about me I'll get fileted.* The thought of his boss having that much control made him angry.

"Are you okay Russ?" The question shook him out of his funk.

"Yeah, trying to figure out how we get this back under control," he lied.

"Let's take it one piece at a time." She drummed her fingernails on the desk. Every action made him sexually uncomfortable; on the verge of arousal.

By 5 P.M. Russell explained to the kids that dinner had to be postponed. They didn't seem disappointed; that cut him emotionally. The crew had reconvened in the conference room. Dinner was delivered as they worked. Barb sat across the table; her eyes heavy on him. She wanted him. He wanted to escape. Allison was not interested. He battled with internal conflict, justifying desire as a way to be closer to the woman he wanted to be.

By half past eight, the team had gone as far as they could on the dilemma. "I'm leaving, but that doesn't mean that you have to. If anyone wants to stay and continue working, feel free," Sylvia announced. The yoke of indentured servitude was more than just imaginary. She was gone five minutes before the others packed up silently not daring to say anything that might become grist for the mill.

In his office, Russell packed his briefcase. He wasn't sure why, he wasn't planning to work at home. By the time he got home it would be bedtime. Barb said goodnight to the others, leaving Russell and her as the only two occupants. Russell was shrugging into his sport jacket when she stepped into his office and closed the door. He felt his sack tighten when he heard the lockset click.

"We're alone, finally," she said, slowly approaching him. She had unbuttoned one of the buttons on her white ruffled blouse that followed her curves. Her voluptuous breasts were barely contained by the bra and blouse. He stopped with the jacket askew across his shoulders.

"I'm really tired and I don't think this is good..." Before he could finish her arms were around him, her lips engulfed his, her tongue probed. Resisting at first, he succumbed to her. She tasted sweet, her lips soft and supple, coaxing him to participate. Her hands found him; gripping and squeezing his butt cheeks. She pulled him close, grinding her expectant mound into his burgeoning hardness.

Torrents of need flooded his senses, drowning his resolve. Russell's hands caressed Barb's shapely hips. As he moved over her he considered how to lose the panties without losing his dignity. Pushing back, he looked deeply into her intoxicating eyes.

"I don't want to ruin this moment. I want you. I've got to pee or I won't last. Make yourself comfortable and when I come back I'll take you to heaven." He sounded confident, believable. She puffed her lower lip before kissing him.

"Hurry; I'm wet and I don't want to cool off. I'll make sure every drop of sweetness is waiting." She pushed him back, lifted her skirt, slipped off her thong and lobbed it to him. She had been wearing pantyhose; she wasn't wearing them now. He caught the thong and brought it to his face. Inhaling he could taste her, pungent and borderline delicious. Scurrying out of the office he closed the door behind him. Moving quickly, he entered the men's room, into a stall and slid the latch into place.

The panties folded neatly and stowed in his front pants pocket, he had checked the mirror to ensure there was nothing telltale. Locking the office door behind him, he faced her sitting in the middle of the work table her legs spread, her skirt pulled up to expose her smooth and clean shaven pussy. She beckoned him with her index finger. He felt himself preparing to enter her, hoping he could hold the erection until after he satisfied her orally.

Dropping to his knees he lifted one leg and then the other, placing them on his shoulders. She moaned with anticipation as he kissed her inner thighs, running his tongue from knee to loin on both legs. She arched her back, wanting his mouth on her. He kissed and he nibbled on the fleshy exterior of her pleasure zone; her fragrance stronger as arousal produced glistening wetness.

Reaching down she grabbed his head with both hands and pulled his face into her wetness. Driving his tongue into her she moaned louder as her hips undulated. Using her calves and heels she urged him on as a rider urges a stallion to excel. Licking and biting he worked until orgasm ripped through her. She held her breath, intensifying the pleasure as he worked over her clitoris. The orgasm seemed to last an eternity as her nails dug into his neck and her heels dug into his back.

When she finally released they were both drenched in sweat, her loins were quivering. "Now fuck me; fuck me hard!" she called desperately. Dropping his pants to the ankles he entered her hard and deep. As his hips moved he drove himself harder and deeper. "Harder!" she called. "Harder, Russell!" As he pumped himself into her he imagined feeling what she was experiencing. He wanted to know what it was like to have somebody want you so badly they would do anything for satisfaction.

He erupted; they arrived at the same time, their moans of

pleasure a lovers' symphony. She took his hands and placed them on her breasts; her nipples were hard. He wanted to suck them; they were plump and his mouth was needy.

Backing away he looked at her pussy, wet and violated. He wanted to know what she was feeling; how the aftershocks impacted her ability to focus. Stepping out of his shoes and shrugging off his pants he removed her shoes, kissed her feet and then moved to her lips. She had dipped two fingers into her pussy and licked them; their combined flavors on her lips. He tried to pull away, but passion was too strong. She made him kiss her until she was satisfied.

"You like tasting my juices mixed with yours? Us?" Her voice was sultry, her eyes soft; stars twinkled in them.

"That was amazing."

"Yes it was. I am glad you decided to come back."

"What do you mean?"

"I thought you would have run for the hills when you left. I didn't expect that you would come back." Her tone was melancholy. He'd seen that reaction from other women. He didn't get it.

"How could I resist after the way you tempted me?"

"Help me up, please?" She extended her hands. He helped her off the table. As he worked to dress himself she dropped to her knees and took his flaccid member into his mouth. Her action took him by surprise.

"What are you doing?" She stopped and took his penis in her hands as she let it slip out of her mouth.

"What's it look like I'm doing?" She looked up at him and smiled before resuming. He had never cum three times in a day and he wasn't sure he was going to be able to accommodate her desire. "Don't worry if you can't cum. I'm enjoying tasting us. It turns me on." As she worked him over, her free hand played with herself. She brought her wet fingers to her lips, purring as she licked them clean. He tried to think of something that would arouse him. He didn't want to disappoint her. That was one of his demons. Mandy hated when he could not perform. She made him see the doctor. The physician told him there was nothing physically wrong with him. Russell was shaken; there was something wrong, he didn't feel the desire to perform as a male.

In a fit of panic he asked the doctor to prescribe an erectile dysfunction drug. The doc was skeptical. After a long pause, he agreed. Russell asked for multiple refills; the doc obliged. Filling the prescription, Russell felt more confident. He would not tell his wife. He didn't want to tell her he needed medication to perform. She would think him less of a man.

His performance with Barb was out of character. Maybe it had something to do with unplanned activity. He wasn't getting hard. Barb didn't seem to mind. When he thought about kissing her feet his cock tingled. Imagining kneeling before her arousal began. His twisted mind took him to the fantasy of Sylvia catching him dressed in pantyhose and heels. Sylvia made him kiss her feet. His cock filled and Barb was purring like a well-fed cat. A little deeper down the erotic humiliation road and he was on the verge of ejaculating.

When he squirted, she swallowed. It wasn't much of a delivery but it seemed to satisfy her. When she stood, she kissed him.

This is what I wanted to do to you last night," she said as she slipped her shoes on. He watched. He wanted to be her. He wished he could tell her. The secret was burning a hole in his brain. "You better get dressed. I think we're done," she said. He pulled up his pants, fastened them, then hooked his belt.

"I suspected as much," he tried to sound grateful.

"What's that supposed to mean?" She sounded hurt. He tried to smile. He didn't want her pissed at him. One problem woman in the office was enough.

"It means that cumming three times in a day was more than I ever could have expected." Before he could correct himself she was all over him.

"We only came twice. When did you cum a third time?" As she spoke she smiled, the realization washing across her complexion. "Naughty boy you did it in the bathroom. That's why you disappeared." Her face twisted into a question mark. "You were worried you couldn't cum three times and you came twice, bang,

bang, then you filled my mouth. I'd say you're pretty amazing. He didn't want to tell her she was mistaken. She didn't seem bothered that he took things into his own hands.

"Thanks for making me feel good. You are beautiful; I couldn't have helped myself even if I wanted to stop." He embraced and then kissed her. "I wanted you since I heard your voice on my answering machine," he lied convincingly.

"Would you like to date me?" she asked as she hugged his neck. Her words surprised him. Did he dare play into her hands? Was she screwing with him? He wasn't sure.

"Do you think it's a good idea that we date? We work in the same office and all." He tried to sound convincing.

"What difference does that make? Do you have any idea what goes on around here?" she asked.

"I know there's a lot of fluid sharing. You don't have a problem being part of that crowd?"

"Honey I will never be part of any crowd. I don't care what others do. But if you're not interested." As she spoke he knew those words were going to bludgeon him if he allowed it.

"I find you very attractive. I'm flattered you are attracted to me. I'm worried that if we break up one of us will have to leave. A break up not only will be bad, it will make it uncomfortable around here." His eyes bored into her searching for her answer. He wanted her to be true to her heart.

"Then we just won't break up." He considered her statement and began to warm to the idea.

"You really want to date?" He kissed her and she pulled him close, squeezing him against her large breasts. "I don't want either of us to get hurt. Can we go slow and keep this out of the office gossip pool?"

"Sure, no problem."

She kissed him. "You wanna go back to my place and screw?" He felt himself shrivel. "I'm just joking." She used her tongue to caress his lips. He nipped at it, causing her to squeak playfully. She was the woman he wanted to be.

"I can't promise you anything more than touching and petting."
He thought about offering her another round of oral sex. She winked
and smiled.

"Follow me; I don't live far from here."

He pulled his car near hers watching as she fussed with her hair,
checked her makeup in the vanity mirror, fished lipstick out of her
handbag and freshened her lips. When she finally fired up the engine
he was imagining Allison following the same ritual although he
didn't know if he could ever allow Allison to be taken like Barb
allowed herself to be taken.

Chapter 10

AWAKE BEFORE THE ALARM, Russell reflected on the evening. His love interest was a bombshell, and their sex had been loud and explosive. He hadn't seen that much attention since he and his ex-wife experimented with his erectile dysfunction drug. Mandy discovered them in his nightstand. After Mandy's typical ball breaking she concluded he had gone the prescription route to please her. She peppered him with questions about side effects and negative reactions.

"They don't bother my system, but they make me hot for you." Passion dripped from every word.

"Hhmm, how do you think I would react if I took one of them?" He considered her question before responding.

"I don't know. Do you think this might only be for men? I mean what if it makes you not want sex with me?" He sounded despondent.

"This is a sex pill, right? It's supposed to make you horny." Her eyes widened to punctuate the statement.

"I don't know about that. I think it's supposed to make me hard."

"It's a horny pill," she said.

"Maybe." He didn't know how to respond. Reaching across him she grabbed the pill vial. Working the childproof cap, she checked the contents before tapping out one of the pills into her palm. Examining it and turning it over in her hand she smiled before dry swallowing it.

"Hand me the water glass." She chased the pill with two gulps of water. "How long before this thing works?" She wanted instant gratification.

"The doctor said about an hour." She frowned. He shrugged his shoulders; *typical Mandy*.

"Well we can have an hour of foreplay." Thirty minutes later she was like a woman possessed. He wasn't sure it was the pill. The power of suggestion could encourage you to do things that were outside the comfort zone. She had multiple orgasms as they explored different techniques and different positions. Her desire was insatiable. He thought she might break his penis; she used it like a dildo; a sexual appendage attached inconveniently to his body.

Hours later she fell asleep curled up next to him. He felt unsettled. If she decided to use his pills on a regular basis he would have difficulty functioning afterwards.

***

Showering felt as if he was washing yesterday's enjoyment away. He contemplated Barb's proposal. It would crimp his ability to be Allison. He would have to play it cool; use her to satisfy his physical need. He worried he might not be able to perform on demand. She probably wouldn't be satisfied with oral sex alone. *Maybe I could imagine my way to an erection.* As he dressed, he considered something feminine but the likelihood that Barb would want an encore was the odds-on favorite. Allison pinged from his subconscious, making him feel uncomfortable.

Early to the office, he decided to stop off to see Bethany. As he entered her coffee shop she was engaged in a heated conversation with one of the patrons. Russell caught the tail end; something about guys using the ladies room.

"Problem?" he asked.

"What'll you have, Russ?" She wasn't interested in small talk. Her color was up; her nostrils flared like a bull readying a charge at the matador.

"Same." She pursed her lips as her eyes narrowed and her brow furrowed. "Double shot skim latte," he said apologetically.

Paying for his purchase he tried to make small talk. Bethany provided only one-word answers or grunts. Russell scooped up the coffee that he didn't really want and skulked out of the shop. Settling uneasily into the car he sipped. The drink was sweet. "Shit, she added sugar." He considered whether it was worth going back to get the corrected version. Turning the key in the ignition he placed the cup into the cup holder in the center console. Dropping the car into gear he backed out of the parking slot.

Traffic was unusually heavy; he cursed himself for stopping off. He wanted to get to the office. He needed to restore order in the sudden turbulence. Pulling into a parking slot at the office he turned off the ignition. Lifting the cup from the holder he sipped the warm, sweet liquid. Exiting the car, he carried the cup to the trashcan and dropped it in. In the elevator, he prepared himself for the onslaught. Sylvia had sent a flurry of emails between three in the morning and sunrise; his mobile phone chirped with the familiar delivery tone. She had insisted all of her employees have the same notification tone for her email, text and ringtone.

Sylvia's door was closed. Either someone was being fired or she was dealing with personal matters. She was the only person in the office permitted to attend to personal matters. Russell scurried to his office hoping he might get to some of the work parceled out before the first interruption of the day. He hoped she would keep her distance. He didn't need the drag of her emotions.

Thirty minutes into his day Sylvia stormed into his office and slammed the door. "What the hell are you doing?" Her arms were crossed under her breasts and she was tapping her right foot. Her gaze burned a hole in him. His first thought was she found out about his little tryst with Barb. Taking a deep breath he told himself to relax; not to let her outburst tilt him.

"I'm working on the emails you sent." He felt his voice beginning to crack. Her blood pressure must have been in the stratosphere; her face was beet red.

"I'm glad you're taking your time. I needed that information an hour ago. I was on the phone with the board chair. He's not happy with our progress on this problem." Her color began to pale slightly.

"I'm sorry; I didn't know you needed this, otherwise I would have been in earlier." He tried to reconcile.

"Then you didn't read my emails in sequence. How many times

98

have I told you to read my messages in sequence?" Her voice jumped several octaves. He cursed himself for being shortsighted. She was right. She expected her direct reports to know how to work with her without constant reminder. Russell sat and took the verbal onslaught. There was nothing he could say to pacify her.

"Let me see what you're working on," she barked. She grunted several times as he walked her through the data.

"I've got maybe another half hour before this is polished enough to present." She cut him off.

"There isn't going to be any presentation. You're going to produce this report for me in fifteen minutes." She turned and headed for the door, turning before she opened it; her demeanor shifted. "Russ, stick around tonight. I have plans for you." She left, closing the door behind her. Slumping into the office chair feelings of dread flooded his mind. She had just turned up the heat on the pressure cooker and the idea that she was planning something for him only fanned the flames and drove him crazy.

By six thirty his nerves had frayed to fine strands, causing him to overreact to the slightest prompting. His lover had stopped by twice to talk. The first time he was sullen. She tried to cheer him up. The second time he almost cried. She wanted to console him. He asked her to leave, not considering her offer to stop by for a nightcap.

At six forty-five his intercom buzzed; he was being summoned. Pushing heavily out of the chair he dragged himself down to Sylvia's office; he and Sylvia were the only two there. Stepping inside he saw her sitting on the settee; a rare sight. She enjoyed the power of the desk. She was surrounded by papers in untidy piles. He walked over to the seating group and stood waiting. He hoped she wouldn't notice him. He wished he could disappear.

Looking over the top of reading glasses she smiled. "How are you, Russell? Get ahead of the work finally?" She was acting like they were good friends. She gathered one of the paper stacks on the seat next to her; attempting to organize it before dropping it unceremoniously on the floor. "The secretary can clean that up in the morning."

Patting the seat next to her she coaxed him to join her. A new wave of dread engulfed him. She watched as he made his way slowly through the maze of papers. They looked like fallen leaves at the base of a tree. She was wearing a button-front scarlet red dress, red pumps with pointy satin gold cap toes and a simple satin-finish gold belt.

"Rough day?"

"Pretty much." He tried to sit up straight.

"I thought you'd be happy to see me." Her Cheshire cat smile made him want to hurl as humiliation crept up his spine.

"I'm tired; haven't been sleeping much."

She made a pouty face. "You should try exercising. It will help you sleep." She paused for a beat. "How would you like to give me a massage?" Her eyes absorbed him, leaving him powerless to refuse.

"Whatever makes you happy." The words sounded like they were coming from another being.

"You can start with my feet. Being in these heels all day isn't kind to them." He started to slide off the sofa.

"You can sit here. I'll shift around and put my feet in your lap." On autopilot, he removed one shoe and placed it beside him on the settee. The fragrance from her warm feet was enticing as he massaged. She purred as hands worked over her heel, toes and instep. As he massaged her foot his eyes were transfixed. She watched as he worked. She flexed her toes on the other foot. He took the cue and slipped off the second shoe. She lifted her leg and exposed her thigh up to the panty of her pantyhose.

"You have my permission to kiss my feet." Her words caught him off guard. Her delivery conveyed privilege, honor. "Don't look shocked. Your expression betrays you. Go ahead." She pointed the toes of her right foot as she touched his lips with them. Unable to help himself, he succumbed to the need. She laughed as the kissing intensified. "Don't kiss off all my nail polish. You love paying homage to your Goddess." He looked over the top of her toes as he kissed them, the answer radiating from his eyes.

By the time he returned to his office to pack up an hour had passed. Sylvia released him for the night after suggesting undergarments for him to wear. She talked with him about panties, garters, hosiery, bustier and camisoles as if they were girlfriends. Every time he tried to escape she mentioned another item. He tried telegraphing his disinterest. She failed to notice.

His mobile phone chirped. Plucking it from his briefcase, he checked the display. Barb had called, left a voice mail and texted. He felt bookended. She was producing demand on the personal side while Sylvia generated ample demand on the professional side.

Escaping to the parking lot he settled behind the wheel. Slipping off shoes and socks he decided to drive barefoot. He had ballerina slippers in the glove compartment. Reaching over he extracted them. Pushing back the twinge of absurdity that infiltrated his psyche he slipped on one, then the other. Allison was assuming control; Russell was happy to recede; he had been exhausted by the day's events.

Climbing into bed after slipping into a silk nightshirt, sleep came quickly. He slept through the missed call and the two text messages sent at 11:00 P.M. Barb wanted him. She told him about her need and what she wanted to do to him. She also told him about the expensive vibrator that would be a poor substitute for him. Rolling over he checked the digital display on his phone. He had ten minutes before rise and shine. Barb's message made him wonder how he had missed this part of the world. Vibrators intrigued him. Sylvia probably had one of those power tools to satisfy her need. The thought of his boss using a vibrator on herself aroused him. He thought about Barb and how he would use her to get off if he had been with her.

Emerging from the house, the morning was beginning its ritual of breaking through the last vestiges of night. Courses of clouds like the slats of window blinds stretched across the sky as sunlight poured through the breaks. He wasn't sure he could face another day with Sylvia using him, although he did pull out a garter belt, silk stockings and matching white lace panties. He didn't think a camisole was going to work. He never gave thought to the exposure if he ended up with Barb.

Katie intercepted him as he entered the suite. "Conference call in Barb's office." He cursed to himself. "Sorry Russ." When he walked into Barb's office she was leaning over the phone talking into the speaker. His eyes fell on her tight ass that pressed the skirt to its limits. The slit at the base of the skirt widened suggestively just above the knee. Light shimmered off the silk hosiery that adorned her smooth legs. As he approached he cleared his mind. There was no way he would fall into her trap of seduction early in the day. He made enough noise to announce his presence. She looked up and then back to the phone to continue her response. Joining the conversation, he took a seat across the desk from her.

The call lasted fifteen minutes. They compared notes and parsed responsibilities. Barb was all business. He tried to make small talk. She dismissed him. "Are you okay?" His voice was soft, almost apologetic.

"I'm fine and I'm busy." She wasn't taking prisoners. As they worked he glanced over at her several times, each time he gazed longer. She refused to engage his stare. Tension was palpable and thick. Russell felt he was suffocating. He wanted to say something; he couldn't find the right words. He didn't think she cared to hear anything that wasn't related to business.

After thirty long minutes he stood, feigning pain in his lower back. As he stretched he hoped she would offer words of sympathy. He grunted for effect.

"You really need to start exercising. Your back's only going to get worse unless you start taking care of yourself." She spoke without looking up.

"I'm going to go back to my office. I've got a few things I need to get to." He approached the door slowly, hoping she would say something that might give him a clue. He hated being in limbo. Mandy did that to him all the time.

Stepping into his office, the feeling of safe harbor evaporated when Barb followed and sat at the small table to the right of the doorway.

"Close the door and come over here." Her tone was authoritative, pricking his spine. "Sit down, Russ."

"Barb." Before he could continue she stopped him.

"I've been trying to reach you." Her gaze burned holes in him.

"I've been swamped."

"You need to do a better job of listening. Just like now you insist on answering before you know the question," she scolded.

"We had sex right here. Right here." She patted the table with the palm of her hand as if there was something sacred about it. "I needed you and you delivered." She puckered her full lips and blew him a kiss. Her expression softened. "I thought we had an understanding. I thought we were going to start dating. But you've been off the reservation since I gave myself to you." Her tone turned serious. "I don't just give myself to men for the hell of it. I thought by your actions you wanted the same thing I wanted." She stopped, her eyes formed a question.

"Can I respond now?"

"Yes." She stood and walked over to the door. His eyes followed her, her hips undulated as she moved. He felt stimulation threatening to compromise him. After locking the door she returned to the table, her large eyes sizing him up.

"I want you, I really do. Every time I think I have an opening Sylvia charges in and sucks the life out of me. She's been riding me hard." He wished he had not used sexually suggestive terms. They struck too close to home.

"You really want to date me?"

"Yes, for sure, absolutely!" It was his turn to sound animated. She dropped to her knees and fiddled with the zipper on his pants.

He tried to stop her. "This isn't such a good idea." She had the zipper down and was searching for the opening in his underpants that would free the bulge. "Barb, please don't." He pleaded trying to restrain her hands. She stopped and looked up.

"You're wearing panties and garters and stockings...oh my!" Barb's voice sounded playful. Embarrassment threatened to crank up the perspiration engine as his body heated. He pushed her hands away and pulled up his zipper. She massaged his loins as he tried to regroup. Another woman at the office knowing his secret meant he could fall farther. He couldn't understand what was up with women wanting to give him blowjobs. Maybe there was something in the water.

"Honey, I think it's cute that you dress feminine." She continued to coax him to cooperate. He couldn't believe his ears.

"What?"

"You think I'm going to make a fool out of you?" she asked from her knees, looking up with wide eyes.

"I can't; I can't risk any office gossip. I'm still recovering from the divorce. The whole thing rubbed my nerves raw." She continued to massage him.

"Russell, you worry too much. I don't care if you dress in diapers. Well maybe diapers would be a little over the top." He removed his hands and allowed her access. She unfastened his belt, unhooked his pants and slid them to his knees exposing taupe stockings and white garters over white lace panties. He was hard and she wanted him. She unsheathed him. He could not believe she was doing this to him in broad daylight while he was wearing feminine clothing.

When she finished she smacked her lips. His legs were unsteady. It felt as if she sucked the essence from him. He struggled to make himself presentable. Barb stood in front of him, a "cat that ate the canary smile" perched on her lips. As he struggled he tried to figure what had just happened.

"Wondering why I did that?" She pointed to his loins as she spoke. He shook his head as he tucked his shirt into his pants. When he had his fly zipped and his belt cinched he relaxed. "I can't resist you. I was excited when I heard you were getting a divorce. It took all of my strength not to attack you when I found out." He tried to figure what made him irresistible. She walked over to the office door, unlocked and opened it. "If you want answers have dinner with me tonight at my place. Seven thirty; bring a bottle of cabernet."

Grabbing her belongings, "Seven thirty," she emphasized, as she exited. He smiled and nodded. She scared him. He wanted to close the door, flood the moat, fortify the battlements. He felt exposed, laid bare, his deed a flashing neon sign on his back.

He needed to regroup. She had flummoxed him. Embarrassment was chased away by intrigue. She knew yet she continued. *Why did she want to have dinner?* He shuddered at the thought of more pain; another layer of epidermis surgically removed. He pondered. Russell knew there was no way he was going to address the quandary. Preparing to dive into work he hoped he could focus before he lost the last vestiges of energy.

The day passed uneventfully. Sylvia demanded several things that he delivered, otherwise she left him alone. At six the office emptied. Barb emailed her address along with directions. He didn't appreciate the pressure but he had to know what she was thinking. Another dilemma. He had to know how exposed he was. Sylvia scared him; his lover intrigued him.

Stopping at the liquor store he purchased a bottle of cabernet and a bottle of champagne. He wasn't sure why; impulse purchase. Checking out he realized he had time to kill. The wait was going to give him an ulcer. He tried to relax as he sat behind the wheel of the coupe. He watched the comings and goings until he couldn't take the tension any longer. Firing up the engine he dropped the transmission into gear and pulled into traffic. He was going to be early. He didn't care.

Pulling up to her house he counted to ten before climbing out of the car, both bottles of booze in tow. He needed a drink. His nerves were frayed. He hoped she wasn't going to pour acid on them. Thoughts of blessed peace that suicide would deliver began to infiltrate. Knocking on the door he drew long breaths trying to relax. He didn't want to appear nervous. He had to show some semblance of control.

She opened the door. His jaw dropped. She was barely covered in a short red silk robe that fell suggestively open revealing more than a glimpse of lace bustier, garter, black thigh high stockings with red bows and black patent leather stiletto heels. Her hair fell in waves across her shoulders. Ruby lips seemed even more full than the last time he kissed her. She extended a manicured hand. He took the offering as she led him inside. As he crossed in front of her his shoulder brushed her voluptuous breasts. He felt control slipping; arousal threatened to destroy any resolve he had mustered.

"Let me take those bottles." She swayed sensually, floating to the dining room leaving him standing in the quaint living room that was furnished in contemporary fabrics and colors. His gaze followed her. "Take off your coat and relax," she called over her shoulder, her fragrance lingering. Slipping out of his jacket he stood waiting, unsure of himself. She was ready; was there was going to be dinner or was she going to take him as the appetizer? He wasn't sure if he would have the courage to ask tough questions after they had sex.

He walked slowly to where she was opening the wine. "Let me do that." He stepped beside her intending to take the bottle and opener. She turned full into him and embraced him. Her lips devoured his. He melted into her as she overpowered him. Her tongue explored every region of his mouth as his hands groped her.

"Do you want an appetizer or dessert?" She asked, her eyes pools of molten desire. The reason for his presence shifted from his need to her desire. He knew dinner would be a blur if he didn't satisfy her. She took his hand and led him up the stairs; his eyes transfixed to the perfect globes that were framed by the silk and lace thong parting them perfectly.

Her bedroom glowed as a forest of candles burned and flickered on the bureau against the far wall, their flame reflecting in the mirror that stretched across the top of the long dresser. The bed's plush duvet had been turned down; a mountain of pillows displayed earthy tones that seemed almost mysterious in the candlelight. Window treatments were long brocade curtains. The tray ceiling was painted with wispy clouds dusting across a pale blue sky.

She stopped after crossing into the bedroom. "No shoes." She stood arms akimbo. Russell dropped to his knees to untie and remove shoes. She closed the gap between them holding the robe open. He looked up to see she had removed the thong. Her sexual fragrance drove him to the ragged edge of sanity. He tried to rise after removing his shoes. She took his head and pulled it into her loins.

His tongue went to work as she moaned with delight and ground her quivering mound into his obedient mouth.

He felt her approaching explosion. His breathing was labored as she pulled him tighter into her. As he tried to free himself to fill his lungs she pushed him down. Climbing on top of him she turned and worked him out of his pants as she lowered herself onto his face; wetness threatening to drip from her. She worked her mouth over his shaft as her hips undulated. His tongue plunged and probed. When orgasm struck she took him deep, muffling her guttural groans.

She worked him hard, almost raw until he ejaculated on her face. She smiled and licked his offering as it dripped toward her lips. He was spent; she was temporarily satiated. Climbing off him she turned and kissed him, her face wet from him. Closing his eyes, he tried not to think of his seed on her lips.

Standing, she reorganized strategically to corral unruly parts that had escaped captivity. Looking down at him she smiled. She was just getting fired up; he was receding. She was going to kill him; he thought it would be an interesting way to die.

"Are you going to lie there or get up and have dinner with me? You're going to need your strength." The words were like the jail cell door closing and the lock being engaged. He held up a finger as he tried to move, his body feeling tight and unresponsive.

Finally standing, he looked at her. She was breathtaking. He thought he saw a glow outlining her body, almost deifying her. She led him down the stairs and to the kitchen where she had set two intimate place settings.

"Light the candles. There are matches on the table." Her back was to him as she worked at the stove. He watched her for a moment. As if she felt his stare she wiggled her ass in rhythm to silent music. Approaching the table, she carried a platter; aroma wafting like the haunting perfume of a prostitute.

"Pasta Puttenesca," she announced. "The pasta of the whore." The words danced off her tongue. Prostitutes would cook delicious meals and place the steaming serving platters on windowsills below open windows to attract male callers.

As they ate he tried to recall the reason for his visit. She made small talk; he added tidbits about his life and his marriage. Barb was a lot like Mandy when Mandy was younger; vibrant with an insatiable sexual desire. She was beautiful in an elusive way. She had a way of capturing your attention and holding it until she allowed you to escape. Once she entered your thoughts you were under her spell and you yearned to experience the submission that only she could deliver. Russell felt the same way about Barb. He wanted and needed her because that's what she wanted.

Helping clean up from dinner he made it a point to touch her; to place soft kisses on her neck; to whisper things in her ear. She giggled when his touch or his breath tickled her.

"Let's sit in the living room. I know you have questions. I think I have answers." They shared the sofa, soft and inviting. She snuggled up to him, her full body warm and supple. Russell took her hand in his and caressed her palm. Crossing her legs, red painted toes peeked from bedroom mules with faux feathers over the sandal strap.

"Why do you wear women's clothes?" The question slapped him hard. She had broken the mood.

"What?" He needed to buy time to find an answer that sounded plausible. She looked at him with a "don't make me have to ask again" look. Swallowing hard he fidgeted. Taking a deep breath, he mustered courage.

"I love the feeling of silk and satin against my body. You girls get to experience it. We just get to look at it." His tone was almost accusatory.

"Hhmm, you enjoy feeling sexy?" she asked. He thought he heard Mandy's voice.

"It's more than that but I can't explain it."

"Try," she said as she shifted to her right and turned her body toward him.

"I've tried to figure it out, really I have. I don't have an answer."

"Sure you do, try." She prodded as if she knew the answer. He sensed that if he tried to dismiss her it would go hard on him. He hemmed and hawed as she waited, her elevated foot tapping at the air. He loved women's feet, especially clad in hosiery and wearing sexy shoes but could not bring himself to say it out loud.

"Let me make it easy for you. This "something," she made quotation marks in the air, "does it have anything to do with a split personality?" She watched for his reaction. He flinched; she saw it. "Why can't you just tell me?" She looked perturbed.

"Why do you think you know about me?" he asked feeling self-conscious and expecting her to ask him to leave.

"Because I was in your position for longer than I can remember." Her expression softened. He tried to process but struggled.

"What does that mean exactly? You wore men's clothes? How does that relate to me?"

"You are dense sometimes, honey. I was a male just like you; a shadow woman, trapped." She let the revelation settle over him. He wasn't getting it. He couldn't get his head around the thought of the beautiful woman sharing the meal formerly as a man. She looked naturally beautiful.

"You're just saying that to make me feel... well I don't know what I'm supposed to feel."

"Listen, Russell; I have no reason to fuck with your head. Well I have lots of reasons, but I'm talking about your organ not your brain."

"You...you were a man? But you're beautiful; naturally beautiful!" She blushed at the compliment.

"Lots of surgeries, facial, body, neck, and so on. If I was going to do this I decided to do it right. It cost me a small fortune but it was worth it wouldn't you say?" She spread her arms. In the candlelight, he saw a flawless woman.

"Wow, that's all I can say."

"I've never told anyone about my gender affirmation surgery; at least not outside my family. I know your situation." She smiled. He felt the warmth.

"I'm torn." He felt the emotional floodgates open. "I don't know how to control it. I struggle every day."

"Honey there's nothing wrong with your male side. I should know."

"Yeah but I don't know if I want to be a male. Sometimes I like it but more times I enjoy being the female side of me."

"What's her name?"

"Who?"

"Your female side."

"Allison." A crooked smile rolled across his lips as he fought the desire to hide the embarrassment.

"Cute name."

"I think so." They proceeded to discuss Russell's problem until he had come clean.

"You want a sex change?" she asked.

"I don't think I can pull it off without destroying what's left of my life. Besides, Sylvia would have a field day with it." He shifted uncomfortably.

"Anything you want to tell me about that bitch?" Barb spoke as if she shared something unspoken about their boss.

"You see the way she is. She barely tolerates me as a guy. After she flayed me she would find a reason to fire me, then I'd really be screwed. What with the divorce and my financial obligations." He rolled his eyes resignedly.

"She has you over a barrel; sounds kinky. Maybe you'd like to have me over a barrel." She tickled his thigh with her nails.

"I can't live in her dungeon. I want to do my job and come home to deal with my gender problem."

"Do you want me to help you?" She turned to kiss him. His response was less than affectionate, causing her to sit back.

"I'm sorry; this bullshit at work has got me emotionally screwed up." He turned and kissed her with passion. She returned the affection.

"That was nice," she purred.

"I can't believe you were…" He paused searching for the right words.

"A guy; is that what you wanted to say? Don't worry honey you can't hurt my feelings. I've been criticized and ridiculed by the best, or is it worst? No matter." She kissed him again. He felt it down to his toes. As she kissed him she felt for his reaction. Her smile radiated through the kiss as she enjoyed his response. Pushing back, she looked at him with deep and penetrating eyes.

"Are you going to be okay with this? I should have told you before we started. It was not fair to you." She looked away. Reaching up he lifted her chin and turned her head to him.

"We're past that point. I have no problems with it. Hell, I'd be an idiot if I did." He kissed her again. She wanted to say something. He placed an index finger on her lips silencing her. "Are you okay with my situation?" It was his turn to peer deeply into her. She looked away, making him feel self-conscious.

"Yes." Her delivery wasn't convincing.

"Don't lead me on. I can't take the emotional roller coaster."

"I'm good; remember I went through it before you did. I don't want to confuse the matter. I want you. I want you as a male. Can you live as a male, with me?" He hesitated. Before he could respond, she continued. "I know and I remember. What I also remember is the overwhelming need to do something radical. I won't be able to take losing you to a sex change."

"Let's go to bed. I want you." He stood and offered his hand. They embraced and kissed before she led him to the bedroom.

Chapter 11

AT 5 A.M. HE padded into the bathroom, the EMHO stiff as a pointer. He thought about rollicking with his bed partner as an encore from the previous night but feared a bladder complaint if he did. When he climbed back into bed she snuggled up to him. They kissed; her hands exploring his body. He needed to go; he didn't have a change of clothes.

He cleared his throat. "I've got to get going; I don't have a change of clothes. I would love to stay, really." She kissed him then bit his ear playfully.

"I've got clothes from my prior life. I think we're about the same size. If you're going to share my female clothes you might as well share my male clothes." Her words stunned him to silence.

"You're not okay with that are you?" Her voice cracked.

He rolled on top of her. He was ready to enter as she opened to encourage him. He worked himself slowly in and out of her. He tried to recall the last time he had been able to rise to the occasion without fear of losing the will.

They arrived together accompanied by alarm bells and fireworks. Spent, he rolled off her. She lay on her back enjoying the aftershocks.

"That was amazing. I never doubted you would be able to perform. Russell, you need to relax like that as often as possible. You owe it to yourself." Barb was expressing feelings that had haunted her when she was a male. There was always an excuse for failure to perform. It got bad; her former male self had refused to engage, fearing emotional destruction.

Several minutes later she stood and worked a kink out of her calf, her ass prominently displayed for Russell's enjoyment.

Strolling over to the closet she placed her right hand between her legs to catch his seed that threatened to run down her leg. Returning from the closet she held two shirts and two pairs of slacks. Dropping them on the bed she watched as he rose.

"Will you date me steady? You can leave some of your stuff here so you can sleep over whenever you want." She was making it easy for him. He wondered if there was going to be an angle that would trap him. He hadn't had sex freely or enjoyably for years. If Barb was this good consistently he could learn to love a relationship with her.

"Okay, if you can accept Allison." His tone was tentative.

"Of course honey. You treat me well and I'll make you happy. I'd even consider going out as girlfriends." She giggled and winked.

They showered together. He had to fend her off; she wanted action. He needed to recharge. They rushed through morsels of breakfast, she was dieting which suited him well. The clothes she had given him were a little baggy, but passable; he tried to feel comfortable in them as he struggled to believe she was a man once.

At the office they were both all business. She allowed him to arrive first. She followed five minutes later looking sensual. They worked together on a project. She behaved herself as she had promised when they kissed in the living room after sharing breakfast and coffee. He felt energized, wondering when the tank would register empty.

By noon he was feeling the effects of the prior night's activities. He needed a jolt. Checking Sylvia's status—he didn't dare leave the office if she was not preoccupied—he stepped outside and headed for his car. He had fought to keep his mind on work. Being close to Barb made it difficult to concentrate. Russell tried to imagine her before the transformation. He wondered if she was playing with him. Could the clothes she gave him to wear belong to another man she was bedding? The thought repulsed him.

Pulling into the parking lot of the coffee shop he watched people scurrying about. Caffeine jolts put a boost in their step. He needed the same boost. If he could focus on work he might get through the day without compromising what little he had salvaged.

The shop was humming. Bethany was engaged in a pleasant discussion with one of her customers. Her smile was intoxicating; full lips moved sensually. He imagined kissing them; being consumed by her. Barb's image filtered into his mind's eye; he saw a corollary. Maybe Bethany was transsexual. He didn't think he could take another of them in his life. He was still trying to reconcile himself and Barb. What would happen if his kids found out he was dating a woman who was a guy?

That thought snapped him back. The weekend was approaching. Had he committed to spend time with Barb? It was his weekend with the kids. They wouldn't forgive him if he stood them up. Plucking the mobile phone from his belt he fumbled through an awkward message to his son. Mark would respond even if he was in the middle of something important. Meghan would ignore him until it was convenient.

Bethany's personality drew him as he approached the counter. She smiled as if she knew something private about each person she saw, making Russell feel self-conscious. "What can I get you, sweetie?" Her toothy smile looked like a dental advertisement. That reminded him he needed to do something about the yellow film on his teeth.

Taking his purchase, he moved to the perimeter of the lobby. He enjoyed people watching, especially the women. Some of them looked fashionable and alluring, while others looked like they needed a makeover. He sipped his coffee; the caffeine had the intended effect.

He watched Bethany move like chocolate silk from the register to the serving counter. His body reacted as if he hadn't had sex in months. Feeling self-conscious, he slid out of the store without looking back. The image of Bethany was going to haunt him.

Back at the office he finished the coffee and tossed the container as Sylvia stepped in radiating energy. That usually meant a late night. Would his strength hold?

"Have a good break?" He tried to read her inflection; was she winding up to unload on him?

"I needed a caffeine jolt; ran over to Bethany's." He thought he saw her expression change for a split second.

"She's got a gold mine there. Who would have thought people would pay five dollars for coffee?" Sylvia's expression looked almost nostalgic.

"Did you need me for something?" He broke her reverie with the question.

"I want you to stick around tonight." She winked and smiled. He felt his heart drop, splashing into the acid that began to churn in his stomach. "I hope you're wearing something sexy under your male shell." She turned and left him to ponder what she had in store for him. He could leave early and suffer the consequences or he could stay and be humiliated. He wanted to believe he had a choice.

Picking up the handset, he dialed Barb's extension. The phone rang twice before she answered. "Hey sweetie, thinking of me?" she asked. He swallowed before answering.

"Yes I am. I really enjoyed last night." He tried not to sound fatalist as disappointment crept into his voice.

"What's wrong?" He felt the pull to tell her about Sylvia; convincing himself that she wouldn't understand, he fought the urge.

"The boss just stopped in. I need to work late."

"You're serious. What's up with her?"

"I don't know how late I will be. Do you want a rain check on tonight?"

"No pressure Russ, really. I know she can be difficult. If you think it would help I can stick around." *Yeah sure then you can see her make a fool out of me; that would do wonders for our relationship.*

"I don't think that's necessary. Besides if Sylvia wanted you to stay I'm sure she would deliver the invitation personally. I think she takes pride in letting us know we are serfs to her nobility."

"I'll be awake tonight. No matter how late, come over. I'll drop a spare key by your office. Keep it close to your heart." *She's serious about the relationship.* He smiled.

"Thanks, I will definitely come by after work. I might stop home to grab a few things. Next time I will have what I need to sleep over."

"Get back to work. Think about wearing pantyhose to bed with me. We can feel silky smooth together." She ended the call leaving him full of anticipation.

***

"We're alone again. It seems like forever since we had our last session." Sylvia circled the chair as he sat; teasing him by drawing the tips of her nails across his cheeks. "Have you been thinking of me; about my clothes, my shoes, my pantyhose?" The blush of embarrassment colored his cheeks. "I have fresh nail polish on my toes. I'm going to allow you to enjoy it. But remember be gentle, this pedicure has to last a week." She cackled an evil laugh.

"Sylvia." He paused summoning strength. "I'm not enjoying your taking advantage of me."

"Did you say you're NOT enjoying worshipping me? I think you're lying. I think you can't get enough of me. I'll bet you whack off in the shower when you think of me." Her words were caustic. He tried to stand up. She placed hands firmly on his shoulders and pushed him back into the seat. "You will sit there until I am through with you." She continued circling like a hawk sizing up its prey.

"Why do you insist on doing this? I'm loyal and hard working. I don't deserve to be treated this way." He tried to sound self-righteous but his tone fell short.

Placing hands on the armrests she bent and looked into his eyes. "You're not looking at this correctly. I am giving you the unique opportunity to worship and adore me. There are men who would kill for the privilege. Consider yourself lucky." She straightened up. Stepping back she eyed him; the bulge in his trousers betrayed him. He tried to cover the betrayal, hating himself for the inability to control his fetish.

"Stand up," she commanded. He stood uncomfortably. She brushed him aside as she sat and crossed her legs. "Now slave, on your knees. Beg me." Her words slammed into him.

"Wwwhhaa…" was all he could muster. Her gaze hardened.

"On your knees. You will beg to kiss my feet." He wanted to turn and run but where? If he ran the next stop would be the unemployment line. He had considered suing for sexual harassment. She had information on his sexual preferences. Even if he won the weight of his dirty laundry would crush him. Dropping slowly to his knees he looked at her as he reached for her leg. She pulled back. "You didn't beg. Don't presume you have the right to take what you want."

"May I have the privilege of kissing your feet?" The words dribbled out of him.

"You will address me as Mistress. And when you beg you will do it with enthusiasm. Otherwise I may conclude that you don't want to worship and adore me." She crossed her arms under her breasts. As he knelt, humiliation fueled his desire.

When she was satisfied Russell had earned the right to pour affection over her feet she watched as he kissed and licked and sucked. His attention to her warm and damp feet made her smile.

"Doesn't that feel good? Now when you go home you can whack off to reality. You can smell your hands and the fragrance of my feet will be with you." He continued to enjoy until she tired of him.

"Put my shoes back on. I've got to run or I'll be late." She stood and left him kneeling in a pool of frustration. Standing on rubbery legs he chastised himself for being weak. Checking his watch, it was still early. He could swing by Barb's and pour himself over her. As he considered her offer, he wondered how long before Sylvia's actions tore him apart and Barb chased him away.

Powering down his computer he called his coworker. Her voice was sultry. "I was hoping you were going to call. How was working with Cruella?" She laughed at the reference. He was too close to the situation to appreciate the humor.

"I'm going to come over. Is it okay if I spend the night?" he asked tentatively.

"Don't be silly hon, of course you can stay. I'm wearing

pantyhose. I've laid out a pair for you. Let's get kinky."

"I'll be there soon. I'm going to need a drink before I pour myself over you." He tried to hide the frustration in his delivery.

"Poor baby. I'll fix you right up. When I'm finished with you everything will be good." He wished that was the truth.

"I'll see you soon." He wanted to close this chapter in his life. The thought of suicide infiltrated his psyche. He had to lose the thought or the evening would be ruined.

Barb's aggressiveness made Russell wonder if his body would hold up. Sex with her was an endurance event; the last one to orgasm was the winner. Sex wasn't about the climax but the journey. Climax was the bell to end the current round.

***

"What's wrong, honey?" She tried to capture his vacant gaze. She was watching, his disinterest sending bad vibes.

"Shitty day at work. Cruella, as you call her, gets her rocks off being queen bee."

"Girls don't have rocks honey, in case you haven't noticed." She lifted the sheet for effect.

"Well she should, she acts like it." Frustration poured out of him.

"What did she do?" He didn't answer. "Was it worse than usual?"

"I really don't want to talk about it." He made a motion in the air with his hand to dismiss her. Incensed, she rolled on top of him and pinned his arms under her.

"You can't bring these feelings here and then let them distract you. When you're here I want all of you. That includes mental and emotional." She kissed him for effect, grinding her damp mound into him. He let her dictate; he didn't feel like fighting. His lack of response emboldened her.

"Would you like to make it up to me by eating me?" The words dug at him like an ice pick.

"Don't; just don't." His words deflated her.

"That bad huh?" She contemplated his reaction. "What did that cunt do to you?"

"Do we really need to talk about my problem?" He wanted to tell her; he didn't slam the door.

"She's what, making you do things for her?" The realization of what she asked settled over her like storm clouds. "She's abusing you!" Barb knelt, pulling her hair back away from her face. Plunging to within inches of his face she stared into his eyes. They seemed vacant; as if he had mentally checked out of the conversation.

"Tell me Russ, talk to me and you'll feel better."

"I doubt it. I doubt that talking about it will make it go away." He opened the door a little more.

"Try me. Hell, if I'm on board with you and Allison and dressing up together what could be any worse?"

"Promise you'll understand. Promise you won't do or say anything." He stared back mustering fragments of strength.

"I promise."

"She tried to have sex with me." He blurted it out stunning her. She blinked back the surprise.

"Sex as in intercourse?" A hint of jealousy in her voice.

"No, not intercourse. She tried to give me a blow job." He looked away ashamed of himself.

She looked at him, a combination of frustration and jealousy bled into her delivery. "You said tried. You stopped her, right?"

"Yes, but not quite. She did it on a day when I wore pantyhose and panties to work." His voice cracked as he spoke. "This was before we started dating." He hoped that would diffuse her jealousy.

"So what, you stopped her?"

"She stopped and told me I was going to have to wear feminine things to work."

"She's blackmailing you?"

"Something like that."

"Did she threaten you?"

"She's Sylvia, you know?" He answered resignedly. They sat in

119

the quicksand of silence that threatened to smother them.

"This is… I don't know what this is." Russell interpreted her comments as a death knell. He figured they were through. She'd be at risk hanging with him.

"I'm sorry that I had to tell you this. And it gets better." He paused, as if he was waiting for the game show announcer to summon the next contestant. "She says she talked with my ex-wife."

"So?" Barb's voice filled with frustration.

"You don't know about the details of my divorce."

"No, but I can put the pieces together. It was about you dressing up."

Russell looked surprised. "How…?" She stopped him.

"Come on honey, the breadcrumbs are the size of buildings. Cross-dressing killed my marriage; I have a good—or bad— reference point." She took his hands in hers. They were warm and inviting; Russell's were cold and clammy.

"Do you think she will fire me?" He felt himself shaking uncontrollably. Barb tried to wrap him in her arms. He was limp; the depth of personal problems soaking him in perspiration.

"Because of something you do personally? I'd say she'd have a lot of explaining to do. I'd like to be on the plaintiff side of that lawsuit." Barb smiled. In the back of her mind she hoped Sylvia would open herself to a career-ruining move. She knew it would be a long shot; Sylvia wasn't stupid.

"I don't like being vulnerable; not with much at stake. My kids already think I'm a pussy."

"Well?" Barb wanted to encourage Allison to bolster Russell's ego. She had been at the bottom of that chasm before the surgery.

"That's not funny; not now." He pushed himself away from her, suddenly uncomfortable with her flip responses.

"I'm not trying to make light of your situation. I've been there. I know how it feels."

"You didn't have kids in the mix." He spoke but refused to look at her. "You don't know what I'm feeling, just like I don't know what you went through." Staring at his hands he couldn't believe he could lose control quickly. Fearing another emotional disaster, he tried to find a middle ground. Turning, he made eye contact again. Her gaze was soft, almost apologetic. He wasn't feeling feminine. He wondered if he could change his outlook if he was to undergo gender correction surgery.

"Russ, I know you're struggling and I know I don't have any idea about your condition except that you can't figure out which gender is your true one." She blinked once as she moved closer to him. Offering her lips, he kissed them. She swept her arms around his neck and forced her mouth onto his. Hands between his legs, she tried to distract him from his low mood. As her hands worked, he warmed to her advances. His hands found her breasts, they were supple, the nipples perky and firm.

Taking his hands in hers she looked deeply into his eyes. She wanted control; he wanted her to have it. "Let's go upstairs and continue what we started. She stood and helped him up. Her ass looked tempting as he followed her up the stairs. Placing hands on the globes above her firm thighs he felt the subtle hint of muscle movements as she stepped.

Stopping on the stairs she grabbed the tread three steps up, bending at the waist. He stopped short, almost running into her. She flexed one leg and then the other making her ass cheeks dance playfully. Spreading them he placed kisses on her smooth skin. "Go ahead honey, enjoy!" She moaned with pleasure as his left hand found her moist clitoris.

"Baby you're there!" She flexed her hips back and forth to the rhythm of his fingers. Taking her right hand, she encouraged his fingers into her. Burying his face between her butt cheeks he tickled her anus with his tongue. As his fingers dug into her, waves of orgasm lapped against the shore of her sexuality. Encouraged by her movement and purrs he worked faster and harder with his fingers and mouth until her body threatened to explode with pleasure. The first tidal wave crashed against her shore. She collapsed onto the stairs, almost crushing the hand that was inside her.

Struggling to keep from injuring himself he leaned against the railing as his face rested on the small of her back, her skin damp with perspiration. Fragrance from her dripping pussy stiffened his already firm erection. Slowly removing his hand, he positioned himself between her legs. Hands on her waist, he encouraged her to kneel. Cock in hand he moved the tip around the rim of her vagina before thrusting into her. Tightening the muscles surrounding her love canal she made him work to enter her completely.

"Come on honey, come all the way inside." Her voice was dreamy, almost distant.

"Move with me," he said as he ground into her, the need to erupt and fill her overpowering his desire to prolong the moment. Moaning and calling her name accompanied uncontrolled ejaculation.

"Yeah honey I can feel your cum filling me." Pressing into him she wanted to feel him and wanted another orgasm. He allowed her to control until a second orgasm ripped through her. Collapsing onto the stairs a second time they decoupled. She climbed to the top of the stairs and fell softly onto the landing. He followed leaving a trail of drips from his flaccid member. Sliding beside her they turned into each other, arms intertwined.

"That was amazing."

"Better than I ever had," he answered. They fit together well as their bodies cooled down.

"Come on, let's get under the covers, I'm getting chilly." She stood. Lying at her feet he grabbed her ankles, freezing her. "What's wrong honey?" He placed soft kisses on the tops of her feet before releasing and standing. Taking her into his arms they embraced and kissed deeply. He wanted the moment to last. She was the real thing; better than any natural born woman he had known.

"Are you okay?" Barb asked. He had faded to sleep; his body twitched and then settled. Her words filtered through the fog of sleep. He had never fallen asleep in Mandy's arms. After he satisfied her he rolled over and slept in his cocoon. Barb wouldn't release him; he enjoyed her continuous need, at least until the desire to escape overwhelmed him.

"I couldn't be better, baby. I love impromptu sex. I never did it on the stairs. And from behind was amazing." He kissed her shoulder. She caressed his head as he nestled between her arm and her breast.

"Is it sex or is it love?" Her delivery was tentative. She had fallen in love and didn't want to be there alone.

"What do you want it to be, Barb? Can you be in love with me?"

"I am not a bed hopper. I don't do this with every man who wanders into my life. Yes, I can be in love. I gave myself to you. It means the world to me. What does it mean to you?" Her voice was just above a whisper.

"It means I love you, Barb. I wasn't sure at first. I've been hurt so many times I've lost count. I don't want this to be another one of those hard lessons." Propping himself on an elbow he touched her face with his free hand and turned it gently toward him. "I don't want to scare you off with words of love."

"I told you I love you first. How could you scare me off?"

"I was thinking about the "L" word as we were eating. I was afraid to tell you." His eyes moistened. She noticed, touching the tears that formed at the corners. She brought fingers to her mouth dabbing the droplets on the tip of her tongue.

"I love you, Barb." It was her turn to mist up. "Now don't you cry; I'm trying to keep myself under control. He saw her gaze stiffen and then soften.

"Promise you will never hold back your feelings. It's okay to be vulnerable. It's okay to show your emotion when you are safe with me." Her eyes bored into his soul. He felt her plant something there; an ache in his chest told him they bonded. He would not be able to escape even if he wanted to. Tears fell across his cheeks. She kissed them away. He loved that he could release; emotion slammed against the walls of his consciousness.

Several minutes later composure gained purchase. He smiled, his lips swollen and wrinkled, she kissed him tasting the salty moisture that accumulated on his upper lip. He hugged her with more strength than he thought possible.

***

The alarm woke them from deep sleep. She reached across to touch him and found an early morning hard on awaiting. Russell wasn't conscious as her mouth closed around the head of his cock. Starting slowly, she used her supple tongue to enjoy the combination of their fluids from the prior night.

Lifting his head, he realized what she was doing. Dropping his head back to the pillow he decided to enjoy the feeling. She moaned and purred as her head bobbed, devouring his cock. Involuntarily his hips moved opposite her movements. As tension built her movements quickened. One hand held the base of his shaft as the other fondled his sack. His hips thrust upwards. Her hand closed around his sack as he exploded. The first ejaculation bathed her throat with his seed. She continued to work him until the second eruption. This time her lips were positioned at the top of his cock.

Cum filled her mouth. She held it as she licked his opening to catch every drop of him. When she swallowed, she watched him. His eyes were on her beaming pleasure and enjoyment. She smiled, her lips wet as she ran her tongue suggestively over them.

"That was amazing! His legs were like rubber, his body unresponsive. Turning toward the nightstand he read the display on the clock. He looked down as her. She was fondling his flaccid cock.

"I set the alarm. Now you can go back to sleep for a little while." She crawled up beside him and nestled against him; his arm wrapped around her shoulder. As he stared at the ceiling he faded off to sleep.

Chapter 12

SYLVIA SLIPPED OUT OF her heels; there was something about lingering in them that made her feel irresistible. Her painted toes cooled against the marble floor in the expansive living room of her palatial home.

"How was your day?" The voice carried interest, devoid of telltale accent.

"Crazy as usual. Keeping all of the inmates in line taxes me. I hate being a bitch but that is all they understand." Sylvia smiled at her proclamation. "How are things at our little experiment?"

Bethany Queralls turned; her brown body glistened in the wash of light in the living room. Wearing a red silk teddy trimmed in white lace, red cotton crotchless panties with black lace bordering the slit that revealed her merchandise, thigh-high nude stockings and five-inch black stiletto heels, she sat with legs softly crossed on the sofa paging through Glamour magazine.

"Busy as usual. Do you want to know how many people hit on me today?" Bethany kept score at Sylvia's request. Sylvia likened Bethany's report to clinical research.

"I enjoy knowing how enticing you are. You also know those people come to your shop to see you. They couldn't care less about your coffee making skills." Sylvia padded over to the blush sofa and leaned over; tapestry fringed with brocade provided an opulent backdrop. Bethany leaned forward as their tongues touched and lips met softly.

"They have no idea what you're really about, do they?" Bethany asked.

"Clueless!" Sylvia said, punctuated with a shrill laugh. Sylvia shared her home with Bethany. The palatial mansion was set alone on ten acres of secluded land with privacy walls and tall trees providing further division from the world at large. It was a hike from the urban sprawl where she earned a living. Cavernous rooms were barely used except for extravagant sexual exploits. Neither woman had time or energy for large gatherings. They got enough external stimulation at work. Sylvia had remodeled the large, previously nondescript, home. Contractors worked for six months laying marble, installing crown moldings on the ten foot ceilings, creating old world effects; Roman-era throughout. She appreciated the trappings of royalty. Her infatuation with the Roman Empire radiated from every room.

The two women met on a hedonism cruise; Sylvia seeking a dominant female, Bethany seeking a sugar momma. They hooked up on the second day at sea; both of them rejecting suitors until the right one surfaced.

After a week of wild intimacy and fulfilling sex they decided to stay connected. Several months later, Bethany sold her belongings and moved into the palace. Bored after a short time being a kept woman, the two conceived a business for Bethany. It was supposed to be more a hobby than a job. Sylvia had money to burn and this would serve as a good tax write off. Neither woman considered a coffee shop to be self-sustaining.

"I missed you, sweetie." Sylvia cooed as Bethany's long manicured fingers found wetness. Moans of pleasure echoed off the marble columns that flanked the wide entranceway across the room from the seating group.

"I know you did. You need mamma to take care of your need." Bethany was the alpha in their sexual relationship. Turning, she opened her legs. Sylvia dropped to her knees at the sight of the strapped-on dildo her lover revealed. "That's right; show mamma how much you missed her." Sylvia's mouth worked over the thick latex toy that Bethany had rubbed with edible flavored gel.

Bethany squeezed the rubber ball that pumped white cream into the hose, through the shaft, and out the slit in the tip of the dildo. Sylvia almost choked on the flow. Bethany held her head down on the shaft forcing her lover to take the offering.

When she finished pumping the fluid Bethany relaxed her grip. Sylvia's mouth released and slid up the shaft until her lips kissed the tip of the toy. Looking up, her eyes were full of lust and need. On cue, she unfastened the strap that held Bethany's play toy. Bethany shifted, bending her knees, she rested the instep of each heeled slipper on the edge of the marble coffee table.

"Go ahead, mamma's ready." Sylvia insisted on the reference to Bethany as the "Black Momma." Spreading the opening in the crotchless panties the fragrance of Bethany's love canal made Sylvia lightheaded. Touching the tip of her tongue to the glistening moisture between the lips of her vulva Sylvia slowly began to work her tongue around the perimeter of Bethany's clean-shaven pussy. Bethany's hips undulated.

She grabbed Sylvia's head and drove it into her wetness, arching her lower back to enable easy access. Sylvia ate hungrily, her pussy dripping, saturating the thong that rubbed against her clitoris.

She found Bethany's firm nipples; squeezing and pulling. Sylvia's tongue massaged faster and faster over her lover's clit. Pulling nipples and sucking clitoris in and out of her supple mouth, she was driving Bethany at break neck speed to the edge. Peaking, she held Sylvia's head in the perfect position as the first orgasm ripped through her. She encouraged her submissive lover. Sylvia squeezed and twisted Bethany's nipples. Bethany released Sylvia's head, slamming her hands on the sofa and digging painted nails into the fabric. Bethany closed her legs, her thighs engulfing Sylvia's compliant head.

The second orgasm was an aftershock, wracking her body. Opening her legs she pushed Sylvia's head away, a silent plea for mercy. Sylvia stood and stripped naked. It was her turn for pleasure. Sylvia snatched the dildo from the sofa and began to work it into her saturated pussy. The toy was big and thick. When Bethany introduced the toy, Sylvia almost swooned at its girth.

"I've never seen anything that big! I'll bet that hurts." Bethany smiled.

127

"Honey you'll never go small once this monster's inside you."

"I don't know if I can do it." Sylvia sounded tentative.

"Take it." Bethany held it out." She stared at it. Bethany pushed it toward her. The submissive reached for it as if it might bite her. Taking it carefully in two hands, a chill cut through her, tingles between her legs dialed up her excitement.

"Now lay on your back," Bethany ordered, "go ahead." Bethany took the toy, licking it like a lollipop and spreading Sylvia's legs took the pleasure instrument and touched its tip to Sylvia's pussy, causing her to jump.

"Relax the muscles between your legs. Once this thing is inside you your body will react, trust me." Bethany added lubricant to the device before working it slowly into her partner. Sylvia's eyes rolled back in her head as the thick log filled her. Sylvia's body reacted by tightening around it, hugging it, encouraging it.

Bethany pushed and pulled it slowly at first, and then faster. Sylvia's body erupted. She pleaded, "Fuck me, fuck me!" Bethany was relentless with the device, pushing and pulling more forcefully against the muscle contractions. The second orgasm was explosive and more powerful than the first. Sylvia nearly passed out from the adrenaline rush.

Lying perspiring and panting in a pool of fluid, her body twitched with aftershocks. Bethany turned the device on herself after enjoying the flavors of her lover that dripped from the power tool. Turning the dial at the base of the device it hummed to life. Massaging her vulva Bethany fell onto the sofa, her knees bent and feet planted firmly on the floor. Inserting the vibrating device slowly into her she braced for the first round of convulsions. As expert as Sylvia was with her lips and tongue, nothing could outperform "the beast" as Bethany called it.

The submissive recovered slowly. She watched Bethany's body shudder and shake. Standing on rubbery legs she stumbled over to the sofa barely avoiding clipping her shin on the edge of the coffee table. Fishing the strap from the sofa she clipped it on. Climbing between Bethany's legs she grabbed the device, slipped it through the opening in the belt and plunged it into her lover. The monster vibrated ferociously. Sylvia felt the effect almost as powerfully as Bethany. Screaming again, Bethany enjoyed a consciousness-robbing jolt as her "g" spot pulsed. The final thrust slammed into Bethany. Holding the vibrator hard and deep against her vagina the two women climaxed simultaneously.

Chapter 13

RUSSELL AND BARB DROVE to the office together, arriving early. They discussed moving his feminine things to her house. She was concerned his children would discover them, giving them another reason to retreat from him. It was a crossover point for her. Having his intimate things at her house would force him to be there whenever the urge to dress was upon him. She knew that urge would strike more often than not; her encouragement would add fuel to the desire for Allison to surface. Barb was more than a little paranoid about Sylvia and Russ's ex-wife knowing about his dressing up. It wouldn't take much for his kids to leave the key to his house where their mother could access it. If there was an unholy connection between the two overbearing women it wouldn't do to ignore it.

She settled into her office as Russ grabbed fresh coffee from the kitchen. She was feeling complete, the memories of the evening vivid. He delivered the coffee and lingered for a long moment, his eyes drinking in the woman who had made his evening memorable. She looked up, a full smile spread from her lips to her eyes. She winked, making him wish they had called in sick, but they both agreed it would have been too obvious.

Stepping across the threshold into his office he saw the sun on the horizon, an angry orange-red ball. He imagined the corollary between how the sun claimed the day and surrendered the night and how his life waxed and waned. Thinking about making a life with Barb, starting over, concerned him. What if things didn't work out? What if she regretted her sex change? He wasn't sure he was ready for another rejection.

His mobile phone jingled. Fishing it out of his pants pocket he checked the display. As he read the text his palms dampened. He ran a nervous hand through his hair and massaged the tension at the base of his neck. It was too early for a problem; this one had the potential to go nuclear. Pressing thumb and middle finger into his temples he closed his eyes; he felt alone and cold. He needed to talk with someone. He wasn't sure Barb was the right person. *Would she understand? Why would she understand?* His son, Mark, was having a meltdown and Mandy was the culprit. She was attempting to turn the kids against him. Mark was the last bastion of family and Russell needed him to be okay. Mandy was pressuring him. Russell read the text message again.

Grabbing the phone from the desk he slipped it into his pocket. Turning, he looked at the sun again, wishing its heat would warm him, its energy would recharge him.

Knocking on the doorjamb, he stared at Barb. Light fell in shimmering waves across her hair. She wore it natural, soft waves gave the hair playful bounce. Looking up, her hazel eyes were full; his image brought a smile of desire to her pouty lips.

"Come in." She tried to sound formal; this was work time, no need to fuel the rumor mill.

"Can I talk to you?" Trouble spilled from his complexion.

"Sure, come in." She fought the feeling that he might be reconsidering their commitment.

"I need to close the door." He said as he pushed the door until the lockset engaged the strike plate. When he turned to sit, her face reflected growing concern.

"Is this about us?"

"Yes and no. Yes, in that it concerns both of us; at least if we are building something together, and no because it is coming from my life."

Her face twisted into a question mark.

"Don't jump to conclusions; I do enough of that for both of us." He forced a smile. "Relax please. I need your advice."

Barb took a deep breath and tried to force the tension from her shoulders. "Okay, I'm relaxed." Plucking the mobile phone from his pocket he opened the most recent text message and considered it before handing the phone across the desk. After reading the message she looked up, a mixture of anger and fear in her eyes.

"Why?" Her voice was soft as she fought the urge to overreact. She read the message again before handing the phone back.

"I wish I knew. I can guess and I'll bet my guess is more right than wrong."

"It's a control thing isn't it? It's her way of taking anger out on anything having to do with you." Barb crossed her arms; blood fury raged in her expression. She had been through all of the stigma, insults and ostracism that accompanied her decision to abandon her birth gender.

"This is really fucked up. My son; for Christ's sake he's my son. He's her flesh and blood. Why would she do this to her flesh and blood?" Russ asked, fearing the answer was retribution and ultimate control.

"How old is your son again?"

"Turns sixteen in two months."

"Are you sure he isn't acting out, trying to get your attention?" Russell swallowed hard before answering. He wanted to chastise her for being naïve. She had no common frame of reference.

"I doubt it. This is not something I think he'd make up to get my attention."

"Then go to him and get to the bottom of it. If you sit around fretting you're going to make yourself a nervous wreck." Her look softened. Russell contemplated. "Is he in school?"

"As far as I know." Barb wanted to reach across the desk and slap sense into him.

"Well find out!" her tone filled with impatience. Grabbing the phone, he texted a short message.

"They can't use phones in the classroom," he said.

"Then I guess you will know pretty soon whether he's in school. If he doesn't respond send him another message telling him you will pick him up after school. This way you can talk it out and if necessary try to reason with your ex."

The thought of talking with Mandy about anything made Russell nauseous. "She's got the cross-dressing thing that she continues to hang over my head. You don't think she told him about me and that's what's making him want to do this, do you?"

"How am I supposed to know that?" Barb's temper was beginning to heat up.

"If she told him about my cross-dressing or showed him pictures, or worse, the kid will never speak to me again!" Panic flooded his voice.

"Keep getting yourself worked up by guessing and in a few minutes, I'll be performing CPR while the paramedics rush here to take you to the hospital." Barb stood and walked to the visitor's side of the desk. She bent and gave him a hug. He was shaking. The mobile phone vibrated and he jumped, almost clocking her on the chin with his elbow. Clutching the phone in both hands he opened the message and read.

"He will wait for me after school." He sat slumped in the visitor's chair.

"Go home; you aren't going to be able to focus on anything today. Do it before Cruella gets in." Russell felt his balls seeking refuge in his groin. He didn't know which problem was harder to handle. After a long delay, he pushed himself out of the chair. Straightening up he motioned to Barb, who walked into his open arms.

"I'm glad you love me. I need you in my life."

"Whatever happens you call me. I want to help you, not just support you."

"Thanks."

"Now go home. I'll tell Sylvia you got sick."

"Wait, how will you get home?"

"You'll come by to pick me up. I'll hang here until you're done with Mark."

He smiled. "I love you Barb." Turning, he opened the door and moved swiftly toward the elevator lobby. He took the stairs, deciding not to chance running into the boss on the elevator.

He wondered what he was doing, the familiar evil twin, suicide, crept onto his shoulder. *Why do you do this to yourself? The world hates you. Show those sons of bitches you hate them back. You keep putting up with all this bullshit. Is it worth it?* The voice prodded him for an answer.

He shook off the funk that threatened to bury him, stabbed the key into the ignition, and the engine roared to life. He felt Barb's energy infiltrating him. She had positive karma. He had no idea why she wanted or needed to be part of his life. The Mandy revelation—*how could I have married a woman with such an evil and selfish streak*—negatively impacted everything in his life.

Barb would kick his ass if she knew these thoughts were sidling up to him, offering friendship and offering intimacy. *Maybe if things worked out with Barb they would work out for my son.* There was that evil twin again. He wondered if his ex-wife was the evil twin. *Don't be stupid. Barb made a conscious choice. Mark is being forced to bend to his mother's will. That's just wrong.* Steeling against what he anticipated to be a knock down drag out fight, he decided to do some research before the meeting with his son.

***

Barb drummed her nails on the desktop. Temper had graduated from simmer to slow boil. She wanted to slap Mandy. She wanted to be with Russell; he needed her strength. She hoped she had enough impact on him to keep him focused. If Mandy was half the bitch Russell intimated, he was going to need the strength of a superhero to overcome her will. Lifting the handset, she held it for a moment before returning it to the cradle. *Timing isn't right. I'll call him after lunch, closer to when he will pick his son up from school.*

Turning attention to work she decided to try to be productive. There was nothing she could do except provide support. As she opened email she caught a glimpse of the boss walking briskly past her office. *Great, she's going for Russell. She's going to be pissed. She will call him and interrogate him about this illness.* She never accepted things at face value, not even from her people. *I hope he doesn't answer the call.*

***

Finishing a quick and late lunch, Barb checked her watch: 2:00 P.M. Closing the door to her office and locking it, despite Sylvia's rules, she lifted the handset and punched in the mobile phone number. Waiting impatiently, he answered on the third ring.

"What time's dismissal?"

Two thirty."

"Russ, I wanted to talk for a few minutes and send you my strength."

"Thanks, I was just getting ready to run over to the school." He wanted to think. Barb's call intruded on him.

"Be calm. Let him explain before you..."

He cut her off. "Barb I need to think. I appreciate your calling but I have to deal with this. I will let you know how it goes, I promise."

She dropped the phone into the cradle without saying goodbye. *Just what I need is a pissed off girlfriend.* Fighting to push the fractured conversation out of his mind he turned attention back to his fragile son.

Pulling up to the school he found an opening in front of the building. He was early. He wasn't ready but knew there was no "ready" that would make their conversation go smoothly.

He scanned the wave of students pouring out of the building. Checking his watch, five minutes had passed since the first student breached the entrance and led the escape from the establishment of learning. Spotting his son, Russell waved. His son was engaged in conversation with a clutch of students. He looked carefree; at least he was smiling.

Mark spotted his father and waved; the smile melted from his lips. His complexion tightened. Russell's spirits dampened. Walking around to the passenger side, Russell opened the door.

"Are you okay?" Russell asked.

"Can we just go Dad?"

"Sure." Russell closed the door and walked slowly to the

135

driver's side. Firing up the engine he pulled slowly into traffic.

"How was your day?"

"It was okay." Mark replied flatly. This was the standard line regardless of the type of day Mark experienced.

"You don't sound okay. Tell me about your text message." Mark fiddled with his fingers and then one of the straps of his backpack.

"I'm scared, Dad. Mom is really mad at you and she's taking it out on me."

"Does Meghan know about this?"

"What does Meghan have to do with this?" Mark lashed at his father.

"I thought maybe you talked with her about it."

"What good would that do? She thinks like Mom. They both think we're wimps. Meghan hates you for not standing up to Mom and now she's getting to be just like Mom." Mark stared straight ahead. Russell glanced over at his son.

"I'm sorry, Mark."

"Well it's too late for that," Mark said.

"You wanna talk about your text message?" Mark was silent as he bit on the tip of his index finger. "I want to help. I'll talk with your mother. I'll talk to the judge if you want to get away from your mother. I'll apply for full custody. You're old enough to make that decision and the court will listen to you."

"That's going to put me in the middle between you and Mom. I can't say anything against Mom." Mark's voice cracked as he fought back tears. Russell knew the situation was near impossible. If he said anything to Mandy she would know Mark ratted her out. If he didn't do anything his son would lose. Either way they would lose. Mandy had a way of building impossible traps for him.

"Look Mark, there's a way out without pitting you against Mom." Russell wondered how he missed the obvious signs that Mandy was like this. He couldn't believe his poor life decisions compromised not only him but also his kids. Didn't the woman have any maternal feelings?

"How Dad, how?" The plea was desperate. Mark turned to look

136

at his father. "You don't know, do you?"

"I have an idea," Russell lied. "It's time I had a conference with your mother. I'll feel her out about you and your sister. I'll get her to tell me why she's doing this without her knowing you told me." Russell looked straight ahead, navigating through traffic.

"Mom's smart. She'll know I told you. You can't..." Mark stopped abruptly.

"I won't compromise you. I know how brutal your mother can be." They drove in silence, reaching the Midtown Diner.

Mark ordered chocolate malt, Russell ordered coffee. The caffeine would boost his brain. He needed to think. He refused to let Mandy win this one. He didn't care what she had over him. Expressing her anger like this was wrong.

"You want something to eat?" Russell asked.

"I'm not hungry yet. Can we just sit here?"

"Sure, no pressure."

***

An hour later they were finishing up burgers. "Where are we going after this?"

"A friend's house, Mom's gonna pick me up there."

"She doesn't know you're out with me?" Russell asked sounding disappointed. Mark shot his father a "come on" look.

"Mom would kill me if she knew I saw you without her permission." Mark was old enough to make his decisions. As he thought about it, Russell realized Mandy hadn't allowed him to make decisions when they were married. Why should he think she would allow a teenager autonomy?

Mark hugged his father before exiting the car. Russell watched as his son climbed the three steps to the front door of the friend's house. He pulled away before the front door opened. Mark had made him promise he wouldn't linger. He didn't want them to know he had been with his father, the risk of this filtering back to Mandy was too great. As Russell drove, bitterness churned in his gut. He hated Mandy. She had to pay for her actions. *Barb will know what to do.*

Chapter 14

POINTING THE CAR TOWARD the office he realized it was still early. He pulled into a convenience store parking lot, shut down the engine, grabbed the mobile phone, and punched Barb's speed dial number. He needed to check the temperature at the office before stopping by to pick her up.

"How did it go?"

"Too early to tell; I've got to figure out how to talk with Mandy, then I'll know."

"When are you planning to do that?"

"Not sure." Russell turned procrastinator when dealing with his ex-wife.

"Maybe you should talk to her now, today."

"What about getting you home? I don't want to leave you stranded at the office."

"Don't worry about me. I've got plenty to do. Remember, someone didn't show for work today and I'm doing two jobs," she teased. Russell didn't appreciate it.

"I don't think I'm up for this."

"Face it, you're never going to be ready." He knew she was right.

"Is she home during the day?" *Lucky bitch,* Barb thought.

"Probably." He was less than enthusiastic.

"Go talk to her. I'll be here waiting patiently. You'll tell me all about it while we're in bed naked, making love."

"If you think it's the right thing to do." Feeling like a condemned prisoner on the cusp of execution he wanted a reprieve.

"It's the right thing before it gets any bigger."

He reluctantly pointed the vehicle toward Mandy's house; the one he financed. *This will be a chance to see where my money's going.* Their custody agreement included a monthly review of the children's progress. He thought he could appeal to the courts for change in custody if she was doing something not in the children's best interest.

Pulling up to the house there was one car in the driveway. Meghan's car was either in the garage or she was out. He didn't see the boyfriend's car. That made him feel a little better.

He knocked at the front door after taking several deep breaths to calm himself. *Maybe she's out.* He hoped. Pressing the doorbell, he convinced himself he had to make an honest effort before folding his tent and going home. Out of the corner of his eye he saw curtains move. *Shit, she's home.* Bracing himself, he waited for the sound of the lockset disengaging.

The door opened slowly. A slight woman dressed in a housecoat answered.

"Is Mandy home?" he asked.

"You mean Miss Mandy?" she asked in choppy English.

"Is she home?" He refused to acknowledge her marital status.

"Wait please. Who I say calling?"

"Her husband." The woman presented a quizzical look before turning and closing the door, leaving him standing on the large portico with semi-circular ceiling and smooth columns standing silent guard. He admired the large wooden mahogany door with beveled, leaded glass panels. Polished nickel hardware finished the expensive look. Pensively, he continued to stand there, unsure whether the unannounced visit would yield an audience. After a long wait the large entry door opened.

"Miss Mandy will see you." The woman held the door and watched him step inside then led him to the formal living room, which proclaimed French Provincial, complete with floor to ceiling wallpaper, heavy and elegant looking window treatments, and moldings that could never be confused for builder's grade.

Pacing the long room, he inventoried its contents; nothing had changed since he moved out. Mandy stepped into the room and watched him. Clearing her throat announced her presence.

"You should call first."

"I was in the neighborhood and thought I'd stop by. We're overdue for our discussion of the children's wellbeing."

"I know." She crossed her arms, taking a defensive posture. He moved toward her stopping while there was safe distance between them. He still loved her, regardless of what she had done. He would take her back in a moment if she… He left the thought unfinished.

"You know the kids don't want the weeknight visits." She grunted and nodded. "I'm not going to force them to spend time with me if it doesn't work for them."

"That's big of you." Her delivery carried a sarcastic edge.

"I would like to trade those weeknight for more time in the summer." He hoped large blocks of time with the kids might short circuit whatever it was she was planning for Mark.

"I'll have to talk with the kids to see what they want." That meant she would make sure they wouldn't go for it. She was the consummate manipulator.

"Let's ask them together." She walked over to one of the two full height windows in the front wall of the room and pretended to straighten the curtains. Turning she stared at him.

"I'm not sure that's a good idea."

"Why not?"

"Look Russell, I'm not interested in negotiating custody or visitation. I like things just the way they are. We spent a small fortune getting this divorce finalized." Her tone implied that it was his fault things were drawn out. "I like things firm and certain. I don't want loose ends." She made it sound like he would screw her out of what was rightfully hers.

"Mandy, the kids are getting old enough to make their own decisions about visitations. You know Mark needs me, just like Meghan needs you. I would never begrudge you that."

"Mark has a man in his life." Her tongue was sharp as a razor.

"Don't you ever stop with the cuts? I'm his father. I'm the man in his life."

"Really?" Arms akimbo her lips pursed and her eyes narrowed. She tapped one foot impatiently on the hardwood floor.

"Really. Can we stick to the facts?" His voice acquired an edge.

"Facts? You want facts? I have plenty of facts for you."

"Can we keep this civil? What I do for a hobby should have nothing to do with the relationship with my children. That hobby cost our marriage and I regret it. Cut me a break and let's keep the secret between us." He thought about drawing her out. He wanted to know if Sylvia was jerking his chain about her friendship with his ex-wife.

"You're accusing *me* of not being civil?"

"I'm not accusing you of anything. I'm asking."

She barked a laugh. "You never learn. When are you going to stand up for yourself?"

"We're going to discuss this and we're going to do it in civil tones," he said, his voice firm.

"Very good; there's a backbone in there." She smiled.

"Let's sit on the sofa and talk civilly." Sitting she crossed her legs. She wore a red button down cotton top with half sleeves. The top two buttons were undone suggestively. The beige wrap skirt opened, exposing her supple thighs. Her feet were clad in red leather mules. Her shoe slipped off her foot and dangled from her toes. Fighting the urge to stare, he lost the battle and she knew it.

"You'd kiss my feet if I let you, wouldn't you?" she cackled making him feel small.

"You wouldn't let me even if I said I would." He shifted his eyes to her legs; they were tanned and smooth.

"I'd let you if you begged me." She laughed again. The thought of Barb walking in on him kneeling before his ex-wife and worshiping her snapped him back.

"No Mandy, that's not going to happen. You didn't want me when I wanted you. It's really over between us." His nerves steeled.

"Fine." She sounded disappointed, as if someone had snatched away her favorite toy. "Are you still dressing?" Her mood shifted quickly; back to the offensive.

Ignoring her question he pressed forward. "Let's talk with the kids on Saturday."

"You didn't answer my question."

"What time Saturday should we meet? I think it might be best to pick a quiet place on neutral ground."

"I'm assuming you are still dressing since you refuse to answer my question."

"How's ten?" He hadn't considered Barb's reaction to him cutting out early Saturday morning; presuming he spent the prior night with her. He began to realize the commitment he was unconsciously making to his new love.

She refused to drop the subject. "How's Sylvia treating you?" The mention of his boss' name struck him hard.

"What's that got to do with anything we're talking about?"

Mandy spotted the chink in his armor and rushed headlong to exploit. "She thinks it's cute that you wear woman's clothes." She paused for a beat. "She told me how you kiss her feet aggressively. She has to warn you not to kiss the polish off her toes. I figured if you kiss her feet you would kiss mine." Her taunting was making him crazy. He was losing control—if he ever had control—of the conversation.

"Can we get back to talking about the kids?" His voice faltered. He stood and walked away from her willing his body to cool down. She watched, then stood and walked around the glass-top coffee table. When he reached the threshold connecting the living room with the hallway he turned. She was standing in the middle of the room slipping her right foot into and out of her shoe slowly.

"I can't do this. You're not taking this situation seriously. I want Mark to come live with me." Russell didn't calculate the impact on his life Mark living with him would have. Hanging at Barb's place would probably stop. Dressing up would be curtailed, if not terminated.

"You keep looking at my feet. Are you sure you don't want to

142

kiss them?" Turning his head away he found something by the large ornate fireplace on the long wall opposite the windows to catch his attention.

"Did you hear me?" she asked.

"I heard you. Did you hear me?"

"Are you planning to tell Mark about your little hobby?"

"That will end. It's ending now. Sylvia did me a favor. Did you know she came on to me in a big way?" He was suddenly smug. She turned and walked over to the fireplace to adjust something on the mantle. When the object was positioned properly she turned.

"Honey, you're naïve. She wasn't coming on to you. Sylvia and I have been friends since you moved out. She wanted to console me. I told her everything. I thought she should know important things about her employee. She was checking out my story. She thought I was jerking her chain; as if women have a chain." She punctuated the statement with a steely gaze.

"She called me that night to tell me I was right. At first she was repulsed. She thought a man should be a man. I said, 'Honey, don't think you're telling me something I don't already know.'" Russell felt the bottom drop from his stomach. He was going to be sick.

"You didn't say anything to the kids?' There was panic in his voice.

"What do you think?"

"I don't know what to think, Mandy. I'd like to think that their mother, who loves them, would not crush them with news they did not need to know."

"You're saying I'm a bad mother. You need to be more careful with your words. Hurtful words will get you in trouble." He threw up his hands in disgust. *How does she sleep at night?* "Look, I didn't come here to fight. I came here to discuss the welfare of our children. Can we put differences aside for once? I don't care what you do to me as long as it doesn't involve the kids."

She took a deep breath before responding. "The kids don't know. I hate you and will make you pay until I am satisfied you've paid enough. But I won't compromise my kids." He tried to read her.

Why would Mark make up a story like he did? He tried to look confident, but confusion fought for equal time.

"How's Meghan? She seems like she's struggling."

"It's hormones. She's a normal teenager with too many boys interested, and too much time trying to be a girlie girl. I'm sure you can relate."

"How are the grades?"

"She's doing okay in school." Mandy didn't want to discuss it. She took his questions as an affront to her parenting. "Let's stay on point. Tell me how you're going to stop with the cross-dressing. Tell me how you are going to control the urge."

He needed to choose his words carefully. "I've made mistakes. One of them cost me our marriage. I'll carry that around for the rest of my life. I don't want to make that same mistake with the kids. The kids are most important. I've got to keep my job to support them. I've got to change things or I risk that too."

She watched him. His body language wasn't convincing her. "She enjoys having you on a string. How's that going to play out when she finds you're not dressing?" Mandy was taking pleasure in watching him squirm.

"You're close with her. You explain to her. She'll listen to you." He wasn't sure Mandy would help him, and even if she did he wasn't sure Sylvia would back off.

"Do you think she'll listen to me? It would be one thing if she had never seen you wearing pantyhose and panties. It's another thing that she's discussing which lingerie styles will work best for you. Either way you're going to have to work that out with her. Until then I don't see the custody arrangement changing." She had him boxed.

"Don't get mad at me. You did this to yourself." Turning, he paced to the front door, beside himself with anger and fury.

"This isn't over. You could have protected me. Instead you chose to feed me to the lions. For Christ's sake Mandy, will you ever stop being selfish?" He opened the front door and bolted out. Storming to the car he thought he felt her watching him

144

Chapter 15

THE PRIVATE LINE RANG several times before the call was directed to voice mail. That line was rarely answered before eight in the evening. The caller knew to leave a call back number and a three-digit code (411). The caller would anticipate a return call before the end of the night.

***

Russell drove toward the office as he tried to digest the confrontation. He wanted to share it with Barb and knew she would press him for specifics. Each recollection raised his frustration level. He called Barb's mobile number.

"How did it go?"

"Not well, I'll explain when I see you. What's going on there?"

"Sylvia was looking for you."

"I figured as much. She'll probably hear from Mandy. I'll be crucified tomorrow."

"She wasn't frantic over your being out. Besides, I took up your slack."

'I'll be by in fifteen. Can you be down by then?" Barb checked the clock on her desk. That would put his ETA at 5:50 P.M., ten minutes before quitting time.

"Sure."

"I'll see you then." Easing off the accelerator, he realized he was speeding. Checking the rear-view mirror there were no flashing strobes to indicate he'd been caught breaking the law. The need to put a stop to the lunacy that had become his life pressed for urgency. Slowing helped him to calm down and return to reality.

Pulling into the parking lot he saw Sylvia's silver sports car parked in her designated spot. Barb was just exiting as he circled around to the front door. She appeared ready for action. He anticipated questions. He wasn't looking forward to the discussion.

"Hi honey!" She bubbled over with enthusiasm. He didn't reply until she was in the car and they were moving.

"No top down? Too beautiful to be inside." She looked over at him. He looked like he might melt into a puddle of dissolved flesh and bones.

"Not good; I wish that text message had never come."

"That bad."

"Worse. I made no progress. She started on the cross-dressing and Sylvia." Pressing the accelerator, he wanted to escape.

"Do you want me to drive? If not you need to slow down." She reached over and took his right hand in her left. Easing off the gas the speedometer dipped below the speed limit.

"I'm stuck and it's my doing. She dredged up the past and used it like a club, beating my nerve endings until they were raw." Barb's temperature rose.

"I'll slap that bitch silly. Let me have five minutes with her. I'll make her regret doing that to you." Barb despised bullies; she had experienced enough of them when she was going through transition.

"I appreciate your offer. I need to handle this alone."

"Are you going home?" she asked sullenly.

"Only if you want me to." He wasn't in the mood to debate. If she didn't want him around he would retreat to his hovel.

"I want you to stay."

"Then I'll stay." He gave her hand a reassuring squeeze. Tears finally came as he pulled into her driveway. Shoulders hunched over and chin on his chest, he cried silently. Barb watched helplessly as she tried to console him.

"Honey, you're a wreck. Let's go in the house. I want to hold you. My arms will make you feel better." She helped herself out of the car. Walking around to the driver's side she opened his door. He stood haltingly, strength abandoning him.

Once in the house, she closed the door and helped him off with his shoes. Taking her hand, he helped her up from her knees and folded into her.

"Sit and let me pour us a drink. I want you relaxed." In the dining room, she extracted two cocktail glasses from the glass doored wall cabinets. Ice cubes from the countertop icemaker and splashes of bourbon filled the glasses. Handing one to him he took the offering with unsteady hands.

Sipping slowly, he summoned the courage to share the events of the day. "She's definitely got a direct line to Sylvia. She described everything that happened between us."

"You and Sylvia, everything?" Barb looked away for a moment. She was jealous. "Everything you told me your ex-wife knows?"

"I told you she was the model for bitch."

"Controlling bitch is how I recall your description."

"Shoot me and send me to hell, straight to hell do not pass heaven do not collect your angel's wings." If she was going to interject something pithy every time he spoke he was going to shut down.

"I'm not trying to give you a hard time. I'm frustrated; maybe as frustrated as you. I hope you know I only want to help."

"I know. This is hard for me. I'm not enjoying having to tell you all of the gory details, but I want you to know everything. I want you to know what you're getting yourself into." He looked at her, desperation fading as resignation settled over him.

"I appreciate that you want to be honest and open. That's one of the things I love about you. And feeling vulnerable and not being afraid to show it is even more appealing to me. There is nothing you can tell me that will surprise me or make me want to run away. Believe it or not, I've been through most of what you are experiencing. The big difference is you have someone to share it with. I didn't have that luxury." As she spoke he strengthened. His eyes told her he appreciated the support.

After draining the drink until there was only ice remaining in the glass he placed it on the end table and rubbed his hands together to warm them.

"Are you cold, do you want a blanket?"

"No blanket, not yet." Sliding off the sofa he knelt before her. She followed his movements. As he began massaging her firm calves she smiled.

***

Sylvia retrieved the message. Smiling, she knew there was something juicy waiting for her. Bethany was out for the evening plying her dominatrix trade. The coffee shop was a front for the sex-for-hire/BDSM business that was brisk and growing. Until meeting Sylvia on the Hedonism Cruise, Bethany ran her business as cash and carry. She would collect the cash, then carry in the tools of her trade. After their connection, Bethany set up a permanent establishment. As part of the deal each of her submissive customers were required to produce steady business for the coffee shop. The majority of the coffee drinkers were clientele of the dark side.

The basement of the coffee shop was adorned with leather, rubber tools, gadgets and restraints of all shapes and sizes that a successful dominatrix needed to address the twisted desires of her customers. Bethany was an equal opportunity Mistress—she dominated women and men.

***

Settling into an overstuffed chair wearing only a thong and camisole, Sylvia pulled the wireless handset from the docking station and punched in the ten-digit number that would enlighten her. On the third ring her call was answered.

"You've got something to share?"

"What do you think?" The two women played this cat and mouse game every time one had information the other coveted.

"You enjoy drawing this out, making me wait," Sylvia said.

"It's worth the wait. This is delicious," Mandy said.

"More news about your ex?"

"He's adorably stupid. He came here to plead with me for new custody arrangements. He thinks I'm stupid." Sylvia knew Russell was business smart; almost brilliant. She also knew that his pliability on the personal side gave her control over him. Sylvia used Mandy as her shill. She tolerated her because Mandy fed her tidbits of useful information.

"He knows that we talk. You should have seen his face. I think I know what castration looks like!" Mandy giggled through her words. "You should have seen him; I played with his mind. He still loves me." Mandy spoke with sudden reverence as if she cared about Russell's feelings for her. Her friend didn't like hearing that she had competition. She wanted singular devotion from Russell. It was imperative that she tighten her grip on him. There would be no repeat performances of Russell cowering before his ex-wife.

"Did you make him do anything?" Sylvia asked.

"He wanted to kiss my feet. I wanted him to beg but he fought me off. Maybe I should have told him he didn't have to beg. I wanted to watch him grovel."

"You should always make him beg for what he wants." Sylvia said, happy Russell didn't give in to her. She wasn't into sharing.

"He wants me to give him more custody of the kids. Can you believe he had the gall to ask?" Mandy prattled. Sylvia calculated that Russell wasn't as docile as she thought. More custody meant a potential change in lifestyle for Russell or a devastating crash when his kids discovered his little hobby. She was concerned Mandy might trash him to the point where it would adversely impact his work. That would be unacceptable.

"How did you leave it with him?"

"There was no way I was going to concede anything; not without legal advice. If he wants to change things he will have to pay for the attorneys." Mandy's voice crackled with electricity. This was another opportunity to bleed him.

"Did you tell him that?"

"No, he stormed out before I could toss him that live

bombshell." Sylvia breathed a sigh of relief. She knew that any further income shrinkage might put Russell in the position of asking for a raise. Things at the office weren't great with the current deal threatening to run aground.

"I'd wait until he comes back for a second opportunity before laying that ultimatum on him."

"I'm playing this for all it's worth."

"I don't think you need him going off the deep end or worse, driving his car off a cliff."

"You're suddenly worried about him. Are you having feelings? Like feelings for a guy who wants to be a woman?"

Sylvia became defensive. "He's your ex-husband, honey. I have no use for seconds from anyone's table." The thought of her employee converting to a woman intrigued her. She might push that button.

Mandy felt a twinge of anger. Did Sylvia think she was too good for Mandy? Attempting to bring the conversation back to point Mandy paused before speaking. "Nothing's changed. He's the same spineless man who let me get away. I can't let the kids get too close to a loser. They might become just like him."

"He didn't kiss your feet?" She didn't want Russell's lips wandering from their rightful place.

"No, but he wanted to." Mandy's voice conveyed disappointment.

"I'll make sure he kisses my feet and sucks my toes. I'll tell him he should show you how good he is at submission. You should see how I've trained him." Control made the overbearing boss feel strong. Wetness formed between her legs. She needed relief. She'd have to revert to a power tool if Bethany didn't come home soon.

"Does he beg to kiss your feet?" Mandy's response conveyed a hint of jealousy. She should have slipped out of her shoes and given her ex-husband what he wanted. It wasn't like she was cheating on her lover.

"No, he doesn't have to beg. His voracious appetite for my feet is enough gratification for me. I swear one of these days he's going to kiss the polish right off my nails!" Sylvia's claws scratched the surface of Mandy's vanity. Suddenly Mandy didn't want to talk. Anger threatened to unravel her. While Mandy stewed, Sylvia wondered how Mandy would be in bed girl on girl. She filed the thought away.

"Gotta go, Syl, the man is home," Mandy proclaimed, to promote her self-worth.

"Talk later." *Not unless I'm interested.* Mandy thought. As Mandy contemplated the call she felt undone by the woman in whom she had confided. Revelations she thought would hurt her ex-husband may have delivered something he needed and wanted. That pissed her off. *Is that bitch using me?* The *man* was home and he would want sex. He was an animal, tossing her about like a rag doll. Today she wasn't feeling like it. He wasn't going to appreciate her problem.

"Where's my sex goddess?" The new man of the house called out as he entered the kitchen. Mandy retreated to the formal living room. They never used the room. The kids were forbidden to enter. Mandy used the room as an oasis. Even her new boyfriend knew not to disturb her when she was in 'recovery mode'.

***

Sylvia retrieved the vibrator from the bathroom cabinet where it had been charging. Her thong was drenched. Bethany would have violated her with the strap on before she knew what hit her. The vibrator would have to suffice; Bethany's dominatrix calendar was full. When she returned from a working evening she was rarely in the mood except to have Sylvia eat her until her mouth hurt and her face was covered with Bethany's love juices. She wasn't in the mood to please anyone but herself. Sylvia applied the vibrator. Her body shuddered as excitement coursed through her. It was as if every nerve ending was connected to her vagina.

Bethany walked in after midnight, the heels of her black patent leather stiletto hip boots click-clacking. Plopping into one of the overstuffed side chairs in the grand foyer she unzipped her boots and slipped them off. She massaged the balls of her feet. She loved the look of the heels but there was a price to pay for style. Rising slowly, her calves and insteps adjusted to the cool marble floor. She recalled the events of the evening. She was raking in cash hand over fist. Sylvia had set her up with a credit card reader and payment tracking system. Customers bought annual memberships to her exclusive club. Sylvia taught her the finer points of marketing. Calling yourself 'exclusive' made people cream their pants for the right to be a member. In return, Bethany educated Sylvia on the finer points of being a dominatrix.

Grabbing a snack from the refrigerator she padded to the kitchen table. Dropping into one of the high-backed cane chairs with comfortable cushions she tore into the food. Abusing and dominating clients always made her hungry. She wanted and needed an orgasm. Maybe she would wake Sylvia and use her. As she ate, she considered the situation. She had to be up early to open the coffee shop; it was her rotation. She wasn't sure why she had to maintain the sham operation, but Sylvia insisted on it. *At what point can I make decisions? I don't like being told what to do all the time.* Bethany convinced herself that everything she had was her doing.

Tossing the remains of the snack into the garbage she zipped out of the liquid leather miniskirt and skintight top, leaving her supple breasts to dangle freely. As she walked, her ass jiggled like a bowl of jelly and her breasts bounced softly. Halfway up the stairs she stopped and dropped to all fours. The index and middle fingers of her right hand found her wet mound and began massaging. She moaned quietly as the need to climax prodded her. When the orgasm struck, it paralyzed her as it ripped through her body like a jagged edged knife.

She tried to stand when the first aftershock hit, causing her to sit down hard as her fingers slipped into her wet vagina. Trying to stand again she propped herself against the railing. Taking the steps slowly allowed herself to catch her breath. Several of her customers offered to pay to watch her get off. They begged her for the privilege. Sylvia's words resonated with her, "Make them believe they are getting something nobody else could give them."

When she reached the second floor landing her legs rediscovered strength. Slipping into the bedroom Bethany found the message her lover barely asleep. In the master bath Bethany applied makeup remover, removed the blonde, shoulder-length wig, brushed her teeth and dug the vibrator from the vanity drawer to the left of the sink. Bringing it close to her nose she inhaled. Smiling, she tasted Sylvia. *My little play toy had fun without me.*

Sylvia was unconsciously fingering her pleasure zone. Bethany took the hint. Moving the fingers out of the way Bethany's went to work. Sylvia kissed her bed partner. Bethany turned and opened the top drawer of the night table. Fumbling around she found the chain with the alligator clips on both ends. She squeezed Sylvia's left nipple and applied one of the clips. Her back arched as the mixture of pleasure and pain radiated from her sensitive nipple. Bethany tugged gently on the chain sending a bolt of pain through her subject. Sylvia moved her body into position and gripped her free breast with both hands.

"What do you want?" Bethany's voice was soft.

"I want you to imprison my nipples please."

"Why?" Bethany teased. This was the ritual; Sylvia pleaded; Bethany made her beg.

"Because it feels good to be controlled by you."

"Who am I?"

"You are my Mistress."

"And what are you?"

"I am your slave." Bethany tugged the chain causing Sylvia to melt under delicious pain. Pulling the free nipple Bethany applied the alligator clip with a flourish, completing the imprisonment loop. Sylvia's body writhed as arousal accompanied the pain that threatened to make her nipples raw.

Bethany pulled the chain until the flesh of the nipples strained. Taking the chain Bethany placed it in Sylvia's mouth. Her lips closed obediently over the metal, maintaining tension and causing spasms of pleasure.

"What does mama's plaything want?" Sylvia kicked off the covers and opened her legs while pulling her knees into her, bringing new waves of pain to her breasts and flooding her vagina. Bethany slipped out of the bed. Opening the top drawer of the night table she extracted a thick dildo, long and brown. Kissing the tip, she moved it toward Sylvia's pulsating loins. Ramming it forcefully into her bed partner, Sylvia's loins moved to enable full penetration.

Bethany pushed and pulled the dildo; Sylvia racing to the verge of orgasm at break neck speed. As sounds and movement intensified Bethany stopped, preempting Sylvia's climax. Desperate and needy Sylvia's hips undulated begging for release.

"It's not that easy my pet. You need to earn your release." Sylvia arched her neck adding tension to the chain intensifying the pain and pleasure. Bethany pulled a thin beaded dildo from the drawer and applied gel lubricant. Pushing against Sylvia's thighs she cleared access to her ass as she teased and tickled with the tip of the toy. Sylvia tried to move to accommodate the promised impalement. As Bethany inserted the toy Sylvia's moans intensified.

"You like that, don't you?" Sylvia's response filtered through the mouthful of chain. After achieving full rectal insertion Bethany resumed with the thick brown object. The vagina dripped and drooled awaiting fulfillment. Bethany teased with the tip of the object before working it slowly into her love canal. Full impalement triggered volcanic convulsions as a powerful orgasm threatened to destroy sanity. As she screamed with pleasure the chain fell from her mouth. The release of tension on her nipples intensified the orgasm as spasm after spasm wracked her body.

Bethany's excitement heightened. She climbed onto the bed and lowered her loins onto Sylvia's waiting mouth. Biting, licking and sucking commenced on the supple wetness until Bethany climaxed. Spent, Sylvia approached unconsciousness. Bethany dismounted and fell onto the bed. Sylvia found the clips and released her raw nipples causing her to yelp with pain. Her nipples would be raw; each movement against her bra threatening to initiate aftershocks.

Chapter 16

BARB DECIDED IT WAS time for a girls' night out. She called Russell as she drove. "I'm dressing tonight. What are you going to wear?" The question caught him off guard.

"Are you serious?" He had been waiting for this and now that it arrived he wasn't sure how to process.

"No, I'm only teasing Russell, boys aren't supposed to wear women's clothes." She paused for effect. "Of course I'm serious. It's time we did this. You need a break as do I."

"I don't know what to say Barb."

"Say you love me."

"I love you, Barb."

"I love you too, Russ. And I love Allison. Let's give Allison a chance to be herself. And when we come home I will show you how a real girl makes her man crazy." Barb ended the call before Russ could respond.

Pulling two large suitcases from the closet in the spare bedroom Russell placed them on the double bed. Returning to the closet that ran the length of one of the walls he pulled back the bi-fold louver doors. Barb had cleared the closet for him; her clothes filled both walk-in closets in the master. Unpacking the suitcases he filled the drawers of the dresser first, placing his jewelry case, perfumes, brushes and makeup kit on the top. Glancing in the mirror he reflected at how his life had reached this point. Completing the unpacking, he surveyed his handiwork. Everything had a place. He didn't have to live out of suitcases and secret hiding places.

The sound of an engine revving and then cutting off caused him to check his watch. "Shit!" Barb was home and he hadn't showered. He had to shave his face and chest to be ready for the outfit he selected for Allison's first girlfriends' night out. The shower let the cares of the day melt away.

Hair removal was a pain in the ass. As the quadruple blade set of his women's razor glided over a thin layer of lather and lubricating agent Russell peeled away, revealing Allison. When he emerged from the shower his body was devoid of hair. The bath towel did not glide smoothly over his skin as it did before shaving.

Barb pushed the door open. She eyed him hungrily. "If we weren't going out I would jump your bones right now. But I'm going to let Allison have her time before I bring Russell to my bed." She grabbed his ass, causing him to jump. "Maybe a little girl on girl might be fun." She left the thought dangling for his stiffening penis.

Allison monopolized the bathroom, trying to move quickly without making a mess of the extensive makeup work needed to complete the feminine face. Exiting the bathroom, she found Barb watching. "I laid out clothes that will work," she said. Barb wore a black liquid miniskirt, her legs caressed by nude silk pantyhose sheer to the toe. The white batwing top sparkled with threads of silver and a low-cut neckline that stopped short of her cleavage. She accentuated with an underwire bra that lifted her ample breasts until they threatened to spill out. The three-quarter sleeve blouse revealed wrists that were a smidge thicker than a gender girl her age. She covered up the minor betrayal with a sleeve of silver bracelets that jingled when she moved. She wore gold ballet slippers. When they were ready to step out, she would slip into side-cutout, peep toe heels. The red patent leather would contrast the black mini skirt and tie nicely into the red belt that was the finishing touch to her outfit.

Allison dressed deliberately; she loved the transformation process. When it was complete she would look like Barb's understudy. That would help her acclimate.

Returning to the full-length mirror Allison picked up the jet-black wig with undulating curves down to the shoulder.

Soft waves of black crossed her forehead like rich curtains framing her soft eyes, and perfect brows. Barb took a fine makeup brush and dipped it into gloss powder, dusting it on Allison's cheekbones before replicating the action on her face.

"Now we look alike." Barb smiled into the mirror watching Allison for reaction. "Come on honey, you've got to loosen up. This is your coming out and our first time out together!." She watched her lover's reaction; color rose above the neckline of the blouse. Allison wanted to speak; to say something pithy, but her throat felt tight, her breathing suddenly labored.

"Are you okay? Maybe this was a bad idea," Barb offered, providing Allison the opportunity to push the 'eject' button. Allison reminded herself to breathe. Barb walked up behind Allison and fussed with her hair until it fell across Allison's shoulders to Barb's liking.

Barb looked over Allison's shoulder. "Red lipstick will complete your look. You look hot!" Allison's confidence took wing. She wasn't alone; she could feel Barb's confidence and reminded herself Barb had done this successfully; she refused to allow doubt to infiltrate.

"I was planning red pencil under gloss."

"That will look delicious! We're going to make all the men drool." The thought of men eye fucking Barb made Allison flinch. Barb caught the reaction. "Don't worry honey, I've been to these places many times they know better than to try. I want to see their reaction to the new girl on the block!" Barb rubbed a palm over Allison's ass. "We're going to knock 'em dead."

Backing the car out of the garage, electricity charged the air. "We're out; how do you feel?" Barb asked. Allison snapped out of her dreamlike state. She was imagining prancing into the bar next to Barb, following her lead. She imagined men buying drinks, plying for action and wondering why men chased women like him.

"I feel weird, comfortable and uncomfortable at the same time. Is that strange?"

"Not at all, I would be worried if you told me you were totally comfortable." Barb pointed the car west. "We're going to a bar that is very accommodating. The men know me and are very friendly." The word 'friendly' rolled deliciously from Barb's full lips. "They're harmless. They come to get what their wives and girlfriends don't give them. They want to get a woody over our pantyhose and heels. They'll treat us like real women." Allison liked how that sounded, being treated like a woman. She couldn't understand what it was about being sexy and sensual that was evasive for gender girls. It was work, but wasn't anything that made you feel good worth doing? She pondered the question as Barb drove.

Pulling into the parking lot of the restaurant and watering hole, Barb negotiated a parking space close to the building. Turning to Allison, Barb reached over and brushed her wrist. Leaning across the center console she touched Allison's lips softly with hers; electricity passed between them.

"Why did you do that?"

"I want you to relax. We're going to put on a show for these frustrated one night bachelors." Allison pulled back.

"What do you mean?"

"Chill, girlfriend. These guys are going to fall all over themselves just to talk with us. Follow my lead and everything will be fine." Barb slipped her hand between Allison's legs and tickled her inner thigh.

"Don't do anything that's going to embarrass me, please," Allison pleaded. Barb exited the vehicle without answering leaving Allison sitting dumbfounded. *What have I gotten myself into? Maybe this isn't such a good idea.*

Slowly extracting herself from the car not feeling particularly interested in taunting a group of strangers, Allison stood on rubbery legs, almost toppling over. Grabbing the top of door, she steadied herself.

"You're not liking this are you?" Barb's voice flattened.

"Now that you mention it…" Allison let the words hang in the air.

"We don't have to go in." Barb sounded nonplussed. Allison

Shadow Woman

thought for a moment that maybe they should retreat. Summoning courage she took several steps, feeling firmer footing.

"No, we're here; let's go in." Her voice was more convincing than the hollow feeling in her stomach. Barb walked around to the front of the car and slipped an arm inside Allison's left. They walked arm in arm. When they reached the entrance, Barb opened the door and followed Allison inside. The room smelled of beer and ancient cigarette smoke from days when smoking was permitted indoors. A low din of conversation competed with the television sports announcers that were competing against each other for eyeballs. The horseshoe-shaped bar dominated the room as two bartenders administered the preferences of patrons on the slow road to oblivion. There were two seats at the far end of the room where the bar turned from north-south to east-west. Allison teetered and wobbled in her heels and was grateful for the support of Barb's arm. She was afraid she would stumble and break her ankle. Embarrassment threatened to ruin her debut. Barb placed a soft hand on her lower back, transferring strength.

"Let's grab those seats." Barb pointed. Bloodshot, hungry eyes followed the two beauties as they walked; heels on the hard floor announcing their approach. Slipping onto the chair, Allison was relieved to be off her feet, but was too nervous to cross her legs and exhibit her wares. Barb was less subdued; her skirt line hiked up to invite lookers. Allison observed and wondered why Barb felt the need to be revealing.

The bartender approached, smiling. He took drink orders and winked at them. He was a player, Allison surmised. Barb leaned over and spoke something softly. Allison's eyes scanned the bar as she tried to relax. They were a minor attraction as conversation hummed. Sipping the fruity drink, Barb insisted on, the combination of sugar and alcohol settled over her, slowly loosening her nerves. As Allison, focused attention across the bar she noticed she was being sized up. She turned to engage the overt stare, unconsciously batting long eyelashes.

"You're beautiful." The words came out slurred carried on stale

159

breath. Allison fought for the strength to respond. Barb leaned over and whispered in her ear.

"Thanks honey, but I'm spoken for." The words floated from Allison effortlessly.

"I'm not looking for anything permanent honey, I just want a taste." He moved his bar stool closer, making Allison uncomfortable.

"Did you hear her? She said she's spoken for!" Barb's voice was sharp.

"I'm talking to her, not to you," he responded with force. Barb was about to get up when the bartender approached.

"Ronnie, leave the women alone or I'm going to have to toss your sorry ass."

"I don't mean no harm, just want to buy the lady a drink," Ronnie said defensively.

"The lady doesn't want to be bothered. You can't go around forcing yourself on people. Now behave or you're gone." Ronnie broke stares with the bartender and shrank back into his stool.

"Thanks, honey." Barb said, reaching a hand out. The bartender took it softly as Barb gave it a squeeze before releasing.

"He's really harmless," the bartender offered.

"Steve, this is my friend Allison."

"Pleased to meet you, Allison." Steve nodded and winked. "You have any problems you let me know. We take our customers' satisfaction seriously."

"Steve's one of the owners. He tends bar to show the customers he appreciates their business," Barb said.

"Thanks for helping me out. I just want to have a pleasant time. I'm not really a barfly," Allison said in beginner's falsetto.

"No worries sweetie, we hope you'll become a barfly here. Is there anything I can do for you?"

Mister Forward receded; he feared Barb but would have loved to exploit Allison's perceived weakness. There wasn't enough reward in conquering Allison that he would risk Barb's ire. He had made an advance to Barb when she first appeared on the scene. The emotional scars were still visible from the verbal beating he took from her.

Several drinks made their way to the ladies from admiring gentlemen as they engaged in light conversation and visual foreplay. As alcohol took residence, Allison loosened up enough to catch the attention of an infatuated admirer. He was partial to trans women. Making his way toward Allison she felt the walls closing. This wasn't what she expected. The thrill of being out and among the public dissolved into concern that she may have crossed the line.

"I could not help but notice how beautiful you are." Perspiration threatened to ruin her makeup as she tried to size up the interloper. She smiled, not wanting to allow the tenor of her voice to betray the reality of her physical nature.

"You can relax; I'm Larry and I love T-Girls. I think you are the true definition of women. You are very beautiful." Larry's eyes moved over Allison's body with reverence.

"Really?" The word slipped out softly.

"Yes, really. Don't be surprised. You are gorgeous and I appreciate how much time you spend to look stunning." He smiled, keeping his hands on the bar showing Allison he was respecting her space.

"Thank you, Larry." Allison blushed as Barb looked on. Larry knew Barb. They had their visits at the bar that made Larry feel like the man his wife could never appreciate. They never dated, but Larry ran Barb's tab for months before she asked him to stop. He was falling in love with her. She wanted nothing but friendship and cut the cord before it connected to her outlet.

"What may I call you besides beautiful?" Larry asked. Barb picked up the conversation. His line of attack hadn't changed.

"Would you excuse us Larry, while we powder our noses?" Barb stood and touched Allison's forearm. "Watch our seats, honey?" Barb asked.

"Larry's harmless unless you let him get close." Barb warned as they freshened their lipstick in the ladies' room.

"What does that mean? Why would I let Larry get close to me?"

"Larry had a thing for me. He bought me drinks every night. I had to tell him to stop; there was no interest beyond friendship. I tried to let him down softly but he took it very hard."

"What am I supposed to do?"

"Tell him you want to be friends. See what he does, how he reacts."

"You don't seem worried."

"Larry's harmless."

"It doesn't sound like it," Allison said warily.

"Just don't lead him on," Barb warned.

"Who said anything about leading him on? He approached me!" Her voice jumped an octave. Barb smiled through the lip pencil.

"Honey you know what men are about. You know men are shallow and easily led. They want only one thing."

"But I can't give them the one thing they want." Allison imagined herself on the bottom being fucked by Larry. The thought was repulsive.

"Blow jobs, men want blow jobs. They don't get it at home. It's their quick road to satisfaction. They don't have to do anything but stand there and let us do all the work." The idea was foreign to Allison. As Russell, there was nothing he would not do for his woman. He would move heaven and earth to satisfy her regardless of what she did or did not do for him.

"You can't think about it from your perspective. Larry is one of the bar losers. He's looking out for himself and will take whatever you are willing to give him."

"Did you do anything with him?" Allison asked dubiously.

"I let him buy me drinks. I even let him kiss me on the cheek. He might have copped a feel of my thigh or my ass. When he touched me I thought he was going to blow his load. Why are you giving me that 'I don't believe you' look?"

"I don't know. This is all new to me." Allison's tone was resigned. "All I wanted was to dress up and go out. I didn't figure on all these complications. And it bothers me to think that men had their way with you." Her tone lowered to almost whisper.

"No man got his way with me unless I wanted it. You're going to have to get over that. And honey, you're going to have to get used to the fact that in the real world men will try to attract your attention. That's just the way the world works." Barb dabbed powder on the tip of her nose to knock down the shine.

"I'm not sure I can."

"You're a woman; at least you are now. You have to act like one. Men expect it."

"Really?" Allison perked up as she finished with the lip-gloss.

"Really. You'd be surprised how much they are willing to put up with just to stand next to you and eye fuck you."

The thought of men visually undressing her made Allison cringe. "I'll try."

"When I get you home I'm going to make you do things to me that will make you forget all about this." Barb kissed Allison softly on the lips. Allison wanted to start now. She saw no benefit from playing prey to screwed up men. "Come on. Larry won't hold our seats for long. Let him ply you with drinks. When we leave, touch his cheek with the back of your hand. You can do that, right?" Barb looked hard at Allison.

"I think so."

Prancing slowly back to the bar they eyed the patrons. They were the eye candy; no real competition from the gender girls. The birth females were looking more than a little weathered; their men disinterested. Larry watched the slow procession, feeling both inadequate and fortunate to have a second chance with one of Barb's friends. He stood trying to look chivalrous holding the stool for Allison. Barb watched. Larry smiled at Barb, who refused to return the pleasantry.

"You have a really cute ass," Larry said reverently. Allison felt her temperature rise, fumbling for an appropriate response.

"I'll bet you say that to all the girls," Allison said.

"No, only you, honey."

"You need to be more original, love." The words flowed smoother than she imagined. Larry looked like someone shot his best friend. His jowls sagged making his sad hooded eyes look even more pathetic. "Don't pout, it's not a good look for you." She sipped the fresh drink Larry had purchased for her. Barb smiled at her friend's newfound confidence. Larry mustered a smile as he leaned closer to Allison, placing an arm on the back of her stool.

"You are beautiful."

"Another tired line. You can do much better than that. I know you can." Allison touched his arm softly. Larry perked up and smiled.

"I'm sorry. You make me nervous." Larry's eyes were tired.

"Try to relax. I could tell you what to say but that would ruin all the fun, right?"

Larry hesitated, wishing seduction wasn't difficult. "I always say the wrong thing," he replied. Allison shot him a skeptical look. He saw the disappointment in her gaze. "See, I did it again."

Allison took a deep breath before shifting in her seat to face him. "You never say things like that. You're telling me you do this often. It lets me know I'm nothing special, just another girl in a long line of girls." She turned to face the bar, his drink offering no longer appealed. Larry's elbows found the bar as his head dropped heavily into his hands.

"You might want to bring Larry here a glass of water," Allison called to the bartender. "He's not looking good." The bartender evaluated the situation. He had seen Larry pull the sad sack routine too many times.

"He'll be fine. Give him a minute."

Chapter 17

SYLVIA CRAWLED OUT OF bed slowly fighting the urge to smash the alarm clock, turn over, and allow her body to recover from the sexual beating Bethany laid on her. After silencing the alarm, she fell back on to the bed praying for a few minutes of precious sleep. Bethany had already risen. The coffee shop would not open without her presence and her submissive playmates awaited the opportunity to drain credit from coffee subscription cards purchased as a condition of her dominance of them.

Out of bed, Sylvia felt the ache in her nipples that promised to blossom when they touched anything. The effects of Bethany's nipple torture were painful, and her breasts would be sore all day. She knew the consequences, but she was unable to stop herself from allowing the torture that felt good in session. The pain was a lasting reminder of the exquisite pleasures of the night before.

As water streamed from the dual overhead jets she allowed the warmth to slowly awaken her. She lathered her body with body wash. The heat of the water stimulated her breasts and she immediately felt the need for an orgasm. Taking the hand-held shower massager, she toggled the switch that channeled water to it. Turning the selector head, she chose single stream pulsing and positioned the showerhead between her legs and pressed her thighs together to hold it in place so she could cup both of her tender breasts with her hands. The rush of water on her clitoris was intensely satisfying and she began to moan. She squeezed her nipples to recreate the prior evening's perilous predicament. Her body shuddered. When climax struck, it was a delicious mixture of pleasure and pain. She took the showerhead and aimed the jet straight at one nipple, which gave her an intense rush of pain. She aimed it at the other for another jolt before replacing the showerhead.

Climbing slowly out of the shower she dried before applying a generous amount of body lotion, then gingerly touched petroleum jelly to her tender, aching nipples and set about applying her morning face. Shifting to work mode, she willed her body to ignore orgasmic aftershocks. She didn't need to be distracted. There were problems to handle and asses to kick.

Dressing in signature navy blue pencil skirt with thin white pinstripe, a billowy white blouse with puffy sleeves was open just above her cleavage. A diamond teardrop necklace rested just above the cleft of her breasts. Diamond stud earrings glittered; an expensive statement about her self-worth. Nude silk stockings fastened to the white garter which matched her white thong and white push up bra. Black patent leather Jimmy Choo stiletto heels adorned her feet and completed the 'dress for fuck you success' look.

Half of a bagel, coffee that Bethany had brewed, and four ounces of fresh squeezed grapefruit juice got her day moving. Placing the used dishes and flatware into the sink, the cleaning lady would handle the mess, Sylvia snagged her keys and dropped them into her black clutch.

Strutting to the garage, the familiar power of authority filled her to overflowing. Settling behind the wheel of the silver Mercedes hard top convertible, she fired up the engine as the garage door rose slowly. The drive to the office pointed her east into the awakening day. The blaze of orange from the semi-circular profile of the sun framed the silhouette of the high rises from the downtown area where she cut her teeth in the securities business. When she decided to move from the concrete jungle to a more low-slung and sprawling suburban campus the men who longed to own her felt a pang of remorse.

Pulling into the parking lot she counted the cars and made a mental note of who were dedicated and who were just clock punchers.

In the office, Delia was busy shuffling papers. "Good morning, boss." Delia's voice was perky, almost too awake for the early hour.

"Good morning," Sylvia responded as she walked into her office. She settled behind her desk and extracted the sheaf of papers from her shoulder bag. She had gotten only halfway through the pile when her secretary interrupted.

"Cream and sugar, just how you like it." Delia placed the steaming mug on the glass coaster to the right of the black onyx blotter where her boss insisted it be located.

"Thank you, Delia. Get the calendar and let me know how busy my day is. I will need an hour thirty to meet with Barb, Russell, and the auditors. Make sure they are all available. We will meet in the conference room."

***

Barb pulled into the office several minutes before Russell. She had stopped to get coffee. As she settled behind the desk, memories of the prior night's festivities swirled in her head. She had made Allison ravage her body. It had been a long time since she had made love with a transgender. The last time was immediately before her final surgical procedures to make the transition to physical womanhood.

Russell fired up the computer and was greeted by a meeting request followed by a flurry of emails. Russell dreaded the meeting, but seeing others on the calendar he was less concerned about the repercussions of being in a room with Sylvia. Barb strolled, coffee in hand, to his office.

Knocking, she surprised him. "Got a minute?" Without waiting for his answer, she invited herself in and settled into one of the guest chairs. "Guess what happened to me this morning?" He wasn't in the mood for twenty questions. She made a sad face when he didn't respond. "What's wrong honey; something bumming you out?"

"It's nothing." She gave him a "really" look.

"Fine, if you don't want to tell me then maybe I'll go back to my hovel with my intelligence." She watched for his reaction.

"Look, I don't want to be here. I want to be anywhere but here. I feel like a caged animal waiting for the trainer to teach me another trick." He felt pushed to the brink of insanity; his life felt like a fiery mess. Pulled by the desire to be both genders, he was in love with two women and enslaved by a boss with twisted fantasies that he was weirdly in tune to. He couldn't decide where his loyalties would land. The night out as girls confused matters more. He thought about how easily he manipulated the sad sack who poured money into drinks just for the privilege of talking to Allison. He wanted to be Allison, but the work to find that place was more than he had energy to devote. When they were in bed after their night out he struggled to perform. He was in it up to his love handles with no way out.

As he was contemplating, he didn't see Barb rise and lock the door. She came around to his desk, slipped out of her thong and lifted her skirt. She placed one bare leg across his desk. Taking two fingers she touched herself before putting them on his lips, startling him.

"What are you doing?" he said as he eyed her. She smiled. Touching her smooth leg, he felt himself arouse to her advances. Sliding her leg slowly off the desk she stood with her skirt up.

"Kiss my pussy; feel how wet I am. Think about me all day and tonight you can enjoy." He kissed her loins and tried to use his tongue. She pulled away and allowed her skirt to fall into place.

"Not here, not now," she chided. Returning to the chair she sat with legs crossed, eyes on him. "I was propositioned at the coffee house." Her words landed like live rounds fired in close proximity stunning him to silence. "It wasn't a guy. It was the woman who runs the coffee shop. You know her, the tall black woman with the magnetic personality." Barb's words indicted him as he thought how he wanted to bed Bethany.

"It's funny how all the men were falling all over her and she was only interested in me."

"Maybe she's lesbian."

"I doubt it. You've been in her place. You see how many men crowd in and talk with her like they want to be intimate. This is the first time she ignored them in favor of me."

"Maybe it's latent realization. You are attractive." Russell smiled. He didn't want to talk about Bethany and her sexual preferences.

"What do you think I should do? Would you be interested in a ménage du troix?"

"We're not married. If she turns you on you should go for it." Russell shuffled paper as he talked. Barb stood, unlocked the door and opened it. Turning she stared at Russell until he looked up.

When their eyes met, she spoke. "I love you, Russell."

"I love you, Barb." She smiled and winked before disappearing. He wondered how he could be weak and pliable. He was under her spell and Barb knew it. The walls were closing in on him. A panic attack loomed on the horizon when his secretary interrupted.

"The boss wants to see you." Katie pronounced 'boss' with undue reverence. Katie felt the negative vibes radiating from *her* boss. "You okay?" Russell looked at her with pained eyes.

"Yeah, late night is all."

"You want me to get you a refill?" She pointed a youthful finger at the coffee mug on his desk.

"That would be great. You can bring it in to Sylvia's." Russell handed her the mug.

"You're meeting in the conference room."

"Thank God," Russell said to himself. Katie stopped and turned. "Did you need anything else?"

"No, I'm good." Now he was lying. He watched his secretary as her tight little body moved rhythmically. *They didn't build 'em like that when I was growing up.* Gathering papers he stood, feeling drained. It was going to be a long day if he didn't find energy. Sylvia would eat him alive.

***

Mandy decided she no longer trusted Sylvia. She had expected a telephone call from her ex-husband pleading with her. She wasn't sure what she wanted from him, except to feel the power she felt the

169

night she played the surveillance video of his cross-dressing. Although she wanted a strong man to protect her, she wanted the control he would never give her.

Am I regretting the divorce? It was too late to undo what had already been done. Walking slowly up the stairs, Mandy admired the trappings of her house. Her boyfriend loved it. She was beginning to think he loved it too much. She didn't want him getting attached. They talked about commitment. He wanted one; at first she tought she did but he worried her. As she contemplated their affair she realized she didn't know much about him. She told him she wasn't ready. He dismissed her. There was no way he was going to call the shots. He had nothing invested. She wasn't about to give up what she worked hard to acquire.

At the top of the stairs she peeked into Meghan's room. Clothes were strewn all over the place. Her daughter was out. Mandy made a mental note to talk with her again about picking up after herself.

Mark was home. He kept to himself most of the time. Mandy wanted to spend time with him. He seemed put off by her need. She knocked on his bedroom door and entered. She stood in the doorway and observed him. Sitting on the bed staring at the centerfold of an adult magazine. He glanced up at his mother before returning to the magazine.

"Busy I see. Can I sit down?" she asked as she approached the bed.

"If you want."

"Those girls aren't really like they look in the photos," she said nonchalantly.

"Like you're not really the way you are with Sam around everyone else?" he asked, looking up from the picture and locking eyes with his mother. Her complexion grayed long enough for Mark to see the effect. "Why did you come in here? Do you like to catch me doing things you can hold against me?"

"I want to spend time with you. Would you like to go to dinner? We'll go to your favorite restaurant." Mark shrugged. He didn't feel like moving but he would be hungry soon and he wasn't in the mood for her marginal cooking.

"If it's just you and me I'll go. I don't feel like spending time with that asshole." Mark hated Sam. When Sam tried to play the adult male Mark unloaded on him. Sam pulled the bigger and stronger adult move that made the alienation deeper. After that, Mark sequestered himself in his room and came out only when Sam wasn't around.

She tried to force reconciliation. Sam tried to apologize but it went badly. Mandy upbraided Sam for fucking up. He stormed out. Mandy's first inkling of doubt arose. The man was amazing in bed, but when it counted it seemed the only brains were in his little head. He wasn't interested in taking counsel from her. He didn't tell her directly; his actions spoke for him.

Mark climbed into desert brown parachute shorts. Stepping into oversized black sneakers that had never been untied he shuffled over to the closet and grabbed a ratty plaid button down shirt. As he passed his mother she reached out to hug him. He didn't resist, giving her a half-hearted hug.

The ride to the restaurant was eerily quiet, tension palpable. Mark fiddled with his mobile phone. Mandy glanced at him but he refused to acknowledge. When she reached across to touch his arm he shrugged her off.

They talked over dinner that consisted of a platter of fried fish and French fries. Mandy selected something healthy although the options were limited.

"I think I want to live with dad." Mark's shoulders slumped as he spoke. Mandy's first reaction was to nix the idea. Watching her son's body language made her think. She didn't want this to come down to a decision between two men. She beat back the thought that life was much less complicated when she was married. Mark glanced up at his mother. He expected a shit storm.

"Mom did you hear me? I said I want to live with dad."

"I heard you." Her delivery was soft. She didn't want to lose control of the situation. Reaching across the table she flexed the fingers of her right hand; the signal for Mark to give her his hand.

He hesitated. Haltingly he slid his hand until their fingers touched. She took his hand softly and gave it a gentle squeeze.

"I know you need your dad. Have you talked with him about this?" She wanted to sound supportive, even if she wasn't. She believed Russell's obsession with cross-dressing would keep things status quo.

"I didn't tell dad." He sheepishly recalled the text message accusing his mother of trying to turn him against his father.

"What do you think he will say when you ask him? How will you get to school?" She looked at him. He was looking through her. Mark shrugged his shoulders.

"I think dad will be okay with it." Mark already knew. His father wanted his son with him.

"Ask him and then tell him to talk to me. If he is okay with this we will need to work things out." She paused and sipped her water. "If this is going to happen it's not going to happen right away."

Mark let out a long breath. "Why not?" Frustration was evident in his delivery. Mandy struggled to respond supportively.

"If you and your dad *both* want this then we will figure out how to make it work." She tried to get him to look at her. His gaze was hollow, vacant.

"You just want to keep punishing dad. He's not that bad really. You and Meghan always dis him." Mark's frustration brought him to the verge of tears.

"I don't want to get into why your dad and I broke up. That happens. It doesn't have anything to do with you or Meghan."

"You didn't even try." Mandy realized her son blamed her for the failed marriage. Mandy needed to change the subject before she lost her temper.

"I can't change what's happened. We need to move past that and get on with life. Can we do that?"

He shrugged. "Daddy still loves you." Mark spoke to the partially empty plate. He looked up for her reaction. She felt a twinge in her heart. Did she still love him? She couldn't let on. It would betray everything she stood for.

"I don't think you ever can completely stop loving somebody when you were married and had kids with them."

"Can I live with dad?"

"I'll talk to your father. I'll see what we can do." He wanted certainty. His facial expression flashed disapproval. Sliding heavily out of the booth he turned and walked toward the restroom. He needed to get away from her. Her eyes followed him. Torn, she pushed the plate away; her appetite gone. She didn't like where this was headed. *Russell must have poisoned him against me.* Confusion reigned as thoughts of retribution collided with thoughts of conciliation. She missed her husband for selfish reasons, but the cross-dressing was a mountain she wasn't willing to climb. *I'm going to tell Sam we need to cool it for a while.* He was a giant fly in her ointment. *Maybe if I focus on the kids Mark will forget about living with Russell.* She considered how she was going to get her lover to back off. *If he loves me he'll do this for me.*

Mark shuffled back to the booth and slid in. "I called dad. He said he can talk about this whenever." Stunned by her son's action, she sat dumbfounded. He stared at her as if he expected to catch her off guard. His eyes radiated defiance. Her will would not be enough to halt the advance of her son's agenda. She expected her phone to ring any moment. She wouldn't take the call. She refused to be jammed up.

"I'm not going to call your father now. This isn't the place to have that discussion. I'm not going to talk to him in front of you. I need time to think about this." Temper leached through, deflating the hopeful look Mark brought back to the table.

"You're not going to talk to him." A tear leaked from his eye. Mandy knew the drill. One tear, then defiance, topped off by the silent treatment. He was like his father.

"I promise I will talk to him. I didn't expect you to call him."

"When?" Mark pressed.

"By the weekend, assuming your father is available." She wanted an "out" but the words sounded like an excuse. She tried eye contact; her way of confirming. Mark would not look at her.

The ride home was loud with silence. Mandy played the possibilities over until they turned sour. This was going to require compromise, not something she was accustomed to. Everything she fought hard to acquire was beginning to tarnish.

***

Barb was lying on the bed in panties and bra. Russell wasn't interested; instead watching a mindless television program. Barb opened her toolbox and selected a vibrator. Russell watched dispassionately as she moaned and squirmed under the actions of her toy. When she climaxed, she drowned out the audio from the television. Russell smiled, thankful there was a stand in for him.

When the phone chirped he grabbed it, fumbling it before answering.

"Dad?"

"Mark?" Russell smiled, momentarily stunned by the call.

"Hey dad." Mark's voice was tentative. Russell's joy turned to concern.

"What's wrong?" Silence greeted Russell's question. "Something happen to you?" Barb watched. She perked up as Russell pressed for an answer.

"I told mom I called you tonight about coming to live with you." Mark paused. "We were at the restaurant and she started trying to be all nice." Russell knew that loss leader. She played the kindness card before slamming your fingers in the door.

"Do you really want to come live with me?" As Russell spoke he felt Barb's eyes on him. He was going to have one chance to get this right. He figured he was going to incur wrath. The question was whose retribution was going to be worse.

"Dad I can't live with mom anymore. Her boyfriend is an asshole!"

"Did he hurt you? Is that what this is about?"

"No, but he got all tough and shit and got in my face about something, trying to tell me about how I'm supposed to act. I walked away and he started after me."

"Was mom there?" Russell's heart pounded in his chest. If Mandy's boyfriend laid hands on his son he would take her to court and contest the custody arrangement.

"Can I come live with you dad?" Mark's voice cracked with emotion. Barb placed a warm hand on Russell's shoulder.

"Can you hold on for a minute?" Russell asked cupping his palm over the mouthpiece.

"Russ you've got to do what's right for Mark. He needs you." She paused, "And you need him." Her voice softened to just above a whisper. She didn't seem upset. He expected her to be possessive. His eyes asked if she was serious. She kissed him on the cheek. "I want you to myself but I will never have you if I don't let you do what you need to do."

"Of course you can live with me. Do you think your mother's going to let you go?"

"Will you talk to her?"

"Yes, this is something I need to do. I will take care of it. You're going to have to be patient. It's probably not going to happen right away." Russell began to imagine what he was going to have to compromise to gain custody. It wasn't a pretty picture.

"Do you have anything to bargain with?" Barb asked after Russell ended the call.

"Only Mark's sanity and what's left of his teenage innocence." He wasn't sure any of that mattered to his ex-wife. Climbing out of bed he paced for a long time. Barb watched, unsure of what to do. He disappeared into the closet and when he emerged he was wearing a black pencil skirt and black stilettos. Dressing up calmed him. Barb smiled. She would do the same thing when she was frustrated. Women's clothing had a calming effect; as if it created a separation from the person experiencing the emotional down stroke.

Chapter 18

TURNING TO HER BOYFRIEND Mandy measured her words. "Sam, I think we need to cool things off for a while." They had just 'tested the bed springs' as he liked to say. She wasn't as energetic as she normally was. He rode her. She had no interest in being the aggressor. They were usually good for two or more positions with a healthy amount of oral foreplay. He wasn't even sure she got off; not that he cared that much about her satisfaction.

"Why?" He sounded surprised.

"I think we started too quickly and too early." Now he was really confused.

"I thought this is what you wanted after that sissy of a husband." She didn't appreciate the characterization. After the dinner with her son Mandy reflected on Sam's actions. He had come on strong about being the man of the house. At first she thought it was cute and acceptable. The more latitude she gave him the more control he exerted. She could see how her son might have been put off.

"I need to figure a few things out. I can't do it with you around."

"What the hell does that mean?"

"It doesn't mean anything except I want some space."

"Space, how much space?" His temperature rose as he felt control slipping through his fingers.

"You can go back to your place and we can date."

"Go back to my place?"

"Don't raise your voice. I can hear you." Her face hardened. "Yes your place, the place where you lived before I met you."

"I didn't plan on this."

"Do it tomorrow please."

"I don't believe you!"

"What's difficult to believe?"

He sat up and ran a hand through his short brown hair.

"You're dismissing me. Nobody dismisses Sam Sharpton." His tone flattened like the calm before a storm. Climbing out of bed he looked down at her with contempt. She stared back coldly.

"Take it any way you want. I'm not going to apologize for what I have to do. This is important to me. You need to understand that," she barked while he gathered his clothes.

"I'm leaving. Enjoy the empty bed." He talked as he stepped into jeans and loafers. Part of her wanted to plead with him, but pride swelled. This was her house. He was her guest. How dare he challenge her?

Pulling his black leather overnight bag from the closet he grabbed things from the one drawer she afforded him. Carrying the bag into the master bath he collected toiletries before zipping it. He stormed out of the bedroom without saying goodbye, slamming the bedroom door behind him and stomping down the steps. Screeching tires announced he was gone. She turned onto her side and curled into a fetal position. She hadn't wanted it to end this way. He gave her no choice.

Several minutes later a knock at the bedroom door caused her to turn toward the sound. "Who's there?"

"It's me."

She sat up and propped two pillows behind her. "Come in, Mark." He opened the door slowly.

"What happened? I heard a bunch of slamming." Mark knew.

"Sam left." She smiled through the disappointment. Mark wandered in and shuffled around to his mother. His eyes were filled with remorse.

"Don't you go mushy on me." She knew her son blamed himself. It was part of his problem, no self-confidence. "I didn't throw him out. He threw himself out." She barked a laugh. "If he was going to be a jerk he deserved everything he got." Mark hugged his mother. His action caught her off guard. He wondered if she had done this to stop him from wanting to live with his father. He refused to allow her to see him weaken further, wary that this might be one of her tricks.

"I still want to live with dad," he said flatly.

"Can we talk about this later?" she said with authority. She had a way of terminating discussions.

***

Sam trudged up to his second-floor apartment. He stopped taking care of it when he started banging his former client. Kicking aside the clothes that lay on the bedroom floor he switched on the solitary lamp on the nightstand. The one bedroom apartment was from another era. He took the unit after his home was repossessed. The job with the police department ended abruptly when he was dismissed for misconduct. He was taking sexual favors from vulnerable women in return for not writing them up for traffic violations. He was getting his share of 'the goodies' until one of the women reported him. His actions were documented in a sting operation that netted Sam and two of his fellow officers. The scandal rattled the department.

He was cut loose in its wake. The municipality that employed him was embroiled in lawsuits over his conduct. Unemployed, he hung out a shingle and went into the private dick business. When Mandy found him he was struggling to make ends meet. She was a dream come true. Easy and lucrative work promised to lead to something more than a paycheck.

Dropping his luggage onto the bed he retraced his steps to the tiny kitchen. He was hungry. Rummaging through the cabinets he found chips and pretzels. He extracted a brown long-neck bottle from the refrigerator. Using the edge of the Formica counter he popped the cap and took a long pull. The cold beer washed away the thirst but had no effect on the frustration that infiltrated him.

"The bitch is going to have to pay for screwing me over. I made her life and she tosses me aside. Who does she think she is?"

A long night ended with Sam finally falling asleep at four in the morning. He had no obligations until the afternoon. Follow up with one of his clients; thankfully he kept his work away from Mandy's, otherwise he'd have to collect his equipment from her house. If he had to confront her he might have done something he'd regret. He convinced himself no woman was worth killing over. That didn't mean he wouldn't attempt another form of revenge.

**

Barb silenced the alarm. When she turned to say good morning to her lover his side of the bed was empty.

Pulling herself out of bed then slipping on a silk robe and white mules, she strolled out of the bedroom and smelled coffee. He was coming around the corner with two steaming mugs.

"I was bringing you coffee."

"I can see that." She kissed him for his thoughtfulness.

"Thanks for last night. Sorry I wasn't attentive to your needs. I don't ever want you to think I'm not attracted to you." He felt himself tensing as the apology poured from him.

"You don't have to apologize, love. I understand. Remember I was there once." She smiled and kissed him between sips of coffee. Even a night in the sack couldn't dampen her beauty. Russell felt a kind of love he had thought impossible to feel. Even when he was married to Mandy what he thought was love was actually just overdeveloped devotion.

The ride to the office was an exercise in silence. She knew he had the weight of the world on his mind. Conversation might be a hindrance. Pulling into the parking lot he finally spoke.

"Can we talk tonight, Barb? I want to discuss this thing with Mark. I need your support and advice. I want to do the right thing and I can't seem to figure it out."

"Sure babe, whatever you need." She smiled, deflecting the feeling that he might be expecting her to make the decision for him. "Let's eat in tonight. This way we can talk for as long as you want."

By 10:00 A.M. an idea had germinated for her. Fishing through her contacts she found the name, email, and mobile phone number. After closing her office door, she called the number. The phone rang several times before the call was answered.

A groggy voice slurred the greeting. "Hello?" Barb wasn't sure she called the right number. At ten in the morning she expected business to be transacted. It sounded like the person on the other end was sleeping off a bender.

"I'm not sure I have the right number. I'm looking for Sam Sharpton." The line was silent for a moment.

"Yeah, this is Sam Sharpton." He didn't recognize the voice. He had received threatening calls from spouses he was investigating. He didn't recall any 'husband investigating wife' clients that might be interested in harassing him.

"Sounds like you had a rough evening." He looked at the phone. The voice sounded vaguely familiar; he was having trouble placing it.

"Who is this?" he grunted into the phone.

"I'm hurt that you don't remember." Barb was feeling playful.

"I'm not into playing twenty questions. Is there something I can do for you?"

"I guess I'm more forgettable than I had hoped." As she spoke the fog from the prior night cleared.

"Barb?"

"I knew that if I gave you enough rope you'd figure it out." She smiled. He pulled himself up and propped onto one elbow. The distant memories of their fleeting romance formed in his mind's eye. They had gone volcanic; almost combusting from passion's heat. He felt an involuntary rise between his legs. Barb had a way of making him crazy. She cut him off when he started to get serious. She knew he was looking for a sugar momma. She had no interest in supporting a man. She could buy what he gave her and there would be no commitment.

"What's up, honey?" He started to think that maybe his luck was changing for the better. Mandy's dumping him might turn out to be a blessing in disguise.

"You still doing the 'cop' thing?" He regaled her with stories of police work when they were dating. His boasting fueled their passion. She wanted to feel the power and he needed the feeling of control. She wondered about his powers of investigation. He never inquired about her past. She never considered revealing her origins.

"Sort of. I had a pretty big dust up with my superiors. We decided to part company. I'm doing investigations full-time." He sounded disappointed that she called to inquire about work. "You seeing anybody?" He could not help himself.

"We had fun while it lasted, but Sam I'm not interested in a date. Before you ask I'll tell you that I'm not in quickie mode either. I want to know if you're interested in doing a little investigative work for me. If I was to employ you what would be your rate?"

"My rate card is $150 an hour, but for you I'll cut you a deal at $100 an hour." He smiled hoping she would consider making up the difference in trade.

"And you'll charge me only for hours worked?" she asked.

"Barb, your question is out of line." He lowered his tone.

"I'm an educated consumer. I want us to have a clear understanding; I don't like surprises."

He chuckled. "You've changed. I can remember when you enjoyed surprises." She allowed things to settle before responding.

"I need you to do some digging on a woman."

"You interested in snagging somebody else's goods?"

"You need to get out the sharpener, your wit is a bit dull. No, this is not about stealing someone's husband. I'm looking for deep background information on a certain individual."

"How deep you want me to go?"

"I'm thinking you're going to tell me how much each level's going to cost."

"A deep dive could take a few days. If we say between $2,500 and five grand that should get you down to the foundation. That is unless this person is into any heavy shit with any of the intelligence agencies. I find that out and the investigation stops. I don't cross those lines," he said reverently. Barb figured his intelligence connections weren't as deep as he wanted her to believe.

"I don't think that's an issue here. I'd like updates at each grand of fees. We may be able to make this short and sweet." Her statement was more a requirement than a request. Sam knew enough to stretch things out without breaking a client's confidence. He fully expected to make the engagement yield his minimum. Barb committed to the number but wanted him to know she would be watching.

"How's your love life?"

"Probably as hot as yours."

"Seeing anybody?"

"Let's just say I'm in good hands." She knew her words would deflate him. He halted the personal advance. If Barb didn't want you to know, she could build impenetrable walls.

"You want to give me the name of the mark?" he asked.

"You have a contract you need me to sign?"

"Where do you want me to mail it? Or do you want to meet me and I can hand it to you?" Barb knew there was no need for them to meet. It would only detract from the contractor-client relationship and he would no doubt try to get into her panties.

***

Barb waited by the fax machine. Sharpton was still operating in the prior century. The contract was three pages. She carried it back to her office, avoiding Russell's. Closing the office door Barb settled behind her desk and reviewed the document. She made a few markups before initialing them and signing at the bottom of the third page. He had written in a five-grand retainer. She marked it down to twenty-five hundred. He tried every angle. She shook her head but wasn't surprised.

After opening the door, she stepped into the hallway. "Do you want me to take that?" Abby, her secretary, asked. The woman had been an early hire; her tenure eclipsed almost everyone in the office. She had a rocky marriage and worked as much for her sanity as to preserve the middle-class lifestyle her husband was busy ruining with his drinking. Abby's body was showing the wear of a failing marriage. She dressed like middle age and her face exhibited worry lines and the beginning of sagging cheeks. Her brown eyes carried the sadness of the world. She tried to please at the office and paid the price of vulnerability.

"Thanks Abby, I've got this one." Abby retreated to her desk as the worry factory kicked into gear. Every time Barb performed a task for herself Abby thought she was on the verge of being fired.

As Barb returned to her office she glanced over at her secretary. *I don't need this.* Stopping at the threshold to her office Barb turned. "Abby, come in and talk to me."

"Should I bring my notepad?" Abby asked hopefully.

"No, just come in and sit down." Barb tried to sand the sharp edge off her voice. Abby fought back nervousness that would eventually bring a downpour. Walking the distance from her cubicle to her boss' office she felt the weight of her world crushing her resolve to be strong. "Close the door, please," Barb asked.

Settling uncomfortably into one of the two visitor's chairs facing the desk Abby's shoulders slumped; she gazed at the desk.

"Relax Abby, I just want to talk."

"Did I do something wrong?" Barb took a deep breath; she wasn't sure she was cut out to be a counselor.

"No, you have been doing everything right." Barb captured Abby's eyes. She smiled to reassure the woman. "I know things aren't always rosy in your world. But you don't have to worry about your job if you keep doing what you are doing. Can I do anything to help you feel better?" Barb asked, realizing she might be practicing for her evening conversation with Russell.

"Help me keep my job." Abby felt tears threatening to ruin her makeup. "Larry's drinking and he's been missing work. I need this job to keep my life together."

"I'm sorry you are struggling. You should try to get Larry into counseling." Abby stared at the fingers knitted together in her lap.

"He won't go; I tried to get him to go. He gets angry." Abby brought the tissue to her face. After a moment of composing herself she lowered the tissue and brought her eyes up to meet Barb's. "You know I've been here longer than almost everybody except Sylvia. I worked for two different people before you."

"Really?" Barb knew that and wondered where this was going.

"Yep, I've seen more than anyone," Abby continued. Barb tried hard not to push the 'eject' button. "I need this job. But I don't know why anybody would work for that monster. She treats everyone like a slave. That's why all those people left." Barb's interest began to pique. "What she's doing to Mr. Radcliffe is wrong but it's not the first time."

"What is she doing to him?" Barb probed, wanting to know how much of Russell's private torture was in the public domain.

"I don't know for sure but if it's anything like what she did to the others it must be evil. I see him going into her office and closing the door. When he comes out it's like the life is drained from him." *It's that obvious?*

"What things did she do to the others?" Barb asked. Abby shifted, suddenly self-conscious about revealing company secrets. Barb's eyes bored into her secretary. Turning, Abby crossed her legs tightly as if she was attempting to restrain the urge to pee.

"She makes them bow down to her. She made one of the men call her 'mistress' and buy her pantyhose and other gifts." Abby's face reddened with embarrassment.

"How do you know this?" Barb's tone conveyed the beginning of anger. Abby stared at something on the floor by her feet.

"Sometimes I stay late. Larry gets in his moods and I can't deal with it." Barb probed Abby's features to see if she was hiding physical abuse.

"How often do you stay late?"

"Probably once or twice a week before. Larry's moods aren't bad now," Abby said defensively.

"And what did you see when you stayed late?"

"Like I said, closed doors and beaten men." She squirmed. Barb knew there was more. "One night I see Mr. Fredricks, he was two bosses before you, come out of Sylvia's office. He was such a gentle man, a wife and family and all. He looked like he had been beaten. Not physically, emotionally. He walked around after that like he was expecting something bad to happen. He looked helpless. Sylvia stood in her doorway and watched. She was smiling; like that big goofy looking cat in Alice in Wonderland."

"The Cheshire cat?"

"That's the one. Anyway, Mr. Fredericks didn't last too long after that. I tried to build up his spirits but she killed him on the inside." Barb wondered how Abby could muster the energy to help someone out of their funk.

"Did you see anything else? And how did you see Mr. Fredericks without him seeing you?"

Abby shifted again, pulling at the hem of her dress. "I was in the library doing some research."

"But not for the company," Barb concluded.

"I wasn't charging the company. I needed to find out what I could do to make things better at home."

"And you didn't work at your desk because?"

"I didn't want anyone to see that I was not doing work stuff." Abby's body began to shake as tears trickled from her eyes. Barb grabbed the tissue box from her credenza and handed it across the desk. Dabbing at her eyes the middle-aged woman tried to compose herself. "I don't care why you were in the library. I want to know everything."

Abby hesitated trying to size up the situation. "You won't make trouble for me? I can't lose this job."

"If you tell me the truth nobody will ever know you told me."

"What are you going to do?" Abby asked.

"I'm going to make sure this stops. Mr. Radcliffe is another one of her victims." Barb crossed her arms, a defiant look on her face.

"You and Mr. Radcliffe are... friends?" Abby's pregnant pause told Barb that Abby liked to know how others lived.

"We are friends." Barb cut it off there. "I don't like people being bullied. If you're the boss that's not a privilege, it's an obligation." Abby processed the statement. She began to relax.

"I can tell you more but I feel uncomfortable talking about this in the office."

"That's fine. I want to hear more; I want to hear everything." Barb stretched the word 'everything' into long drawn syllables.

***

The mobile phone chirped. Barb fished through her oversized handbag to find it.

"Hi Sam."

"Barb why did you change the retainer?" She knew that would rankle him.

"I want control over this investigation. At two and a half grands, you have twenty-five hours to prove you can produce."

"The hourly rate was based on you paying the full retainer." He raised his voice for effect.

"Sam, I understand your position. You need to understand mine. I pay for performance. If I give you the full retainer and you don't deliver would you refund the unused portion?" She knew the answer.

"You think I would keep your money if I didn't earn it?" Sam sounded offended.

"Now you don't have to worry about that," she said in a singsong voice. "Do we have a deal?" Silence greeted her. She waited patiently; she knew she had the advantage as long as she held the purse strings.

"You drive a hard bargain. I start work as soon as I get your check," Sam said, knowing he could take a small victory away.

"Give me your bank account information and I'll wire the money in. I want you to start today." He scratched his head. He had to find his checkbook.

"Let me call you back with that information."

"Sure, I'll be here." She ended the call and held the phone to her lips before dropping it in her bag.

***

Five fifty-nine and Russell was preparing to wrap up for the evening. The intercom buzzed. Dread wrapped a cold bony hand around his heart. Lifting the receiver, he knew better than to use the speaker. "Come to my office." He was cut off before he could reply. Dropping the handset back in the cradle he wanted to scream. He and Barb had planned an evening out. Rising slowly, his shoes felt as if they weighed a hundred pounds.

"You wanted to see me?" He stepped across the threshold, the feeling of captivity palpable.

"Close the door... and lock it." He wanted to complain but knew there was no averting whatever she had in store for him. He stood as if naked and needing to run for cover.

"Come over here." Sylvia was sitting on the settee, her feet, in ruby red heels, perched on the edge of the coffee table. Russell obliged her, although his pace didn't convey enthusiasm. "You're acting like you aren't happy to see me." Her lower lip formed a pout.

"I'm tired. I want to go home and crash."

"Come sit next to me." She patted the seat cushion as an owner would encourage a pet. Her action made him feel small and insignificant. Lowering himself onto the cushion she watched him with interest.

"Did you want me for something?" Reaching over she placed a manicured hand in his lap. He recoiled at her touch. "What..." Her hand rubbed him as he hardened.

"Shush, just sit there for a minute." She watched his reaction; he was squirming. "I have a present for you." She said with a flourish as she moved her feet to the floor and reached for the brown box on the coffee table and handed it to him. His eyes followed her movements. He could not help but desire to kiss her feet. He hated himself for the dark desires he was unable to control.

"Why did you do this?" he asked.

"Open it," she said playfully. His fingers fumbled with the packing tape. After lifting the outer flaps he peered inside. Plucking at the newspaper packing, he found another box. He lifted it out and placed the smaller box on his lap.

"You're going to love this." She was almost giddy. He looked from her to the box and back. The silver markings on the black box did not register. Opening the second box he tried to make out the foreign device.

"What is it?" he asked, looking at her as the bottom dropped out of his stomach.

"You don't recognize it. I'm sorry. I thought you would know. It's a male chastity device." Her singsong tone made him want to vomit as reality slapped him.

"Why? What is this about? This isn't for me," he stammered.

She blinked twice. "Of course it is." Her delivery was matter-of-fact. "I think it's time we reached an understanding." When she started a conversation with that phrase it meant the listener was going to be told the way things had to be.

"What understanding? You expect me to wear a chastity device? Why? We aren't dating!" He couldn't form the appropriate response. "You want to own me, own my orgasms!" As he spoke he imagined Barb's volcanic reaction.

"I know you go home and beat off to my feet. If you're going to worship me you'll do it on my terms." Her inflection conveyed superiority.

"I don't do that." His voice betrayed him.

"Russell, you don't have to lie. I know all about your sexual flexibility." She cackled a wicked laugh, making his skin crawl. "Of course you beat off to my feet. Don't get me wrong, I'm flattered that my feet can have that effect on you. I want to use your desire to heighten your sexual experience. I'm not planning to deny you release. I want it done when I can watch." She paused for two beats.

"Stand up, pull down your pants and put it on," she said. He looked at her as the emotional walls closed in. His cock was erect; he was out of control. Her gaze hardened as he hesitated. "Stand up and put it on!" He stood on rubbery legs. She reached across for his belt. He moved out of reach.

"You want to do it yourself, I understand." He looked at her, trying to summon willpower.

"Don't you even think about walking out of here without your

188

chastity device. You do this or you can look for another job." He felt his spine seize. His hands moved as if he was having an out of body experience. Unfastening the belt, then the button on his waistband, he pulled down the zipper and his pants slipped to his ankles. His erection strained against the triangle of cotton of his string bikini panties.

"See how out of control you are! Get on your knees and relieve the pressure." She turned toward him, swinging her legs up onto the settee. His eyes followed her actions, his penis pulsing. "You're never going to be able to put this on while your little guy is showing off." She held the cage in the palm of her hand. Embarrassment skewered him. "You can ravage my feet after you are in your chastity device." She accentuated the word "your" conveying transfer of ownership.

He felt her power, the air was electric with it as resolve drained from him. Slipping the panties down to his knees, embarrassment mixed with supplication; he wanted to submit to her. He needed release as submission beckoned him to follow her command. Dropping to his knees brought him closer to her feet. The haunting fragrance of Sylvia's feet confined to heels all day made his penis leak.

"I kept my shoes on all day for you to enjoy every bit of flavor and fragrance," she said. Had they been in church Sylvia might have blessed herself. "You're not the first man to submit to me this way." His mistress' smile turned to a frown as she watched him deflate. "Here, put it on now. You'll need to take care of that but not until I tell you it's okay." Her words cut him. He looked at the unit. He fought for the courage to defend himself. Every argument for his dignity was dampened by desire to submit.

Reaching over he took the device. "Are there instructions?" he asked softly. She handed him the small glossy enclosure. He opened it and after removing the retention ring from the cage he slipped it over his receding member until the plastic ring with the single post protruding from the top was seated against his loins. Sylvia handed him the cage. Tucking his penis into it he pushed the cage into place, engaging the two posts on the cage into the receivers on the seating ring. He watched the post on the seating ring slip through the opening in the top of the cage. This post had a hole in it to receive a locking mechanism. A surge of sensuality radiated through him. The act of confinement thrilled him in a dark way.

"How does it fit?" she asked as if she was inquiring about a pair of shoes. He looked at her, his eyes answering. Picking the small brass lock out of the box he turned the key and the lock opened.

"Uh no honey, not the lock. Let me have it." Holding out her hand as if she was waiting for change at a fast food restaurant, he handed over the lock. "And the key." She handed him one of the plastic latches that accompanied the device. "Use one of these, but first write down the number and hand it to me." She handed him a piece of paper and pen. Jotting down the numbers he handed it over.

"Add today's date." He complied. "Now fasten it." Russell fumbled with the plastic tab trying to first slip it through the circular opening on the top post of the chastity device. When he secured it, a feeling of humiliation rocketed through him as his loins reacted. "There now, you are officially my slave. And this lock better not be broken. That's why there's a number on it. Don't try to replace it." She was ecstatic; she'd always wanted a man slave; the others refused to submit. She encouraged them to leave and paid generous severance. She held the specter of their sexual deviations if they tried to sue.

"Stand and let me see." Her voice was playful. She tapped the plastic cage with the nail of her index finger. "So cute and secure." She tugged it, causing him to wince. His face reddened with embarrassment.

"Now pull up your pants; put yourself back together. You won't even know you're wearing your CD, until you want to play. Then you'll know who's in control."

Turning her feet slowly and seductively she encouraged him. "Go ahead, I promised." Russell fought and lost again, dropping to his knees. When he finished, he buried his nose in her shoes, inhaling the intoxicating fragrance and feeling lightheaded. As he slipped her

190

shoes back on her supple feet he looked at her, lost in the reverie of the moment.

"I will see you tomorrow. Dream of my feet and how you will enjoy performing for me tomorrow." She swung her legs around and planted her feet on the floor before standing. Russell rose slowly and watched as she moved toward the desk. She went about gathering reading materials, then scanning recent emails as if he wasn't there. He slinked out of her office trying to make sense of his predicament. Most of the employees had left for the day, including Barb. They had driven in separate cars. She was planning an evening for them and wanted to get home before he arrived. He began to sweat, thinking about how he was going to explain this to her.

He couldn't face her; he needed an excuse. She would not be easy to convince but he could not allow her to see him this way. He would be the laughing stock. Settling into his office chair he felt the chastity device positioned uncomfortably between his legs. Dropping his head into his hands he fought for composure.

Falling back into the chair his hands moved to his loins as if touching might make things easier. Everything he had done in his life had brought him to this point. Life was crumbling to a fine powder. He was going to lose Barb and become a slave to his boss. An ironic smile crackled across his lips. *At least I'll have a job.*

"Come over anyway, I'll let you have your space. I made a very nice dinner for us. I don't want to let that go to waste." He could hear disappointment leaking through her delivery.

"I'm really tired; I won't be good company." Resignation in his voice told Barb there was something seriously wrong. She remembered the days when she was on the ragged edge, considering suicide to end the emotional pain.

"Just come over and don't worry," she insisted. He hesitated. He wanted to see her, to tell her, to take a hacksaw and cut the chastity device into a million pieces.

"I'll come for dinner but I might go home afterwards." He wanted an escape hatch.

"Just come over and leave whenever you want." Barb's voice

expressed disappointment. He knew he was hurting her, and knew he was helplessly and hopelessly trapped between love for her and lust and desire to submit to the she-demon.

Halfway to Barb's he knew seeing her was a bad idea. She would hug and kiss him; grind her mound into him. She would feel the problem and when she opened his pants and saw the cage she would flip. That would be the beginning of the end.

As he drove he spun the tale to make it sound like he was wearing the device to show his commitment to her. Pulling onto a side street five minutes past his house he pulled at the cage, sending shocks of sensuality through him. He was beginning to like the surrender of control the device provided. *Maybe Barb will get into this with me.* Suddenly confident he could sell the situation, he drove on. When he arrived at Barb's he walked through the front door to the aroma of home cooking.

"Hi honey," he announced as he walked up behind Barb who was laboring over the stove. He kissed her on the neck.

"Hi Russ," she said as she stirred one of her creations. "Be a doll and open that bottle of red wine." She turned and pointed to the six-bottle wine rack sitting on the counter. She was giving him the ability to bide his time. He wasn't sure when he was going to break the news, but he hoped he could wait until after dinner.

Pouring two glasses he handed one to Barb, who was placing her creations in white serving platters. He watched her as he raised his glass. She raised her glass and touched it to his. "To us," she smiled before sipping, her full lips leaving merlot-colored lipstick on the rim.

"Help me carry these to the dining room." He put his wine glass on the counter and lifted two platters as aroma wafted and steam rose.

"This smells awesome."

"It should; I've been slaving over the stove for hours." She laughed at her exaggeration. After retrieving his wine glass Russell took a seat beside Barb. She liked arranging the seating close together so they could feed each other.

"Were you in Sylvia's office when I left? I came by to see you and your office was empty," she asked as she served him before serving herself.

"Yeah, she knows how to stretch a day."

"The door was closed, must have been something important." She was probing.

"Everything with Sylvia is important. Don't you know that by now?" He tried to sound amusing. "This is really delicious. You're going to make someone a great wife." She smiled as she moved her left hand onto his thigh, caressing it with her nails. He shuddered.

"That tickles!" he said playfully.

"There's more where that came from," she said as she brought a forkful of poached salmon to his mouth. He fed her a forkful of steamed asparagus.

He helped her clear the dishes from dinner. They talked about their day. Russell tried to avoid anything suggestive until he could reveal his little secret.

"Would you like dessert now or later?" She winked as she loaded the dishwasher. Russell washed pots.

"Not feeling like dessert. Let's finish here and relax for a little." She hesitated. He realized she had probably made dessert from scratch. This was one of Barb's needs, to have her creations acknowledged and doted over.

Russell settled on the sofa turned at an angle with one leg bent and resting on the sofa. He needed physical separation, at least until he explained. Barb looked at his seating position and hesitated before sitting, his body language not lost on her.

"Something's wrong; you didn't like dinner."

"It's not you Barb, dinner was wonderful."

"Then what is it?"

He looked down at his hands, courage abandoning him.

"You don't want to be with me." Her voice cracked.

"Barb..." He paused, making her more uncomfortable. She wanted to hug him. Sensing her need, he reached out and took her hand. His palm was sweaty. She squeezed his hand in hers. "I don't know how to say it." He hitched as he took a deep breath. "Sylvia is really applying the pressure, putting the screws to me."

"Is that what this is about?" Her eyes probed his.

"It's not work pressure."

"Then what pressure is it?" she asked as her face twisted into a question. Realization dawned. "What is she doing to you now?" Barb's temperature rose as she spoke, color flushing her cheeks.

"She is making me wear a chastity device." Barb blinked; she didn't get it at first.

"What? A chastity device? How is she making you wear one?" Russell's face contorted, radiating a "come on Barb you know" look. "She threatened you."

"And she's good at it."

"You're wearing it now." Perspiration blossomed on Russell's forehead and upper lip. He losing the tenuous grip on his emotions.

"How did my life get fucked up? How did I get myself into this shitty situation?" He was on the verge of tears as she pushed his leg until she could snuggle up to him. She held him for a long moment before releasing and sitting back.

"We're going to get even. This shit is going to stop now." Barb spoke in even tones. She wanted to tell him about Sam Sharpton.

"She told me if I don't wear this thing she would fire me."

"She can't do that," Barb said matter-of-factly.

"She can force me to quite if she has information that will ruin my reputation." He responded in desperate tones, stopping Barb's verbal advance. "I could sue and after she drags my name through the mud and my lawyer fees drain my bank account my kids will disown me and I'll never work in this field again." He was shivering uncontrollably.

"Fuck! There's got to be something in that bitch's life that will compromise her. My secretary...you know Abby...told me a few things." Russell was trying to process what this had to do with anything. "You're not the first she's abused. She said others submitted to her. "

"We've got to do something about this bitch. She thinks she can

194

just use people until they have nothing left. It's time somebody stopped her." She worked herself into his pants over his objections, fingering the plastic lock trying to figure out how to open it.

"Stop Barb, if you break the damn thing she'll crucify me!" His voice was shrill with panic. Barb looked at him in disbelief. He grabbed her hands and held them. She felt him shaking.

"Okay, I get it. I'm not trying to screw things up for you any more than they are already." She pulled back and stood, flexing outstretched hands to beckon him. He looked up at her with puppy dog eyes. He was unsure what she wanted.

She took his right hand in her left. "Come on. I have a way to use this to our advantage." She led him to the stairs. He stopped, causing her to tug on his arm. "Come on. I won't do anything you won't enjoy and I won't break your new toy."

In the bedroom she dropped to her knees and unfastened his belt. She helped him remove his shoes before helping him step out of his slacks. After unbuttoning his shirt, she nipped at his nipples, causing him to moan. She looked down and saw him straining against the cage.

"This feels weird and thrilling at the same time," he said, his voice crackling with desire. She pushed his naked body onto the bed.

"Don't go anywhere," she said as she disappeared into the closet. When she emerged she was wearing a red silk and lace negligee, her ample breasts bounced playfully to the seductive swaying of her hips, her hands were at her back concealing something. When she reached the bed she revealed her surprise.

"These will make the evening memorable." She held up two substantial vibrators, one shaped like a "J" was purple and white. The second looked like a red torpedo. She sat on the bed facing his loins, his penis swelled, filling the cage. She turned on the vibrators. The low hum sounded like background noise.

"Lie there and try to relax," she said as she giggled a schoolgirl laugh. She placed the vibrators strategically, one at the base of his sack and the other against the shaft of his penis as it strained against confinement. His body twitched as the two electric marvels worked magic.

"That feels amazing," he said.

"I'll let you use them on me after we take care of you." She repositioned her face to hover just above the cage. "You just need to tell me when you are ready to make your delivery." That was her description of an orgasm. She moved the vibrators until she found the right spot. She knew by his moans and how his penis pulsed.

"I'm cumming!" He struggled to speak as his body wracked. Barb lowered her mouth to the top of the cage, the tip of Russell's penis was proud of the end. As he ejaculated Barb's mouth absorbed every drop. She kept the vibrators in place until he was firing blanks.

"That was amazing!" he moaned.

"I am wet. I want you to do the same for me. She climbed atop his chest and handed him the two vibrators. He applied them to her dripping vagina, her clitoris standing at attention. As he worked the red torpedo around her clit, anticipation coursed through her. He watched the soft light glisten off her pleasure zone. He helped her over to her back before burying his face between her legs. She wrapped them around his head encouraging him. As she approached the top of the emotional roller coaster run her thighs tightened. Russell's tongue moved rapidly until she screamed. Wetness poured from her as the first orgasm ripped through her like a tornado. Her hands moved to his head coaxing him to her clit. He licked and sucked until the second orgasm blasted through her; this longer and steady.

When she released him, she was perspiring and panting. "That felt amazing! Russell your mouth is a treasure." She pulled him to her and kissed him deeply, enjoying her fragrance and flavors.

"I think I might like this chastity device. The only thing I would change is being able to let you out. I want to feel you inside me." Her words reminded him of his situation, tarnishing what they shared. He rolled onto his side. After a long time holding each other they fell asleep.

On the way to the office he recalled the events of the evening. They were shattered when he tried to wash himself in the shower and how the nylon scrubber caught on the edges of the plastic locking device. Barb tried to assuage his concerns. She seemed to be taking this well. He wondered how black her dark side was.

When he pulled into the office parking lot his throat constricted when he saw Sylvia's car. The walls felt as if they were closing in. Retreating to his office he wanted to lock the door and hole up until quitting time. Dropping his briefcase, on the work table he pulled out papers he had taken home. He should have read them but he was too busy trying to deal with his predicament. There were twenty-five new e-mails, most from Sylvia. If she wasn't such a bitch she would have been a good mentor. The woman seemed to work on little sleep and was always fresh as a flower.

His intercom buzzed. Lifting the handset dread gripped him. "Come in when you have a moment." Sylvia's tone was all business. Carrying his coffee in one hand and a pad and pen in the other, he trudged down the hall to find her engaged in conversation with Simon and Garfunkel. He watched, not wanting to interrupt. *Maybe they would stick around and this would be a group meeting.* Sylvia looked up.

"Russ, come in. I was going over some of the financing assumptions. S&G tell me we have some room to maneuver." She sounded almost sanguine. The Simon look alkie summarized. She watched as if she was sending telepathic waves that carried the words the man spoke. When Simon finished, Russell asked a few questions. The Garfunkel look alike answered as he referred to papers in front of him for confirming facts.

"Thanks, you guys have some additional work to do. Get back to me this afternoon with scenarios." Sylvia dismissed them leaving Russell alone. She walked to the door, closed it and locked it. He didn't know why she insisted on locking the door. Nobody dared interrupt her when the door was closed.

"How's my little caged pet today?" Sylvia's tone was playful, making Russell more uncomfortable. She knew how to rub a beach full of sand in his open wound.

"Not good. I didn't sleep well. This thing is uncomfortable. I need to take it off." He tried to sound self-assured. Sylvia watched his body language.

"You can take it off." She paused. Russell's spirits lifted. "Tonight, if you are going to do what I asked you to do last night." His expression clouded. He might have choked her to death if he thought he could escape the consequences.

"Why? Why do I have to do this? I don't like being abused!" Russell's anger fired up. Sylvia's expression hardened.

"Don't take that tone with me. I'm not the one who's into submission. I'm helping you experience your fantasies." She spoke as if she was fulfilling a contractual obligation.

"I never said I was into submission."

"You aren't? That's not what your wife tells me. She thought this would be a good idea. Maybe she would take you back if you accepted this." Russell dropped his head into his hands. He felt the last vestiges of strength being sucked out of him.

"Go back to your office and take care of the emails I sent. I will see you back here at six sharp. I have to leave at seven; we only have an hour and I want to make the most of that time." She turned to her desk and began typing.

***

Russell worked for two hours, trying unsuccessfully to focus. He was making mistakes; formulas weren't working and the report he produced was disjointed and almost incomprehensible. *I can't let her affect me like this. If she sees it's getting to me she will never let up.* Rising, he walked to the kitchen for a glass of water. He hadn't peed all morning and was afraid to go to the men's room. This humiliation was crushing.

He returned to his desk totally distracted. He thought about leaving early, claiming sickness. That would only delay the inevitable.

***

Barb jotted names and contact information for the men Abby

had indicated were objects of Sylvia's twisted attention. After closing her office door, she returned to the desk and lifted the handset before dropping it back into the cradle. *Am I losing my mind?* Digging through her black leather handbag she found her mobile phone and selected Sam's number. He answered after three rings.

"Sharpton."

"Hi Sam, it's Barb."

"Hi Barb, I recognized your voice. I don't have anything yet on the Mandy chick." He didn't want to confess he had been screwing her before she tossed him.

"I have something to add to your work." Barb read the names and last known address and telephone number.

"These guys bothering you?" he asked.

"Nothing like that. I need you to run these guys down. I want a face to face with them."

"Wait a minute. I investigate, I don't make introductions." Sam's voice was firm.

"Make these introductions and there will probably be a bigger payday for you. These guys may have information that will lead to an investigation."

"Now you're talking," Sam sounded enthusiastic.

"Sam, what you told me about Mandy Radcliffe and how she fucked with her husband, how did you know that?" When Barb gave Sam Mandy's name to start the investigation Sam acted as if he knew her. At first, Barb shrugged it off. She wanted intelligence. She didn't care how Sam got it.

"I can't reveal client confidences."

"This isn't some attorney-client relationship," Barb chided.

"Barb, don't push me on this."

"Fine, I'll take my business to another private dick." Barb's voice acquired an edge. Silence ensued. "You can return the retainer as soon as you can."

"Wait…I helped her set up some surveillance. Caught her husband dressing up. The dude looked really good. I think that pissed her off." It was Barb's turn to be circumspect.

"How do I know you're not still sleeping with her?"

"Barb, I may be a lot of things but I'm not like that."

"I find out you're compromising me as your client and I'll make sure you never work again in this town. Is that clear?"

"Are you finished? My word is my bond. Besides, what she did to her ex was wrong. The guy was strange but she didn't need to bury him like that."

"Since we're both into full disclosure I'm going to give you another piece of information. The boss is doing to him what the ex-wife did. There's a connection I want you to dig up."

"That's fucked up."

"And it's got to stop. Help me get this situation straightened out."

"And you'll date me?" he asked hopefully.

"I'm not promising. There will be no payment in trade," she said. "I want your best work and I will pay you." She left the unanswered to hang like an expectation.

"Give me a few days and I'll be back at you."

***

Five fifty-seven found Russell finishing up the last of the assignment Sylvia had dumped that morning. *Three minutes until doomsday.* Russell felt his body betraying him. He couldn't escape the hold she had on him. He pondered whether being her sex slave would somehow bring her to respect him. Maybe she would find him indispensable.

At one minute after six his phone rang. He moved quickly toward her office.

"You're late. I told you I have an hour. Come in and lock the door." She snapped her fingers. Russell blinked before moving slowly toward her. "Get a move on. I don't have all night. Unless of course you want to go another night without relief." She spoke as if she had total control over his orgasms. He wanted to tell her he had beaten her system. He didn't think it would make her happy. Pointing a manicured finger at her shoes, he knew.

Dropping slowly to his knees he felt himself sliding. He was out of control at the feet of the woman who threatened to turn him into a slave to his dark desires.

"If you want to kiss my feet you will need to beg me. His mouth was dry as he searched for the words that might satisfy her. Before he could begin, a knock on her door interrupted.

"What the fuck! I don't want to be interrupted," she barked at the door. Another knock infuriated her. "Go see who that is," she ordered. Russell stood on rubbery legs. Opening the door he saw Barb's smiling face. She pushed her way in.

"I know you don't like to be interrupted when your door is closed, but something urgent just came up. I thought it was worth breaking your rule." Barb handed a thin sheaf of papers to her boss. Sylvia took the papers acting bothered. She looked up after flipping through the first three pages.

"You just received this?" she asked.

"Ten minutes ago by email. I needed to read them through before bothering you." Barb's tone was apologetic. Sylvia shifted her focus back to the papers. "I'll see you in the morning," she said to Barb dismissively. Barb stood for a long moment. "Did you hear me?" Sylvia snapped.

"Sorry, I thought you were talking to Russell," Barb said innocently. Sylvia's eyes bored into her female employee, who absorbed the stare as if she were a sponge. Barb turned slowly and as she approached the threshold she stopped. "Do you want the door open or closed?" Barb knew the answer but wanted to hear it.

"The same way you found the door before you interrupted us." Impatience dripped from the reply.

"Okay, good night." Barb said as she pulled the door slowly closed, stopping before the lockset engaged. Pushing the door open she poked her head in. "What time do you want to get together?" Barb asked, knowing her question was like pulling sandpaper over road rash.

"Check with my secretary. First open time slot," Sylvia said, trying not to lose control.

"Okay, good night again," Barb said before exiting and pulling the door closed.

"Lock the fucking door and get down on your knees," she barked. Russell moved deliberately. The clock on her credenza read six twenty. He silently thanked Barb for interrupting.

"Beg!" She spoke as if she was giving direction to an uncooperative pet. As he started the phone rang. "Stop!" she commanded. He wanted to hide, to push the eject button, hating himself and wishing he had sat in that garage with the engine running. Blissful sleep would be welcome.

"Hello," Sylvia conveyed annoyance. Russell was too busy feeling sorry for himself to notice her expression change. She was engrossed in the conversation as she turned away from him. Grabbing a pen and a notepad she began to scribble furiously. Russell remained on his knees unsure what to do.

"Hold on for a minute." Sylvia punched the 'hold' button.

"You can go. We'll pick this up tomorrow." She dismissed him as she might dismiss a secretary. The intimacy he hoped she would feel for him in exchange for his devotion dissipated like mist in the summer sun.

Collecting what was left of his dignity he exited her office. When the lockset engaged the strike plate he felt weight lift from his shoulders. When he reached the doorway to his office he saw Barb sitting at his desk, her shapely legs propped up, the edges of papers kissing her calves. She looked beautiful and confident.

"Did I do good?" she asked as a playful smile danced across her lips.

"Your interruption was perfect. You almost rescued me."

"What do you mean 'almost'?"

"The phone call saved me." He stopped to consider. "You didn't arrange that call, did you?"

"Honey, there is no such thing as coincidence. I made sure that stack of papers I handed her didn't get to wait until tomorrow." Come over here." Russell took her into his arms and kissed her. She pushed him back. "Let's be careful. This should be done with the door closed."

"I have a better idea, let's get out of here,"

***

At nine thirty Barb's mobile phone chirped. She looked at the display. "I've got to take this call. She sat up as Russell unfolded himself from her naked body. She had snipped the plastic lock and removed the chastity device. She needed him and refused to allow his objections to stop her. "You think Sylvia is persistent, you haven't seen anything, honey. Remember I have the strength of both genders." He let her control; he had no fight left.

"Hello Sam." The name made Russell pay attention.

"Right, you tracked them down. Wait, I don't have a pen and paper." Barb put the phone down on the bed as she dug through the top drawer of the nightstand. "Okay go ahead." Barb scribbled as Sam dictated names, addresses and phone numbers.

"Have you contacted any of them?"

"No, do you want me to?"

"No I'll take it from here. Thanks Sam." She listened for a moment before ending the call.

"Who was that?" Russell asked.

"A private investigator friend."

"Friend?" Russell was suddenly uncomfortable.

"Not that kind of friend," she said matter-of-factly.

"A private investigator named Sam was fucking my ex. He helped her bury me."

"I know all about Sam. Your ex tossed him like yesterday's garbage. He's pissed."

"Yeah, well shit works out if you wait long enough." His voice acquired an edge.

"Sam's going to help us bury your ex. He's also going to help us bury Sylvia." Barb held up the paper with the information from the call. "These people are all ex-employees that were abused, at least according to my secretary. I have no reason to doubt her."

"And what are you going to do with that list?" he asked.

203

"We're going to talk with them and find out what Sylvia did. Then we're going to talk with a lawyer friend of mine to see what we can do to stop the bitch from screwing with people's lives." Russell looked at her, unsure what to say. "Don't thank me yet. There's work to do. Tomorrow's Friday, we're both going to call in sick and make calls to these people. Then we can use the weekend to visit with them."

Chapter 19

SYLVIA WALKED IN ON one of Bethany's sessions at the dungeon. She was frustrated and aggravated. She needed relief and she wanted it immediately. She had expected to find Bethany at home. Temper threatened to boil over into anger when she found the house empty.

"I'm in the middle of a session," Bethany said as she administered a caning to one of her subjects whose bare ass was beet red. Sylvia watched as her lover used and abused.

"When are you coming home?"

"Mamma will be right back." Bethany whispered in the ear of her subject as she reached around and squeezed his ball sack to punctuate the promise. Bethany waved Sylvia to an anteroom.

"Why did you come here? I can't allow interruptions. These clients pay top dollar for my attention. They could go anywhere but they come here because I give them what they want."

"I don't appreciate your tone. I know all about business and customer satisfaction." Sylvia's tone hardened. Bethany paused to weigh her options. She didn't want her skids to lose their grease. Her business was flourishing, but Sylvia owned the building and could evict her.

"I'll be home as soon as I can," Bethany said as she walked over to a metal cabinet. Opening it she extracted a vibrator inside latex panties, velvet-covered handcuffs and a ball gag. "Take these home. Put this on." Bethany showed the panty/vibrator combination. "Put on this ball gag then turn on the vibrator and cuff yourself to the bedpost. When I come home I will take care of the rest of you." Sylvia took the toys; the attention temporarily assuaged her need.

On the drive home Sylvia called Mandy. She wanted to report

the latest humiliation for her ex-husband. They talked for thirty minutes. "Honey you should have used a chastity device. You might still be married." Sylvia's suggestion sounded like an elbow to the ribs. Mandy didn't appreciate the bedside quarterbacking. Mandy probed with a few questions. She wondered if her victory over Russell was really a victory at all. Mark hated her for standing between him and his father and Meghan refused to allow her mother to control her life. Mandy had lost touch with Sam; he didn't attempt to call her and she was too proud to call him. The more Sylvia talked the less engaged Mandy became. "Remember he's got an obligation to pay child support and alimony. If you push him over the edge you will lose him as an employee." Mandy left the balance of the statement unspoken.

***

Russell sent an email to his boss announcing sudden illness. He attributed it to something he ate. He added graphic details of vomiting and diarrhea at Barb's suggestion. Barb called and left a message with her secretary to pass the message that she was running a fever and didn't want to infect the office.

"We're clear for the morning. Now let's see if we can finish what we started. What was it you said you needed?" Barb teased as she crossed her legs suggestively and flexed her painted toes peeking from white mules. Russell was all over them with his hungry mouth. As he kissed and sucked her toes her hips undulated, wetness threatening to soak the white thong that barely covered her landing strip. A trill escaped her lips.

Breakfast consisted of Barb's famous oatmeal, apple, cinnamon and raisin pancakes. The combination of the evening's activities, the morning greeting and Barb's delicacies helped Russell feel like a new man. She made him forget the horrors of the week, at least for a time.

"Lester Wexler expects us at eleven. You think we can make it?" she asked.

"Two hours, how far is his office?"

"Fifteen minutes in traffic," Barb replied. Russell finished the last of his pancakes, chasing it with his second cup of coffee. Barb watched and smiled. She was madly in love with the man and would do anything to protect him and make him happy.

***

Sylvia fumed over the absence of two of her top lieutenants. She commanded her secretary to get them on the line.

"Do you want them on at the same time? I can conference them in."

"No, not unless they are together." The thought of Russell cheating on her with a coworker made her angry.

Fifteen minutes later her secretary reported no success. The boss sat distracted, thinking about Russell and how interruptions ruined her plans. Bethany had taken care of the physical for her but the emotional continued unattended.

Russell's mobile phone chirped while he and Barb were meeting with the attorney. Russell recognized the number as one from the office. He figured it was Sylvia; he wasn't sure why it had taken her so long to bother him on a sick day. He let the call go to voice mail.

Lester Wexler's six-foot frame was tucked neatly behind a polished wooden desk in a leather executive chair. The office carried an air of success with ten-foot ceilings, the walls were five feet of walnut wainscoting and the balance neutral wallpaper with a faint geometric pattern. Tall windows to the left of the desk bathed the room in natural light. Wexler's desk was arranged as if staged by a decorator.

Barb introduced Wexler to Russell and explained the situation. Russell added color. Wexler listened attentively and jotted notes with a fountain pen onto a white legal pad. He interrupted the conversation at intervals to ask clarifying questions.

"You've got hard evidence of this systematic harassment?" Wexler asked.

"Russell is the most recent example. We have others we plan to contact to join the lawsuit," Barb said.

Wexler fixed his gaze on Russell. "No disrespect. but I've got to hear this from you." Barb took Russell's hand in hers for reassurance.

"The woman is a destroyer. She insists on sexually abusing."

"Can you provide specifics? Specific examples make a stronger case." Wexler continued to stare at Russell, sizing him up.

"How about telling me what feminine undergarments to wear to work?" Russell felt embarrassment threaten perspiration. Wexler scribbled notes as Russell spoke.

"What else?" Wexler asked. Russell swallowed hard. "It's okay, everything you tell me is privileged information." Barb squeezed his hand harder.

"She made me put on a chastity device." Wexler put the pen down.

"A chastity device?" he asked incredulously. Barb opened her handbag and extracted the device. His gaze shifted to the unit. Sitting back in the chair he steepled his fingers and touched his chin with his index fingers.

"She will argue that you bought the device," he stated. Russell felt his blood pressure rise.

"Why would I buy this device? I didn't even know these things existed before she gave it to me." Russell's voice was approaching frantic.

"Without corroboration we don't have the ammunition. If she's smart, and she sounds cagey, she probably paid cash for the unit. There won't be any trail." Wexler paused and watched Russell for betraying body language.

"I told you this was a bad idea," Russell barked at Barb. "Now somebody else knows my humiliation and I'm no better off." He wanted to leave.

"Lester, what do we need to produce from the others?" Barb asked, trying to salvage something before Russell pulled out.

"Get them to agree to provide details and testify and we have a case." Turning to Russell he continued. "I understand your frustration Mr. Radcliffe, but I want to save you money and time. I want you to win and in order for that to happen we need more than just your word." Wexler make a few more notes before opening the desk drawer. Pulling out papers he looked them over.

"Get as much of this information as you can and then come back." He handed the papers across the desk. Barb took and perused them.

"Do you need all of this?" Barb asked.

"Not all, but the more the better."

In the car, the couple sat quietly for a long time before Barb broke the silence. "I don't blame you if you are frustrated, if you want to give up." He looked deflated. "Can we at least try to contact these people?" Barb had the list in front of her. His lack of response made her think the effort was over.

"I don't know. On one hand, I think I've got to do something to stop her." He took a long breath. "On the other hand I'm trying to figure out why it has to be me. What if the others already tried this and failed? Do we want to spend all this time and money only to get crushed?" His eyes carried the weight of the world. Barb took his hand in hers.

"We won't know unless we try. If we find out there's no 'there' there I'll back off." Barb wasn't sure what she was promising but she needed to assure him she would be there for him. They stopped for coffee and found a table in the far corner of the small shop, windows on two sides fronting a bustling community street.

Barb's mobile phone rang. She dug it out of the handbag and checked the display before answering. "Hello, Sam." Her voice was bubbly. Russell wished he could turn the emotions on and off like Barb.

"I have something interesting on the boss," Sam said.

"Really?"

"She's hooked up with a woman who runs a fantasy shop."

"What's that mean? Why should that interest me?" Barb asked.

"It's the kinky kind, they sell services." Sam strung out the facts.

"Services, what kind of services?"

"BDSM, you know what that stands for, right? You want the

information on the business?"

"Where is the business located?"

Sam read the address.

"I know that address," she questioned, unable to visualize it. "When are you sending the information?"

"You'll have it in your email in a few minutes."

"Thanks Sam, you done good." She ended the call and placed the phone on the table as she fingered the tall coffee cup.

"Well, are you going to keep me in suspense?" Russell asked. She held up an index finger as she thought.

"I've got it, of course!" Barb's voice spiked. A few of the patrons looked her way.

"What?"

"Our beloved boss owns a BDSM business." Barb announced derisively.

"You're sure?"

"We're going to have the information and we can check it out." She lifted her coffee cup and sipped, then checked email on her phone. Sam sent a multi-page document. Barb opened it and sipped as she read. There was another name on the registration that sounded familiar. As she digested the information she dropped tidbits for Russell to absorb.

"Wait, did you say Bethany?"

Barb nodded.

"It can't be; got to be a coincidence," Russell reflected. "No wait, it makes perfect sense."

"The coffee lady," Barb said as the light bulb went on.

"Sylvia would never fund a low-brow operation like a coffee shop," Russell said. Barb figured the chastity device came from Bethany's shop. And she would probably swear that Russell was a client. The situation was getting more complicated and at the same time more interesting.

"I could see her in one of these places. I wouldn't be surprised if the shit she pulls on you she learns from the coffee lady."

"It also explains why the business is booming. The Starbucks down the road wishes it had this much foot traffic," Russell stated.

"You think there's a connection?" Barb asked as her wheels continued to turn.

"Got to be," Russell said. "Gives her business legitimacy and keeps the connection. The more touches, the longer the business relationship."

"Let's go home. We have phone calls to make and all this talk is making me hungry and horny." Barb's erotic dial was never in the "off" position.

Barb made calls while Russell cobbled together a meal from leftovers in the refrigerator. By the time he had set two places and finished the presentation Barb wrapped up the second call. She settled onto the chair as Russell held it for her. He knew she would reveal the results of the call when she was ready. After one bite of the sandwich and chasing it with sugar-free iced tea, she dabbed the sides of her mouth with a white banquet napkin.

"First call was a dud; he's not interested. Second call was more interesting. He's unemployed and has time to talk with us." Barb sounded almost giddy. Russell wasn't sure. He was going to have to reveal his secret to another stranger.

After lunch she made the third call. This person was more hesitant to discuss the topic. He was gainfully employed and feared losing his job if the scandal broke. Barb spent twenty minutes cajoling him to open up. She told him he would not have to testify; his information would be used to prompt a settlement. She assured him they didn't want this to end up in court. They wanted to make amends for the lunacy that was Sylvia Hutchison's management style. She mentioned that if this person wanted to share in any settlement he would need to sign on as a plaintiff and agree to Wexler's representation.

After wrapping up the call and jotting down a few notes Barb found Russell sitting in the living room staring out the window, a vacant look on his face.

"What's wrong?" she asked. He continued to stare, not looking at her.

"I'm trying to get a grip on this problem. I'm not sure I'm keen on the idea of going after Sylvia like this. Things are going to get worse before they get better." Barb listened, wanting to be sympathetic yet struggling with the desire to halt the evil her boss insisted on bringing to the office every day.

"It can't get much worse," Barb said. Russell turned and looked her.

"You think so?" he asked, skeptically. Barb looked at him, her eyes soft. Dropping onto the chair beside him she caressed his cheek.

"I can imagine what you are going through. If I was still a guy she would probably be doing the same thing to me." Russell thought that maybe a sex change might free him.

"When are we supposed to see contestant number two?"

"Tomorrow at ten. I'm going to try number three again tomorrow morning to see if I can convince him to at least see us. Maybe seeing us will give him the juice to talk." Russell felt the walls closing in again.

"What are we going to do until then?"

She stood and took his hand. "Come with me. We're going to think this out and write down a few questions. Then I'm going to take you to bed and make you forget all your troubles." She winked. He wanted to believe her.

***

Darkness pushed the last vestiges of daylight back to the horizon as Barb and Russell awoke. A long bout of foreplay lightened his mood. His orgasm wasn't volcanic and hers was subdued; the weight of the work situation impacting them.

"Russ, it's Friday night. Let's get dressed and go out."

"Guy and girl date?"

"How about as girlfriends?" She hoped Allison would break him from the slump.

"Sure." Russell didn't sound enthusiastic.

"Let's take a shower. You'll feel better. She started the shower and when the bathroom was steamy she stripped and stepped under

212

the hot stream of water. Russell followed her trying to pull his emotions together.

Barb handed him the pouf and then the soap. Pouring body wash over the fuchsia ball he stepped toward Barb and began to wash her supple body. She gave a playful yelp. "That's cold honey!"

She stepped under the shower. Russell waited for her to emerge before continuing. He washed her ample and youthful breasts, using his free hand to caress the areas slickened by the soap. She moaned as he teased her nipples. Her reaction was giving him a rise. She watched as he moved to her waist, wrapping his arms around her to access her back and bulbous ass. She moved into him, her thighs massaging his erect member. As he dropped to his knees to wash her legs and feet she parted her thighs. Water washed bubbles across her landing strip. Russell knew that area well, his mouth provided pleasure to her and fulfilled his need to taste her delicious flavors and enjoy her fragrances.

His hands moved up and down her legs, the thought of shaving her strengthened his erection. He felt vulnerable and needy. Her hands found him and began stroking. He wanted inside; she wanted to please him with her hands. As tension built in his loins Barb worked him until he was ready to explode. Drawing him in slowly she extended the climax. Slow and tantalizing movement from tip the shaft made him shudder as his legs shimmied and shook. He needed to erupt, to explode with fury.

When she released him she was smiling. She hugged him, feeling the exhaustion. "I love you, Russell," she whispered in his ear. He hugged her tightly as if trying to pull her into him.

"I love you, Barb." This time he said it without reservation, without the chill that had accompanied prior deliveries. She cared about him in ways he wasn't accustomed to. She would do anything for him. He needed to get to that place before she left him for greener pastures.

Drying each other with oversized pink terrycloth bath towels they worked quietly until Barb broke the silence. "Are you okay with going out tonight?" He listened closely. He wanted to detect how much it meant to her.

"I'm up for whatever you want to do. I want to spend time with you."

"Let's do it. We don't have to stay out long." She knew that once she got him out he would want to prolong the night. They selected wardrobe. Barb chose provocative. Russell conservative. Barb looked over his combination that included midnight blue knee-length half sleeve boat neck dress, three-inch black heels, taupe hosiery and half sweater and made a face as if something odiferous infiltrated the room.

"Let's see if we can do better," she said as she approached his closet. She pushed aside hanger after hanger until she found the perfect dress: merlot, sleeveless, plunge cut neckline, hem cut mid-thigh and ruched to one side for interest.

Taupe pantyhose were replaced by nude, red patent leather stilettos replaced the black. Barb selected rhinestone jewelry set in silver, a gaudy necklace with large teardrop-shaped hunk of cubic zirconia, matching dangly teardrop earrings, thick rhinestone bracelets, rhinestone rings and an ankle bracelet.

Russell applied concealer and foundation while Barb worked on the wardrobe. When she joined him in the bathroom he had just selected eye shadow. Barb stopped him.

"Try this combination." She handed him a palette of red, silver and white along with a tube of silver glitter. He looked at her. It wasn't worth arguing. She watched as he worked meticulously.

"That looks really good." Barb smiled as she admired the artistry. "Try adding this." She presented the vial of sparkles.

"You do it, show me."

"Turn toward me. You can watch me in the mirror." Barb dabbed the applicator brush lightly around the corners of the eye then over and under the eye. "Finished."

He turned and looked. The light twinkling in the sparkles made his eyes pop. "I love it."

"Okay, get dressed and let me get ready." She pinched his left nipple playfully.

Barb emerged from the bathroom her face glowing as smoky eyes glistened with flecks of glossy black eye liner. Her body seemed to move sensually as she slipped into silver sleeveless top the waves of sequins flowed over her rack like the current moving with the tide. Black liquid leather skirt accentuated her hips and contrasted her bare legs.

Allison watched, feeling her male parts reacting. "You look delicious!" Allison's compliment halted and hitched as she tried to use her feminine voice. Barb winked as she raised one leg and slipped on a leather sling back. She held the pose as if for a photographer. After slipping on the second shoe she stood before the full-length mirror admiring her creation.

"Come over here Allison, and let's see how we look together." Barb beckoned her lover with a sultry index finger. Allison wrapped an arm around Barb's waist. Their colors were perfect contrast and compliment.

Barb made small talk during the commute. Allison wasn't talkative; she stared straight ahead. Barb reached over, flipped down the visor, and pulled back the cover to the vanity mirror.

"Look at that beautiful girl!" Barb said playfully. "The guys are going to be tripping over their tongues tonight." Barb rolled her shoulders feeling sensual energy coursing through her. She mentally prepared for the game that would ensue when they entered the club.

Pulling into the parking lot Barb checked her hair and makeup, tossing a kiss to the reflection in the mirror. "Let's go, they're waiting for us." Allison shot her a look.

"Who is?"

"The people in the club. Honey, they're not waiting for us specifically but when they see us they're going to realize they were." Allison tensed. Barb took her hand and squeezed it. "The sooner we get inside the more relaxed you will feel." Barb pulled her cell phone from her black shoulder bag and snapped a picture of herself, then of Allison. She pulled Allison close to her and took a picture of them together. Checking the picture, she showed it to Allison.

"You look amazing and we look amazing together."

Barb led the way as they entered the club. She paid the cover as the bouncer eyed her lustfully. She ignored him as if he was one of the fixtures. A rectangular bar dominated the left side of the room. Mirrored ceiling tiles reflected low voltage lighting. Behind the bar three tiered shelves held the raw offerings as bartenders scurried about serving customers. To the right a hardwood dance floor spread from the bar area to the mirrored walls. Barb had been to the club at the height of activity, patrons standing three deep around the bar attempting to order liquid oblivion and the dance floor thick the dancers emulated lazy ocean waves on a warm evening.

They were early for that level of activity. She directed Allison to one of the open pub tables that filled the area adjacent to the wall. "Let's grab a table before things get nuts." Allison didn't like the idea of being flesh in a meat market. She cringed at the thought of Meghan frequenting these establishments when she reached the age of enlightenment. She remembered how Russell acted in his early twenties. He had met Mandy at one of these places. She was a barfly and he was a wannabe. He should have known from the venue how things would turn out.

The waitress stopped by the table and dropped two menus. "What can I get you ladies?" They ordered cosmopolitans. Barb knew they would loosen Allison. As the waitress departed Allison watched her tight ass move, committing her movements to memory and hoping to emulate them.

"This is fun," Barb announced. Allison looked at her as she fought to remain positive. "Relax honey, one drink and you will be fine." Barb reached across the table and touched Allison's wrist to reassure her.

When the drinks arrived Barb raised her glass and toasted their evening and the coming success. Allison sipped slowly as she watched the activity at the bar. Men cruised by, some stared while others glanced and looked away. Barb winked at some and ignored others. Allison tried not to make eye contact.

They chatted. Barb did most of the talking. "Smile, it will make you feel better. You're beautiful!" Barb said loud enough to attract attention. She caught a few furtive glances in her field of vision. "Isn't she beautiful?" she asked in a louder voice as she turned toward the bar. A smattering of agreement was offered. Two men decided to approach. Barb watched, Allison receded.

"You ladies are hot!" one of them said. Barb rolled her eyes. "You are!" the other one chimed in.

"You boys need to get another opening line. It's not what ladies want to hear up front," Barb engaged. Allison prayed Barb would leave it alone. She wasn't in the mood to fight. The larger of the two men, six feet and thick through the chest and waist, moved closer to Barb and put his arm on the back of her chair.

"Time to back off, buddy," Barb said, her stare hard.

"Hey Larry, the little lady's got spunk." Larry laughed.

"You boys paid a cover charge to get in, right?" Barb asked. The two interlopers looked at each other.

"Why?" They both shrugged.

"I'm about to signal the bartender who will call the bouncers and have you ejected." Barb's voice was firm, matching her stare.

"Little lady wouldn't do that, would you?" Steve moved closer to Barb, his chest brushing the tips of the sequins covering her bust. Barb thrust an elbow into Steve's gut.

"And don't you ever touch my breast again, you pig!" Seconds later the bouncers were escorting Steve and Larry out.

"Bitch elbowed me," Barb heard Steve say as the towers of security cleaned up the mess. After a few minutes the melee settled and normalcy resumed. Complimentary drinks were delivered to Barb and Allison.

Allison swallowed a healthy portion of her drink and leaned forward. "Did you have to do that?" she asked just above a whisper.

"I'm not going to let some asshole touch me."

"That's not what I mean."

"What do you mean?" Barb asked in the same tone she used on Steve.

"Encouraging them to come over. I wanted a nice quiet evening. I wasn't expecting a fight." Barb sat back and sipped before replying.

"Okay, maybe I encouraged them... a little." She wasn't about to admit full guilt. Half an hour later the club was jumping. The DJ was spinning kick ass music and the crowd began to respond.

"Come on, let's dance," Barb said as she slipped off the seat. Allison was hesitant. She wasn't interested in being picked up.

On the dance floor, they danced together. Sporadically a guy would join and dance with them. When neither girl showed interest he moved on. The crowd filtered onto the floor making it more difficult to dance; Barb tired of the exercise. Taking Allison's hand she led her to the exit.

When they reached the car Barb pulled Allison to her, embraced and kissed her passionately. Their actions elicited a few whistles and catcalls. Allison's face flushed with color. When Barb released her Allison moved away to her side of the car. "Unlock the door, please." She had enough of Barb's antics. When she slid behind the wheel she felt tension radiating from Allison.

"You need to relax, honey. Life is never as bad as it seems. You have to be ready to control outcomes. Don't let people take advantage of you." Barb was on a roll. Allison listened. "If you let life shit all over you all you will get is brown and smelly."

"Okay Barb, I get the point. I don't need graphs and charts," Allison said as she fought a nervous laugh. Barb smiled as she felt the tension level drop.

"Let's go home."

***

Russell lay in bed replaying the events of the evening. They played fantasy girl on girl. Barb made Allison stay in character until Allison pleaded to be released. Barb enjoyed the control; Allison felt uncomfortable. When Barb finally relented Allison retreated to the bathroom and emerged as Russell.

Barb watched. Russell looked defeated; his naked body lacked the confidence a male lover brought to bed. After a few moments, Barb apologized and beckoned him to join her. At first he wasn't responsive. She was patient. When he finally began to respond, she pleasured him. After his orgasm, he tried to return the favor. She pulled him close and whispered words of reassurance, "Relax love, you already gave me what I wanted by going out with me tonight. There's nothing more you need to do but lay here with me."

Russell breathed. He felt his heart soften, the frustration over the evening melting away.

Barb awoke and slipped out of bed quietly. "I'm awake," Russell said.

"I'll be back in a sec," Barb said as she disappeared into the bathroom. Russell thought about their plans for the day. He wasn't thrilled pursuing this angle against their boss. Nothing good could come from squeezing her. She was like a boil. Lancing it would produce nasty stuff.

Russell was standing by the double-hung window in his pajamas, fingers parting the horizontal slats of the white wooden blinds.

"Anything exciting going on out there?" He turned before responding.

"All quiet." He took two steps toward her and stopped. "Are you sure we're doing the right thing?" Barb's expression grayed before she smiled.

"I thought we agreed this was the right thing to do. I thought you didn't enjoy indentured servitude." He looked away, trying to collect his thoughts.

"What if this blows up in our face? Do you think she's lasted this long on pure luck?"

"We have an appointment at eleven. We have an hour to decide before we have to leave. If you don't want to do this I'll call and say we're not coming. There is the possibility he initiates a law suit now that he knows there are others she abused." Barb tried to box him in. She didn't want to give up the chance to nail her boss.

"I'm going down to make coffee," he announced as he walked out of the bedroom. Barb's frustration level rose. She didn't like indecision. She had enough of that when she was going through transition. Pulling on a pink three quarter length cotton robe then slipping into pink ballerina slippers she moved quickly to the stairs. In the kitchen, she watched Russell measure out coffee into the filter basket. He looked defeated. She wanted to embrace him but knew it would only encourage the mood.

Dropping the basket into the top of the coffeemaker and closing the lid, he pushed the 'on' button. The machine popped and hissed as the first droplets of brown liquid landed in the carafe. Sensing her eyes on him, he turned.

"Maybe I'm not cut out for this. I seem to have lost the will to fight. I'm not looking at this logically. If you think this is the right thing I will work with you."

"Sounds like you're putting this on me. Why is this suddenly my decision?" She couldn't hide her frustration. He moved toward her, needing a hug. At first she didn't respond. When she relented, she pulled him into her.

"I feel like such a loser," he tried to laugh, "she's broken me. You must hate me for being weak."

"If you don't want this I'll forget we even started." He turned and filled two mugs he had placed on the counter. Pouring half and half into each he watched the cream bubble as it reacted to the hot liquid. He handed a mug to Barb.

After sipping he carried the mug to the table in the corner of the kitchen. "Would you come and sit with me?" he asked. Barb moved slowly, trying to assess him. She sat and sipped her coffee in silence. Russell watched her body language as he sipped coffee without tasting it.

"I wish I knew how this was going to turn out."

"We are going to the eleven o'clock. We'll see what we learn. If we have an eager witness we will proceed. If it feels weak we'll reassess," Barb said.

In the bedroom, they prepared to shower. Russell's mobile phone rang. He walked over to the bureau and checked the display. He felt his back seize. Picking up the phone he carried it across the room and hesitated before stepping into the hallway.

"Hello?" Silence answered him. Checking the phone's display

the readout indicated the call was connected.

"Hello Russell." He heard the reply and placed the phone to his ear. "How are you?" He wasn't prepared for a civil conversation.

"Good morning," was all he could muster. On top of the tension that was about to unfold, a Mandy pile-on would be crushing.

"Sorry to call on a Saturday morning."

"That's okay," he lied.

"How's work?" *Suddenly she's interested in my job? Was this a setup for her wanting something?* "Fine." He wished he had let the call go to voice mail.

"Look Russ, I wanted to apologize for all the trouble you're having with your boss." Her words stunned him. He didn't think she was capable of remorse.

"Why did you have to tell her?"

"I was hurt and angry. I thought she wanted to be my friend." Mandy's tone was soft, almost a whisper.

"Well the damage is done." He wanted to lash out.

"You have every right to be angry. I really made a mess of things." Sobs broke up her delivery. He tried to remember the last time Mandy apologized and meant it.

"Well life is a living hell with her. She humiliates me and thinks it's funny. As if I'm one of her pets, her toys." He wasn't going to let her off the hook easily.

"I'm sorry." *Wow, two apologies in one conversation!*

"Sorry can't make all this shit go away, you know," he fired back. There was a pause before Mandy answered.

"She told me about the chastity device."

"What?" he yelled. Barb appeared in the doorway, a look of concern on her face. Russell's face was red with anger and embarrassment.

"I think it's wrong and I tried to tell her but she wouldn't listen."

"I'm going to have to quit my job. That is if she doesn't fire me first."

"I don't think she'll fire you," Mandy offered, as if she knew something.

"How do you know that?"

"I don't, but I think she's having too much fun to get rid of you. She loves the power trip."

"Do ya think?"

"Are you doing anything later today?" She changed the subject. He tried to analyze the purpose for her question.

"Why?"

"I was hoping we could get together and talk." *She wants to talk? How can I trust her?*

"I'm busy. I'm not sure how long my appointment's going to take."

"Doctor?" she asked. Russell was tiring of her concern.

"No, not a doctor. And does it matter?"

"Maybe it shouldn't but it does," Mandy said. Barb tapped her wrist signaling they needed to go.

"I gotta go. Can we talk later?"

"I would like that." He ended the call and turned to Barb.

"That was the obscenest call," he said.

"Really? Kinda early for telephone sex."

"That was Mandy."

"I figured as much. What did she want?" Barb crossed her arms under her breasts.

"She wanted to talk," Russell shrugged.

"Maybe she wants you back," Barb said, a slight edge to her delivery.

"Not a chance. I don't trust her."

They rode mostly in silence. Russell reflected on the conversation with his ex. Barb focused on the questions she wanted to ask. Pulling up to the nondescript townhome in a small development, Barb pushed the transmission into park and unfastened her seat belt.

"I need you to be mentally here for this interview. If you show you're not invested in the process this guy will wilt."

When the front door opened Frank Singleton, a tall man casually dressed in blue jeans and three button gray sweater with a full head of gray hair neatly combed into a swirl across his forehead, looked out from behind the full-length glass storm door. A slight smile greeted them as he held open the door.

Barb introduced herself and Russell before crossing the threshold. He invited them to sit down in his living room.

"May I offer you something to drink, a cup of coffee, or tea, or water?"

"Coffee would be great," Barb said.

"Me too," Russell added. Frank walked to the kitchen, his penny loafers clicking softly on the hardwood kitchen floor. He returned with a wooden tray holding three steaming mugs, cream pitcher, sugar bowl, three teaspoons and a dessert plate with a perfect circle of shortbread cookies. Placing the tray on the coffee table he sat on the settee facing the television. Barb and Russell shared a second settee to Singleton's left.

"Mr. Singleton..." Barb began.

"Please call me Frank." He looked at both of them through gentle eyes.

"Frank, we spoke briefly about why we're here. We want to thank you for seeing us." He nodded. "We both work for your former boss, Sylvia Hutchison." Singleton shifted uncomfortably. "She's done despicable things to Russell, things no human should have to put up with." Barb turned to Russell. It was Russell's turn to be uncomfortable.

"She's been abusing me." His voice quivered as he spoke. "I am really uncomfortable going into details." Russell knitted his fingers together and watched them as she spoke. Singleton watched Russell, the pain of his encounters with his former boss churning bile and black thoughts.

After sipping coffee and placing the mug on a coaster on the coffee table Singleton leaned forward elbows on his knees. "If it will help I can give you details about what I went through." Barb nodded. Russell wasn't sure he wanted to hear. Singleton stood and walked over to the server in the dining room. He extracted a large manila envelope from the bottom drawer. Pulling at the flap he opened it and extracted a black laboratory notebook. Returning to his seat he opened it on his lap and began to read in a disconnected voice. After reading several episodes Barb interrupted.

"You wrote down everything?" she asked.

"Not everything. After the first few times I began journaling. It was the only way I could cope with all the nonsense. She was merciless. All of this (he held up the journal) forced me to leave." His face hardened.

"Why didn't you come forward?" Russell asked.

"Ha! Against that woman, thinking I was the only one? I considered it. She was shrewd, covering all her bases. It would have been a stretch if I went after her. Besides she gave me a large severance to shut me up. I had to sign a confidentiality agreement and she paid me out over months. She loved to hold the leash, know what I mean?"

"Why now?" Russell asked.

"Because now I know I was not the only one. Anyway, with at least two of us we stand a chance," Singleton said.

"Are you willing to testify against her?" Russell asked. Singleton contemplated before answering.

"Are there any others involved?"

"So far just the two of you," Barb said.

"Do you think you can get others?"

"We have another meeting after this one. We'll know after that. May I see your journal?" Barb asked. Singleton held it for a moment before relinquishing it. Barb flipped through, stopping to read various entries. After a few minutes she looked up. "All of this stuff really happened?" She handed the book to Russell pointing him to three entries.

As he read, his expression changed, as if he was experiencing what was written. Looking up his eyes were bloodshot. "She really did this shit to you. I thought I had problems." Russell tried to sound sympathetic.

"It wasn't that intense all the time. And it didn't start all at once. I'm sure she's got the same plans for you. Give her time. If she's anything she's consistent." Russell grunted agreement.

"Barb, do you have that paperwork from the lawyer?" Russell asked, suddenly energized. Imagining Sylvia doing more lewd things to him was enough to push him over the top.

Chapter 20

BARB TALKED AS SHE drove. "It's a wonder he's not still in therapy."

"I know. He's been to hell and back. And I don't want to go there." Barb fought back a smile. She was thrilled he had finally come around. "I know you're happy we'reon the same page. I know it's going to be ugly but I don't want to end up like Singleton. He's got demons and they terrorize him. I saw it in his eyes."

At 2:00 P.M. Barb pulled into the semi-circular driveway of the two-story brick colonial at the end of a cul-de-sac. The house sat on a triangular lot bordered on the left and right by towering pine trees. The street was quiet; the lawn well manicured, the planting beds neatly organized and filled with color. There were no cars parked in the driveway leading to a three-car garage.

They ascended the three steps and onto a large portico covered by an A-frame roof. The large solid white front door was bookended by sidelights that were shielded by sheer white curtains. Barb pushed the illuminated door chime button and listened. Several seconds later incessant barking announced them.

The curtain on their right moved. An eye spied them before the curtain snapped back into position and the lockset disengaged. The door opened. A dark-skinned man in a dark gray cardigan over a white oxford shirt, black slacks and black wingtip shoes stood before them. His hair was close cropped, complexion clear and youthful. His average frame was complemented by the outfit.

"Are you Quentin Wescott?" Barb asked. He looked too put together to have suffered trauma.

"Who's asking?" Barb felt cold radiating from the man.

"I'm Barb and this is Russ. We called yesterday." He continued to stare at them.

"You two have last names?" Barb was beginning to think this visit might be cut short.

"Barb Collins and Russell Radcliffe," Barb said as she extended her right hand. The black man shook it firmly.

"I guess you want to come in." He stepped aside, allowing his guests to step in front of him. He led them down a wide foyer and into the formal living room and invited them to sit down. The living room was decorated in colonial motif; patterned sofa with light brown wood accents, matching side chairs, end tables matching the oval coffee table. The lamps atop the end tables were ornate black wrought iron with southwestern flair. The little furry dog sat in his bed, preoccupied with a chew bone.

"Mr. Wescott, thank you for seeing us on short notice," Russell said. Their host eyed them with what felt like contempt.

"You came all the way out here to right a wrong's been done to this black man?" he asked.

"We're here for you, for Russell, for Mr. Singleton, and for all the people Hutchison has wronged."

"How many others?" Wescott asked.

"We know of four; three have agreed to talk with us," Barb said.

"You really think you've got a snowball's chance in hell of defeating that bitch?"

"Singleton kept a journal, Russell is living the hell now. If you're willing to testify we have a good shot."

Wescott sized up his visitors. "Russell what have you got to say about all this?"

"It's a living hell. The woman makes me do things that nobody should have to put up with. No job is worth what I have to do to make her happy."

"You think she's dumb enough to leave any trail even a smart lawyer could follow?" Wescott asked.

"I'll admit she's clever. I'm sure she's covered her tracks pretty

227

well. Our lawyer thinks witnesses will be able to make the case without much trouble. There's probably a good chance the company settles out of court and you never have to testify." Russell sounded hopeful.

"She's a big rainmaker for the company. I think they'd go pretty far to protect her," Westcott said.

"Why do you say that?" Barb asked.

"Singleton say anything about a severance package?" Wescott asked. "Did he mention a confidentiality agreement?" As Wescott spoke he opened a manila envelope and extracted a thick document. Reaching across the coffee table he handed it to Barb. As she flipped through it Russell read over her shoulder.

"She made you sign this?" Russell asked.

"If I didn't sign I wouldn't get the severance. Money talks. I violate this and I gotta give the money back, maybe even get sued for breach of contract. Probably why one of your people didn't want to talk. I think you need to go back to Singleton and find out about his confidentiality agreement. Russell and Barb looked deflated as they stood to leave.

"Sorry to have wasted your time. I wish we would have known about," Barb said. Wescott stood and shifted his gaze from Russell to Barb and back to Russell.

"I'm not much for the legal end of things but I think there might be grounds for this confidentiality to be null and void." Wescott was beginning to warm to the conversation. The couple stood silently allowing their host to continue.

"Seems like Sylvia's using the law to hide harassment. I'm not sure she can do that."

"What are you saying exactly?" Russell asked.

"I'm saying you need to go back to your lawyer with a copy of this confidentiality agreement to see if he agrees with me."

"And if he does?" Barb asked.

"Then we meet; you, Singleton, me and your lawyer, to talk about a strategy." Wescott paused. "I want you to know up front that I expect two things out of this. One, Sylvia loses her job, and two I get more than an equal share of the settlement."

"I can't guarantee either one of your conditions."

"If they want to keep us from going public with our case the company will do whatever it takes to protect their good name. Do you think they'll get the same business deals if it comes out their key rainmaker sexually abused her employees? That shit won't flush."

"I could see how that would be a problem for them," Russell said.

"Can we have a copy of this agreement?" Barb asked.

"That's your copy. All of my contact information is on the last page. Have your lawyer call me if he has questions," Wescott said as he escorted them to the door.

In the car, Barb settled into the driver's seat while Russell paged through the agreement. "This is a lawyer's wet dream. I'll bet this cost a small fortune to draft."

"Let's get this to Wexler and let him give us his take on it," Barb said.

"What's the deal with Wexler? We might be bankrupt before the case gets far enough down the line to make a difference."

"Wexler owes me a favor. He's taking the case on contingency," Barb said as she wove from lane to lane moving around slower traffic.

Pulling into the parking lot of Wexler's building Barb sat for a moment. "I know you want to ask." Her voice was flat. "I helped him with a financial problem. He handled my sex change legal work; that's how I met him. After his divorce his life was a mess. He asked if I could help. I did and he's whole. He told me he owed me one. When I called him he was anxious to help. He knows all about me. And besides he's not my type." Barb stopped abruptly, staring straight ahead. Russell felt frost coming from her side of the car.

"Look Barb, this is hitting me all at once and it's hitting me hard." Russell stopped. Reaching over he took her hand; it was clammy. She squeezed as she turned, her eyes filled with tears.

"I guess you'll never understand that I love you and would never do anything to hurt you." He turned to face her.

"I know. Let's go see Wexler. I want to know whether I'm going to be able to sleep tonight." He climbed out of the car and moved around to open Barb's door. When she emerged, he kissed her. She fought back tears as they walked together to the three-story brown brick building.

***

Sylvia spent Saturday at the office. She was distracted. Two of her employees had called out sick on the same day and in the middle of heavy crunch to wrap up their biggest and most complex assignment of the year. She began to consider a conspiracy to make her fail. She couldn't understand. *I've done everything to make them successful; paid them well, gave them challenging work. This is how they repay me?*

She had called them both wanting to convey her concern for their well-being and to see if they were well enough to come to the office over the weekend. She convinced herself she cared about them. When neither answered, she left curt messages. She didn't like working alone. When she talked it over with Bethany she found the woman no help. All she could think of was her business and how she didn't have these problems. It was her and her hourly employees. When one didn't show up she called another. They wanted to work and there was no drama. All of the drama took place one floor below and clients paid for it.

"Why don't you quit that racket and join me? We would have fun and there would be no stress. Guys and girls pay to have you treat them like shit," Bethany said. Sylvia waved her off. She was many things but she wasn't a quitter. Besides, she was having too much fun toying with Russell to give it up. Sylvia loved his helplessness. She wanted to break his will. If he paid her to feminize him it would not be as much fun.

She convinced herself that revenge would be hers and it would be sweet. *If Russell comes to the office with his chastity device intact I'll forgive him. If not I'm going to make him wish he crawled to work with boils on his back.*

230

Shadow Woman

***

Mandy spent Saturday afternoon with the kids. They had plans. "Push them back. I don't get to see the both of you together very much. I want to spend the day with you."

"Mom, you don't see us together much because we don't hang out together. We don't have the same friends," Mark said. Meghan was half-listening as she texted her friends to tell them her mother was making her change plans. When Meghan finished messaging she placed the phone on the table in front of her.

"Dad doesn't make us hang out together," she said. Mandy didn't like to be compared to Russell but speaking ill of their father would do nothing to ease the tension.

"That's up to him. This is up to me." Mandy tried to sound understanding; she needed to practice her delivery. As she laid out plans for the afternoon she couldn't help but think it would be nice to have a male companion. Maybe they could do a family togetherness day once in a while. She wasn't sure she could convince her ex-husband. She didn't think he wanted to be in the same universe as her. That made her sad. He had worshiped and adored her once. She craved the attention and its absence left her empty.

"Let's make the most of this. Before long you'll be off to college and I won't see you very much." She tried to sound positive; it wasn't working. Meghan mumbled something under her breath. Mandy tried to ignore the remark, fighting not to lash out.

***

Wexler reviewed the agreement. He needed time to research the precedent around such a complex and comprehensive document. If there was going to be any chance of winning the day he would have to overcome the breach of confidentiality argument. Without clearing that hurdle there was little chance their case would ever see the inside of a courtroom.

He didn't like how the conversation with Quentin Wescott concluded. Wescott figured he controlled the process. Maybe he knew more than he was telling. Wexler hoped neither of the two new variables would feel compelled to call Sylvia to alert her. He didn't think of that angle until he read one of the clauses that created the obligation to report any malicious or defamatory statements. He would never had advised his client to sign such a restrictive agreement. The settlement was substantial; three years' severance and health benefits for the same period.

***

Mandy's time with her children was less than she had hoped. They had become bored with parental participation in their lives, making her feel isolated. As she drove from the bowling alley to the restaurant she reflected. Sam was at one extreme and Russell the other. Her need for control would make it difficult for her to find that "perfect" relationship.

Meghan sat in the back, sending text messages about boys and boredom. Mark rode shotgun watching his mother's driving techniques. He itched to try his hand at it. Driving would be the next liberating event in his life.

"Mom will you teach me how to drive?" The question drew her back.

"Don't you want your father to teach you?"

"Yeah but I want you both to teach me," he said sincerely. Mandy reached across and squeezed his hand. He smiled. He knew that two teachers would make the time from permit to license shorter. Mandy interpreted his statement as a connector between her and Russell.

After dinner she dropped Mark at a friend's. Meghan grabbed her car keys and was gone. *Alone again, this is not how I expected to spend my time.* Flipping through channels she could find nothing to capture her interest. Grabbing a fashion magazine, she turned pages until she found an article on relationships; trying to connect the threads of intelligence to her life. When she finished she closed her eyes; her heart suddenly heavy.

Chapter 21

RUSSELL MIXED TWO SHAKERS of drinks; Barb's favorite martini and his scotch. Chilled oblivion in hand, he sat next to her on the sofa. His mind drifted in and out of the legal tussle they were about to undertake; the call from Mandy left him unsettled. He couldn't get over the damage she had caused by disclosing his fetishes. If they were going to get resolution to the problem she would have to step up.

"Barb, I've been thinking about this thing."

"What thing?" she asked.

"The law suit." Russell spoke as he leaned forward and placed his drink on a cocktail napkin on the coffee table.

"What have you been thinking?"

"You know the Mandy-Sylvia connection is at the root of this problem. If Mandy had kept her trap shut Sylvia might not have done any of these things to me."

"Russ, if it was only you under her heel I would agree. But these other guys went through what you did. I think she played on the weaknesses of the spouses of each of these men. Did you notice there were no wedding rings or pictures of a significant other in their homes?" Russell stared at her. He had not noticed. Barb felt a chill cut through her. She worked in hell and the devil was the taskmaster.

***

Sunday morning started slowly. Russell rose first. He left Barb sleeping soundly. Descending to the kitchen, he brewed a pot of coffee. Pushing the power button on the remote he watched as the nineteen-inch flat screen television mounted on the wall in the dining room awakened. He flipped channels until he found something interesting. Pouring the first cup he added creamer until the coffee was a pleasant shade of brown. Settling into one of the chairs in the dining room he found yesterday's paper. Flipping through the pages an article in the business section caught his attention. When he was finished, he was suddenly hungry.

Grabbing granola and a clean bowl he poured until it was full. Picking at the granola clusters atop the mound of dry cereal he crunched and chased it with coffee.

Barb shuffled down and past him into the kitchen. After preparing coffee she settled into the chair to Russell's right.

"Sleep okay?" she asked as she leaned over to kiss him.

"I did, couldn't stay in bed any longer, feeling restless." He forced himself to look at her. She reached across and took his hand; it was cold.

"I know you're not feeling good. I promise it will get better."

"When are we going to hear from Wexler? You know tomorrow's another workday. I'd like to know whether I can go in confidently or if I'm going to have to grovel." His shoulders slumped as he spoke. As he wrestled with the demons Barb's manicured toes touched his calf causing him to flinch. She watched him out of the corner of her eye. She smiled, her lips on the rim of the coffee mug. He couldn't stop his body's natural reaction. Barb reached her left hand under the table and began caressing the burgeoning activity in Russell's loins. He moaned as her hand slipped through the opening in his pajamas. He wasn't wearing underpants. "You're not worried are you?" she asked. He shifted to give her better access.

"No, not worried," he replied in a labored voice, his attention just below his waist. Barb slipped out of the chair and moved it aside.

"Turn toward me," she said in a soft voice. On her knees she took him in her mouth as fireworks exploded in Russell's sky. When she finished she settled back into her chair. Russell sat exhausted. He couldn't remember the last time Mandy had done that for him.

"Can I get you another cup of coffee?" she asked, calling him back from his thoughts.

"I'll help you." He tried to stand. She placed a hand on his shoulder and kissed him, his flavor and fragrance on her. "Sit, I'll be back in a minute." His thoughts became jumbled. Reaching across him she refilled his coffee mug, her breasts threatened to spill out of her robe. He watched their rhythmic movement. Barb was better endowed than Mandy. He chastised himself for thinking about his ex. He felt like he was cheating on Barb.

They finished breakfast quietly, Russell engrossed in the television and Barb reading the newspaper. Barb was clearing the breakfast dishes her mobile phone rang.

"Would you get that sweetie?" Russell had been drying dishes. He flipped the towel over his shoulder and walked to the other side of the kitchen. He checked the display on the phone before answering.

"Hello, Lester. Yes, she's here." Russell handed the phone to Barb as she dried her hands.

"Good morning, Les." Barb placed the phone on the counter and tapped the "speaker: icon. "Les I put you on the speaker so Russ can hear.

"Hello again, Russ. I was starting to tell Barb the law is pretty clear on contracts where significant consideration is given. The contract Wescott signed would be valid and enforceable against him. If he breaches the agreement he could be sued for everything he was paid and then some." There was a pregnant pause before Wexler continued. "Do you think he understands his exposure?" Russell felt his stomach bottom out. His life would be toast, burning him to a crisp. He tried to listen to the balance of Wexler's information but his attention was diverted to what he believed would be his execution.

Barb ended the call and stood with her arms crossed under her breasts. She was processing. "It's not the end of the world. I think there's big upside for Wescott. The man lost his livelihood and Wexler thinks he should have gotten more than the paltry package he got." Russell didn't remember hearing that from the attorney, he was too consumed with his demise to remember much of the conversation.

Barb unfolded her arms and wrapped them around her lover. "It will be all right." Russell wasn't buying it. He finished drying while Barb finished washing. Tension was palpable, unspoken words seemed to pass between them.

Barb finally broke the ice. "Russ there's no way you can go on living like this. She's breaking your spirit. I see you crumbling a little every day. Soon there won't be much left of you and she will have won… again!" She almost shouted the word "again." Russell listened. He didn't have anything to offer. After she put the last dish away she walked over to him. "I wish there was something I could do. If things get too tough at work you can move in here. I'd love to have you with me full time. Get rid of your house, save the payment. I've got some money saved and can loan you until you find something else."

He stepped back and leaned on the edge of the counter. "I'm not going to leave. Where am I going to go without a reference?" His voice cracked.

"You've got to get on top of this or it will bury you. You have a few bumps and then the road levels out."

"Easy for you to say. You're not the horse she's riding. I feel her spurs digging into my side constantly." His tone was alarm.

She knew there wasn't anything she could say to change the outcome of the conversation with the attorney. She was frustrated and needed time to think. Could they really come out of this whole? She was beginning to doubt her enthusiasm. "I've got a nail appointment at noon. Maybe you want to come with me?" Her tone was hopeful.

"Not feeling like it. I want to try to figure things out." Barb looked at him, concerned. He detected it. "I'll be fine, go ahead and get your nails done. Maybe I'll call the kids; I haven't talked with them for a few days."

She left him nursing a glass of water and two NSAIDs. There were times during her sexual transition that she considered overdosing. She had been down the road to hell; unsure whether she was strong enough for a second trip. As she prepared for the shower she wondered how she had survived the turbulence. She knew that if she could survive that, Russell could survive the ensuing battle.

***

The house phone rang three times before Mandy answered. "Hello?" Momentary silence preceded a reply.

"Hi."

"Russ?"

"Hi Mandy." His delivery was tentative, making her wary.

"The kids aren't here," she said, feeling him out.

"I didn't call to talk to them. I called to talk to you." She smiled. Maybe her call to him yesterday had an effect.

"I'm glad you called. I've been thinking a lot lately and was hoping we could sit down and try to iron things out." Her voice was soft. It made him think of the days when they were together.

"So have I. I just wasn't sure how to approach you. When do you want to talk?" he asked.

"I've got no plans. Are you available now?"

"I could be ready in an hour."

In the shower he decided not to shave his legs, he could survive one day without primping. Besides, he wanted to give Allison a rest. She didn't like or trust Mandy, she was a threat to Allison's well-being. He felt restive. Meeting with Mandy without telling Barb began to feel like cheating. He shrugged off the thought convincing himself this was about the kids and his relationship with them.

Driving to the restaurant he played out the conversation; promising to listen more and talk less. Pulling into the parking lot he searched for Mandy's car.

Checking the rear-view mirror, he saw Mandy pull in. As she passed him she waved before parking the powder blue Range Rover. Taking a deep breath, he exited the car, clicked the fob to lock it, and walked toward Mandy. Her hair was pulled back into a tight ponytail, face freshly made up, eyes dark and sultry, lips plum-colored and pouty. This was the woman he remembered, the one he adored. As she moved away from the car he saw she was dressed in a tangerine and white horizontal striped half-sleeve scoop neck top over a mid-thigh white wrap skirt. Her legs were tanned and natural, her feet in white strappy sandals. Her toes and fingers were painted to match her lipstick. She looked radiant. He reminded himself this was her way of manipulating.

"Hi Russ." Her voice was bubbly. She approached him and kissed him softly on the cheek, scattering his thoughts like wind through a pile of dry leaves. He touched her bare forearms and slid his hands down until they touched hers. They were soft and dainty in contrast to Barb's larger hands. He felt control slowly slipping away; she knew it and squeezed his hands as if to acknowledge his weakness.

"Let's go inside and sit down," she said. The waitress led them to a corner booth, the diner was mostly empty, a few patrons at the long counter and in a couple of booths.

"I don't think we've been here," she said.

"Nope, that's why I picked it. I thought a change of scenery would be good." He didn't want the albatross of memories to cloud their conversation. A new place might mean a new beginning.

They ordered coffee and water. He sipped water until the silence was broken. "Look Russ, I'm glad you decided to see me. I know things have been bad between us." She stopped as if her mind seized up. He refused to respond, wanting her to finish. He remembered how his jumping into their conversations made her crazy. "I was angry. I didn't understand what you wanted or what I wanted." She paused to sip coffee. Placing the cup on the table her eyes probed his.

"Did you come here to ask questions?" he asked and swallowed hard before continuing. "I'm willing to answer if we can keep this on a level plane. I hope we can make it good conversation. We haven't had much success doing that."

"I know, and I didn't come here to fight with you." Her gaze was soft, almost inviting. The waitress took their order and refilled the coffee. They made small talk, almost afraid to broach anything that resembled a touchy subject.

Halfway through the meal Mandy dropped her fork onto her plate and pushed the dish aside. "Russ, can you stop eating for a minute." Her voice acquired an edge. Russell stopped in mid-chew as his stomach tightened. Placing his fork delicately into his dish as if anything more forceful might have exploded it into shrapnel, he looked at her.

"I don't know how to say this." He was puzzled. She never expressed lack of confidence. "I'm just going to say it. I wish I hadn't talked to Sylvia." She stopped and watched for his reaction. He wanted to shake her.

"Why did you do it?" He knew the answer.

"I was angry. I thought she might help straighten you out."

"Straighten me out, really?"

"You hurt me, Russ. I wasn't sure how to react to your dressing. And the..." She stopped short.

"The what?" He felt his temperature rising. He and Mandy had never talked about what happened, really talked about it without trying to hurt each other.

"I know what I did was unexpected. And if I know what you mean about the other thing I'm sorry I did it. I should have waited for you to come home. I should have poured myself all over you and showed you how much I adored you." Emotion threatened to derail his delivery.

"Adored, does that mean things are really over between us?"

"What do you want me to say?"

"Would you worship and adore me?" His loins were filling as she spoke. He couldn't help himself.

"I would have done anything for you." Her complexion stiffened.

"Does that mean you wouldn't want to do those things now?" she asked as she closed the distance between them, the hint of her perfume reaching him in sensual ways.

"Would you take me back?" he asked. *Could it be this easy?*

239

"Things have been different since you left."

"What does that mean? You had another man in your bed. What's up with that relationship?"

"That was my anger and frustration. He meant nothing. He's out of my life."

"What if he wants to come back?" He could not believe he was pushing her away.

"It's over, that's it. I would take you back under certain conditions," she said. This was the woman he knew, always a footnote, a condition, a proviso. "I want a fantasy relationship."

"A what?" He sat back as if slapped.

"I want you to dress for me in private. I want to be dominant and I want you to be submissive. I want to play out your fantasies."

"Why?" He looked around as if someone might be eavesdropping. "You told me you wanted a real man and I wasn't a real man."

"I told you I was angry. I said things to get back at you. I've been reading up on your situation." He frowned as if "situation" was a dirty word. "I am beginning to understand it. If you're using it to express things that have been buried deep inside you I can handle it." She paused. "If you want to have a sex change that's a different story. I want a husband, not a sister or roommate." She sat back and crossed her arms under her breasts. This was the signal that she was finished, statement made, conclusion drawn.

"Look Mandy, I can't explain why I need to dress except to say that I am overwhelmed at how beautiful you are. I am envious and wanted to feel what you feel. I can tell you that feeling feminine like you made me want to love you, worship you and adore you." Mandy blushed. He could not remember the last time she blushed when he complimented her.

"This is going to be complicated. I've got that... Sylvia to deal with. Do you know what she did?"

"She told me." Mandy looked away, embarrassed for him.

"Yeah, you know how small I felt?"

"I know. I felt bad for you. I realized I was wrong, about all of it. She did things to you that are wrong."

"Are you still close to her? She didn't put you up to this, did she?"

Her gaze hardened, her face set like granite. "I'm nobody's spy or errand girl. I'm here because I am serious about this. If you don't believe me we should probably go." He reached across the table to stop her.

"Don't leave. I had to ask." He tried to regroup. He wanted to tell her about the lawsuit, about how he was sticking up for himself.

"Don't put me in the same league as that manipulating bitch. She used me to get to you and I let her." That was the closest she would get to an apology.

"I wasn't trying to do that. I can't take any more of this aggravation. She's making me doubt myself and hate my life."

"Russ, I know she put you in that chastity device. When I heard it at first I thought it might be a good idea, but as she talked I realized she was trying to break you." Mandy didn't have the heart to tell him she would love the control of having him locked up. Control over his orgasms would ensure that she was the center of his universe.

"Would you be willing to state that under oath?" he asked.

"What, you need me to tell you under oath before you believe me?"

"Keep your voice down. Let me explain." He summoned courage. "I talked to a lawyer about this nonsense. I did a little digging and came up with three other men who preceded me. Sylvia tortured them as well."

"What did the lawyer say?"

"If we can prove a case it could mean the end of her."

"Are you going to sue for pain and suffering?" she asked. Russell looked for the dollar signs in her eyes, then dismissed the thought.

"Yes, but not sure how much I could get since I *am* still employed." He sipped warm coffee then pushed the mug aside. "I want her gone. I want this nightmare to end." Mandy searched him. She felt unease. Reaching across the table she took his hand.

"If you need me to testify I will." He felt skepticism pulling at him.

***

Barb walked in. The house was quiet. "Russ? Russell?" she called as she walked through the living room and into the kitchen. She looked for a note. Extracting the mobile phone from her purse she was about to dial when the phone rang. After checking the display, she answered it.

"Hello Barb this is Sam."

"I know. I programmed your number into my address book."

"Oh." She wondered how he made a living as a private dick. "I did a little more digging. The business under the coffee shop isn't registered as far as I can tell. And the woman running it is in the country illegally."

"Really, and you know that how?" She wanted verification before hurtling down another rabbit hole.

"Checked with people in the know. I have contacts in some very key places."

"Such as?" she prodded.

"I C E." He spelled out the initials. "Immigration and Customs Enforcement." He spoke the name reverently.

"Sounds threatening."

"Yeah, well they wanted to know why I wanted to know."

"And what did you tell them?" Barb asked.

"Told them I was working on a case."

"I'll bet that made them happy," Barb said.

"They're pretty jammed up with all this amnesty bullshit."

"You free to get together? I'd rather not talk about this over the phone." Barb was beginning to feel paranoid.

"Sure, nothing I couldn't move." Barb interpreted that to mean he wasn't busy.

"Meet me at Gino's; I'm leaving now."

"See you in a few."

Barb sat quietly for a moment before grabbing her coat. She

wished Russ could join her. She knew Sam would draw the wrong conclusions about getting together. After starting the car she called Russ. She got voice mail and left a short message. Her heart was in her throat; she felt like he might be slipping away.

***

Sylvia awoke, her thighs sore. Bethany had worked her over leaving her spent and whimpering. Moving slowly, she pushed herself out of bed. Bethany was already up, the aroma of coffee wafted to the bedroom. After relieving herself she dabbed her sensitive vagina with a cool damp washcloth. She hadn't felt like this since the cruise. That's when she knew the woman would be good for her. She descended the stairs gingerly. As she reached the opulent landing she heard Bethany's voice heavy with authority and eastern island accent. She was ripping into someone, probably a client. She didn't enjoy phone sex but if a client was willing to pay she would accommodate. Pouring her first cup of coffee Sylvia listened to the technique. Bethany was smooth and powerful. She could love you one minute and rage on you the next. It made her wet to know a woman who could overpower her. No man in her life had achieved such a status.

Settling into one of the cushioned bar stools at the center island Sylvia watched and listened. Bethany flashed a pearly smile as she wielded her feminine powers. The smile was deceptive; it hid darkness that was blacker than night.

As she was pouring her second cup of coffee the conversation ended.

"Son of a bitch insisted I give him a session," Bethany laughed. "For the next few days he will remember it." Sylvia pieced together the threads of the portion of the conversation she heard. The anal penetration ritual Bethany imposed on her victim sounded painful.

"Are you free for the day?"

"You need more of last night?" Bethany asked.

"No, I wanted to spend the day with you, no agenda." Sylvia had work to do but wasn't in the mood. She was still distracted by her employees' failure to respond to her calls. If she didn't find a distraction her day would be ruined by growing anger.

"What did you have in mind?" Bethany asked, as she spooned Greek yogurt over granola.

"Let's take in a movie and then go into town for an expensive dinner. I want to be free and easy today." Bethany smiled. She loved when her meal ticket treated her like the queen she believed herself to be.

***

An hour later Russell picked up the check. He had pressed Mandy for conditions of their reunion. She tried to put her feelings into words. She wanted emotional and physical control. After a bout of cat and mouse she finally told him she wanted his attention exclusively. He would commit without conditions. She wanted the docile husband she'd had before she found him dressing.

"I'm asking a lot but I'm offering a lot. I feel how you look at me. I know what you want. Give me what I want and I'll give you what you want."

"Can I think about it? I didn't come here expecting this. I thought…" He stopped and looked down at his hands. "I didn't know what to expect. This is emotional overload after the last few days of abuse."

Sitting in the car he pondered the conversation. He felt squeezed between lust, submissiveness and femininity. The emotions that drove a wedge between him and Mandy threatened to bury him. Mandy would not allow him to dress and go out. Barb would give him the freedom but he'd have a failed marriage and the regret of never giving it a second chance.

Checking his mobile he saw the message from Barb. His heart beat faster, panic looming on the horizon. Listening to her message he sensed distress in her voice. He hadn't left a note. He didn't think he would have been out long. Firing up the engine he pushed the car to the speed limit wanting to get home.

Pulling into the driveway he cursed himself for rushing. Barb wasn't home. He trudged to the front door. Letting himself in the emptiness surrounded him, conflicting thoughts fought for marquee space. Climbing the stairs he felt Allison pushing him toward the bedroom. Slipping out of his clothes he left them in a pile. Moving to the closet, he selected a navy-blue pencil skirt from the lower rack. He pulled down a pair of navy blue sling back peep toe heels and slipped them on.

Looking at himself in the mirror he realized how ridiculous he looked with a bulge in the front of his skirt. Fumbling through the pantyhose drawer he extracted a pair of black tights to hide unsightly stubble. Finding a bra and breast forms he dropped them into the cups once he fastened the bra and positioned the shoulder straps. Topping off the outfit, a white silk blouse.

Standing before the full-length mirror he focused from the neck down. Allison was comforting him, reminding him of the freedom he worked hard to achieve. Strolling into the bathroom he washed and dried his face. He used the electric razor to smooth out early stubble, applied moisturizer and then concealer.

Dabbing on liquid foundation his complexion softened. He hoped Barb would be happy to see Allison. The last time the two girls were together Allison wasn't feeling as feminine as she felt now. She wanted to show Barb how much she appreciated the unqualified acceptance.

Deep red lipstick and clear lip-gloss finished the look. Pulling on the blonde wig Allison adjusted it until the bangs fell softly across her forehead. She softened the sides and back with a few strokes of the hair pick. Not even the thought of Sylvia excoriating on Monday could dampen the mood.

***

Barb sat across the table from Sam. He was undressing her with his eyes. He called her "eye candy." She warned him not to treat her like an object. He persisted; she ripped him to shreds verbally before he finally stopped.

"Sam, eyes front and center. Looking at my breasts won't make them pop out of my bra." She pointed two fingers at him and then at her eyes.

After swallowing a large gulp of coffee he cleared his throat, another quality she adored in him. "Here's what I have." He pulled several folded pages from a manila envelope. After unfolding them and flattening out the crease he reviewed them before handing them to his client. Barb looked them over.

"Official-looking," she said looking over at Sam. "Can I keep these?"

"Sure. We need to talk about my fees." Sam's complexion firmed. Barb's eyes narrowed. "Those papers are included in my fees."

"I know," Barb responded.

"I've already burned through the retainer. I'm going to need another two and a half after today."

"You burned through twenty-five hundred? We agreed you would give me warning before you spent more than the retainer," she said, her voice expressing displeasure.

"I thought you wanted me to push forward." Barb considered the situation. She had two agendas. Her second item might not fly if she made a stink about his fees.

"I'm not happy about your racking up the dollars. It stops now."

"Fair enough. Can you write me a check today?"

"I'm not prepared to do that. If I had known I might have brought the checkbook. Do you have an invoice?" she asked, his expectation to be paid on the spot annoyed her.

"I'll send you one; I'll do it when I get home. Unless you want it hand delivered?"

"That won't be necessary, mail will do just fine." She didn't want him getting the wrong impression. She wanted him chasing Mandy and hopefully catching her. Suggesting that to him was not going to be easy.

"I'm finished for now?" he asked. Barb thought about it before responding.

"Is there something you haven't finished?"

"There's always more work I can do. The question is whether you are willing to pay for it." His tone was sarcastic. She liked him less and less, making him just the man for Russell's ex-wife.

"How about you give me a summary of what you want to investigate and I tell you whether I want you to do the work," she said. He looked her over, another eye fuck.

"You're the client." As he spoke she signaled the waitress for a refill on the water.

***

Pulling up to the house she felt drained. Sam had a way of sucking the life out of you. Their conversation had migrated to Mandy and his relationship with her. Barb listened without commenting. It wasn't as if she cared, except she did. She suspected that his revelations about Mandy were designed to make her jealous. After five minutes of banter he stopped, realizing Barb wasn't biting.

She stepped over the threshold and felt better. "Russ, are you home?" She listened for a reply. She heard movement above. Walking over to the stairs she was about to ascend when she saw Allison at the top of the stairs making her way down. Barb smiled. "You look wonderful."

"Thanks honey, I feel wonderful." When Allison reached the bottom of the stairs she embraced Barb. They kissed. Allison's hands wandered around the curves of Barb's figure. "I couldn't help it. I needed to dress," Allison explained.

"I thought you went AWOL. You weren't here when I got back from the salon."

"I went to talk with Mandy." Barb's smile faded. "She told me she knows all about what Sylvia did to Russell. Get this, she even agreed to verify what Sylvia has been doing to him." Allison looked at Barb knowing the conversation wasn't pleasant.

"Is that all you talked about?" Barb asked, taking half a step back.

"We talked about the kids and how she wished she had never talked with Sylvia. She was really upset."

247

"Sounds like she might have been after more than just forgiveness."

"I've been doing a lot of thinking about my life." Barb's hands fell to her side anticipating bad news. "I've been through a lot. Most days I wonder whether I'll have enough energy to go another day."

"Do I want to hear this? What are you telling me?" Taking her hand Allison led Barb to the sofa.

"Please sit." Allison watched as Barb reluctantly complied. "Please cross your legs." Barb crossed her left leg over her right. Allison dropped to her knees and placed soft kisses on Barb's ankle before removing her shoes and kissing her feet. The warmth and moist fragrance of her feet was making Allison crazy. Barb watched, enjoying the attention. She understood the unspoken message.

When Allison finished, Barb beckoned her to sit on the sofa next to her. "That felt good. I needed that more than you know." Barb smiled; Allison returned the smile.

"Not as much as I needed it. I want to make love with you girl on girl."

"You sure you don't want to go out first? You look cute, seems a shame to waste all that work." Allison stood and lifted her dress. The pantyhose were straining to hold the erection. Barb took the cue as Allison moved closer. Barb teased, slowly her lips caressed and kissed. Her tongue probed. Allison's legs quivered. She felt comfortable, at ease and finally home. When Barb finished, Allison kissed her wet lips, the taste of cum palpable.

***

Mandy sat at the computer and began to type. The meeting with her ex made her yearn. She knew there was still something about him that pulled at her. The father of her children, she recalled the early days of their marriage. They had been in love. *Where did things go wrong? How did he get into being feminine?* Two pages into documenting all of the things Sylvia revealed to her the mobile phone rang. The sound startled her.

"Hello?"

"Mandy it's Sam." He had struck out with Barb. He needed to know if he could mend a fence.

"Hi Sam." She tried to sound cordial, her defenses rose.

"I wanted to call to say how sorry I am things didn't work out." He sounded sincere. Mandy was torn between the masculinity he exuded that made her feel like a complete woman and his need to dominate. She needed a fuck but wasn't sure she was ready for the baggage that came with the delivery.

"I know things ended badly," she said, knowing what was coming next.

"You interested in trying again?" She was silent. "You're not interested. I know why. That was my mistake; I was trying to help."

"Sometimes helping only hurts."

"Well you learn from your mistakes."

"Look Sam, I appreciate the call but I'm a little busy. Let's talk about this later."

"Okay, when can we talk again?"

"I don't know but not now." Her voice danced up the octave scale.

"Fine, I'll call you tomorrow, okay?"

"I'll talk to you then." She pushed the mobile phone away as if distance might prevent it from ringing. She wasn't sure she would be interested in talking with him tomorrow; she would deal with it then.

Rereading the last paragraph, a chill gripped her spine. The reality made her shudder. She added a few closing facts, then saved the document before reading it again. When she was finished, she emailed it to Russell and printed it. She wanted a record of what she was agreeing to say.

Punching the 'power' button of the remote control she waited for the television to awaken. Flipping through the channels she found a favorite program. Lounging on the sofa she propped her feet on the coffee table and admired her pedicure. She wanted him there to worship at her feet.

Chapter 22

MONDAY MORNING ARRIVED EARLY. Russell rose first, dread hanging over him like storm clouds. He didn't want to go to the office. Walking over to the dresser he lifted the Ziploc bag that held the male chastity device. He and Barb discussed how to handle things knowing Sylvia would expect him to have worn it all weekend. There was no way he could reattach the locking tag. He was going to be flayed. He considered taking another sick day. They had talked to Wexler late last night after they forwarded the letter from Mandy. He wanted to talk with Mandy in order to confirm that she would go on record with her allegations. Russell called Mandy and asked. After a long conversation, she agreed. Wexler planned to call her as soon as he reached the office on Monday. If she was willing to step up, Wexler thought it best there not be any confrontations. He suggested his client take another sick day. There was no reason to suffer any further.

After talking with Mandy, Wexler was convinced she was credible; he could file the complaint and have it served quickly. He had already drafted the bulk of it. Barb asked to see it. They huddled around her laptop and read it. Barb thought it looked straightforward; Russell was less convinced. "What if she fights and wins?"

"Do you think the company's going to back her? The publicity alone will drop a building on them. They'll abandon her like a hot potato."

"I guess you're right."

***

Shadow Woman

Sylvia awoke feeling woozy. She and Bethany had spent the previous day together. They bickered about the coffee shop. Sylvia wanted Bethany to pick up the tab for the mortgage since the business was doing well. Bethany thought her dominatrix role was more than enough compensation. Sylvia laughed, mocking her roommate. Bethany's anger blossomed. As their voices rose they attracted the attention of several patrons at the restaurant.

"I'm not talking about this here. If you want to debate the topic we'll take it back to the house. I'm not making this a public spectacle," Sylvia said in an even tone. Bethany's eyes burned. When they returned home the bickering resumed. Sylvia was insistent. Bethany was petulant; she threatened to leave. Sylvia held her ground. She was financing Bethany's enterprise and receiving no return on her investment.

After an hour of squabbling Bethany changed and left for a brief period before returning in a better frame of mind. Sylvia watched her as she walked in smiling.

"I didn't come back to fight. I came back to try to work things out," Bethany said, her eyes radiating confidence.

"You know what I expect." Sylvia continued to press her case.

"Yes, I know."

"Well?"

"I pay you to run my business out of that building, I want my payments to be paying off the building. I want to own it when the mortgage is paid off." Bethany's Jamaican accent thickened as she talked.

Sylvia smiled, feeling the power. "That was never the deal. I'm the landlord, you're the tenant."

"That's not what we agreed," Bethany said. Sylvia dismissed her with the wave of a hand. Bethany moved closer, coming almost nose-to-nose; her frame large and imposing.

"Bigger and badder people than you tried that approach. It didn't work for them," Sylvia said.

"No money until I get the deal on the building."

"I can have you evicted for failure to pay rent."

251

"How would your bosses act if they found out you were financing a sex operation?"

"Ha! They wouldn't care. They've got more important things to do than meddle into the private affairs of their employees." Sylvia sounded more confident than she was. She was on thin ice with the board. They had little tolerance for rogue employees.

When Sylvia went to bed Bethany went out. She wasn't interested in being somewhere she wasn't appreciated. Before leaving she grabbed her assortment of toys. She wasn't going to leave anything for Sylvia until she deserved it.

Sylvia tried to shake the funk. She could not remember the last time she felt lousy. Cup of coffee in hand, she wandered up the stairs and into the master bath. Fishing through the medicine cabinet for the bottle of pills she found they were gone. She could have sworn the bottle was almost full but the clouds in her mind wouldn't allow her to concentrate. She checked her face in the medicine cabinet mirror. She felt as if she was looking through a light fog, her peripheral vision limited. Bloodshot eyes told her something was wrong; alarm bells clanged in the distance.

Taking a long pull from the coffee mug her stomach rejected the offering. Placing the mug on the edge of the sink it crashed to the marble floor and exploded as brown liquid splattered everywhere. Two retches and the contents of her stomach were deposited in the sink. She braced her hands on the sides of the bowl for the next shockwave.

When the upheaval subsided she felt drained, her face a sunken mass. Looking down she surveyed the mess strewn across the cream-colored marble, the brown relief tiles blending nicely with the spilled coffee. Pulling a plush towel from the bar on the wall she opened it and dropped it over the area between the sink and the shower to keep from cutting her feet on the ceramic shards.

She stumbled before catching herself on the towel bar. Stepping gingerly, she made it to the shower. Turning on the water the blast of cold shocked her as she stood counting the seconds until the water turned hot. Several minutes later her soaked body shook off the chill.

She tried to clear her head. She grabbed a towel from the heated rack on the back wall of the shower. Drying off she tried to avoid the mess on the floor but nicked her heel on a shard.

"Fuck!" Blood dripped from the cut as she pulled a remnant of the mug from it. She ran a washcloth under cold water before applying it to the cut. Dropping heavily onto the toilet seat she grabbed the edge of the polished mahogany vanity to keep from falling over.

Frustrated, Sylvia tried to recall the events of the prior evening. Something she did or didn't do made her feel like death warmed over. After applying antibiotic and a bandage to the cut she made her way into the bedroom to dress.

In the kitchen, she toasted two slices of bread and boiled water for tea. She was running late but didn't care. Rushing wasn't going to make her feel any better. Spreading butter on the bread she thought about adding orange marmalade, her favorite spread. After two bites of the toast she decided the sugary spread was the only way she was going to finish the Spartan meal.

Back in the bedroom she applied makeup and completed her outfit: navy blue blazer over navy blue pencil skirt, white blouse and black leather pumps, no pantyhose. Walking toward the garage, nausea struck again. Rushing to the powder room, she dropped to her knees and vomited into the toilet. Her forehead was cool and clammy. "No fever," she said relieved. The problem had to be something she had eaten the prior night.

After brushing her teeth and clearing her sinuses she gargled with mint-flavored mouthwash. She felt drained but her stomach had stopped hurting. Grabbing a sports drink from the refrigerator she picked up her briefcase and proceeded to the garage. Settling behind the wheel of her car she tried to put on her game face. The issue with Bethany really angered her. She wanted things to work out but not unless Bethany paid her way.

Pulling into the parking lot, the clock on the dashboard read nine thirty-five. She scanned the lot. There were some empty spots. She didn't see Russell's car. Another layer of anger and her day was barely underway. Punching the voice command button on the steering wheel she said, "Call Radcliffe." After five rings the call went to voice mail.

"Russell, this is your boss. I don't see your car in the parking lot. I assume you're not in the office yet. Call me with your ETA. We've got work to do." She punched the end button and sat for a moment to compose herself.

The office was humming with activity. She walked by Russell's office, miraculously expecting him to appear. Proceeding to her office she dropped her briefcase and called to her secretary. Delia walked in carrying two items. "These were just delivered. I didn't have time to put them on your desk." Sylvia took them, a small square box wrapped in shimmering gold paper and topped with a red bow, and a large white manila envelope.

Dropping the envelope on her desk she tore through the wrapping paper and bow on the box.

"Belgian chocolates, my favorite." Delia watched and waited for orders. Looking up she saw her secretary waiting.

"Track down Radcliffe. I want him in the office immediately." Sylvia dropped into the executive armchair and held the box in both hands. Returning it to the desk she opened it. There was a card that read, "You will always be the queen of my life." The card was not signed. She turned it over in her hands before placing it next to the box.

Plucking one of the nine neatly arranged truffles she brought it reverently to the tip of her nose. The aroma of quality chocolate encouraged her. Taking a bite, she allowed the flavor to wash slowly over her palate. She didn't spend time enjoying much in life, expensive chocolate was the exception.

"I left a message on his mobile phone and I sent him an urgent email." Delia interrupted her boss's reverie; her complexion darkened.

"When he comes in I want to see him immediately," she said, frustration apparent in her voice. Moving the box of chocolates to her desk drawer she pulled the large manila envelope to the center of the desk. She read the address label; she didn't recognize the name of the attorney. Opening the envelope with the letter opener she removed the contents. Reading the cover letter her blood pressure rose; the names of the plaintiffs igniting rage. Rising she marched to the office door and closed it.

"Son of a bitch, what do they think they're going to get? I'll expose their asses to the world. They want to play rough? They have no idea what they're in for." She paced as she collected her thoughts, memories of prior settlements making her uneasy. Grabbing her headset, she dialed the number from memory.

"Hello?"

Sylvia charged in. "Do you know your husband's suing me and the firm for harassment?" She paused before continuing. "He'll lose, then lose his job, and you'll lose your precious alimony and child support. I suggest you talk to him before this gets ugly. If he withdraws the lawsuit I'll forgive him. If not I'll expose him to the world."

"Why are you barking at me? You brought this on yourself," Mandy replied.

"You helped. If you hadn't told me about him I would never have played the game."

"Nice try. I know all about the other guys. Russell told me about them. Besides, I think your job is more important right now."

"You little bitch, you have no idea."

"Yes I do. I may be a bitch but I can deal with it. You, on the other hand, have bigger problems."

"Like what? He'll never be able to prove the allegations. I'll call you as a witness. You'll corroborate my story." Sylvia sounded smug and confident.

"Sorry to break the news to you but I'm a witness for the plaintiff. I can corroborate Russell's story and I will."

"How far do you think you will get? You're a tramp and my lawyers will rip your credibility to shreds."

"I don't think you'll get very far with that threat."

"Really!"

"My husband has done his homework and he's got a really good lawyer. He knows all about the other guys and your little side business under the coffee shop." Russell had told Mandy all the details to convince her their lawsuit was strong.

"Your husband? Now he's your husband? That won't matter at all. My personal business has nothing to do with my work life."

"The lawyer thinks differently. I guess we'll see what the jury says."

"This whole thing is going to blow up in your faces. I'll give Russell twenty-four hours to take back the complaint before I turn this over to my shark lawyers."

"I'll tell him but I doubt he will budge."

"When you talk to him tell him to get his worthless ass to the office. I have work for him to do." Sylvia punched the 'end' button.

"Mother fucker!" she shouted to the walls. Her stomach was churning acid as her temperature rose. Walking over to the under counter refrigerator for a bottle of water she felt her knees weaken. Catching herself on the back of a nearby chair she stood for a moment before opening the refrigerator. She unscrewed the cap and took a large gulp. As she swallowed the last mouthful her stomach flipped and tightened. Rushing to the desk she grabbed the trashcan as the contents of her stomach rushed for the exit at lightning speed.

Dropping heavily into the desk chair she felt lightheaded; chiding herself for eating the chocolate.

Grabbing the cover letter Sylvia checked the addressee. *It's addressed to me in my capacity as CEO of this office.* Checking the bottom of the letter she saw what she expected but hoped wasn't going to be there. A copy of the letter with attachments was addressed to her company's general counsel. "Son of a bitch." Picking up the handset she punched the intercom.

"Yes Sylvia," Delia's voice was perky.

"Get me Stanley Wang." Sylvia dropped the receiver into the cradle before Delia answered. Thirty seconds later the telephone rang. She slipped the wireless headset over her ear and punched the intercom button.

"Mr. Wang is in a meeting and asked not to be disturbed. I left a message that you needed to speak with him as soon as possible."

"Find me as soon as he calls."

"I will," Delia said. Sylvia pulled the headset from her ear, almost catching her earring before dropping it disgustedly onto the desk. She was unnerved. Working was going to be impossible. Rising she extracted her car keys as she opened the door to her office.

"I'll be in the car. Find me if Stanley calls." She didn't wait for a response. Once Sylvia was out of range Delia rolled her eyes.

Dropping the car into gear she pulled out of the parking lot, preoccupied with the lawsuit. Stanley Wang was a legal genius. The company lured him away from a partnership position at a major New York law firm. She ran up against him during a merger negotiation. He dismantled their position and reconstructed it for the benefit of his client. Sylvia and her team were impressed by the man. They encouraged the company to approach him.

Wang had been instrumental in fixing "the problem" as he called the last two incidents. She had been fortunate that her star was on the rise. Her boss told her as much. He was less accepting the second-time things happened, he had experienced employees with "management challenges." Those employees had to be top performers; there was a tradeoff. The company calculated the cost/benefit of Sylvia's personnel problems. They extracted the cost of the settlement from her annual bonus, no harm no foul.

Had she been a lesser light she would have been cast to the wolves. She presumed the situation would be the same this time. Her earning potential was still high and any settlement would be merely a nuisance to her overall earnings. She wanted assurances from Wang before her boss confronted her.

She drove oblivious to the traffic, her mind wandering to the last time she had been alone with Bethany. The unresolved problem grated on her. She needed closure. *The best time to confront is when you have the advantage,* she reminded herself. Pulling into the parking lot of the dual-purpose building Sylvia took her time exiting the car. Standing, she felt queasy. *I must have the beginning of the flu.* Walking slowly to the front entrance she surveyed the foot traffic. There was a short line waiting for service. Bethany was working the crowd as she assisted the servers. Sylvia couldn't figure why Bethany insisted on working. As she entered Bethany saw her and smiled. Heads turned to catch a glance of the well-dressed woman with the attitude. Sylvia acted as if she was alone in the store.

As she approached the counter she greeted Bethany. "We have unfinished business to discuss. I want to leave here with an understanding so we can put this behind us." Sylvia probed Bethany's expression, it was unchanged. Two employees buzzed behind Bethany extracting individual servings of fresh brewed coffee from stainless steel machines that hissed and wheezed, depositing steaming long thin streams of brown liquid into waiting cups. Handwritten descriptions and prices in a rainbow of colors appeared on the black boards above the coffee machines.

"Sure, but this is not the best time. I have customers and it would be wrong to let them see this."

"Get your staff to take care of the customers. We can go to the back room and work this through." Bethany considered the statement. "Okay, give me a minute and I'll see you in the back room." She lifted a section of the hinged portion of the counter and unlatched the counter height door, swinging it inward. "Go on back. Can I get you something? Coffee?" Bethany asked.

"Stomach's not right, no coffee."

"How about herbal tea. I have just the recipe to help." Bethany smiled. Sylvia returned the smile thinking her lover was a cool customer. She made her way down a short corridor lined with shelves holding supplies. The back room was small; stainless tables against the two parallel walls; the rear exit door in the far wall was ajar. She walked over to the door and opened it. There was nothing to see except the parking area devoid of vehicles. Scanning the room, she spotted a chair. After removing an empty box that was filled with paper trash, she wiped the seat with clean paper towel before sitting. She was feeling ill and hoped Bethany's recipe would fix her up. She had too much work to do to be sick.

After several minutes Bethany joined her, carrying two tall hot drinks. She handed one over. "That should fix you up. I'll make you another to take when you leave. You can never have too much of mamma's special brew." Bethany smiled as she sipped her coffee. "Reggae cinnamon spice, my tribute to Bob Marley." Bethany spoke with pronounced Jamaican undertones. Then her tone flattened. "But you didn't come to hear about my recipes, you came to finish our conversation."

"It was never my intention to support you. I wanted to get you started until you were self-sufficient. Looking at the numbers and the traffic I'd say you're doing well enough to begin paying me back." Sylvia sipped the tea. "This is delicious."

"Thanks." Bethany smiled as she processed her response. "I guess I should show you the books to give you a better idea how well I *am* doing. I think you will be surprised," she said, gazing with eyes that hid secrets.

"Which books are you going to show me?" Her lover was well aware of the tricks business people played with their bookkeeping.

"The only set I have. I'll show you tonight," Bethany stalled.

"We're going to resolve this tonight. I don't want any misunderstandings," Sylvia said as her gaze hardened.

"Drink your tea, it will make you feel better." She sipped, her stomach feeling settled. They talked for several minutes. Bethany flitted around the edges of their erotic encounters. Sylvia listened but she wasn't in the mood.

"I've got to get back to the office. I'll be home early tonight; plan to be around when I get home." Bethany didn't like being told what to do.

"Let me make another one of those for the road." Bethany pointed to the tall red travel cup. The liquid had cooled enough for Sylvia to drink it down. "Wait here, I'll be back." Bethany left Sylvia in the storeroom alone. Her stomach was settled but she felt lightheaded. Waiting a moment before moving she looked around. "There must be something here." She checked the wall mounted cabinets opening each door and scanning the contents; mostly coffee and tea.

The click clack of heels on the tile floor announced Bethany's approach. Sylvia turned and walked to the doorway feeling as if she had overlooked something obvious.

"Here you are." Bethany handed the large travel cup in a protective heat sleeve.

"Can you throw this out?" Sylvia handed over the empty cup without waiting for acknowledgment.

Bethany escorted her to the front of the store, lifted the counter and opened the knee-height door. Watching Sylvia leave she stood engrossed for a moment before lowering the counter and returning to work.

Sylvia slipped the cup into the cup holder in the center console of the car before pulling onto the street. She still wasn't feeling right. The tea sloshed around in her stomach making her feel bloated. Returning to the office she carried her handbag over her shoulder and the drink absentmindedly in her right hand. She walked by Delia without a word. Delia rose from her desk after scooping up three pink phone messages. She approached her boss' office to find the door closing slowly. She knocked before pushing the door open.

"Three calls, Mr. Wang hasn't called back yet. Now that you are in the office would you like me to try to get him on the line? Sylvia's eyes were glassy and unfocused as she looked over the rim of the cup from which she was sipping.

"See if you can get him." Delia held the three messages out. Sylvia looked at them before reaching across the desk to take them. She sipped more of the tea before placing the cup on the desk and reading each message. She crumpled each one and deposited them in the trashcan. Delia turned and walked out; she'd never seen her boss disconnected. Delia knew at least one of those calls was important. Either her boss had committed the number to memory or she didn't care. Neither option seemed conceivable.

An hour later Sylvia was cloistered in her office. She had ignored two telephone calls. When Stan Wang called and Sylvia didn't respond to the intercom Delia moved quickly to her boss' office and knocked twice. There was no answer. She knocked again before opening the door. The executive sat slumped over the desk. Delia called to her as she approached. Sylvia didn't move, her face turned to her left obscuring her expression from Delia as she rushed to her employer's side.

Delia shook her gently. "Sylvia, Sylvia are you okay?" Alarm rose in her throat. "Sylvia wake up." Delia grabbed her boss' arm and shook hard. She continued to be unresponsive. Delia was scared. "Somebody help, Sylvia's not moving!" she called as she tried to lift Sylvia's head. It was a dead weight. Her face was cool and pasty. Delia's hands were clammy as her nerves frayed. She didn't like her boss, but seeing her dead wasn't an outcome she desired.

Two female coworkers entered the office. "What's wrong Delia?" Delia looked up teary-eyed.

"I think she's… she's…" Delia couldn't bring herself to say it. A third person, Jonas Sterling, entered.

"Did someone call 911?" he asked. The three women looked as him blankly. He moved to the desk, lifted the handset and punched in the three numbers. After a moment, a 911 Operator answered. Jonas answered the opening questions and described the situation.

"Send an EMT unit, hurry, I think she's dying," he barked, tiring of the questions. He shooed Delia aside as he approached the body, grabbed Sylvia's right wrist and checked her pulse. "Pulse faint but there is a pulse."

"They're closed, I'm not going to touch her eyes!" he said incredulously into the telephone. "Send help here now!" He barked before dropping the handset into the cradle.

"Honestly these people." Jonas left the comment hanging. "Let's try to get her to sit up."

"You think that's a good idea?" Delia asked.

"Do you think I would suggest it if I thought it was a bad idea?" He lifted her limp body gently. She opened her eyes momentarily; eyelids fluttering. She appeared to recognize Jonas as she smiled. Closing her eyes, she dropped her chin onto her chest.

"Sylvia," Jonas called in an authoritative voice. He called her name again, grabbing her shoulders firmly in large calloused hands and shaking her. Turning to Delia, "Help me to get her to the sofa. She's going to flop onto the desk if we leave her in the chair." Delia shied away. "For Christ's sake woman buck up and help me." Jonas' booming voice snapped her out of her funk. Each grabbing an arm, Delia and Jonas lifted Sylvia; heavy and unwieldy, her feet dragged as they moved her slowly from the desk to the settee.

***

Mandy tapped the screen selecting the number from the address book. When Russell answered, she spoke nervously. "Are you at work?"

"No, I'm home."

"Your boss is really upset, she called me to tell me she got the lawsuit." The statement made his stomach lurch.

"You're going through with this right?" Mandy sounded desperate.

"We filed the lawsuit. Yes, we're going through with it. Do I have any choice? I'm screwed if I try to pull back. She'll crush me." He stopped as it dawned on him she might be pulling back her support.

"What are you trying to tell me?" he asked, skepticism in his voice.

"I'm telling you to stick to your guns. Don't back down. She thinks you'll crumble."

"I might crumble but I won't back down. I've had enough of her abuse. Are you still in my corner?" He felt strange asking since she hadn't been on his side for longer than he could remember.

"Yes. Why wouldn't I be? Look Russ, no matter what happened between us I don't want this to end badly for you, okay? This is about you and the kids. I don't want them to have to deal with any fallout. I hope your lawyer is good enough to get this thing settled before it gets to court."

"I hope so too." Russell knew Mandy's interest was in the continuing payment of support and alimony. Leopards don't change their spots.

After he ended the call he looked over at Barb. She was sitting quietly absorbing the conversation.

"You still have feelings for her, don't you?"

"She's the mother of my children and she's finally doing the right thing. The only feelings I have are the ones that have to do with Mark and Meghan." He walked over to her and took her hand encouraging her to stand. Taking her in his arms he pulled her into him. They kissed. Barb pushed him back gently.

"I wonder if we shouldn't see each other until this thing is settled." Barb's delivery was soft, gentle. Russell looked at her questioningly. "I'm trying to keep a low profile. I don't think we need anyone digging into our relationship." He interpreted the statement to mean Barb didn't want the reality of her situation to be discovered.

"We probably shouldn't dress up either," he added. As he spoke the mobile phone rang. He didn't recognize the number, allowing the call to go to voicemail. When the voicemail indicator flashed, he checked the message. Listening intently, he replayed it over the speaker for Barb to hear. She smiled as she listened. The caller ended the message with his name and telephone number. Barb grabbed a pen and jotted down the information.

"That's a big deal," she said. "It sounds like you could add gender discrimination to the list."

"Do you think Wexler put them up to the call?" Russell asked.

"I'm sure he did. He's going to use every angle if it means his client wins," Barb said. "You should call him back." Russell thought about it. He wanted to hear about Mandy's call with Wexler before hurtling into the frontier.

"You know that if we work with this other group my secret will come out."

"Sweetie, if this thing goes to court all bets are off for concealing your identity. You're going to have to think about telling the kids before they hear it in the media."

"I know. It's got me worried. My life with my kids will be

ruined. I know she figured on that angle to keep me under control."
The more he thought about her cunning the more he hated her. If she
had left him alone he would have gladly worshipped her. If only she
hadn't pushed him to the breaking point.

"The more pressure you put on her the more likely she is to
settle."

"I'm not comfortable telling my kids until I know it's going to
trial." He turned as he spoke. "I'm not going to subject myself to that
punishment until I can't avoid it." Russell sounded desperate.

Chapter 23

THE EMERGENCY MEDICAL TEAM checked vital signs as the vehicle sped to the nearby hospital. Sylvia wasn't responsive. They relayed her condition to the emergency room physician on the other end of the phone. Under her direction they administered CPR and pressed the defibrillator into service. Rushing the patient from the ambulance to the hospital the attending ER physician met them and fired questions. Steering the gurney past the entryway, through double glass doors and into the bustling emergency department to an open examination area the doctor called to a nurse for assistance.

"Thanks, we'll take it from here." The doctor dismissed the EMT technicians as the nurse entered the examination area and pulled the curtains to cordon off the area. The medical team attacked the patient as she clung precariously to life. The doctor barked orders; the nurse complied. A second nurse was summoned to connect the patient to various monitoring devices.

***

Delia and the others sat quietly in Sylvia's office until Jonas broke the silence. He sounded like Alexander Haig after President Reagan was shot. "We all need to get back to productive work."

Delia rose from the settee and walked out of the office slowly. She was troubled by the sudden illness. As much as she thought her boss needed to take a chill pill, she admired her ascent to the top of the heap and her ability to cut through all the bullshit to get things done. She didn't aspire to be a Sylvia clone but had learned much about how to run her life without unwanted influence.

After the others cleared out of the office Delia rose from her desk and collected the mail. She carried it into Sylvia's office and under the pretense of organizing the desk she scanned the legal document. *Someone's calling her out for her actions.* Delia suspected there was something going on to keep Sylvia's people on a short leash. She had no idea it had gotten to the point of a lawsuit. She read the first two pages of the complaint before realizing she had lingered too long. Moving to the seating group she reorganized until things looked pristine. She couldn't help but think that maybe Sylvia had burned out, worked herself to death.

***

The patient was moved to the intensive care unit. Her vital signs continued to weaken. As she lay silent, except for the sounds from the apparatus attached to her body, the world continued to function without her input or control.

Bethany smiled as she considered Sylvia's fate. The tea she brewed contained the chemical Cerbera odollam, commonly known as the suicide tree, that continued the work of the drugs Bethany had mixed into the drinks she prepared the prior evening. One of the things Bethany had not disclosed to Sylvia was her penchant for toxic cocktails. Those who crossed her ended up violently ill or dead. This was one of the prime reasons for her emigration from Jamaica; she had worn out her welcome.

***

Delia decided to enjoy her boss's absence and take an hour for lunch. During the reign of terror employees rarely left work for the frivolous waste of an hour to dine outside the office. Sylvia was a proponent of eating while you work. She did it, there was no reason her employees couldn't follow suit. She made it a point to circulate during lunch to see who the loyalists were.

When Delia reached the parking lot she connected with Katie. The two shared concerns about the boss's condition but were also euphoric over the light mood and relaxed atmosphere with her gone.

"I should call my boss and let him know," Katie said.

"Yeah, what's up with him? He took two sick days in a row. I can't remember the last time that happened," Delia said. Katie extracted her mobile phone from her handbag. Delia touched Katie's arm. "Wait, don't do that yet. Let's enjoy the lunch hour."

At lunch Katie's mind was on calling Russell. She loved her boss. This was her first job; he'd taught her about professionalism. She excused herself midway through the meal and called from the ladies' room. He answered on the third ring.

"Hi Katie."

"You don't sound sick," she said playfully.

"There's different types of sick."

"I'm teasing," she said.

"Things must be slow for you to miss me enough to call."

"I wanted you to know that they rushed Sylvia to the hospital this morning."

His jaw dropped. "Why?"

"Not sure; she bugged out at her desk them passed out. She was acting weird, like she didn't know where she was or didn't care. It freaked me out." Katie's voice was animated.

"Do you know the name of the hospital?" he asked.

"No, I'm not at the office. Delia and I needed to get out of there for a while. I think Delia's taking it hard," Katie lied. He doubted it.

"Who's keeping an eye on things?"

"Jonas is acting like the boss." Katie was not one of Jonas' fans but she appreciated that he took control of the situation. "He got the EMT there and made sure they had her insurance information."

"Who's letting corporate know?" He didn't know if there was next of kin. He figured she had destroyed her siblings like she destroyed everyone else for the fun of it.

"I thought you should do that. Jonas didn't agree. I think he called. I think you're the boss while she's out," Katie offered. Russell blanched at taking the reins especially since he filed the lawsuit. "Delia told me about the lawsuit you filed." Katie paused. She thought she heard something drop. "It's about time somebody did something about it."

"Katie, I hope you didn't read it. What did Delia tell you?" He held his breath. He didn't need news of his extracurricular activities becoming grist for the mill. "Maybe I need to come in make sure things continue to function." Barb was listening to the call. She signaled to him to nix the idea. He had his reasons, including retrieving the complaint before it became public knowledge.

"She didn't tell me anything except you and a few other people were suing her and the company." She tried to sound convincing.

"Katie do me a favor, get that paperwork and lock it in the file cabinet in my office." He had to head off the problem before it took flight. "If I'm going to take charge while Sylvia's out of commission I might as well start by keeping this under wraps." Russell hoped he sounded convincing.

"Sure boss, I'll do it as soon as I get back to the office." She figured it would give her time to read it before locking it away.

"Thanks Katie. I might stop by later. Let me know when you hear something from the hospital. I'm worried about her."

**

Wexler's secretary punched the intercom. "Mr. Wexler, Mr. Wang on the line."

"His company?" Wexler asked.

"He's calling about the complaint against Ms. Hutchison and her company."

"Okay, put him through."

"Stanley Wang here."

"Good afternoon Mr. Wang."

"You can call me Stanley. You know why I'm calling."

"You have our complaint. As much as we regret having to take these steps, the actions of Ms. Hutchison leave us no alternative. We believe every point in the complaint and we can substantiate them." Wexler cut through the pleasantries. He wasn't being retained to make nice.

"You know the company will vigorously defend itself."

"Of course, I would expect nothing else," Wexler said.

"You should know that I was just informed that Ms. Hutchison has been hospitalized. We are awaiting an update on her condition."

"We're sorry to hear that. We hope she's okay." Wexler sounded almost sincere. The two attorneys talked for several minutes before agreeing to a pretrial conference.

***

The on-duty nurse rushed to address the Code Blue alarm. The patient's vital signs flat lined. The doctor and another nurse rushed to the area, the doctor barking orders as the nurse followed his lead. Ten minutes later the attending physician called an end to the efforts to revive the patient.

***

"Why do you have to go to the office if your secretary took care of retrieving the document?" Barb stood with her arms folded, her breasts resting heavily on them.

"Barb, this is my life we're talking about. I'm already on thin ice. I have my kids to worry about. And even if Mandy testifies, I have no assurance she won't hold it over my head with the kids." He tried to remain calm as his blood pressure rose.

If Sylvia lived he would go forward with the litigation even if it meant exposure. He would deal with the fallout. He would talk with Mandy and seek her support. He didn't want the revelation to ruin his life; it was already in the shitter, it couldn't get much worse. Being able to support the kids was worth the pain of exposure. If she died, and he realized it was a big if, he would table the action pending the naming of a replacement. There wasn't anyone in the office he saw as her successor.

In the midst of the discussion Barb's mobile phone rang. She answered it as she listened to Russell. Barb brought an index finger to her lips for silence as she walked toward him. Tapping the "speaker" icon she held the phone between them. "I have you on the speaker phone; Russ is here," Barb announced. Wexler reported his discussion with Stan Wang.

"Wang's a slick bastard. Be careful," Russell cautioned. "I've been involved with a few deals he's worked on. He can lull you into a coma before he lowers the boom." There was a long silence as the couple exchanged looks.

"I appreciate the warning. I've dealt with his type before. I don't think he wants to litigate this," Wexler said.

"Did he say that?" Russell asked hopefully.

"He didn't have to say it. I know it from how he handled himself."

***

Word reached Bethany of her partner's death. She finished the workday and traveled to the hospital. The body had already been turned over to the authorities. Tracking down the body led her to the police. Uncomfortable with the situation she girded herself before presenting at the precinct handling the case.

The attending ICU physician wasn't accustomed to losing healthy patients. Her observations led her to believe foul play contributed to the patient's death. She called the authorities, relayed her assumptions and insisted on a visit from a detective and an examination by the coroner.

The lead detective, Bennett "Benny" Acavedo, fielded the case. His lieutenant provided background before sending him into the field to meet the physician. After taking a statement at the hospital he processed the information. Things had been slow; a murder case would provide some much-needed spice to an otherwise bland schedule.

Bethany had arrived at the hospital moments before the detective. He asked her to wait while he spoke with the doc. She felt put out, waiting to talk to the last person she expected to see. Acavedo met with Bethany and collected personal information then provided details about the situation with the body. Since Bethany could not prove next of kin she had no standing in any decisions regarding the body.

"Detective, why are you here?" Bethany tried to hide her concern. She knew this would not be a police matter unless there was suspicion surrounding the death.

Acavedo looked up from his notepad. "You two were a couple?" He sized her up.

"Yes, we were a couple."

"Married?" His eyebrows arched to punctuate the question.

"No."

"Do you know where we can find next of kin?" the detective asked. He was young and aggressive, dark smooth skin exhibiting more than a hint of interracial roots; his wavy black hair was styled short and shiny, deep brown eyes were inquisitive and strong. His clean-shaven face accentuated a rock-solid jaw. He was medium build with a muscular frame. In a button down gray shirt and thin black tie he looked youthful, not threatening.

"I don't know of any family. And I've known Sylvia for over a year." She choked up as she spoke. He wasn't buying it; he had been played by countless women of Bethany's ilk. After taking her information he escorted her to the medical examiner's office. Bethany identified the body. At first she was stoic, finally tears flowed slowly and silently. The detective's eyes were on her.

Bethany pushed emotion to the surface and allowed her body to wrack as she cried. "I...I can't believe she's dead." More sobs and tears flowed as she fished tissues from her handbag. "How did she die?"

"We're going to let the coroner help us with that. We don't know enough to rule out foul play. Did she have health problems?" he asked as she watched her.

"Not that I was aware of. She was healthy." More tears accompanied the statement. The detective consoled her. "She worked all the time. She never went to the doctor, even when she was feeling rundown." More sobs, her ample chest heaving. "I tried to tell her to slow down. She kept taking all those miracle remedies to keep herself going." Bethany collected herself, thanked the detective for his interest in the case before making her way slowly to the parking lot.

Sitting in the car she pondered the situation. *The cops are going to investigate this. I've got to get myself ready for the worst. I'm not going to jail.*

The coroner scheduled the autopsy. Initial examination by the attending physician at the hospital supported the premise that the decease was a healthy woman for whom sudden death was unexpected.

A visit to Sylvia's home by the detective found Bethany there, comfortable and relaxing.

"Hello detective, it's nice to see you again considering the circumstances. Won't you come in?" The detective absorbed the opulent surroundings.

"Nice place."

"It's comfortable. Is this business or a social call?" Bethany asked, her voice soft and sultry. Black capris with fuchsia stripe down each leg, form-fitting spandex top with scoop neck and half sleeve made her look athletic. White sneakers with matching fuchsia stripe finished off her look. Hair tied back in a tight ponytail accentuated high cheekbones and silky smooth skin. Desire burned just below the surface of her eyes. Acavedo sensed it and pushed carnal thoughts from his mind.

"I would like to ask you a few questions about Ms. Hutchison." Bethany's shoulders slumped. She had practiced the move in front of a full-length mirror until she felt she mastered the technique. "I know this is difficult. We need to figure out why she died suddenly." Bethany broke into sobs and tears He had seen murderers put on amazing displays of sorrow. He waited while Bethany pulled herself together.

"May I offer you something to drink?" she asked.

"Water if you have it."

"I'll be back, make yourself comfortable." Bethany turned; Acavedo's eyes followed her tantalizing movements. He imagined what the two women did in this cavernous abode. While Bethany retrieved water the detective poked around the spacious living room looking for clues.

"Tell me more about your relationship with Ms. Hutchison," he requested before sipping, watching her over the rim of the glass. Sitting next to him on the settee they were positioned at forty-five degree angles. She knitted her hands in her lap; another practiced move. Looking down as if she was examining something Bethany measured her response.

"We were soul mates." The statement brought precipitation as puppy dog eyes begged empathy. "Everything was going well. She loved her work and most of her employees loved her. How could this have happened?" More tears accompanied by sobs as she reached for the tissues from the designer box.

Acavedo asked several questions, his voice soft but the questions sharp. Bethany fought the urge to be defensive. She stood and walked over to the stately fireplace with massive carved white marble mantle exhibiting two scantily clad maidens. She glanced into the gold-framed mirror hanging over the mantle, spying the detective. He eyed her impassively.

Turning, she stood suggestively. "When will you be releasing the body? I want to start to make the, um, arrangements." She dabbed the edges of her eyes.

"It's not up to me. Once the coroner concludes the autopsy we'll know more. Bethany turned away for a brief moment to hide the reaction. She wanted to wrap this thing up without worrying about repercussions. In her home country, the autopsies revealed nothing unusual. She hoped as much would be concluded here.

The young detective stood and took several steps in her direction. She girded. He stopped short and folded his arms. "Is there anything you think I should know about your soul mate? Even if you think it's unimportant you should tell me. Sometimes the tiniest of things become significant." His gaze was intense, boring into her. Fighting the urge to shiver she folded her arms accentuating her endowment.

Tapping her foot, she became reflective. "I really want to help.

If I think of anything I'll let you know." He fished a business card from his jacket and handed it over. She walked him to the door and let him out. He paused before stepping over the threshold and onto the portico. She lingered at the door as he descended the steps and approached the black Crown Victoria.

After closing and locking the door she breathed normally again. Up the curved winding staircase she stopped to recall their exploits. The stairs had been a favorite place to fuck. Bethany smiled and continued climbing. When she reached the second floor she turned her attention to the master bedroom. In the cavernous closet, she approached the floor to ceiling shoe rack filled to overflowing with stiletto heels. Pulling at one corner the large bank of shelves swung effortlessly on hidden hinges exposing a wall safe.

During one of their sexual exploits that spilled into the bedroom Sylvia had shown this to her lover. Bethany discovered the combination. She opened the safe and found a hoard of cash. Grabbing a roll-aboard suitcase she extracted the stacks of bills and filled the bag. Closing the safe she locked it and wiped the surface clean. Moving to her closet, the master bedroom had two, she gathered belongings and packed another suitcase. She repeated the all too familiar routine. As she descended to the first floor she thought about the offshore bank account where she had stashed the profits from two previous businesses. This relationship had been financially fruitful. She could escape and lie low for a while before resurfacing. The quandary was how to get the cash from the safe out of the country without drawing attention. She couldn't deposit and transfer it. She wished she had planned this part of the scheme better. She couldn't take it on an airplane. A cruise ship was her best bet. She would disembark at one of the Caribbean islands and not reboard. She hoped her forged passport documents would work.

After dropping the bags by the front door, she grabbed the computer tablet and searched for last minute cruise deals on one of the popular travel sites. There was one leaving in two days for the Bahamas. Booking the cruise, she selected an inside cabin and used her debit card to pay. It would leave a trail, but once she disappeared they would never be able to trace her beyond the cruise line.

**

Jonas notified the corporate office and received instructions to inform the office pool. He gathered the troops to convey the bad news. After the gathering, Katie called her boss. Abby also called her boss, hysterical. As Barb was calming her secretary Russell was feeling the relief in his assistant's voice. Katie had a way of keeping things in perspective. She knew her boss was on the receiving end of some of life's unpleasantness at the hands of the dearly departed.

The two lovers sat quietly after the calls and pondered the future. Although he loved her, Russell thought Barb was too headstrong and impetuous. He wished he had not agreed to the lawsuit.

"The company's going to settle," Barb concluded, since the defendant was gone and there was less of a chance to build a defense to the charges. She smiled as Russell fretted. He hoped those words would not be part of his epitaph.

"Do we need to talk about something?" She reached across the gap between them and directed his gaze to hers. She was strong, like Mandy, but she also cared.

"I'm worried." He tried to hide the conflict that raged in his heart. He hadn't seen his kids in two weeks; the emptiness weighed heavily. If he went back with his ex-wife he could have his family but he would need to give up Allison. The emotional push and pull threatened to tear him apart.

**

The mobile phone played a sultry tune. Acavedo fished it from his jacket pocket. "Yeah lieu. Uh huh, I'll get on it right away." He pointed the sedan toward the downtown area. He had been heading to Sylvia's office to canvass the employees when he received the call from his lieutenant. After pulling into the parking lot of the Medical Examiner's offices he sat for a moment. The place gave him the creeps. No matter how long he investigated murders he still could not reconcile dealing in death. He didn't understand people and became more disoriented by peoples' hatred, compulsiveness and disregard for life.

The smell of death accosted him as he entered, causing his stomach to constrict. The deputy medical examiner approached. "Benny, good to see you." Lisander Morris was tall, rail thin and gaunt. Aquiline features and sunken eyes made him a leading contender for one of the characters out of the Headless Horseman story.

"Sander what have you got?" Acavedo asked.

"Found something interesting in the blood and tissue samples." The detective looked at his host awaiting the continuation. "Had to run the samples twice before I was sure. Found remnants of an obscure vegetable-based poison in the liver. It expressed like early precancerous cells."

Morris had more initials after his name than most doctors in his field. He had a pharmacology background on top of a few other specialties. When asked why he took a thankless job dealing with autopsies he replied, 'the dead don't talk back.' Although the man was off center he was brilliant.

"She was poisoned. You're sure?" Acavedo asked. Morris shot him a look of disbelief. "I'm sure."

Morris walked out of the examination room; Acavedo followed. Settling behind a cluttered metal desk that was new several generations ago he leaned back and propped his worn shoes on the desk, finding a small clearing without disturbing any of the folders stacked on either side.

"Have a seat for a few minutes and I'll try to explain." Acavedo extracted a small spiral notepad from his jacket. Reaching over to one of the stacks, Morris grabbed a thick textbook and opened it to where he had placed a marker.

"The poison is Cerbera odollam, commonly known as the suicide tree. The seeds contain cerberin, a potent toxin related to digoxin. The poison blocks the calcium ion channels in the heart muscle, causing disruption of the heartbeat. This is typically fatal and can result from ingesting a single seed. Cerberin is difficult to detect in autopsies and its taste can be masked with strong spices, such as a curry. It is often used in homicide and suicide in India; Kerala's suicide rate is about three times the Indian average. In 2004, a team led by Yvan Gaillard of the Laboratory of Analytical Toxicology in La Voulte-sur-Rhône, France, documented more than five hundred cases of fatal Cerbera poisoning between 1989 and 1999 in Kerala. He paused to give Acavedo a chance to catch up.

"They go on to say, 'To the best of our knowledge, no plant in the world is responsible for as many deaths by suicide as the odollam tree. A related species is Cerbera tanghin the seeds of which are known as tanghin poison nut and have been used as an ordeal poison.'" Morris closed the book with a flourish.

"The poison could be masked by herbal tea?"

"Tea with nutmeg and other spices."

Acavedo contemplated before responding. "How did you know?"

"Studying poisons is one of my hobbies. Conan Doyle is one of my favorite authors." Morris folded his arms and smiled. Acavedo finished jotting notes, slipped the notepad and pen into his jacket and stood.

"Sander, you're incredible. Thanks. I'll take the report back to the office." Acavedo waved. He couldn't muster enough nerve to shake hands with the doctor. On the drive back to the precinct he called the lieutenant.

After briefing her and rounding up his partner he decided to resume his canvass. They arrived at the office. On the drive the two police caught up on the coroner's report. Benny's partner was a young detective who reminded him of himself a few years earlier. He was average height with broad shoulders and barrel chest. His nappy hair was trimmed close, his complexion milk chocolate.

"Follow my lead, Chili." Acavedo said to Dante Peppers. When the young detective joined the ranks of the plain clothes his fellow detectives branded him Chili. He didn't mind. He considered it a rite of passage and a sign of acceptance.

After an hour at the office they determined there wasn't much to learn. The staff weren't crying rivers over her death. The detectives checked Sylvia's office and bagged a cup from the trashcan and an open beverage container from her refrigerator. The cup had the coffee shop logo.

*****

Russell called Mandy and told her about Sylvia. There was a long pause before she responded. "You didn't have anything to do with that, did you?" She tried to maintain composure.

"Do you think I could kill someone?" Two beats later he continued. "If you do, then you don't know me. If I was going to do something like that don't you think I had grounds prior to my little adventure with my former boss?" Silence continued to pour through the phone as his words indicted his ex-wife.

"No I don't think you would do such a thing." After a beat, Mandy continued, "Are you relieved?"

"I don't know. I don't know what to think." Russell shook his head. He was alone in the living room. Barb was in the shower. She was struggling with her lover's depressed state; the memories of her battle with depression too much for her to deal with.

"Does this mean you don't need to sue the company?"

"What do you think? Do you think I can turn off all the shit that happened to me? Do you think I forgive her because she's dead?" His voice rose. Was she having second thoughts. Suddenly he disliked himself for calling.

"I don't know. I thought maybe it would save you from being exposed to all that legal business. I know how much this hurt you. I know she almost ruined you." He wanted to tell her it was her fault. Had she not made a fool out of him for cross-dressing this would never have happened. He wanted to blame her. As bile churned in his gut he realized he was making himself sick over something he couldn't change. He thought he wanted her back and was willing to forgive what she had done. Could he trust her? Was he imagining that everything could be all right?

"Are you listening to me?" The words brought him back.

"I am listening. I'm trying to figure this out. The lawsuit was filed and the company knows all about it. How do I take it all back? How do they act like this never happened? This is their fault by codoning this." Regret filled him to bursting.

"I think you should talk to the company and explain everything," she offered.

"Sure, just like when I tried to explain everything to you. Remember how you reacted? You were forgiving." He couldn't believe he was telling her. "Do you really think they are in the business of forgiving and forgetting?" he asked, willing himself to stop shaking.

There was a long pause. "I don't know," she said.

"Look Mandy, I forgot why I called. I gotta go." He ended the call before she could respond. Dropping heavily onto the sofa, his head in his hands; anger and frustration raged.

Barb discovered the hot mess of humanity. Her nerve endings were beginning to fray from the strain. She contemplated whether she could handle his weakness and bring him around. She was being haunted by memories of her long and arduous transition.

"Russ," she called, in a voice more confident than she felt. "Russell?" He looked up through bloodshot eyes. "What's wrong?"

He shook his head trying to clear it. "Too many feelings, too much conflict. I don't know." Moving to the sofa she sat next to him. She wanted to touch him. He was wrapped in gloom. She wasn't sure she could handle transference, absorb any of the pain.

***

Acavedo and Peppers decided to visit the coffee shop. A few patrons waited for their orders; the detectives eyed the activity. Approaching the counter Acavedo flashed his shield. "We'd like to ask you a few questions," he said as he introduced himself and his partner. Extracting Sylvia's picture from his inside breast pocket he handed it to the clerk. "Do you recognize this woman?" The counter clerk, a thirty-something woman with shoulder length brown hair streaked by gray pulled into a tight ponytail took the photo. Her brow wrinkled as she stared intently at the photo with deep brown eyes.

"Yeah, seen her in here several times."

"What does she usually buy?"

"Don't know. She gets service from the owner. She won't let any of us help her." Acavedo looked over at his partner.

"Is the owner here?" Peppers scanned the counter.

"You mean Bethany? She didn't come in today." Acavedo looked over at his partner.

"Did she call?"

"She said something about arrangements."

"You want coffee?" Acavedo asked his partner. He ordered two mediums with cream and sugar to go, then dropped two dollars into the tip jar after the barista told him they were free.

Sitting in the cruiser Acavedo took a long pull from the cup. "Interesting the owner wasn't there today. I guess she's mourning the loss of her soul mate," Peppers said.

Acavedo punched up the lieutenant. "Hey lieu, we need the crime lab to dust those articles we retrieved from the dead woman's office. And need them to check the cup for anything peculiar."

"Why?"

"If the woman was poisoned we might find poison in the cup. And if the cup has traces of poison we can look for fingerprints. One set might be the killer's."

"I'll make the call and tell them to put a rush on it."

"Thanks. We're gonna run down a hunch. We'll check in later." Benny turned to his partner. "I think it's time you met the owner of the coffee shop."

Bethany heard the car stop in front of the house. She hustled the suitcases out of the foyer and dropped them into the large coat closet off the foyer.

"Hi detective. I didn't expect to see you again." Peppers sized her up; chasing unhealthy thoughts from his mind.

"We have some follow up questions. Mind if we come in?"

"Please." She swung the door open and turned. Her body swayed to a silent rhythm as she walked. They settled into the cavernous and ornate living room. "Can I offer you something to drink?"

Peppers spoke first, "Anything carbonated," he smiled. Bethany looked down her nose at him. She wasn't into unhealthy habits; at least not for herself.

"Best I can do is pomegranate juice. It's not carbonated." Her voice carried the hint of indictment.

"Never too soon to start healthy. But no glass. I want to see about this stuff. If it tastes good maybe I'll work it into my diet."

"Nothing for me," Acavedo said.

"Nice," Acavedo said as he paced slowly before the ornate fireplace. Bethany returned a minute later with the drink in its original plastic container.

"Brought you a glass in case you find drinking from the bottle beneath you." The intrusion was beginning to bother her. She sat across from them in a wingback chair and crossed her legs. "How can I help you?" The playfulness from the prior meeting was gone.

"Wondering if you can tell us about medical problems, drugs Sylvia might have been taking. Recent visits to the doctor that might have indicated a health problem?"

"No; there was nothing I was aware of. But it's possible she was having a problem and didn't want to worry me. If she was seeing a doctor she never let me know."

"Would you mind if we checked the medicine cabinet in her bathroom?" Peppers asked. Their hostess projected discomfort before the look faded.

"If you think it would help, you can follow me." She stood slowly, as if the effort was taxing. Climbing the stairs, foreboding danced threateningly up her spine. "This is the master bedroom." The room was pristine.

"Nice room; my wife would kill for something like this, Peppers said.

"As soon as you make police commissioner," his partner teased.

"There's the master bath." Bethany pointed as she settled softly onto the opulent bedspread adorning the king size bed. "There's a medicine cabinet over the sink. You can check the linen closet too, if you like." After several minutes the two detectives emerged. Acavedo's phone vibrated and played a sultry ring tone.

"Excuse me." He left his partner with their hostess as he walked back into the bathroom. Emerging, his expression was cold, his eyes narrow. "We're going to have to ask you to come down to our office to continue this conversation."

Bethany's expression turned ashen. She tried valiantly to appear nonplussed. "Why?"

"Something's turned up in the autopsy. We need to clear it up and my lieutenant needs to hear from you," Acavedo lied. The district attorney was already informed and was interested in the chemical findings in the cup and the unidentified second set of fingerprints. Coincidences were beginning to line up like ducklings.

***

Russell turned and placed his head in Barb's lap. She stroked his head, haltingly at first. Nestling closer to her she relented and embraced his pain. "It will be okay, we'll work this out together." He sat up and wiped his eyes.

"You want to talk about this?" she asked.

"If you promise to let me talk it all out and don't respond." She looked away and then back at him.

"Okay, I promise I'll try." She felt the pain she had shackled and sequestered, threaten to emerge.

"I'm scared. I'm really scared." He paused. "I want you and I also want this. I know, I'm not making sense. Can you wait a few minutes? I'll be back." He stood and walked out of the room and up the stairs. He returned in a skirt and heels.

"This is what I mean. I want this." He tried to express confidence through his partially transformed image. "I can't give up Allison. I've been wrestling with it; beating myself up emotionally. I don't know how to handle all the conflict. The job, my kids, us. I want what you have, what you are. I want the inner me to be the outer me but I don't know how to figure this out." He sat next to her, crossed his legs and folded his hands in his lap. Barb looked at him, processing the statements.

***

When they arrived at the precinct Acavedo escorted their disgruntled guest as Peppers split off with the bottle of juice in tow. The Crime Scene Investigation unit dusted the bottle, lifted prints and compared them to the unidentified prints from the coffee cup. They were a ten-point match. Peppers smiled. Another circumstantial puzzle piece fell into place. He approached the interrogation room, knocked on the door, entered and signaled to the lieutenant. She rose and walked out of the room leaving Bethany with Acavedo.

Opening the folder, he shared the report with his superior. "Did you call the D.A.?" she asked.

"Montgomery's on the way. I explained the findings. She's ready to support an arrest," Peppers said.

"Let's wait until she arrives. I want to hear this first-hand. The lieutenant had been burned once before by acting capriciously. She wasn't taking chances.

"I'm not sure why you brought me down here. I feel like you want to blame me for something. I know what you're up to. You need somebody to accuse. That's how you make your promotions." Bethany folded her arms and tried to look upset. She was getting too close to the flame and didn't want to get burned. "I know my rights. You can't force me to stay here. She shot a withering glance at her host before looking away. She needed to get out, gather up her belongings and get away before the opportunity was gone.

"This should not take much longer. Can I get you something to drink?" Acavedo asked. The withering glance turned into a glare. The detective smiled. The more they complained the more convinced he was of their guilt.

"No," she barked as she shifted uncomfortably before rising. "If there are no more questions I'm leaving. You know where I live and I wish you didn't. Acavedo rose to meet her. As he did, the door opened and the lieutenant walked in holding the folder.

"Miss Queralls, please sit down." The lieutenant's voice was hard as steel.

"I will not." Bethany's stare was cold, her teeth bared into a smile of hatred.

"Fine, cuff her and Mirandize her." Acavedo stepped forward. Bethany froze, reality struck her hard.

"Bethany Queralls you are under arrest for the murder of Sylvia Hutchison." He took her hands and applied the bracelets.

***

Barb processed the statement. She liked men; it was one of the reasons she transitioned. But there was something at her core that carried a kernel of masculinity. Could she handle a roommate; a female roommate who held desires for women? She wasn't sure. Memories of the pain and anxiety of changing not only her appearance but all the relationships that connected to her life made her circumspect. She couldn't answer the call for help, at least not without coming to grips with how it would impact her emotional state.

Taking his hands in hers she swallowed the consternation that threatened to unnerve her. "Honey, I understand what you are going through. You know I do. I have scars. You need to know about them." He looked at her, questions forming in his eyes.

"Not those types of scars." You've seen all of me. You know that's not what I mean." He looked away; knowing full well where she was going. "This is hard; not only on you. The changes in your body are the easy part. Injections, pills, a few nips here, a few tucks there and you have the outer shell of a woman." She washed her arms across her body as if on display.

"I know about the body thing. I'm not comfortable in this body." He shrugged off the urge to break down again.

She needed to draw him out. No five-minute wonder therapy was going to make him realize what was in store. "A few minutes ago you were afraid to let your little secret out. Are you feeling differently now?"

"I know." The realization that he could not go back to Mandy slapped him hard. All of the wishes and the hopes were fantasies. There was no way he could go back and leave Allison in the cold calculating claws of the woman who made his life a living hell.

"What are you thinking?" Barb's question pulled him back.

"I tried subduing this. I played with fire and got burned." She looked on, trying to make sense of the statements. "I should have been honest with myself and with my ex. I hated her for what she did to me." His breath hitched as he fought for strength. "I did this to me. And the more I think about it, the more I realize it needed to happen. I don't want to live a lie anymore. As much as it hurt for all the changes to happen, I think I was powerless to stop them." He lifted his head and thrust his shoulders back. Barb saw something in his eyes, something she hadn't noticed before. He took her hands and placed them firmly in his lap. He was hard! She took the cue and lifted his skirt. As she encouraged him he touched her cheek with the back of his hand.

"I love you, Barbara Collins. More than I can ever tell you." He wanted to kneel and kiss her feet. She knew it but this was her show. She was on her knees, her mouth on him. When he climaxed the pitch of his voice was higher. He imagined his orgasm vaginally and it sent him into orbit.

Preview
Out of the Shadows
Book Two of New Boundaries

The judge slammed the gavel three times, sending shockwaves down the defendant's spine; how could she be on trial for murder? "It's not possible! I got away with it before; how did they figure it out?" Bethany spoke the question to herself. The defense had argued successfully that Bethany's alleged prior bad acts were not permitted to be introduced, causing the prosecutor to almost be held in contempt for her virulent comments on the judge's ruling. The trial had been sensational and filled with fireworks as the prosecutor built a mountain of circumstantial evidence against the defendant. But no one in the packed courtroom who glanced over at defendant, would have sensed the shock and dismay that she felt.

Seated at the defense table, Bethany Querrals wore a navy-blue skirt cut just above the knee, matching jacket, demure white blouse, and muted navy blue three inch heels. Her defense attorney had had to purchase the outfit for her—one more expense she was being overcharged for, Bethany thought in disgust. Nothing in her wardrobe had suited her defense attorney's idea of proper dress for her trial for the murder of her lover, Sylvia Hutchinson. Of course, most of her clothing had been spandex, faux leather with flex panels to follow every voluptuous curve of her sculpted body, patent leather stilettos and massive rhinestone-studded silver earrings. If the defense attorney could have populated the jury with lustful closet submissives, she would have had a riding crop, bamboo caning sticks and nipple clamps on the defense table and submitted into evidence.

The trial, which had garnered national coverage because of the defense team's desire to try the case in the media—lessons learned from lead counsel's tutelage at the elbow of Johnny Cochran of O.J. Simpson fame—was wrapping up its fourth day. It didn't hurt the defense's strategy that Sylvia Hutchison was a high-profile female executive for a bulge bracket investment banking firm. Recent sex scandals emanating from national government lit the fuse for extensive publicity, and the defense counsel was eager to add logs and gasoline to the fire. Blaming the deceased for fomenting hatred from his clients or their shamed family members might create reasonable doubt. That's all she needed for an acquittal. Defense counsel opened the afternoon with cross-examination of one of Bethany's bondage clients. Her attorney was completing the thrashing of the man's dignity. His wife, the daughter of a prominent philanthropist, was in the gallery sobbing loudly, causing the judge to train vengeful eyes on her. The scene stirred commotion around the grieving and betrayed woman.

"I will clear this courtroom if I don't have order!" the judge bellowed. The jury's attention was torn between the grieving, soon-to-be divorcee and the defense attorney.

"Your honor! These outbursts from the gallery are prejudicing the people's case." The lead prosecutor, a milk white middle-aged woman with twenty years of experience as an overworked and underpaid assistant district attorney, stood. Her frustration with the circus that was unfolding tore through her thin professional veneer.

"Sit down!" the judge shouted. She and the prosecutor had their differences, both strong-willed and passionate about their profession. The prosecutor shot the judge a look of disdain. The judge muted a smile of superiority.

Bethany sat expressionless.

In the gallery, Russell Radcliffe's eyes were drawn to her like moths to light. He'd spent every day at her trial. He still couldn't believe how their lives had intertwined. If Bethany hadn't killed her lover—his boss—he might be the one sitting in the courtroom right now. Oh, not for murder. It would have been a civil suit naming his employer and Sylvia Hutchison as co-defendants in a sexual harassment suit. Sylvia humiliated him in ways that even the most experienced discrimination legal counsel would have found incredulous. That was of course except for Stanley Wang, corporate counsel for Russell's company who had saved Sylvia's sexually abusive ass at least twice. Wang negotiated hefty financial settlements with at least two former employees that also included the threat of public exposure if the details of the settlement were revealed.

Russell wasn't interested in losing his job. He had no appetite for a financial settlement. Until he and Barb hired an attorney to pursue legal recourse against Sylvia, and the company by association, he had not known Sylvia's history or the company's desire to pay hush money. Russell wanted Sylvia gone. But he never considered vanishing her from the planet as the solution to what ailed him. Part of him pined for her. She was beautiful and dominating. She aroused eroticism in him he never knew he possessed. Humiliation aside, he may have been a victim of the Florence Nightingale effect. Except for Sylvia imposing the male chastity device he might have not only tolerated but possibly enjoyed submitting to her.

As he absorbed the courtroom theatrics he was having a hard time believing Bethany had been Sylvia's dominatrix lover. He couldn't see Sylvia as submissive to anyone. His overbearing boss lady had made him kneel and worship her by kissing her feet, giving her foot massages, showering her with attention, and ultimately subjugating his orgasms to her total control. How could she be submissive to anyone?

Bethany intoxicated him and he wished he had gotten to know her better. He missed the coffee shop and the sometimes teasingly inviting dialogue. The shop bustled every time he had stopped, and he figured serving coffee was a hobby since the numbers didn't seem to generate enough money to support a woman who looked like she demanded a lifestyle well above the work-a-day life the coffee shop represented. Sam Sharpton, a private detective hired by his Russell's lover, Barb, had uncovered the dark enterprise flourishing in the basement of the once active building. Russell couldn't believe Sylvia was party to the dom/sub business. The courtroom drama was slowly enlightening him.

The first three days of testimony cast the deceased in an unfavorable light. The defense put poor dead Sylvia on trial. Russell worried her extracurricular activities at the office would surface and expose him. He convinced himself that his presence in the gallery was fact finding and reputation monitoring. Refusing to acknowledge his crush on Bethany, he sat transfixed by the proceedings. The longer the trial dragged on the more his mind wandered off the beaten path. Noir thoughts of bondage made him wonder whether there was another level of eroticism he had missed in his pursuit of pleasure. Barb was dominating, but their rollicking didn't approach what was being revealed about Sylvia in the courtroom. Russell began to paint a picture of emotions sharpened to a fine point, then used to deprive until sexual release brought Bethany's subject to the edge of hysteria.

As day four wound to a close Russell struggled. He wanted to approach Bethany. He had fantasized on numerous occasions about talking to her and maybe hooking up. He and Barb argued about Russell's preoccupation with the trial. She wanted him to spend the mental and emotional recovery time the interim boss had granted building his resume and looking for greener pastures. Barb knew memories of Russell's sordid relationship with Sylvia haunted him from every corner of the office. She also surmised that the lawsuit they had threatened had become grist for the mill and Russell would never again feel comfortable in the office, presuming everyone knew his secret. Russell tried to explain he needed closure. The conversation fell apart when he told her he thought she would understand. After all she had obtained closure when she completed her gender transition. She excoriated him for being heartless and using her situation to justify his faulty reasoning. She also told him for what sounded like the thousandth time this was a perfect opportunity to transition, if he was really serious about it. Russell began to wonder if she was using reverse psychology to make him forget Allison and cling to her.

He exited the courtroom and took a position opposite the dual wooden doors in plain view of the traffic. Bethany glanced his way before turning her attention to her legal team and the reporters her lawyer had cultivated.

The defense attorney knew how to use the media to gain

advantage. As she headed for the semi-circular marble staircase leading to the main level of the courthouse he followed. He thought something ephemeral passed between him and Bethany. He wondered if he was imagining things. He wasn't sure anymore.

Bethany's entourage stopped at the foot of the staircase. Russell had to sidestep to avoid running into them. Spilling out of the building he struggled between waiting to attempt a conversation with the accused or dragging his unbalanced desires to his car and returning to his life. After five minutes of milling around outside trying not to look conspicuous he trudged to the parking lot, chastising himself for faulty resolve. The inner voice warned that if he didn't deal with the issue it would forever haunt him, just like all the other opportunities he had failed to capitalize on.

Made in United States
North Haven, CT
09 November 2023